A CHANCEY DETOUR

6

A
Chancey
DETOUR

6

KAY DEW SHOSTAK

Kay Dew Shostak

August South

So great to meet you!
love, Kay ♡

A CHANCEY DETOUR

ISBN: 978-0-9991064-4-0

Library of Congress Control Number: 2018906835

SOUTHERN FICTION: Women's Fiction / Small Town / Railroad / Bed & Breakfast / Mountains / Georgia / Family

Text Layout and Cover Design by Roseanna White Designs
Cover Images from www.Shutterstock.com

Published by August South Publishing. You may contact the publisher at:
AugustSouthPublisher@gmail.com

Dedicated to my Wednesday Lunch Group
Especially to Pat Kaminski who keeps us on track
and out of trouble

Character List at end of book

Hi there,

This is Anna, and I feel like y'all might've gotten the wrong idea about me. But that's no real surprise, is it? Look who does all the talking in these books. Not that Carolina hasn't treated me fine, but Will is her son. Plus, I think they've had a pretty sorry summer up there on the hill. What with the air conditioning going out, Bryan stalking that girl Brittani, and Savannah moping around about Alex Carrera. How funny was it that he ended up with Angie Conner? Never saw that coming! And then there's all this stuff with Will and me.

Let's face it, Will is just a boy. I know he's gone to college and looks grown up, but he's not so much, really. He can be sweet, but he's really kind of clueless. I know that old saying, it takes two to tango, (and I was definitely there for the tangoing, you can tell by the way my jeans don't fit anymore), but... naw, I guess there's no but. We made a mistake. Big one. Then we went and got married! What in the world were we thinking?

Best part of the summer for me was the opening of the Dollar Store. There I get treated like an adult, not some wayward teenager or poor relation. You've met my grandmother Missus, right? Now, can you imagine living with her? Depending on her for everything? She wanted to run my life, and I had to get out of there. She's paying for the apartment, so maybe I'm being too mean to her, but seriously, you've met her.

I know y'all are thinking I like the Dollar Store so much because of Kyle—Mr. Kendrick. Okay, maybe some. I think people have the wrong idea about him, too, but I don't have time to go into all that. Let's just say... no, never mind.

So, I don't know if I've explained things any, but at least I tried. One thing I do agree with Carolina on, this living in a small town isn't easy. Everyone knowing everything you do and having an opinion on it stinks. But guess I gotta get used to it. With the baby coming in only four months, I don't think things will get any easier.

Now, I need to go find some pants that'll fit before I head off to work. Stop in and see me at the Dollar Store. I'm the one wearing the assistant manager badge. Just between us – I think it'll be the manager's badge before long!

Anna

CHAPTER 1

"You're going to burn up in that," I say. However, since I'm saying it to my teenage daughter I have absolutely no faith that it will be heeded, acknowledged, or even heard.

Wait, she rolled her eyes. She did hear me. Savannah pulls out a Little Debbie oatmeal cake and drops it in her purse as she swivels to the refrigerator. "We're going to the Varsity before the game. Isaac's parents love that place. Guess they went there when they were dating." She grabs a bottle of water, closes the refrigerator, and shudders. "I don't know why people love it so much. It's confusing to even try and order."

The Varsity is an Atlanta eating institution. If you have history with the place, it's the greatest food on the planet. If you don't, then it seems very greasy, common, and, well, greasy. And she's right, ordering is confusing. They yell, "What'll ya have?" practically when you walk in the door and they expect a knowledgeable, and fast, answer. With my lack of ability to make quick decisions, I avoid the Varsity like the plague. (Hmm, wonder if the plague started at some place everybody ate and... never mind.)

Since she's apparently actually talking to me, I try again. "Honey, you're going to burn up in that. It's going to be near ninety degrees at kickoff."

She stops at the door from the kitchen in to the living room, turns, and looks at her reflection in the glass doors going outside to the back deck. She pushes her fingers through her long dark hair, widens her blue eyes, and shrugs. "I'll be fine. It's a college football game. Everyone will be dressed like this." Then she turns back around and looks out the front window before dashing up the stairs. "Holler when they get here."

Clomping up the stairs are the reason for her outfit. New knee-high boots. She worked hard all summer at the Dollar Store and rewarded herself with those boots. Of course, she *must* wear them immediately. And while I thought they looked fine with the skirt—yes, girls wear skirts to football games in the South—she liked them better with her new black jeans. Georgia Tech's colors are gold and white with accents of black, so her short-sleeve gold sweater with the turtleneck is perfect.

Except she's going to burn up. The game is at noon. It's the first week of September. In Atlanta, Georgia. In an open stadium. But, *she* knows best.

Of course, the main reason I'm so smart is that I remember my first college football game at the University of Tennessee wearing the cutest, three-quarter length orange sweater, jeans, and loafers. Did you know when it's too hot to wear socks with new loafers there is nothing between your blisters and all that new leather except more blisters? My mother knew that and I remember her telling me all about it. Along with her saying, "You're going to burn up."

Silly woman.

"They're here!" I yell up the stairs. It's early on a Saturday, but I'm dressed in a shirt with no food stains and have lipstick on because the boy Savannah's going to the game with is Isaac Rivers. Of course, she's not just going with Isaac, she's also going with Mr. and Mrs. Rivers. Isaac is a senior at Chancey High, like Savannah, but he's not allowed to date the way the other kids do. He can only go out with either his parents or his older sister and her husband along.

I learned this the hard way when he—no, they—picked up Savannah Wednesday night to take her to church with them. They *all* came to the door and inside to meet me. Me, who was sitting on the couch watching a recorded episode of the Real Housewives of Somewhere, eating a warmed-over sloppy joe that had dribbled on my faded tee shirt. And of course, I was braless. Hey, it had been a long day. Besides, what happened to guys sitting in the car, looking at their phone, honking the horn? Seems like good old-fashioned common courtesy to me now.

So, today, I learned my lesson and I cleaned up ahead of time.

"Hello, Isaac. Mr. Rivers, Mrs. Rivers." They are all tall and blond. Not especially beautiful as the statement 'tall and blond' implies, but how bad-looking can you be if you're tall and blond? His parents look like normal parents, but apparently they run a huge church out near the interstate. Huge. One of those that doesn't have a particular denomination.

"Hello, Mrs. Jessup," they all say in a jumble and then as Savannah comes running down the stairs they look up as one and smile, greeting her. As she leaves the last step, she leans toward me—I might've flinched—and kisses me on my cheek. "Bye, Mother. Hope you have a nice day."

Mother? I start to laugh, but she frowns at me. So I swallow and wish her a lovely day also, adding, "Hope y'all win the game."

"Me, too," Mrs. Rivers says with a laugh. "It's real hard for me to get good with the Lord on Sunday morning when we lose on Saturday."

Mr. Rivers joins her laughter. "My prayers get quite somber and long after a loss, so the whole congregation hopes for a Tech win each Saturday."

11

Savannah leads them out the door, and as she does she says, "Give Daddy my love, and hope Pawpaw feels better."

"How is your father-in-law?" Isaac's mother asks, hanging back a bit from leaving.

"Seems to be doing okay, now," I say. "Thanks for asking." Jackson's father, Hank, had fallen from a ladder and been knocked unconscious almost two weeks ago. Jackson and his brothers all went home to Kentucky immediately, and while his dad was now out of the woods, his recovery was taking some time. Jackson is still up there with him.

She pats my arm as she passes me. "He's in all our prayers."

I say, "Thanks," and Mr. Rivers shakes my hand as he follows his wife.

Isaac is the last out the door, and as he shakes my hand he winks at me. "You have a good day, Mrs. Jessup," he says, as he winks again. He has movie-star looks, not leading-man looks, but more like the boy-next-door, best-friend-of-the-leading-man looks. Sandy blonde hair that flops toward his eyes, a slow smile that makes *you* smile, and sweet eyes that crinkle just a bit at the corners. He's lanky and wears his clothes like a young Jimmy Stewart, or Ryan Reynolds for the younger crowd.

Savannah usually dates the leading guy, so it's interesting to see her with the best friend, the safe one. But I'll take it after *The Summer of Chasing Alex Carrera*. The older, New York born-and-bred, gorgeous, worldly man with his own apartment she set her sights on earlier this year.

Isaac Rivers makes me smile as I close the front door. Then my laugh finally bursts out. "Mother!"

It's strange to not have Jackson home on a weekend. Now that they've moved Hank out of ICU, Jackson is hoping to be coming home soon. Hank's young wife, Shelby, is proving to be a pretty good caretaker. Makes my mouth taste like cat spit to say that, but I guess I should be appreciative.

"Speak of the devil," I say into the phone, answering it on the first ring. "Hey sweetie, I was just thinking about you. How are things going?"

Jackson sighs. "Tired of being here. Ready to come home. Which I'm planning on doing tomorrow. That way I can get back on the job site Monday."

"Good. I miss you. Saturday's just not as much fun without you." I wedge my phone under my chin and talk as I pour another cup of coffee and then head out to the deck. "Whew, no, too hot to sit out there," I say as I close the door. "What's the weather like up there?"

"Cooler than there, but still pretty warm. Hey, listen, Colt's going to be in the area this fall, and I told him he could stay with us."

"Oh, okay. I think the B&B rooms are full all the weekends in September. When's he coming? I mean, we can make it work even if there's no room in the B&B. But how is he getting away in the middle of his football season?" Jackson's brother coaches the local high school football team in their hometown of Painter, Kentucky. He's single and eats, lives, and breathes Painter Football.

"Well, that's the problem." Jackson takes a breath. "He got let go."

"What?!" This news legitimately shocks me. "They went to state last year. He lives for that team!"

"Yeah, he's taking it kind of rough, especially now with the season starting. I think it'll be good for him to get away for a bit when he gets the chance."

This is sounding like more than just a little visit. "Um, sure. But is it really a good time with your dad and all?"

"Dad is going to rehab in the morning," Jackson says, "so he's going to be busy there. And, well, Shelby and Colt don't exactly get along."

Makes him okay in my book. "Then, sure. We'll find a place

to put him. It'll be good to see him again. We can talk about it later when you get more details."

"Thanks, honey. And I'll see you tomorrow. Leaving first thing in the morning. It'll be good to be home. Been weird being at the house here with neither Mom nor Dad. Love you. Bye."

I say, "Love you, too. Bye," and hang up my phone. For a minute I start to worry about Jackson and Shelby being there together. They were married for a short bit a long time ago. But then I remember what it was like having her here last Christmas and realize she makes me look good. Jackson's dad, better known as Hillbilly Hank of the book series and senior center talk circuit, had been carrying on with sweet Shelby behind everyone's backs, including his wife Etta's, for years. It all came out right here in this house. Etta let go with grace and bought a beach house in South Carolina. Shelby went about expanding Hillbilly Hank's territory and married Mr. Hillbilly in the spring. We weren't invited or notified, but she's wearing a ring and changed her name, so we assume they took the leap.

Turns out being up and dressed so early on a Saturday is nice. Bonnie opens our side of the store, Blooming Books, on Saturdays, so I usually lay around drinking coffee too long and then run around like a crazy woman getting ready to go. Saturdays are early days for Shannon and her flower business, as most of her weddings are on Saturday. Meanwhile, I don't have to be there until closer to eleven or even noon. I pour another cup of coffee, but before I can sit back down, I hear footsteps coming down the B&B hall.

"Good morning, is that coffee I smell?" The woman in shorts and a T-shirt, carrying hiking boots, asks as she enters the kitchen.

"Yes, can I pour you a cup? There are also muffins."

"No coffee for me, but Allen would love some. No muffins

for either of us. He's com—oh, there he is." She turns to her husband. "Coffee's ready."

"Wonderful," the man says. He's older than the woman by a lot, but he's also carrying hiking boots. "Can we sit out on the porch?"

"Absolutely!" I say. "Wherever you feel comfortable. Although it's pretty warm out there."

She pipes up. "Oh, we love the heat. Sweating is good for you. I'll meet you out there, babe." She steps onto the deck, which is in full morning sun.

Allen takes the cup of coffee I hand him, and I point to the muffins. "Help yourself to a muffin if you'd like."

He glances towards the back deck as he reaches for the muffin plate. "I've got to have something more than yogurt if we're going to hike in this heat."

"You have your choice," I say, although he's already taken a huge bite from a blueberry muffin and is chasing it down with a swig of water. "Our other guests went out for a big breakfast earlier. They only had a day of train-watching planned, but felt they needed bacon to sustain them."

"Umm, bacon." Allen rolls his eyes in pleasure at the thought. "She'd flip out if she caught me with this muffin, let alone bacon!"

"Your wife has more willpower than me," I say with a laugh.

"Oh, she's not my wife." He wipes his hands on his shorts, takes another swig of water, and tosses the bottle in the trash, then tops off his coffee. "Better get out there. Am I crumb free?" he asks as he turns toward me.

"Crumb free," I nod. "Y'all have a good day. Feel free to take some ice for a cooler or some waters from the door of the fridge. You hiking the beginning of the Appalachian Trail?"

"Yeah. We'll see how it goes. I'm not much of a hiker, but well…" He nods his head toward the outside deck.

"But she is," I say with a smile. "Good luck." We exchange thumbs up and he joins his girlfriend.

"Glad I only have to try and keep up with young people who are my kids. As a partner? No, thank you," I mumble, then pause as I hear sounds in the basement. "Who could be down there so early?" Bryan spent the night at Grant's so they could hit the golf course early for caddying tips, and I believe Will is still upstairs asleep. He doesn't go into work until noon. Saturdays are late nights at the car dealership.

I open the basement door, and shout, "Hello?"

"Mom, come look at this," Will shouts back.

Walking down the steep wooden stairs, my anger grows. He's moved the den furniture up against my washer and dryer and then filled where the couch and chairs and coffee table were with junk from the spare rooms. It looks like it did when we first moved in.

"Will! What in the world have you done?" My oldest is beaming with pride, which doesn't even hit a glitch at the tone of my question or the anger on my face.

"Mom, it's going to be great," he says. "That room there will be my bedroom, this can be my living room area, and here, where there's water for the washer, we can put in a little sink and a counter for a makeshift kitchen. The bathroom is already here, I'll just need to add a shower somehow. It's perfect for me."

I fold my arms. "But it's not for you. This is our house. Our den, our laundry room, our bathroom. Now clean all this up, like it was. Don't you have to work late today? Shouldn't you be sleeping in?"

He shakes his head. "Too excited to sleep. Mom, you didn't think I was going to stay up in that little room beside yours, did ya? That room will be a great nursery for the baby when it stays here, but I can't live there like I'm back in high school. Besides, I'll need quiet to study for my classes."

Okay, you might be wondering if I ever had that talk with Will, the one about pulling his own weight around here now that he's moved back in to get his degree to teach. One look at this scene, and you know for sure that I never did. But it's never too late to start. "First, the baby is your responsibility. How will you hear it cry all the way down here?"

Will's head jerks back, and I see him realizing this won't work. He's actually concerned. Good. Then he shakes his head at me.

"Mom? You'd put a baby down here with all this dampness? Your grandchild staying in your basement?"

"Well, no, but…"

"You want me to be successful in my classes, right?" His big brown eyes are stretched wide, and he looks so helpful, so concerned. Right.

I close my eyes and turn away from him. He's got to grow up. He's got to bear the consequences. He's got to know how I feel. I'm all the way on the third stair when I say, "Your daddy will be home tomorrow. Talk to him."

If Jackson didn't want to get the unpleasant parenting jobs sloughed off on him, he should stick around here more.

Chapter 2

"Who knew school was so exhausting?" Zoe Kendrick exclaims as she flops in one of the wing chairs beside Blooming Books' front window. "Now I know why everyone loves Saturdays. I *need* this day off!"

I move from behind a bookshelf to dash to the front door to keep the little hands of the Kendrick clan, which are never far from Zoe, from destroying the store. Zoe is their twelve-year-old half-sister and basically the live-in nanny. When I don't find any smudgy fingerprints to prevent, I stop short. "Wait, you're by yourself? Where are the kids?"

Zoe sits up a bit and lets the weariness of the world slide down her face. She's more mature than any of my children, including the college grad arranging his new pad in my basement. "Kimmy took them to the Dollar Store to see their daddy," she explains. "Says she don't want them up where he's living due to, well, you know. Him and Anna? But says she's not going to take care of them all seven days a week either. Said she was dropping them off at the store."

Shannon creeps out from behind her worktable, a bunch of white flowers in one hand and open scissors in the other. Bonnie leans around the sales counter, one hand on her hip and a smile growing on her face. Zoe shrugs, and I burst out laughing.

"She's dropping off all three kids at the Dollar Store!" I exclaim in the midst of laughing. Shannon and Bonnie join in.

"Couldn't happen to a nicer guy," Bonnie, our number one, and only, employee says. "They'll destroy that place. Remember what they did in only a few minutes last time we let them in the door?"

"Since when has Kimmy had the guts to do something like that?" I ask.

"She's been going to some women's thing at church," Zoe answers. "I thought it was just for free babysitting now that I'm going to school, but they've been getting her all fired up about saving her family. She says she's making it too easy on Dad."

"Well," Shannon says, turning back to her arranging, "she's got a point there. Him shacking up with a woman pregnant with someone else's child." She catches herself. "Oh, sorry, Carolina. I sometimes kinda forget it's your grandbaby. Peter can't *stand* Kyle Kendrick. Sorry, Zoe, I know he's your father, but, well, it's the truth."

"No offense taken," the girl says, then she sits up straighter and smiles. "But I've got a day to myself. Had Kimmy drop me off here so I can walk around and see everyone. I miss being around during the week."

I sit in the other wing chair. "So how is school? Are you glad you got moved up? High school is hard even when you're the same age as everyone else."

"Oh yes, I'm glad. It didn't take any time for the teachers at the middle school to see I needed to be moved up."

Bonnie comes out to lay a hand on the girl's shoulder. "Skipping a grade is a lot, especially going from middle to high school. How are you finding the high school classes?"

"Good," she says. "Not really hard. I read most of everything last weekend."

"You mean you didn't read all your assignments? Just most?" I ask. "How will you keep up with the rest of the class? Bryan seems like he's got hours of homework every night."

"Oh, Miss Carolina, of course I read the assignments. I just went on ahead and read most of the books. Well, not the math book. But the history and literature ones were just too interesting to stop, you know?"

Bonnie pats Zoe's shoulder and chuckles. "Oh, honey, you'll do just fine."

Zoe closes her eyes and lays back against the chair. "But it's so tiring! Sitting in classes even though you already figured out what the teacher is trying to say, riding the bus back and forth, and then all the rushing around between classes."

"More tiring than watching Cayden and taking care of things at Laney's?" I ask as I go back to straightening the bookshelves. "More tiring than watching your siblings all the time?"

"Most definitely," she says as she also stands up. "I'm going over to Mr. Peter's place to get something to eat. Can I get anyone anything?"

Shannon calls out from behind a large pink and white arrangement. "Just tell Peter I said hi and that I had a wonderful time last night."

As my mouth opens, Bonnie glares laser beams at me and shakes her head, mouthing, "Don't ask her!" Zoe watches Bonnie and me and then says into the pause. "Okay, Miss Shannon, I'll tell him. Who are those flowers for?"

"I've gotten a new account, thanks to Savannah." Shannon continues placing the flowers as she asks, "Did I tell y'all? That new boy she's with now, his parents run the big church out at the highway. They came in to see your store, Carolina, and said they wanted to switch their weekly flower order to here. Want to support Savannah's mother, they said."

"Really? That's nice." *I guess.*

Shannon turns the arrangement toward the front and stands beside it. "They want two this size every week, so it's *very* nice for me. However, we all know that Savannah dating a preacher's son can't last long. She'll wear him out in no time."

"Shannon!" I exclaim.

"For crying out loud, Carolina," she answers my indignation. "You know she will, right?" Looking to Zoe and Bonnie for validation, she smirks when they both only grin.

Zoe turns to leave. "See y'all later," she says walking through our big old door. She holds the door open for someone I can't see, but who is apparently coming in. I cringe when I do see who it is.

Missus stops for a moment to talk to the girl, then marches in. "Did you hear that Zoe girl has been allowed to skip a grade into the high school? How mediocre must our educational system in Chancey be if a girl who is basically self-taught can skip a grade? This explains why Susan has taken her son out of the public school and is sending him to Darien Academy. As I will also do with my great-grandchild."

Bonnie smiles and welcomes Missus. "Can I get you a cup of coffee, Missus? I just made a new pot. It's hazelnut-flavored."

"Pshaw, might as well be serving hot chocolate." As Missus passes Bonnie at the counter, she stops and turns back. "You taught at Darien, correct?"

Bonnie, who's as old as Missus, but has lived in the South (and Chancey) long enough, answers, "Yes, ma'am."

"Did you find it adequate?"

"More than adequate. Very good actually."

"Would you be so kind as to look into reserving a spot for my great-grandchild?"

Bonnie flattens her eyebrows. "Um, the one who's not born yet?"

"Yes. I know how these things work." Missus turns back around and looks for me. I'm not actually *hiding,* per se, but I am arranging our new fiction releases with intense focus. "Carolina, are you hiding again? Please tell me you agree. Please say that you don't have some notion of wanting the child educated in the public school system for some equalitarian, common-man nonsense."

I grab a book off the shelf to show I was working and not hiding, and step out. "You mean the school system two of my children currently attend?"

"Oh, Carolina, stop trying to argue. You just love to argue."

Shannon comes out of her cooler with a bucket of greenery. "You are right, Missus. I'm constantly amazed at how smart Peter is, and everyone knows you gave your son the best education possible."

Missus doesn't even turn toward the young woman. "I didn't ask you. Now, Carolina, come with me to Ruby's. I have something to discuss with you, and when we are here it is impossible for me to have your undivided attention." She tugs on her white gloves to make sure they are in place, turns, and nods at Bonnie, who understands she's to open the door.

Missus in her black skirt, black heels, and red silk shirt is dressed like half the state of Georgia on a Football Saturday. She leaves, and Bonnie keeps the door open.

"Are you waiting on me?" I ask her. "I have work to do. She can't just come in here and tell me to follow her like she's some Georgia Bulldog version of Jesus."

Bonnie shrugs and lets go of the heavy door. But before it closes, I stomp in that direction. "Okay, might as well. The sooner I go, the sooner I can leave. Right?"

She reaches for the door and pulls it open again. "Right. Whatever you say, Boss."

"Shut up."

After the flare of business we enjoyed this summer, things are really pretty quiet in downtown Chancey for a nice Saturday morning. Once the Georgia liquor commission discovered Gertie giving out moonshine samples at Andy's Place, she was shut down. No more weekend road trip features in the Atlanta paper. No more men encouraging their wives to shop, shop, shop while they retire to Gertie's basement for just a sip or two.

Peter's Bistro's lunch business has dried up, too, so that he just has hot dogs sitting in water in a crockpot, and a hunk of bologna and hoop cheese to slice and put on white bread. However, it's true that the lunch counter might suffer more from the absence of Alex Carrera and the success of Alex and Angie's food truck. Alex runs all over the northern suburbs of Atlanta, going from office building to park to festival, selling his creations. Apparently, Angie Conner is as much a taskmaster as her mother. Still hard to get my head around the vampire wannabe not only holding onto Alex, but keeping him in line. She's only going to school half days her senior year and building her empire the rest of her time.

Out on the sidewalk, the air is close and heavy. The trees are green, but tired-looking. Any flowers that survived the summer are leggy and have more dead leaves on them than live ones. The flower heads are small and dull-colored. Summer is definitely over, but autumn isn't in any hurry apparently.

Pulling open the door of Ruby's, I notice it even looks sadder than usual. Only half the tables are full and there's no life, no bustling. However, the smells are just as wonderful as always. Coffee and muffins. I detect hints of fruit and, hmmm, fruit? "Hey Libby," I say. "I'm sitting with Missus there. What's the muffin I smell?"

Libby leans against the back of the chair near her and looks to the back and the kitchen. "Berry apple nut is the muffin we liked the best. She's not figured out the strawberry cream cheese one just yet. It tasted good, but wouldn't hold together. You know how Ruby feels about having to use cupcake holders for a muffin." Libby rolls her eyes and walks away as she says she'll bring me some coffee and a warm muffin.

Missus is seated at one of the tables in the middle of the stuck-in-time café. She's facing the front, but looking at her notebook so she doesn't see me.

"Sit there," she says without looking up. Okay, so she did see me. "We have a few things to discuss before the others get here."

"The others? Who?" I ask, sitting down in the chair across from her.

Missus rolls her eyes up to look at me. "Honestly? That's what you want to discuss?"

"No, just asking. Go on, what do you want to discuss?"

She lays down her pen and grits her teeth, pulling a breath between them. "What are we going to do about Anna? I cannot abide her living with that man any longer. *And on my dime.* But FM thinks if I, *we*, quit paying for the apartment, she'll move in with him where I, *we*, have no control whatsoever. What does Will think?"

Libby places a cup of coffee and a muffin in front of me. I smile at her and then sigh. "Will is taking over my basement and making an apartment for himself. Honestly, it reminds me of coming down on Saturday mornings when the kids would turn the living room into a huge tent city. I don't think he misses Anna at all. And he has no clue about what the baby will mean."

"I'm worried about FM. He's taking this all so hard." She swallows and looks down for a moment. Her voice is just a mumble. "Last night I woke up, and he wasn't in bed. After a while I went looking for him. He was up in the rooms we remodeled for Anna and Will and the baby. There's no furniture since I gave it all to Anna when she moved. He was laying on the floor of the room. Just lying on the carpet in there. I, well, I couldn't bother him, or let him know I'd found him there. What are we going to do?"

Missus is worried about FM, and I am, too, but I'm also worried about her. I've only known her a little over a year, but she's never been at a loss for what to do. Never. She might've been wrong, but she always had a plan. I repeat what I've said to her every time she's brought this subject up. "I think we just have to let it play out. The baby will be born in a few months, and we will have to see how everything changes. Kyle Kendrick strikes me as someone who just likes hurting people." She rears back and her eyes fly open, so I rush to correct myself. "Oh, no, Missus. I don't think he's physically hurting Anna, I mean emotionally. He's just a bully, but I think you put a stop to him actually putting his hands on anyone for a while."

"Oh, dear God in heaven, Carolina! What if my confronting him caused him to go after my granddaughter?"

"I think it's more that Anna saw in him someone to tell her what to do, and to respect her, which honestly we didn't. We saw her as someone we could help. He not only gave her a job, but he gave her a title. Anna thinks he's a god, we just have to hope her eyes are opened soon. Or that he decides to go back home."

Missus frowns as my lips curl up into a big smile. I tell her, "Get this. Kimmy has decided to work on her marriage and is forcing him to spend time with the kids. Zoe says she took the three little ones up to the Dollar Store and let them loose to spend the morning with their daddy."

Missus can't help but smile, then she takes a deep breath and sits straighter. "Okay, I'll take your advice to just wait things out. Only I hope this time your advice proves to be well thought-out. You tend to steer us into disasters." She looks

25

over my head at someone. "Ah, there you are. Sit down and let's get to business."

Peter sits beside me. "So you're on board with this festival idea of Mother's?"

"Festival? No, I, I just…" I look around as Charles Spoon, the town's newspaper editor, pulls out the chair beside Missus; Jed Taylor, the mayor settles at one end of the table; and the new head of the chamber of commerce, our old real estate agent Retta Bainbridge, sits at the other end.

"I'll sit here beside, Carolina," says a dusky voice that makes me cringe. I've spent the past year avoiding a place I love, the library, because of Ida Faye, and now here we are, sitting side by side.

"Hi, Ida Faye," I squeak.

She settles her bulk in and looks at me. "I'm here because you and that one," she tilts her head toward Missus, "have done enough to ruin this town in the past year."

Missus speaks up. "Oh, please. You're here because Jed forced me to ask you. You must be holding some mighty fine gossip over our young mayor."

"Hey!" Jed blusters. "Ida Faye is a respected member of the, ah, community, and she'll be an asset to this committee."

Retta laughs out loud. "Sure, Jed. That's the ticket. Act innocent until ya can't no longer. Hey, Carolina, how's things with your kids all back under your roof? When I sold you that house you were worried about how they were turning out, and looks like you were right to worry, weren't ya?"

Before I can glower in response to Retta, Cathy Stone rushes in and sits down. "Whew, made it just in time. These lingerie parties every night are crazy!" She yells over to the waitress, who is also her mother. "Mama, can I get some coffee? Anyone else need anything?" In the lull, she pats our mayor's hand. "Hey handsome, how's Betty liking that thong you bought her? Sexy, isn't it?"

Jed's round face turns dark red, and he gets to coughing. Libby arrives at that moment with baskets of muffins and a fresh pot of coffee, and Missus takes the opportunity to wrestle back some control.

"All right people, I've determined the date for our festival. The second weekend in October. Now, we just need to come up with what the festival will be about." She holds out a hand to her side, to cut off Cathy, who had started to talk. "No. It will not be a lingerie festival. Despite your best efforts, this is not yet Las Vegas East."

Cathy slumps. Then, as she grabs a muffin, she says, "Maybe not, but we sure do have the Wicked *Witch* of the East living here. Pass the butter, y'all."

Chapter 3

"Missus has really gone and done it now!" Susan exclaims when I answer the phone. I'm sitting at one of the tables outside Peter's Bistro eating a boiled hot dog on a partially stale bun. Luckily, there's no limit on the spicy mustard, so it's not *completely* bad. I swallow before I ask my friend what Missus has done now.

"She's stepping all over the opening of Nine Mile. It's been set for the second weekend in October for months."

"Oh, yeah. Maybe that's why that weekend sounded so familiar when she mentioned it."

"Yes," Susan snips. "I heard you're on her committee. Like, co-chair or something."

"No. You heard wrong, well, at least that part." I try a different tack. "But maybe it's good to have the festival the same weekend. More people to come up to Nine Mile. Y'all haven't really advertised it much."

Nine Mile is a living history kind of museum set up near the Lake Park on some land confiscated due to the drug business being done there. The whole druggy family was run off or put in jail, and Mountain Electric, the company that was putting in the power plant in that area, offered to pay for a living history setup.

"We haven't advertised because we wanted it to be a slow opening," Susan says. "They're not set up for crowds yet. The idea was to provide examples of old country living. Folks making jams, blacksmithing, baking bread, weaving baskets. You know, like Dolly Parton did up in Tennessee."

"I love Dollywood," I say. "We haven't been there in years. We used to go—"

Susan shouts, "I know! Everyone loves Dollywood and apparently everyone has copied her. Now the old-time crafts people want to be paid. A lot! It's not enough to be passing down their knowledge and their experiences anymore. They're artisans and expect to be paid!" She stops, and I can hear her taking deep breaths. "I'm sorry. I don't mean to yell at you, but we thought we'd find lots of grandparent-type folk with nothing to do. Instead, well, instead it's kind of a disaster."

"Really?" I say this with an appropriate amount of compassion in my voice. But my voice is lying. Carter May, the woman whom I had big problems with last winter, is working on the Nine Mile project along with her husband, Todd. Their failure isn't *really* a disaster in my book.

Susan apparently doesn't hear the appropriate amount of compassion. "You're funny. I know what you're thinking. Believe it or not, Todd is everything Carter May said he was: lazy, unorganized, and basically just a knot on a log. No wonder she thought Jackson hung the moon."

"Leave Jackson out of this," I snap. "So, is it even going to open? What do the folks at Mountain Electric think? They're funding all of it, right?"

"Yeah, including the Lake Park and my job."

Now I understand what I'm hearing. "So, you think it's all tied together? One failure will reflect badly on everything else? What's Griffin say?" Susan's husband, Griffin, took a new, high-powered job with Mountain Electric last spring. He and Susan moved into a mansion up in the la-di-da community of Laurel Cove at the beginning of the summer.

"He doesn't say anything," Susan says. "Oh, never mind, I'm just acting crazy. I'm sure it'll all be fine, but I would appreciate you keeping me in the loop with the festival plans. How's Hank? Jackson coming home soon?"

"Tomorrow, last I heard. Hank is in the rehab, and apparently Shelby is a wonderful nurse." I crumple up my napkin. "Well, I better get back in the store. Things are really slow down here today. Maybe all Missus is doing is trying to drum up some business. Guess I can't be too sorry if Missus' festival brings more folks to Chancey, even if it'll mess up Nine Mile's quiet opening."

Susan sighs. "Yeah, I know. Hey, you want to come up here for dinner and watch the game?"

"Oh, you're showing the Tennessee game up at your house?" I laugh and add, "No thanks, I'll watch my team and leave the Georgia game to y'all. Besides, I have a ton of wash to do. I slacked off with Jackson gone. Y'all have fun, and I'll make sure to fill you in on what happens with the festival."

"Okay, thanks." Then as she's hanging up she yells, "Go Dawgs!"

Putting my phone back in my purse, I see the muffin half I wrapped up earlier at Ruby's. The mustard on the hot dog has dried, so I push it to the side and unwrap the muffin. Berry apple nut, I think Libby said. There are pieces of berry making the muffin dark and then lighter pieces of apple. It's not very sweet, but moist and warm from being in my purse. Speaking of being warm, the shade is moving away from my table, so as I pop the last piece of muffin in my mouth, I stand.

"Hey, Carolina. What ya doing?" Gertie's daughter, Patty, comes from around the corner.

"Oh, hey, Patty. Just eating a late lunch. What about you?" Patty has taken to wearing dresses all the time. At first I was glad. They looked cuter on her than the shapeless pants and big tops she hid in before. But now the dresses are getting about as shapeless. I haven't asked, but I think wearing the dresses has something to do with Andy's family. His father is minister at one of those little churches out on the back roads. They're pretty fundamentalist. They picketed when the coffee shop opened on Sunday mornings.

"Oh, not much," she answers. "Going to Peter's to get Mama a fountain Coke, but I was also supposed to stop in and see you."

She stops talking, and so I prod. "What did you want to see me for?"

"Mama wants you to stop by before you go home. She says you've never seen Andy's Place, and she has something to ask you." She turns toward Peter's front door.

She shuffles along, and I realize I have another command performance. What is it makes people think they can just tell me to follow them, or show up, and I'll do it? Well, I suppose I don't have anything else to do. And she's right, I've yet to go into Andy's Place. Having tried to run a business with Andy and Patty, I have an idea that their store looks like one of the worst episodes of *Hoarders*. Makes my skin crawl a bit just thinking about it. But, well, can't hurt to stop by.

With all my garbage in one hand, my purse over my shoulder, and my plans for the afternoon laid out, I go back to the shop. I reach the door just in time to open it for Shannon as she comes out with one of the big arrangements she was working on earlier.

"I'm delivering these and then I'm done. We've not done enough business today to pay for the toilet paper we used in the store. Hope that festival you're in charge of works magic." Beeping heralds the back door of her van opening, just as Bonnie sticks her head out the door.

"If you'll hold the door, I'll take this one out to her." she says. "Sooner we can get her gone, the better."

Once Bonnie is through, I enter our store. It's still hard to believe how Gertie's decorating this summer changed it completely. Patty's mama has owned this building for decades. No telling what other property she owns, but now that she lives in Chancey again, little bit by little bit, we are finding out just how much control Gertie Samson has over our little town. She seems to have unlimited resources and no fear.

Wait—what did Patty say? Gertie wants to ask me something? Okay, forewarned is forearmed. I push my purse under the counter and state out loud. "Just say no. No. No."

Bonnie sails in the door and then stops. "No, what?"

"Never mind. So, Shannon's been a pill? Sorry I was in the back working when I came back from Ruby's and then ate lunch out there."

Bonnie waves her hand in dismissal. "No worse than usual. She's just so depressing and negative."

"Surely Peter isn't dating her, is he?" I used to like Shannon, but ever since her stepfather made her start carrying her own weight at their house, she's gotten so grouchy.

"Oh no," I groan. Then I sigh and grimace. "Think when I finally have it out with Will he'll get all moody like that?"

Bonnie's eyes widen, her eyebrows arch, and her mouth stays shut. She picks up the duster from where she'd laid it earlier and decides she needs to dust at the other end of the store.

I laugh. "Okay, I get it. Not giving parenting advice."

She waves with the duster and makes me roll my eyes.

I hate when I know what I have to do and can't find anyone to talk me out of it.

CHAPTER 4

"I'm going to walk up and see Andy's Place, want to come?" I ask Bonnie as we close and lock the door to Blooming Books. She lifts her head to look up at the house-turned-store at the end of the street.

"I haven't actually been in there yet, so it's enticing. However, Cal and I are going to an exhibit at the High Museum of Art in Atlanta tonight. I better go home and get changed." She turns toward the corner where her car is parked, but says over her shoulder, "I'll expect a full report on Monday. Bye."

"Bye," I say, still standing and watching her walk away. *An exhibit at The High?* Now that's an excuse you don't hear every day. Matter of fact, I don't think I've ever had someone say that to me before, especially on a Football Saturday. Dropping my keys into my purse, I turn and say out loud, "Oh well, forget The High, I've got a date with a junk store slash moonshine parlor!"

It's four o'clock and last I checked Georgia Tech was tied in the fourth quarter. Maybe the game will go into overtime. Avoiding the heat of the sun, I walk close to the buildings and can't imagine how hot Savannah is in the stadium. Especially since she's wearing a sweater. Oh, well, I tried to tell her. One good thing of her being on a campus is maybe it'll prod her to apply to colleges. So far, she's resisted applying anywhere. Only saying, she'll do it later and she has plenty of time. And she does, I guess, but…

Chancey is the quietest it's been all day. I'm the only one visible right now and the only sound is the broadcast from some football game, but it's too dim for me to decide who the teams are or even where it's coming from.

At the end of the block, I look up at Andy's Place. Situated next door to Missus and FM Bedwell's beautifully restored antebellum home, it's hard to not compare the two buildings. Although it's not a comparison that takes very long. Actually, you don't get much past the paint choices. Historically accurate, pleasing to the eye, and well-coordinated colors on one house. On the other, well, not so much. Neon green paint covers the wooden siding. Elaborate gingerbread trim accents the green with swirls of bright purple. The shutters are orange. Highway safety vest orange. And then there's the elegant brass plate under the one doorbell spelling out "Bedwells" to compare to the big letters on the other roof spelling out "ANDY'S" in kindergartner handwriting.

Folks do not get the two places confused.

Stepping up onto the porch, I first think the solid wooden front door is standing open, but then I realize there is not a wooden front door. It's a solid glass door, like on a strip mall store. It's set between two wall-sized windows so that the interior is immediately visible. A soft bell chimes when I open the door and step in. The big door quietly falls closed behind me just as Patty comes down the hall to my left.

"Hey Carolina!" She laughs. "Look at you. Surprised?"

My mouth is hanging open, full of questions I can't get out. Where's the clutter? The junk? Any evidence whatsoever that Andy Taylor is in charge here? Finally I ask, "Where is everything? This place is amazing."

Soft gray carpet spreads out in the big, open room, down

the hall, and up the stairs. The walls are painted white. The wide historical ceiling's trim is the same shiny purple from the outside and the windows are trimmed with the neon green. All the furniture is bright orange, like the shutters.

"What's all the furniture for?" In the big room, there are small gathering spots of chairs, each surrounding a clear coffee table with a laptop opened on it.

"This is our viewing room. Everything we sell is loaded on the computers so you can look through everything from right here. Of course, you can also look around the rooms, which is where the things are." She shakes her head and beams, adding, "But we also have stuff we sell all over! Like all over the world!"

While she's talking I walk to the hall and start down it. At the first doorway, I stick my head in and she's right. It looks like a regular old antique store. Crowded shelves and small aisles. "So all the rooms, even upstairs, look like this?"

"Yep. Well, most of them. We do have one we use for shipping stuff."

"Oh, there you are, Carolina," Gertie booms from behind us. "'Bout time you came to visit, don't ya think?"

"Gertie, this place is really something." I walk back out. "Was this all your idea?"

"Mine and Andy's." She pauses. "We let Patty pick the colors." The big woman shrugs at me and comes as close to rolling her eyes as I've ever seen her. "My apartment is behind there," she says pointing to the right side of the big room. The wall is solid, with an entrance towards the back. "But forget all this, let's go downstairs. We need to talk."

Patty chirps, "This way, down the hall."

As I follow her, Gertie dismisses her daughter. "Not you. Get them orders packaged up. UPS is picking them up in less than an hour."

Patty peels off and opens the last door on the left as she

points me to the right, where the hall ends with a landing. In that area the gray carpet is matched with walls and trim of the same gray, the first break in orange, green, and purple accents.

Gertie moves around me and begins walking down the wide stairs. There are small light strips at the floor and ceiling to give some light and a carved sign at the entrance saying, "The Cave."

"So this is it? The place with the moonshine?" I ask as we descend.

"This is it." At the bottom she moves to the side and looks back, I'm sure wanting to see my reaction. She's not disappointed.

Again, my mouth is hanging open. The gray carpet no longer only covers the floor, but the walls and ceiling. The same furniture in orange upstairs is gray down here. Same gray as the carpet so it does look like a cave. The clear Lucite tables from upstairs are replaced by low tables made of thick wood slabs. The gray is only broken by a large stone fireplace, where a dozen candles are now lit.

"Of course we'll have a big fire going there in the winter. Can't wait for it to get cold enough. What do you think?"

"It's… it's beautiful, cozy. Oh, look, the bar!" Behind me, on the other side of the stairs is a wooden bar with a wall of televisions.

"Did ya hear I got my license all worked out? We're reopening this week. I kinda liked the idea of it being illegal, brought back those good old memories of running shine in the mountains, you know?"

"Except it was illegal," I add.

She waves a hand at me. "Law, shmaw, but guess it's not all bad being on the right side of the police. Seeing as I got Patty and Andy wrapped up in it and hope to get me a grandbaby real soon." As she moves toward the bar, she points me to a chair.

"Sit down. Let's have a drink. Play with that remote there and you can find a game to watch."

The chair is so comfortable, I just sink into it for a minute. Then I grab the remote and point it at the wall behind her. One by one, the screens jump to life and light fills the cave.

Now how will I ever watch a game in my house again? This is perfect.

"Your smile says you like it. You like the cave?" Gertie asks as she sits in the chair beside me. "Try this. Smell it first."

She hands me a cold glass that looks like it's carved out of rock. It's rough, but feels right in my hand. "Smells like, um, I don't know. Smells good." Then I take a sip. "Oh, Gertie, that tastes like, like…" I grin at her. "It's pecan pie."

"Very good, Carolina. Take a look at my moonshine menu." She points toward the wooden sign at the bar.

"Apple crisp, peach cobbler, banana pudding, pecan pie, blackberry muffin, and strawberry shortcake. These are moonshine flavors?"

"Yep. Brand name is 'Southern Sweets.' Finish that and you can taste the others," she says as she starts to get up.

"No, no, thanks. I'll just sip this. Gotta say, I'm really impressed. I pictured it, well, different."

"Yeah, that's the problem. Having trouble convincing folks it's not a junky basement."

"Gertie, how can you afford all this? You can't have that much business, upstairs or down here for all this." I clamp my mouth shut and grimace. "I'm sorry. Never mind, it's rude of me to ask."

"No worries. If I don't want to tell ya something, I won't. Now, the junk stuff upstairs, over ninety percent is sold online. Got to get Patty some help with the shipping. That's all just to keep her and Andy happy. Andy loves looking for junk, both real and online. I don't give a bullfrog's tail about all that. This…" She lays her head back and looks around. "This is my passion. Been waiting my whole life for moonshine to make its comeback. Been saving my money."

She takes a heavy drink from her cup and motions for me to join her, so I lift mine and take another sip of the sweet, smooth liquid. It warms me all the way down to my toes, and I giggle. "Gertie, I don't usually like strong liquor, but this? Yum."

"Glad you approve and glad you could come by. Make yourself at home. Have to tell you, I do miss getting to visit with you like I did all those weeks living up at your place. Come to think of you as a friend, Carolina."

"Really?" I had no idea. "Oh, that's nice. You aren't exactly what you seem, are you, Gertie? Like the way you had them paint and fix up Blooming Books? It's as good as any Atlanta interior designer. And come to think of it, I enjoyed your company, too, up at the house." I take another sip, well, maybe a bit more than a sip.

Gertie leans forward. "Did you see the rock cubes in your cup? You freeze them and then put them in the drink. They don't melt so no watering down your drink."

"What will they think of next? It goes with the theme. Cave and rocks. Oh, I don't think I want anymore," I protest when she lifts up the bottle she'd retrieved from the bar.

"Please, just a taste. It's my newest one. Peach cobbler. Do you like peaches?"

"They are *just* my favorite!" That was a tad over enthusiastic, probably should slow down. "Okay, a sip, then I need to get home." She pours and settles back down across from me. We watch in the quiet as Georgia Tech wins in overtime. My eyes travel from one screen to the next. Wait'll Jackson sees this. With peaches on my tongue and a new appreciation for Gertie Samson, I smile at her and tip my glass towards my gracious host.

"Back at ya, friend," she says, tilting her own glass. "So, Carolina, this festival you're in charge of…"

Oh.

"…I have a couple questions."

CHAPTER 5

"I know it sounds tacky, but it wasn't," I whisper with a slap at Laney's leg. "Stop laughing so loud."

We're getting rude looks from the congregation, and the organist seems to be playing louder to cover Laney's laughter. This is why I don't sit with my friends during church. Confession time—I have this problem: can't help talking during the service if I'm sitting next to anyone that'll talk back.

Jackson won't and my kids would rather die than be caught whispering with their mother, so usually I'm forced to be good. But with Jackson gone and Laney's husband, Shaw, sitting up front as the lay reader, it's just the two of us in the third row. And it's not going well. Susan is two rows behind us, and I keep hearing her clear her throat, louder and louder. She really thinks that'll stop us? Any minute I expect her to come up here, push us apart, and sit in between us.

When the preacher walks up to the altar, he gives us a look before beginning the sermon. I really try to not talk during the sermon. Really. Laney has also calmed down and is actually taking notes about the sermon. Hmm, if it's that good maybe I should actually be listening instead of wondering what the Quinbys are fighting about. Look at their body language, sitting so rigid, not touching. And who in the world lets their six-year-old dye their hair *that* color? Brandy Chambliss, that's who. She doesn't have the brains God gave a goose. Laney lays a piece of paper on my lap, then primly looks up at the pastor, drinking in his every word. Okay, okay. Taking a deep breath, I focus for a moment, then take a look at the paper.

New Moonshine Flavors – Peanut Butter, Margarine, Celery, Chicken Soup, Chicken and Dumpling, Taco Casserole.

I scrape my teeth along my tongue trying to keep from laughing out loud. Laney is still acting focused and serious, but her crossed leg is shaking and her foot is swinging up and down in midair. She turns slightly towards me and whispers, "Aluminum Foil Moonshine."

Hopefully, my coughing fit seemed legit. Or at least the final hymn covered it up.

"You two are never sitting together again," Susan says as she grips the fat on the back of my arm and squeezes it at the end of service. "You were worse than any of the kids in church today."

"Ow, that hurts!" I jerk my arm away.

Laney smirks at her sister and says, "What if we let you sit with us next time? Jealousy is such an *ugly* emotion."

Susan shakes her head. "Jealous? Okay, well, maybe a bit. What in the world were y'all talking about?"

Laney grins. "Carolina went to Gertie's, well, Andy's place yesterday. She was in the moonshine basement."

"Really? What'd you think? Is there even any room to sit down?"

"Get this, sis, there's carpet on the walls and ceiling," Laney says. "And you drink out of rocks."

"I'm not talking about this here." I turn my back on them and walk down the aisle toward the front doors. "Good morning, Missus, FM. How are y'all doing?"

Missus raises one eyebrow, sniffs, then walks out the open front doors. FM chuckles. "You're lucky she didn't come over there and snatch you and Laney bald-headed. Few years back, she would've. Lucky for you she's softened up."

"Softened up? I don't think so. How are you doing, FM?"

He winks. "Oh, I'm 'bout the best ya ever saw, if you ain't seen much. How about you? When's Jackson get back?"

"Today. You want to join us for Chinese? He's planning on just coming there when he gets in town." We walk out into the sunshine. "Laney will also be there, so Missus can put us in our place. She'd enjoy that."

"Now that is an offer she can't refuse. We'll see you there." He waves as he walks on to where Missus is holding court on the other side of the steps. FM sounds like always, but there's a light in his eyes that's gone out and he seems to shuffle along more than before. Anna moving out makes him look his age for the first time since I've known him.

I look down over the crowd leaving, trying to see if Anna might have come in to church late, but I don't see her. The teenagers are gathered in one corner of the parking lot, and I watch as the group ebbs and flows. Savannah went to church with Isaac this morning, but is meeting us for lunch, so she's not down there.

Bryan is in the middle of all the youth, but I'm not crazy about where the group's ebb and flow has taken him. With Grant going to school at Darien Academy and him making the transition to high school, Bryan has found some new friends. Smart-aleck guys and sullen girls. Kids that come to church Sunday morning to keep their parents happy, but wouldn't be caught dead at a youth group function.

Reaching the bottom of the steps, I catch my son's eye and smile as I walk towards him. "Hey, ready to head to lunch? Hi guys." What I wouldn't give for a little of the smarmy, fake good manners of Savannah's friends. These kids stare at me like I just asked to drug-test them. Bryan ignores me, but nods at them and starts walking toward me. Well, not exactly toward me, but to the side of me where he never even looks my direction as he passes. When I look back at his friends, there's a black wall of their backs. Okay. Lovely children I can't wait to get to know better!

"Dad will be there, right?" Bryan says as I join him in the van.

"Yep, just got a text from him. He'll be there in fifteen minutes. It'll be good to see him, won't it?"

He shrugs and starts playing with his phone. He grew about a foot this summer and developed muscles with his new attitude and a recurring crop of acne.

"So, your friends back there," I start. "What're their names?"

"They're just people."

"But do I know them?"

"How would I know if you know them? They're just kids I know from school. Aren't I supposed to reach out to people at church?"

"I guess. So who are they?" He's busy pressing stuff on his phone, so I wait. "Bryan?" He still doesn't look up. "Bryan!" I finally yell.

"What?" he asks, looking at me.

"Those people you were talking with at church, who are they?"

"I don't know, okay? Just people."

Well, that was a productive talk. You'd think this being my third teenager I'd know to shut up. But... "So, does Grant like Darien?"

Bryan scoffs. "I don't know."

"Did you ask him about it?"

"Some."

"What did he say?"

"I don't know."

I slam on the brakes at the stop sign. No real need to slam

on the brakes except I needed to hit or stomp on something. I also wanted to get my son's attention. As the van shudders to its stop, Bryan looks at me. So see, it worked. Feeling superior, I slide my eyes toward him as I smoothly pull my foot off the pedal and press the gas.

Wait—did he roll his eyes at me?

He rolled his eyes at me!

Then he shakes his head and makes it worse. "Mom, just chill, okay?"

Then he makes it even worser, worse, worst? Whatever! He mumbles under his breath. "Good thing Dad gets home today."

Tires spin as I jerk the van into the Chinese restaurant's gravel parking lot. That makes me feel some better. I resist another superior glance at my son. There's only so much teenage judgment one can stand this early in the day.

CHAPTER 6

"That's what she's worried about. Folks here think of it as a junky basement, but I'm telling you it's not." I hand my used plate to the waitress.

"Keep your fork," she reminds me, so I grab it and use it to point at Laney. "And the carpet on the walls and ceiling is *not* creepy. It's nice, it's cozy."

Our heads all turn as we hear a commotion near the front door. "There's Jackson," Missus says. The restaurant was crowded when we got there, so we all ended up at small tables around the place. The men are at a table up front and the kids are on the other side of the large fish tank, out of sight, out of mind. We ladies—me, Susan, Missus, and Laney—are at a tiny table way in the back and I'm facing the back wall.

"Hey honey," Jackson says as he grasps my shoulders and kisses my cheek. "Sorry we got held up. Construction had the highway down to one lane. Guess there's no room for me back here."

I wipe my mouth and then lay my napkin on the table as I struggle to get out of my chair. There was little room before, but with Jackson standing there, it's even tighter.

He says, "Don't try to get up. Guys have seats for us up front. We'll talk later. I'm starving."

"Okay," I acquiesce as I settle back down. "Your dad doing okay when you left?"

"Yep, just doing the rehab thing. I'm going to go eat. I'm starving."

He leaves, and Susan asks, "So who's with him? He said *us*, and then *we* got held up."

"Oh, he did." Standing up is much easier since he's moved and since Susan left the table, headed to the buffet again. "I'm not sure."

ollowing her, I look for Jackson and come up behind him as he fills his plate to give him a little hug. "I'm so glad you're home."

He steps to the side, stringing noodles off his plate. "Me, too."

Then through the clear plastic sneeze guards I see who the *us* and *we* meant. "Colt. Hi."

"Hey Carolina," my young brother-in-law says as he picks a piece of broccoli off his plate and shoves it in his mouth before continuing down his side of the buffet line.

Turning my head, I look to see my husband, but he's already moved from the noodles down to the eggrolls. I catch up with him. "Colt came with you?"

He moves around the end, saying, "Yeah. I told you."

I scurry around the end. "No, it was very open-ended. Like, in the future at some point. Not right now."

He dribbles hot mustard over his plate of food. "Oh, thought you knew. Aren't you getting food? Y'all aren't done yet, are you?"

"No, we're not done, but..." People in line cause us to separate. My husband shrugs and smiles before turning toward their table. Stepping out of folks' way, I go back to the beginning of the line and get a clean plate.

Back at the table, Missus is waiting since she only eats one plate of food. Ever. If you think she's superior at other times, try sitting with her at a buffet. I mean, why come to a buffet if you're only eating one plate? She speaks as soon as my plate hits the table. "So, Jackson's younger brother Colt came with him. I never had the opportunity to talk to him at the wedding."

"I did. I talked to him at the wedding," Laney says with a grin and a wink as she sits.

Missus smirks. "Of course you did. Never one to let being pregnant deter your flirting. How long is he here for, Carolina?"

Putting a piece of sweet and sour chicken in my mouth, I shrug, keeping my eyes on my plate.

Susan laughs. "You didn't know he was coming, did you?"

Swallowing, I shrug again. "I knew he was coming at some point, but not right now. And I don't have any idea how long he's staying. Colt's okay, but I don't really know him. He's so young and he's single. We've never had a lot in common."

"Isn't he a football coach? Shouldn't he be busy this time of year?" Laney asks as she stands up. "I hear Cayden starting to fuss. It was kind of nice not having enough room for his carrier back here, but it doesn't take much fussing for Shaw to freak out. Keep me in the loop on what Colt's doing. We need more interesting young people in Chancey, I think." She gets almost to the fish tank when she turns and says loudly, "Maybe he'll move here!"

Now that'll kill your appetite. More family moving in.

Missus clears her throat and primly leans on the empty table in front of her, empty due to her one-plate rule. "Carolina Jessup, you and your family have done more to increase Chancey's census figures than when General Sherman came through with the entire Union army. There's the four of you who moved here, then add Will. And now your brother-in-law?"

Susan wipes her hands and balls her napkin up. As she drops it on her plate, she says, "It's just more fun to be where Carolina is, apparently."

Pushing my chair back, I moan, and not only from a full stomach. "Then remind me to not be so much fun. Did I tell you Will is already trying to turn our basement into his pad? Hopefully Colt's just here for a little visit."

We walk towards the front, then I turn to speak to them quietly. "Used to be I worried about having complete strangers sleeping in our house with the B&B. Now, it's the people I *know* that worry me!"

We laugh and continue to the front where the rest of our crew are paying bills and wandering out to the sidewalk. Jackson holds up four fingers for the number of meals we're paying for. I nod yes and follow the rest into the afternoon humidity.

"Savannah, how did your face get so sunburned?" Missus demands.

My daughter sighs. "I went to the Tech game yesterday. It was brutal."

"Brutal? But they won, right?" Susan says.

"Sure, but you wouldn't believe how hot it was. And we were in the full sun. I don't ever burn, so I didn't put any sunscreen on. It makes my face looks so greasy."

"Well, I hate to say I told you so, but I told you so!" I crow as I step up to the edge of the sidewalk beside her. "She had to wear her new boots and jeans and sweater. Just *had* to!"

"Mom…" She groans with an obligatory eye roll.

I smile wide at her and mentally pat myself on my back as we walk into the parking lot. Rare to get to put a teenager in their place with an audience. Yes, I'm being mean, but… okay no excuse, I'm just being mean.

"Mom?" Savannah says again. This time with a bit of a lilt and a bit of a question.

A look to my right where she's standing tells me she's stopped and is pointing at the truck she's next to. It's a big pickup truck with the rear loaded down with furniture and boxes. Then she points to the bumper where a sticker says "Painter Football."

Bryan wanders up to her, looks at the pickup, and says, "That's Uncle Colt's truck."

Laney starts laughing. Susan joins her. Missus shakes her head and walks on. Suddenly a big hand lands on my shoulders.

"Sure do appreciate y'all letting me stay with you a while, Carolina," Colt says. "Think Chancey and me are going to get along just fine."

CHAPTER 7

"What's going on in the basement?" Jackson asks as he enters our bedroom.

I'm pulling off the shirt I wore to church, and that stops him in his tracks. "Whoa," he says. "Forget the basement. What's going on in here? Need some help getting undressed?" He closes the door and starts unbuttoning his shirt with a grin. "Can't believe you've had to do all this undressing by yourself while I've been gone."

"And I can manage a bit longer by myself," I say as I step away from him into the bathroom and close the door. "Is Colt moving here? You never mentioned he'd have a truck full of furniture," I yell through the closed bathroom door.

"He needs a break from home. Guess it hit him pretty hard, Mom and Dad breaking up. He and Dad were always pretty close, but now Dad needs no one but Shelby." He pauses, then weariness creeps into his voice. "Apparently Colt slacked off with his job and got fired. I felt kind of sorry for him."

Okay. That does make sense, but I'm not letting Jackson off the hook this easily. As I change into my old shorts and worn T-shirt for a Sunday afternoon chilling out, I say, again through the door, "You still should've told me. Not hit me in the face with it in front of God and everybody. I thought we agreed to talk more, right?"

He doesn't say anything, and I wait while I brush my hair. "Jackson?" I finally call. When he still doesn't answer, I open the door and look out. At first I don't see him, then he clears his throat and I spot him. In the bed. No clothes in sight. And he's *not* asleep.

"Yes," he agrees. "You're right. I should've talked to you more. So, come here, lay right down here and we can talk."

"I don't think we'll get much talking done," I say.

"Yes, we will. We need to talk. Really do." He winks at me then widens his eyes in mock innocence. "Come on, I've got a lot, a whole lot to say to you." He pats the bed and tries to look serious. Then he gasps. "Why, Mrs. Jessup! If all we're going to do is talk, why are you taking off your clothes?"

"Oh, shut up, Mr. Jessup. Sometimes you talk too much."

Leaving our bedroom I pause to hear where everyone is, but there's no sound. The house feels empty. No pulse of music seeping through headphones, no TV, no one stirring on any of the floors except for Jackson getting into the shower. I can't help but smile closing the door behind me. What a great idea it was to get some talking done.

In the kitchen I open the basement door, but hear no one down there either. Movement catches my eye out the back doors, and I look to see Savannah on the deck. She's sitting at the table waving at someone walking up the hill.

"Hey," I say, stepping outside, then I extend my greeting to Bryan and Colt as they near the steps.

Colt puts his arm across Bryan's shoulders. "Bryan was showing me around the garden. Never paid much attention to your yard when I was here for the wedding. Nice how it goes all the way down to the river. Pretty hot out here, though."

"Y'all want some water or tea? I'll bring it out. Savannah, you want a refill on tea?" As I take her offered glass, I notice she's got a textbook open on the table. "You're studying?" Oops, the direct question slipped out, and I'm duly rewarded with an eye roll.

I bring the boys the bottles of water they requested and glasses of tea for me and Savannah. Bryan or Colt haven't sat down yet.

Colt is holding Savannah's school book. "I think we use this same text at Painter High. Seems like I've seen it around the halls. So you're a senior this year? Whew, time flies."

When I see the book is for math class, I can't help my involuntary grimace. "Ugh, math. You have a test tomorrow?"

"What classes did you teach?" my daughter asks her uncle, ignoring me. But there wasn't an eye roll this time.

"Civics, or it may be American Government here, and Phys Ed. Did some weight training classes, too." He punches at Bryan's arm. "I hear Bryan is playing football. What about you, Savannah? Any sports?"

"Cheer, but it's not that much of a sport here. Not like at our old school." She stands up and takes her book back from her uncle. "But that's not all bad. It's pretty low-key and just fun." She turns to me. "And no, I don't have a test tomorrow, like I would need to study for math. Isaac is having a hard time in this class, so I'm going to help him in a little bit, before church."

"You're going to youth group at his church?" I ask as she heads for the kitchen.

"They don't do youth group," she says. "Their church doesn't believe in dividing the ages from each other. It's all very modern. Not like our church."

"But they chaperone their kids' dates," I mumble, then raise my voice. "Bryan, if Savannah isn't going I guess you'll need a ride, if you're still going to youth group."

Bryan nods. "Think I'm going. I'll let you know." He also enters the kitchen, and I'm left with Colt. Not sure my brother-in-law and I have ever actually been alone together.

Colt leans back on the deck railing. "I like teaching teenagers, but I'm not sure I'd ever want to parent one."

"It is not for the weak of heart."

And there we are. That's the extent of our conversation. Finally, just as I decide to go inside and avoid him all together, Jackson walks out. "Shower felt great. I'm all unpacked. Colt, did you get unpacked?"

Colt opens his mouth, then closes it.

I open my mouth and then just before I close it in an imitation of Colt, everything I've been thinking falls out in a jumble. "Where will you stay? And how much stuff did you bring? For how long? Do we need a storage unit? Is all that stuff in your truck supposed to go in our house? Will's planning on moving into the basement. There's the baby coming in December, so we need to make a nursery, right? The B&B rooms are booked pretty much every weekend this fall." Then my mouth closes, popping back open just to say, "But it's good to have you here, Colt."

His face darkens, and he looks down at his feet. "Yeah, sounds like it."

Jackson steps over to his brother. "I messed up. Guess I thought I'd told Carolina more than I had. Let's get you into one of the B&B rooms for a couple nights to start with." He looks at me. "That'll be okay, right, until the weekend?"

I take a deep breath. "Sure. Chessie Room is open. It won't take but a minute to put clean sheets on and straighten it up." I stand up and swallow as I look at Colt. Seems like I should apologize, but now the words are stuck in my throat again. So I turn inside. "Okay, I'll go do that."

Well. Isn't this going to be fun?

I grab sheets from the laundry basket in the B&B office and take them into the Chessie Room on the right side of the hall. The Chessie Room is based on the advertising campaign for the Chesapeake & Ohio Railroad in 1933. Chessie, the cuddly kitten tucked in fast asleep on snow-white linens, starred in the ads. "Sleep Like a Kitten and Wake Up Fresh as a Daisy in Air-Conditioned Comfort" was the slogan. Even now, Chessie calendars are popular, and I found several on eBay cheap. So I ordered them, then cut out and framed the cutest pictures to cover the walls. A current calendar hangs beside the small secretary desk near the door. We painted the room dusky blue and the furniture antique white.

The curtains are yards and yards of unironed, unbleached muslin. We hemmed the bottoms but left the edges frayed, again for that well-loved look. On the bed, the same white comforter we use in all three rooms is coupled with a light gray cashmere throw. The comforter and throw are piled in the desk chair. I yank the dirty sheets off and dump them in another corner. I tuck one corner of the elastic fitting onto the corner nearest me, then help arrives.

"Here, let me get this side," Jackson says entering the room. "You just said Will wants to move into the basement, is that what's happened down there? That's what I came upstairs to ask you about before we got busy talking. Throw me that pillow," he says with a smile and a waggle of his eyebrows.

So I chuck the pillow at him. "It's a mess down there, isn't it? I was so mad when I saw it yesterday, didn't go back down when I got home last night. Oh, I forgot to tell you about last night, you are not going to believe me when you hear about Gertie's moonshine thing. *That* basement is amazing."

"Wait, first back to our basement. It's not a mess. I was thinking it looked great. No idea Will did it, or even *could* do it. Where did he get the furniture?"

I stand up straight, letting the soft gray cover fall from my hand. "Furniture? Guess I need to go take a look. Come on." Jackson follows me down the stairs. At the bottom step he has to nudge me forward so he can also see. Our old couch is still there, but there's also nice-looking end tables and a new coffee table. Where's the old one covered with crayon marks from our kids' coloring days? And there's a pretty rug in blues and greens covering most of the living room area. Straight ahead of us, the door to the middle junk room is open, and there's no junk in sight. As I step to it and then inside the door, I see a double bed made up with a red bedspread. There's a matching bedside table and dresser, both painted white.

"Look at this," Jackson says as he steps out of the bedroom doorway and pulls on my arm to me turn around.

The washer and dryer, as usual, sit side by side to the right of the stairs. They are tucked against the back wall of the house near a high-up window, which lets in very little light as it's practically at ground level. The table I had for sorting clothes and folding is still there. However, it's now a kitchen counter beside the big old laundry tub, which I've never used. Apparently, the faucet for the tub works, as it looks cleaner than the last time I remember looking in it. There's dish soap, a dish strainer, a cutlery basket, and stacks of dishes. Four plates, saucers, bowls, and mugs for a new coffee pot, which is also sitting there.

The shelf that held detergent, dryer sheets, and other laundry stuff now holds kitchen items. My laundry things are in a cardboard box on the floor, wedged in beside the washer. There's a small refrigerator sitting in front of the dryer, off to the side just enough to allow me to open the dryer door, kind of. There's a toaster oven on top of the dryer, facing towards the kitchen area, of course, and on top of the refrigerator there's a basket of nonperishable food. Maybe I should be flattered that my son chose the same items I buy at the store, but I think not.

I think I did choose them, and that they came from my cabinets upstairs.

Jackson crosses his arms, then shakes his head. "You think Will did all this?"

"No. Absolutely not. There's a rug on the floor—some woman has helped him. But look at my laundry space. We run a bed-and-breakfast, laundry is important. But it did *not* look like this yesterday morning." I pull my phone out of my pocket and rant. "He is totally out of control. He's an adult. This is our house. He can't just do… this! You need to have a talk with him!"

Jackson takes a step back from me. "Calm down. I'm actually kind of impressed. It looks pretty good, I think. He's an adult, I think we need to give him some space."

"Space? Like our entire basement? What about the laundry or a place for Bryan and his friends to hang out? You think Will is going to let them hang out here now?"

Jackson shrugs and turns toward the stairs. "He'll be home soon. I need to go pack for next week. We can talk about it when Will gets home, but for now it's all good. Colt and Will are both settled for now."

He's halfway up the stairs when he adds, "What are you thinking for dinner?"

"I'm thinking about running away," I say loudly.

I can hear his raised eyebrows all the way down here.

Chapter 8

"You are obsessed with basements," Laney says as she opens the door to Ruby's. "First it was Gertie's and now your own. So Will spruced it up. I'm not getting the angry part. Hey, Libby, we need a table. Cayden's carrier won't fit in a booth."

"But it's not his basement to fix up!" I protest. "Wait'll you see where we have to do laundry. Nowhere to fold things or even move. Hey, Libby. How you doing?"

Libby sighs as she rests her empty hand on a bony hip and keeps the full coffee pot upright in her other fist. "All right, I guess. Working here all day, then taking care of a five-year-old every night is getting old. At least when she lived with us, Cathy was there to help. Now she's all over north Georgia doing them lingerie shows, and she gets home so late, he just sleeps over most nights. His grandpa didn't retire to have to get up, pack his lunch, and haul him to school every day. I'd do it, but I'm here so early. Anyway. Best muffins today are banana nut, she put some granola stuff on top that's real good, or the spiced apple ones. Those have those little cinnamon candies in them. Strange, but pretty good."

"One of each. We'll share. Wait, is Susan coming?" I ask Laney.

She's clutching the handle of a pacifier in her teeth. She

doesn't look at me as she's trying to settle Cayden, but she mumbles, "I don't know."

Libby nods and turns. "I'll bring more if ya need them."

With her son settled and the other end of the pacifier in his mouth, Laney leans back against her chair and lifts her coffee cup. "Would it be bad of me to ask Zoe to drop out of school?"

I chuckle. "Yes, it would be. And don't you dare joke about it to her. She's struggling with being there all day as it is. The girl needs to think about herself for once, unlike the rest of the young people in this town who only think of themselves. Did you hear Libby? Cathy just assumes her folks will make her life easier. Sorry to say, it's the same with Will. And you aren't angry at him yet, but just wait until you have to do laundry for the B&B." I smugly sip my coffee and wait for her to realize how this will impact her.

"So just tell him that the price for him having the basement is he has to do all the laundry. Thanks, Libby." She takes the apple muffin onto her plate and cuts it in half. "Look, you can see the little red spots where the candies were." She pinches a bite marked in red. "Umm, cinnamony, just like the candy."

"But... but what if... I mean... Will do all the laundry? That won't work."

Her mouth is full, so she scrunches her eyes at me and lifts a hand in question.

"Because," I say, "he'll forget, or mess it up, or something."

"He's got a degree from the University of Georgia," she says. "If he can't do laundry then we taxpayers need to demand our money back from that esteemed institution."

"But what if he doesn't want to do it?"

This she doesn't even grace with words. Just a cocked eyebrow and pinched lips.

My phone rings. I find it in my purse and answer it. "Hey, Miss Susan. You coming to Ruby's?"

"Can't. I'm waiting on the police at the Lake Park. Someone broke into the concession stand last night."

My eyes widen at this news, and Laney shoots me a puzzled but intrigued look. "No way! Was there any money there?"

"No, just candy and cups and things. They took the candy and then made a mess. I'm so mad!"

"I bet. How did they get in?"

"Through the window. My fault for not having a real lock on it. Listen, I've got to go. Police are here."

"Did you hear that?" I ask Laney as I hang up. Susan usually talks pretty clearly, and this time she was talking really loud, too.

"Yes. That's awful. Who could've done that?"

"Bet it was some kids," I say. "Can't wait to hear what the police think. Okay, but before Cayden wakes up and you have to go, I want to run an idea by you about the festival. Tell me if I'm crazy."

"Okay, shoot. So far all the ideas I've heard are old repeats or just stupid."

I take a deep breath and tell her. "Southern Desserts – banana pudding, peach pie, blackberry cobbler, chocolate pie, buttermilk pie, all of them. We could have food booths offering desserts done by businesses and fundraising groups. Like the high school band doing – oh, strawberry shortcakes."

Laney nods, smiles, then leans up and adds, "And you know how they do that world's largest ice cream sundae thing? We could do something like that with banana pudding! Layers of vanilla wafers, pudding, sliced bananas, cool whip?"

"Oh, yes! There are all kind of ideas, like pie-eating contests and a bake-off that can be done in different age groups. We could even do one of those 3K runs, like a Sugar Sprint or Dessert Dash." I clap my hands and laugh. "Or the Pudding Prance, and for walkers, the Pudding Plod!"

Cayden startles as I clap again. He stretches his mouth

wide to let his displeasure be known. Laney scoops him up and bounces to quiet him. "Okay, time's up. He's ready to eat and my boobs are just too famous to pull out right here in Ruby's. Plus, my mother would die. Well, she'd die *after* she killed me."

I help her gather her things, and we are headed for the door when she stops, nearly causing me to run into her. She looks back at me. "And don't think I don't know that this little dessert idea originated in Gertie's basement."

"Well, some, but—"

She continues walking. "Oh, I don't have a problem with it at all. However, I'd get it all nailed down before Missus gets a look at Gertie's moonshine list."

"That is the plan," I say as I slip around her to open the door. As Laney walks through the door, she smiles at me and bats her eyes.

"Why, Carolina Jessup, you're becoming more Chanceyfied every single little ol' day. Bless your heart!"

Andy keeps the store supplied with used books he picks up when he's out junking. Like most Mondays, this morning there are several boxes full in the back of Blooming Books for me to go through. Bonnie is great with running the store and coming up with ideas for decorating and promoting, but the books are my main focus. Monday mornings are my favorite, and coming in to go over Andy's haul kept me going last night after Will got home and we confronted him.

Jackson is too soft. I think it's because he's gone so much that he likes the idea of Will living here. I am going to try out Laney's laundry idea on Will. Yeah, right. Oops, guess my attitude of doubt won't help it work, will it? Okay. Will *is* going to do the laundry, all the laundry, in return for taking over my basement. I repeat it to myself, hoping it'll stick. Will is going to do all the laundry in return for living in the basement. That's better. Will is going to do all the laundry in return for living in the basement. Now, I just need to repeat that to myself all day.

I take a deep breath over the boxes. I think I've become addicted to the smell of old books, like in a library or an antique store. Old books that have sat in a cardboard box for a few years. There's a musty, interesting smell. Like fresh-dug dirt combined with that well-known and well-loved book smell and mushrooms. Yep, that's pretty much it.

Bonnie can't stand the smell, though, so I have a fan dispersing it. I turn it on, move a box next to my chair and the card table, and start sorting. The store doesn't open for a few more minutes, and even then Bonnie doesn't come in right at that time when she knows I'm here. Shannon comes in depending on her orders, which are usually slim on Monday mornings, so when I hear a knock on the front door, I assume it's time to unlock the front door and open up. However, it's not a customer. It's Anna.

"Anna. Come in. Sit down." I point her to one of the chairs in the midst of the shelves and displays. "Want a bottle of water or anything?"

"No, I have some," she says as she sets her aluminum bottle on the table next to her. She pulls herself forward to sit straight, but her growing stomach gets in her way.

"You look great," I say as I sit in the chair across from her. "How do you feel?"

She nods quickly, then looks up at me and smiles. "Better. Morning sickness is going away some. They say that happens at the end of the first trimester, but mine hung on longer." She takes another deep breath. I remember that feeling of not having enough room for my lungs. As she releases her breath, words come with it. "I wanted to ask you something." She rubs her lips together in a way that looks so much like the unsure girl who came home with my son as an almost-stowaway last Thanksgiving.

"Sure. Ask me anything."

"I have an ultrasound is tomorrow. Do you want to come with me?"

"Oh, Anna. I'd love to. I'll drive," I pause, "or is Will driving? Can't believe y'all are asking me."

She twists her lips again. "Not Will. He's not coming. Just you."

And with that, my heart falls. "Oh, honey... why not? Wouldn't it be good for him to see it? Might make the baby more real to him."

"No," she says. "He and I fight every time we're together. I don't want to be upset at the doctor's. Figured you being there would be all right, but you can't tell Will or my grandmother until I say it's okay. Okay?"

She pushes out of the chair and stands, not waiting for me to answer. This doesn't feel like a good idea, but I can sense how hard it was for her to ask me. I'm afraid any pushback will cause my invitation to be rescinded. "Here, let me get the door," I say as I jump up from my seat and dash to the door. "It's so heavy and... well, heavy."

She gives me a quick smile and pulls a card out of her pocket. "Here, this is the doctor. I'll just meet you there tomorrow at ten, okay?"

"Sure, but honey, you let me know if you decide you want me to tell Will. I can make him behave."

Her smiles tightens, and she shakes her head as she stares at me. "Then why haven't you up to now?" She turns to leave, and again she doesn't wait for an answer.

Good thing.

I don't have one.

Chapter 9

The door barely closes before my phone rings. The name "Missus" screams at me from the screen. In my panic, I accidentally answer it. "Shoot! Hello?"

"What is wrong, Carolina? Is Anna all right? I was looking out my bedroom window when I saw her go in your shop, so I couldn't get down there fast enough. She didn't stay very long. You didn't upset her, did you? Never mind. I'll be there in a minute."

She hangs up just as I hear the bell over our door ring. I whip around. "Missus, it's— Oh, sorry, I thought you were someone else." Two women I don't know push on through the door. I welcome them and ask if they are looking for anything special. They say no and make their way to the shelves behind me. Dang. Now I can't disappear out the back door before Missus gets here.

And there she is. "Good morning, Missus," I try. "You look nice." She has on a kelly-green skirt and shirt with a short-sleeved white jacket. Her shoes are navy blue and green low-heeled pumps. Meanwhile, I have on clothes for working with boxes of old books.

"Of course you'd think so, but I'm having what the young people would call a 'wardrobe malfunction.'" She holds out her navy blue purse towards me. "For some reason FM removed the extra set of gloves I always carry in every purse."

"Now, come on. Why would he take your gloves?"

"I'm sure I don't know. He's the only other one in our house, so it was obviously him." She walks into the center of the store, eyeing the two ladies who are chatting amongst the books. She turns to me and whispers, "Anna? What did she want?"

"Just stopped in to say hi, I guess. She looks good," I say as I move toward the counter. "Wonder what time Shannon is coming in? I need to look that up." Digging around underneath the counter, I come up with a notebook that looks like it could hold important notes, and I start flipping the pages. Then, even better, the customers come toward the counter each carrying a couple books. "Did you ladies find something you want?"

"Yes," one says. "I love this mystery series. I read it years ago."

"Oh, they are good. I almost took these home when they came in," I say as I take the books and put them in a bag for her. "That'll be six dollars."

Her friend speaks up. "We love your shop. We're coming back for the book signing later this month."

"That'll be wonderful," I say. "There's a lot more activity on the weekends usually. It's pretty quiet on Monday mornings." I take the second woman's money and continue rambling. Anything to get them to stay. Missus hates small talk, so maybe she'll leave. "It'll be our first book signing. Author is from Dalton. Are y'all from near here?"

"Not too far. We live up towards Laurel Cove, but not *in* Laurel Cove. We're headed to our Monday morning Bible study, and our leader last week said we should stop in here. Do you know Di Rivers?"

"Oh, yes, Mrs. Rivers. Well, that was awful nice of her. I mostly know her son, Isaac. He's a friend of my daughter's."

"Savannah. We know." The first woman reaches out and touches my hand. "She is as beautiful on the inside as she is on the outside."

Well, that stops my rambling. "Thank you. Yes, she... thank you."

"We better get going. Don't want to be late!"

"Tell Mrs. Rivers I said hello, and you ladies come back soon."

As they leave, Missus makes her way to the counter. "Di Rivers? Do I know her?"

"Her husband is the preacher at that big church out at the interstate. They just moved here this summer. Isaac and Savannah met at school."

"Is it that nondenominational one? How can people not just pick a denomination? Not like there aren't plenty to choose from. You're not letting Savannah go to church with him, are you?"

"Of course we are, Missus. They're nice people, and if a teenager *wants* to go to church, I say let 'em!"

She's rubbing her bare hands. "This is ridiculous. FM knows better than to go into my purse. I've got to go home and get some gloves right now. Anna has me so worried, I rushed out half-dressed. Although, if FM would mind his own business and leave my purse alone, then I would have my gloves." She's uncharacteristically rambling now, and I'm just holding my breath hoping she'll leave.

"So, tomorrow morning. Nine sharp," she says before marking to the door. "We will make our final decision then."

She's almost out the door, but I have to ask, "What decision? What's tomorrow morning at nine sharp?"

She sighs. "Don't you listen? Or read your email? Festival meeting. Nine a.m. at Ruby's. Mandatory."

"Okay, but..."

She closes her eyes as she stops. "But what, Carolina? You act like you don't even care about the festival."

"Nothing. I'll be there."

She pushes on through the doorway and leaves. Okay, so I'll only be at her meeting for a little bit. I'll drop off my idea for the Southern Dessert Festival and then leave for Anna's doctor's appointment.

Bonnie waves as she walks past our front window and then enters. "Good morning. Have you had some nice quiet time with the new books?"

"Honestly, no. It's been like Grand Central Station in here this morning."

"Well, doesn't look like things are going to change," she says. "Kimmy Kendrick is headed this way with her kids. Looks like they all have half-eaten muffins from Ruby's. Okay if I tell them they have to stay on the tile until they're done? No sense in having to clean up crumbs from the whole store."

I take a page from my daughter's book and roll my eyes. "Sure, if you think it'll work. I'll stay up here to help." Again, the bell over the door rings, and the Kendricks enter. Bonnie holds the door open while also playing goalie at the edge of the tile. I'm a few feet behind her acting like the net.

We're ready, but there's nothing to be ready for. K.J. is holding his little sister Katherine's hand and they stay close to their mother, who holds baby Kevin on her hip. "You two sit down right there on the floor and eat your muffin. Don't get up until I tell ya ya can, ya hear me?"

Both kids nod from where they've slid down to sit against the wall beside the door, but then K.J. seems to remember and says, "Yes, ma'am."

Kimmy tilts her head at her daughter. "Katherine Elizabeth?"

"Yes, ma'am," the toddler answers through a mouthful of muffin.

Kimmy shifts her attention to us now. "Morning, Miss

Carolina. Miss Bonnie. I need to look at some books and figured this was the best way to keep the kids quiet. Hope it's okay with y'all."

"Oh, yes," Bonnie and I say as we take a step back from our defensive positions.

"How are you, Kimmy? I haven't seen you much lately," I add as I step towards her and pat the baby's back. "Hi Kevin, you look sleepy."

"He is, so I'll just hold him. Here's what I'm looking for, some kid books. We wore our welcome out at the library, so we can't go there no more. Plus, when the kids tore them books up they were expensive to replace. Figure we might as well buy our own now that the kids are going to behave and not mess up the books." She looks back over her shoulder. "Right, kids? You ain't messing these books up, are you?"

K.J. yells, "No, ma'am!"

Katherine grins wide and mimics him. "No, ma'am!" They giggle together and make me and Bonnie smile, too.

Bonnie bends toward them. "Would you like a little cup of water if your mommy says it's okay?"

Kimmy nods, and Bonnie goes back towards the bathroom where we have disposable paper cups.

"Here, our children's books are down here. Why don't you just pick which ones you want and you can have them? No charge," I say. "Kimmy, I'm just so impressed with how you're handling things."

She beams. "To be truthful, Miss Carolina, so am I. Right impressed with myself, but don't want to be too prideful. And thank you for the offer of the free books, but I need to buy them. Need to do something good that costs me for my kids. It's kind of, well, an assignment."

"An assignment? Like for a class?" I lift a handful of books up for us to look through.

"Yep, exactly like that. I'm going to a parenting class at church."

"Oh, yes. I did hear that. Well, it sure is working. Good for you."

She bends her head down, but I can still see her smile. Same flat, sand-colored hair, but she looks like a different person. Same gray eyes and pale complexion, but her eyes have some life and her mannerisms have strength, whereas before she seemed to just drag herself from one place to another. "Well, thanks. Let's take those three. One for each of them. How much'll that be?"

"Two dollars. Children's books are three for two dollars." We walk to the counter, where Bonnie has pulled up a little stool and is reading a book to K.J. and Katherine.

My partner pauses and says, "But I thought children's books were four for two dollars this week?"

"Oh, that's right!" I exclaim. "How about the one you're reading? *Where the Wild Things Are* was one of my kids' favorites. Bryan put it in the window last week himself."

Kimmy frowns at first, then I can see her talking to herself inside. She takes a breath, lifts her chin, and says, "Thank you. We'd like that." Then like she's reading it from a book she says, "It's good to be grateful when people do nice things for you. Kids, say thank you. Now stand up here and help me pay for your books."

She hands each of her older children a dollar bill, and they give it to me. Bonnie puts the books into two bags and says, "There you go, each of you have a bag to carry to help your mother."

Kimmy smiles at her and whispers, "Thanks," so as to not disturb Kevin, who is asleep on her shoulder. She herds them toward the door, where Bonnie has hustled to hold it open. "It was a delight reading to you, K.J. and Katherine. Come by anytime."

Suddenly K.J. halts the procession as he stops in his tracks. "Wait!" Then he turns around to his mother. "Thank you for the books, Mommy."

Kimmy looks startled, and her mouth opens as she stares at her son. With her eyes open wide, we see them get shiny. She sniffles, then she lets out a breath, pats his head, and says, "You're welcome, son."

Bonnie closes the door as we watch the little family walk up the sidewalk. Her voice is husky as she turns to me and says, "Not every day you get to witness a walking, talking miracle." All I can do is nod.

CHAPTER 10

I'm going to tell Will about Anna's doctor appointment. About the sonogram.

Working through two boxes of old books gave me lots of time to think, and I've made my decision. As soon as I get home I'm going to tell him, and then I'm going to lay the law down about his behavior and how he needs to treat Anna. I've never been a big fan of the term 'man up.' Seems sexist. Too macho. But it's the phrase that keeps running through my head. It's time for him to man up. With Anna, who is still his wife. With me and his dad. And even with Rose, his girlfriend and the one who probably picked out the rug in my basement. If he wants a relationship with her at some future point, then he needs to do right and let her be until he's single again.

As I drive up the hill toward home, the afternoon sun barely penetrates the thick shade provided by the trees planted decades ago. The large lots are filled with thick grass and flowers. Cooler nights dipping into the fifties have put some bounce back into the flowers. They are lifting their heads and showing brighter colors. Or maybe it's just the reduction of that harsh summer lighting. The shade looks comfortable, instead of only tolerable.

"Looks about perfect for reading on the deck," I say with

a glance at the stack of books I culled from the boxes at the store. When you own a bookshop part of your job is reading the books, right? Taking the last curve at the top of the hill, I lean to look up our driveway as I turn in to it. Good. Just Savannah's car. Bryan has football practice, but I wasn't sure who else might be waiting on me. Since moving here, I never take for granted that pulling into my home means simply being at home. Too many times it's been like driving straight into an ambush.

"Savannah," I call as I unlock the front door. "I'm home."

"Finally!" she yells from her third-floor room. She's left her door open apparently to hear me come in. She's bounding down the stairs before I even get to the kitchen.

"Mom. You are not going to believe it! The Rivers are taking me with them on a cruise for fall break. How amazing is that?"

"Um, pretty amazing, I guess." I wander around the kitchen, putting my purse and keys away, getting a bottle of water, cleaning up from where someone ate lunch and didn't wipe up any crumbs while my daughter talks about this cruise she's going on. Yes, see, *you* caught that. The cruise she *is* going on. I do not remember any permission being sought, or granted.

She's perched on the kitchen table, her bare feet in one of the chairs. Her long, black hair is tied up in a loose bun, which she keeps having to mess with as in her excitement it's trying to fall. Finally she undoes it and lets her hair fall past her shoulders. She stops talking as she holds the hair tie between her teeth, and she bends her head forward, pulling her hair up with both hands.

I take a slug of water and lean against the counter, waiting. Waiting for her to realize she's the only one talking.

When she turns her head back up, hair tie back in place, my chest crunches a little. She looks so completely happy. Eyes wide and sparkling, the color on her face only from her excitement, not makeup. Like the little girl who used to hug me and tell me I was the best mommy in the world. This is a Savannah her friends are familiar with, but I have to visit in memories and photo albums.

I watch the moment she takes in my face and a cloud crosses her face. "What?" she asks. "What's wrong?"

"Honey, I just don't know if I'm comfortable with you going on a vacation with your... is he even your official boyfriend? Last I heard you were just friends who might be dating. You've not known him but a couple weeks."

She hops off the table, losing all sparkle by the time her feet hit the floor. "Mom, his parents will be there. It's a family thing."

"Exactly! A family thing, and you're not family. Besides, how much would this cost?"

"See, that's the perfect thing. I know how all tied up you get about money, but they're paying my way. Some kind of group rate they get because they do a lot of cruises or something. It's perfect. I get to go on a really cool vacation, and it doesn't cost you anything. I won't even ask for new clothes or swimsuits. It'll be cheap."

She holds out her hands to stop me from saying anything. "Mom. No, just wait. Mrs. Rivers is going to call you tonight to give you all the information. Don't make up your mind until you talk to her, okay?" As she's talking she's working her way out of the kitchen. "Just relax, Mom, and chill. Talk to Mrs. Rivers, okay? I'm going to finish my homework and I'll come help with dinner in a bit, okay?"

She's already at the bottom of the staircase when I yell, "And I also have to talk to your dad." She goes up the stairs much slower than she came down. I finish my bottle of water and crunch it as small as I can.

Parenting: crushing your children's hopes and dreams one idea at a time.

Speaking of which—what time does Will get home? A check of the clock says its twenty minutes until four, which means I should read for twenty minutes and then get started on dinner. I'm glad Bryan is doing football, but he comes home starving. Filling him up with easy food is possible, it's just expensive. Plus, I've now got Colt to feed. My days of frozen pizza or chicken nuggets for dinner when Jackson is out of town have seen their last hurrah. I take a bag of frozen chicken breasts from the freezer, put some on a plate to thaw in the microwave, and choose a book from the pile I brought home.

Shade from the house gives me a place to sit out of the sun, so I pull a chair up next to the house, sit down, and open the British cozy mystery I brought out. It's number seven in a series I found a few years ago. I love series, as it's so easy to become immersed in the next story. I know the main people, the place, and even the personalities. It's like visiting with old friends.

As a matter of fact, my immersion was so complete that I didn't look up until four-thirty when Colt opens the deck door.

"Oh, there you are. Wanted to let you know I'm home. Think I'll join you out here. Can I get you anything?"

"No," I say as I stand and stretch. "Been out here longer than I intended. Need to get dinner going." He holds the door open for me to come inside.

"Carolina, I don't want you feeling like you gotta cook for me. I told Jackson I don't want to be a pain."

"No worries. The kids have to eat, and Bryan has become a human eating machine."

As I pull out two pots and place them on the stove, Colt pours himself a glass of iced tea.

"I stopped by football practice. Saw Bryan. Shame there's not a freshman team this year."

Shrugging as I fill the pots with water, I laugh. "Gotta admit, I don't know much about it. Will was never into football, and

I'd just as soon Bryan not be." After I place the pots on the heating burners and put their lids on, I turn to Colt. "But I do highly approve of teenagers running off those hormones and being as tired as possible, so football is fine with me."

"True, true about running off those hormones." He's leaning against the counter, holding his tea, and looking down at his feet. Reminds me of when the kids have something to say, but don't know how to say it.

So, I do the parent thing and go back in our conversation to the last thing he said. "So, you said there's not a freshman team this year?"

The way his head jerks up tells me I'm good at this.

"Yeah, guess the guy that's done it for years had a small heart attack in the summer. They hoped he'd be back, but he didn't want to continue. They tried to get a couple of the other teachers to fill in, but football takes up a whole lot of time." He shrugs at me and waits. This time I know the question I'm supposed to ask, but really? Do I have to?

Sighing, I dump the thawed breasts into one of the pots and ask, "So are you thinking about offering to help?"

"Yeah, I am. Get to spend time with Bryan—that would be cool, right? And I'm liking this place." At the look on my face, he says, "Of course I'd get another place to live. There are some rental places around, right?"

"A few. But you already had a football job. Won't you miss Kentucky? You were head coach, right? And you did good. Didn't y'all go to state last year?"

"Yeah, we did. And I'm not thinking this is forever, I just need a break." He shoves his hands in his jeans pockets. "So, Jackson didn't tell you?"

"Nope." I lean against the counter next to the stove, holding a handful of spaghetti noodles, waiting for the other pot of water to boil, and I stare at him. "He didn't say a word."

"Well, it's like this. I was ready for a change. Dad getting hurt so bad really shook me up, you know? And then, well, you know there's that old saying about how you should go while the going is good? Well, it was a good time to go."

After dropping the noodles into the pot, I turn to face him and cross my arms. "Why?"

He leans up and walks across the room, looks out into the living room and up the stairs, then walks back toward me. "One of the school board members had it out for me. He and my dad have never gotten along, you understand how hard it can be to get along with Dad. And they were rivals back when they were in high school, if you can believe it. They still carried on like some old Kentucky backwoods feud. But when you take your team to state, all that can be pushed to the side. Forgotten. But then…"

"I'm home!" Bryan's voice in the hallway cuts Colt off. "What's for dinner? Hey Uncle Colt! Saw you at practice." My youngest comes rushing into the kitchen, bringing a whole houseful of smell with him.

Much like Savannah did to me earlier, I hold my hands up at my son and his odor. "We'll eat when you get out of the shower. Go."

He drops his cleats and backpack on the kitchen floor, along with a shower of red clay chunks and grass clippings.

"Bryan!" I yell. "Take those shoes outside. Not wearing them inside also means not *bringing* them inside. Look at the mess."

Colt hands the shoes to their owner. "Here, you take these to the porch and I'll clean this up."

Bryan heads to the front door, and Colt reaches for the broom leaning in the corner of the kitchen. We hear Savannah in the living room declare, "You are disgusting!" and Colt and I share a smile.

"Hey, Uncle Colt," she says entering the kitchen. "Who all's eating? I'll set the table."

I roll my eyes and turn to stir the spaghetti. Gotta love a kid who wants something. "Guess there's us four. Will won't be home for a bit, but go ahead and set him a place."

While they do their cleaning and setting of the table, I unwrap the Velveeta, then open the can of soup and the can of Rotel tomatoes. Chicken Spaghetti is one of the kids' favorite meals. Mine, too, since it's so easy. After dumping the water, I put the boiled chicken onto a plate. Then I put the soup, Rotel, and cheese in the pot to warm and melt together. "Savannah, get those two bags of spinach out of the bottom drawer in the fridge and open them. Put it into the big white bowl on the top shelf."

Colt grabs the bowl down for her. "Is it okay if I put ice in the glasses yet?"

"Sure," I say. "Savannah, quit playing, just push it all in there and then put it in the microwave for a minute. Move so I can drain the noodles."

When she finally moves, after acting like putting spinach in a bowl deserves a medal, I drain off most of the liquid.

"I'm starving. Is it ready?" Bryan pushes into the crowded kitchen as he puts on his shirt. He smells much better.

"In a minute. Grab the Hawaiian rolls and go sit down." I know he'll eat at least two before we all get to the table, but there are no worries about it ruining his appetite. Moms of teenage boys spend their lives trying to ruin their appetites.

I put the sauce along with the cut-up chicken into the spaghetti and mix it. "Here, put the lid on it and it can go on the table," I instruct Colt.

The spinach has magically wilted down into the bowl, so I stir it a bit and add a pat of butter.

Savannah is waiting to carry it to the table, so I give it to her and follow her. Colt is sitting across from me in Jackson's seat. It's weird, but apparently only for me.

We say a quick grace. The amen is barely said before Bryan

lifts his plate to me so that I can serve him. He's grinning from ear to ear, which means the roll stuffed in it is threatening to pop out. I ladle a hefty portion of chicken spaghetti onto his plate and then add a scoop of spinach. The look on his face as he sits the full plate in front of him causes me to smile and reminds me of those midnight feedings when they were all eyes and mouth.

Is there anything better in this world than feeding your kid?

Chapter 11

"Please, call me Di," Isaac's mother says to me at the beginning of our call then she laughs. "Yes, Di like Princess Diana. However I came a couple years before the royal wedding, so even though my mother didn't name me after her, she did seem to keep my hair cut like Princess Di's my whole childhood. You know that short haircut with the long bangs?"

"Yes, I do remember it. But don't worry, my parents had a fascination with *Gone with the Wind*. Still do. All their dogs have names from it, and I barely escaped being Scarlett." I take my phone upstairs to talk in my bedroom, although Savannah is begging me with her eyes and exaggerated hand signals to let her listen.

Di laughs. "Oh my, Scarlett. That would be bad. Wonder what our children will complain about with their names. I can imagine Isaac complaining about being named after a baby its father tried to sacrifice."

"And Savannah has already informed me being named after a town is not as clever as I seem to have thought it was. Especially since my name is a state, but I honestly didn't think about that at the time. Oh well, guess it's good to give them something to talk about in therapy sessions."

Di laughs. "That is true. So, did Savannah fill you in on our plans for fall break? The cruise?"

"Yes, she did, but I don't know how I feel about her going on a cruise with her boyfriend. If they even are officially boyfriend and girlfriend."

"I completely understand your hesitation," she says in a soothing tone, "but Paul and I will be there. She would be staying in a cabin with our married daughter, Bea. Bea's husband can't join us. It's a cruise put together by one of the small groups in our church and given to us a gift."

"Well, okay, but I'd have to talk it over with her father and he's out of town. I'm just not sure…"

"You don't think we'd put our son in a bad situation, do you?"

I jump up off the bed and start pacing my room. "No, of course not."

"Paul and I feel very strongly that showing a child they have your trust is important. We trust Isaac. We trust Savannah."

"Glad you do!" I say with a laugh.

She pauses. "Doesn't Savannah deserve your trust?"

"Well, sure, I guess. As far as I know, but…"

"You talk to your husband and let us know. The space is available and we think our trip would be enhanced having Savannah along. And as Savannah has never been on a cruise, it would be especially nice for her, don't you think?" Di has found her royal voice.

"I have no doubt it would be very nice for Savannah, but I don't… listen, I'll talk to Jackson and get back to you. We really do appreciate the invitation."

"Absolutely. And by the way, the ladies from my study loved your bookshop this morning."

I'm a little relieved by the change in subject. "That was so nice you telling them about us. I enjoyed getting to meet them. Thanks."

"You're welcome. Anything I can do to help your little store. Now you have a good night. I know it's difficult with your husband working out of town so much. That can be taxing on a marriage for sure."

"Well, yeah. You have a good night, too. And I'll let you know, you know, about the cruise. Bye."

I sink back down onto our bed. Maybe she's right. Maybe we should trust Savannah more. Families down in Marietta went on cruises all the time, and it would be nice for Savannah to get to go. Saying yes would be so easy and would make my daughter so happy. Remembering her lit-up face this afternoon, how like a little girl she looked. I can have all that again with just one word. Of course, Jackson might not like it, but honestly, I could sway him. If I wanted to sway him.

I mean, he already trusts our kids. Taking a deep breath, I stand up and leave the room. When I hit the stairs, Savannah turns from the couch to look up at me. "Can I go?"

"I have to talk to your dad," I say. As her mouth pops open, I add, "Don't bug me about it." She closes her mouth, nods, and turns back toward the television. I ask, "Is Will home?"

She answers with a shrug. I enter the kitchen and see the door to the basement is open and there's light down there. Then I notice the back door is standing wide open. "The house will be full of mosquitos!" I complain as I grab hold of the door to close, then Will steps in off the deck.

"Oh, sorry, Mom. I was just outside for a minute. Rose is looking for any ripe tomatoes in the garden. We're cooking dinner."

I walk to the stove and lift the lid sitting there. "I left you Chicken Spaghetti. Just need to warm it up a bit."

He puts his hands in his back pockets and rocks on the balls of his feet. "Yeah, well, Rose is vegetarian, and I guess I am too, now. Kind of."

"Really?" I look back in the pot. "But you always loved Chicken Spaghetti."

"Hey, maybe I can just take the chunks of chicken out." He joins me looking down into the pot. "They're pretty big." He takes two plates out of the cabinet and is beginning his vegetarian meal preparation when the back door opens and Rose comes in with one good red tomato and three mostly green ones.

"Found some," she says. "Hi, Carolina. Garden looks to be on its last leg. Guess it needs some care. I could help out with that. I love gardening."

"Good someone does. I thought I wanted to be a gardener until I had a garden. Glad you found at least one good tomato. Salad will be good with the spaghetti. We ate all the spinach we had."

She's stepped over to see what Will is doing. "Spaghetti? No we're just having a salad. Will, what are you doing?"

"I'm taking the chicken out," he says. "Making it vegetarian. You'll love this. It's my favorite."

"Will, it was cooked with chicken and chicken broth. Right?" she asks as she looks back at me.

I nod. Really nothing I need to say right here.

"We're not eating that," she says in a soft voice to him. But the way his mouth is moving says that he's already eating it. "At least *I'm* not eating it." She walks away from him toward the basement door. "I'm going downstairs to fix dinner. Bye, Carolina, thanks for letting me raid your garden." She smiles at me, but cuts her eyes at my son. The tall, clueless one standing at the stove—chewing.

He wipes his mouth, grins at me, and starts putting the spaghetti from the plates back into the pot.

"Never mind. I'll do that. You go have dinner with Rose." He takes another bite and then steps away from the stove as I step up to it.

"Okay. Thanks, Mom. And it's as good as always. Love me some chicken spaghetti."

I lower my voice. "Listen, Will. When Rose leaves can you come see me? I need to talk to you about something."

"Sure, Mom." He leans back toward me and picks a chunk of chicken off the plate I'm holding over the pot. As he pops it in his mouth he winks. "Don't tell!"

I shake my head at him and laugh. "Go enjoy your salad. Don't forget to come talk later."

"Okay."

Chapter 12

I woke up from a dead sleep on the couch last night around midnight. TV still on, every light blazing, and the doors unlocked, but not a kid in sight. Last thing I remember was sitting down to watch whatever Savannah and Bryan were watching. A note from Will saying he came up, saw I was asleep, and decided to not wake me, was lying beside me on the end table.

So I'm up extra early to catch him, but I'm rethinking telling him about Anna's appointment. He has school this morning, and there will be more sonograms. Maybe it's best if I just do like Anna asked. The coffee finishes just as I hear him on the basement stairs, so I get up to pour us a couple cups, keeping my back to the door so I can decide what to say. Should I tell him?

"Good morning, Carolina."

Rose's voice makes my head jerk around. "Rose?"

Will joins her. "Morning, Mom. Oh, you've already made coffee. Thank you!" he says as he sets his backpack on the table and comes toward me.

"Why is Rose here?"

He stops and looks down at me. "We have school. Is that cup for me?" He takes the cup then opens the refrigerator.

"Figured we'd just make coffee up here since we don't have any half-and-half downstairs."

Rose sits down at the table and starts looking at a notebook she's holding. "Will, can you put on water for my tea? I want to look over these notes one more time, but I think I'm ready for my test."

This is way too comfortable. Way too familiar. "Rose, you didn't sleep here last night, did you? Will, what's going on?"

"Mom, we were studying late last night, and you know Tuesdays are our early day at school." Will runs water into my teakettle and puts it on the stove as he so calmly explains that he's moved his girlfriend into my house.

I feel like a pressure cooker building up steam. "No. No, this isn't going to happen. This isn't happening."

Will turns and shakes his head at me. "What do you mean? Where did you think all that stuff downstairs came from?"

"I didn't know, I…" Then I remember looking at the rug and thinking a woman was involved, the extra furniture and bedspread. "I don't know, but no, she is not living here." Then I turn to face the table. "Rose, you can't live here. This isn't going to work."

She focuses on closing her notebook and putting it into her backpack, then she stands. She finally looks up, but not at me, at Will. "Told you." She walks back toward the basement door and as she descends the stairs, she yells, "I'll be in the car."

The whistle of the teapot scares me and I jump. Will moves the pot off the burner, then makes a big deal out of getting one of my to-go cups to pour his coffee into. His back is to me as he goes through the cabinets finding a matching top. He finally turns and stares at me. "You wanted to talk to me? You were asleep last night."

Oh, yeah. "No, not now." When he hears the word no, he walks past me, slings his backpack up, and begins loping down the stairs. "I'll be at work late tonight. Bye."

Sometimes coffee can taste so bitter.

"Hey, Libby," I say as I push through Ruby's door. "I'm early for the festival meeting with Missus. Okay if I just sit here, since I'm sure she'll want the big table?"

"Absolutely. Once the before-school rush is over, there's plenty of room. I'll bring you coffee, ready for a muffin?"

"Sure. What's hot?"

"Cheesy-corn ones just came out. That okay?"

I nod as I read a text Susan just sent. The police say the vandalism at the concession shed wasn't the first. Not big things, but items missing off front porches and mail found that must've been taken out of mailboxes.

Libby sets my cup down and fills it.

"Libby, have you heard about the vandalism going on?"

"Wait!" Ruby yells from back by the stoves. "Wait, til I get up there. Libby, come finish filling this tin and get it in the oven."

Ruby wipes her hands on her apron as she's yanking it over her head and walking my way. "If I catch who's doing this crap I'll strangle 'em. No room for vandals, I hate 'em. There are sins that are understandable, absolutely understandable, Carolina, but just messing up other folks' things for no good reason? Not on my watch!" She sits down, but her sharp behind is barely on the seat of the chair next to me. She's turned the chair so that just a corner sticks out and she's sitting on that corner. Her elbow is leaning hard on the table and she's jutted her neck out so far that her face is closer to my coffee than mine is.

"Took my silk flowers," she says. "One day they're there

pretty as can be, next day it's just plain dirt. Took every last one of them. I'll not have it, I tell you!"

Now, the silk flowers she's talking about, well, I'd noticed they were missing from her window boxes out front. I thought good sense had finally caught up with Ruby. Sometimes she plants real flowers in the window boxes. Well, she basically just transfers flowers out of the little cartons from the Walmart Garden Center into her bigger containers hanging below her front windows. No fertilizer and no care, so they last a few weeks. As they begin dying she fills in the holes with old, really old, bunches of grave flowers. The cheap ones that fade and fall apart.

But I push this aside to ask innocently, "Really? I wondered where they were."

She slaps the table. "Why, of course you did! They was a tradition. A real part of Chancey and now they're gone. If you think I'm going to go spend the money to replace them just to have them stolen again, well, you got another think coming!" She lowers her voice and leans even closer. "This is how it begins. Little crimes, then we're no better than living in downtown Atlanta. We've got to figure this out. Start one of them crime watchers groups. Hell's Angels or something like that, no, Guardian Angels, or you know. They get to wear them red berets." She leans back and yells, "Libby! Remind me to look them up and see about joining."

Behind us a voice says, "Carolina is early and Ruby has on a clean shirt. My, my, it *is* the end times."

Ruby's mouth puckers up, and her nostrils flare as she takes in a deep breath. I pat her arm and laugh. "Oh, Missus. Good morning to you, too. We were just talking about the vandalism around town." I don't mention Ruby's flowers because Missus will say what I was thinking. "I have to leave the meeting early, that's why I'm already here."

Ruby relaxes her mouth and lets her breath out as she

stands up. She ignores Missus as she walks toward the back counter, but we're all waiting for her retort. There's a pause in conversation as Ruby stops at the opening in the counter and turns. "Missus, I forgive you. Have a blessed day." She nods and continues back to the kitchen area.

Missus' face has developed two bright red spots on her cheeks. She shakes her head quickly as she moves around the table and sits down facing the front windows, away from Ruby. "Here come the others. Since you have to leave early, you can explain your idea, then we can move the meeting to your store to finish. Bonnie need more dental work? She must have exemplary dental insurance."

"No, it's not work I need to leave for. You can't meet at the store. I won't be there. So…" I let my comment string out as I bow my head. Hoping against hope Missus will leave it at that. Yeah, that's a stupid thing to hope.

"Where are you going?" Missus asks as she waves to the people coming in. "Everyone, get seated quickly. Carolina has something more important than this meeting to attend to this morning. Tell everyone why you have to leave."

"Um, a doctor's appointment. That's all."

"Well. It would be appreciated by all if you would refrain from planning them during our meetings in the future. As you should all know, we are on an extremely tight schedule."

Retta Bainbridge has selected a seat next to me, but now she pulls away from me. "Doctor! You're not sick, are you? I can't possibly get sick. I leave this afternoon for a real estate conference in Las Vegas."

"Ooh, you're going to Vegas?" Cathy Stone asks as she rushes in to sit on the other side of the table next to Missus. She straightens her back and holds her chest out as she sways toward tall, trim Peter who is taking the end seat next to her. "Peter, wouldn't you love to be going to Las Vegas this very afternoon?" Cathy is young and attractive, but I'm trying to remember if I ever realized she had such big, well, breasts. She's wearing a very low-cut shirt, so maybe I've just never seen her with everything out front, but...

Missus waves a hand for Libby, Cathy's mother, to refresh her coffee and says, "Libby, your daughter is apparently missing some buttons on her shirt. Surely you've taught her how to sew on a button."

"Mother!" Peter scolds as Libby stutters an apology.

Cathy laughs and stands up. "It's one of the new bras I'm selling. First time I've ever had cleavage. Isn't it great?"

Libby gasps and disappears behind the counter. Missus rolls her eyes, and the rest of us watch Cathy. Because, well, the bra *is* rather remarkable.

"And Carolina, I've been wanting to talk to you," Cathy says, leaning forward at me ever so slowly. "Since you have a larger bust, you of course don't need *this* bra, but I have a bra that will fit you better than anything you've been wearing. You must make an appointment with me. I know! Ask Jed," she says pointing at our red-haired, now red-faced, mayor. "Betty's hosting a party next week." She sits down as she concludes, "Jed, tell Betty to invite Carolina."

Missus speaks up. For the first time, Jed and I are thankful for her bossiness. "Before Carolina gets distracted any more by your chest, let her share her idea for the festival since she has to leave."

"Thank you, Missus. Here it is, all laid out." I stand up and hand out the papers I'd typed up at work yesterday. The Southern Dessert Festival. "Here are some extra, if someone can get one to Ida Faye since she's not here yet. I really have to leave." I pick up my purse and back away. "Sorry," I say as I turn around and walk as fast as possible for the door.

Can't help but cringe when I hear my name called before I can get the door open. Jed calls again, "Carolina!"

I push on the door as I turn and look back. Jed waves the

paper I'd given him. "I love it. Great idea! Good luck at the doctor."

With a wave, I push on through to the sidewalk. Okay. The meeting wasn't too bad, and I should be on time for the appointment. Not bad at all! Got most of my cup of coffee down and the half of the muffin I had left is wrapped in a napkin to eat on the ride. As I get a glance at my reflection in the shop window, though, there's only one thing at the front of my brain...

Cathy's boobs looked amazing.

Chapter 13

"I didn't think I was supposed to eat before the ultrasound," Anna says around the chicken sandwich she's devouring in huge bites. "Haven't eaten since dinner last night and that was just half a box of Wheat Thins. Didn't even have hummus or peanut butter to eat with them." She takes a long slurp of her Coke and then pauses in eating and talking for a long breath. One of the ones where you feel like you're physically lifting your lungs out from underneath the baby so you can fill them up.

Then she continues. "I'm just so tired by the end of the day, I can't even think about eating."

Dipping a waffle fry in my pile of ketchup, I nod. "Totally understand. Pregnancy tired is unlike every other kind of tired. But you heard the doctor, she wants you eating better."

We eat in silence for a minute. The morning has gone so well, I'm afraid to jinx it. But I don't know when I'll get this chance again. "You know you can always move back in with your grandmother. She'd love to take care of things like groceries and meals for you."

"I know, but…"

I find it so hard to even imagine her being with Kyle

Kendrick that I can't bring it up. Can hardly say his name, but it is what it is. So, I'll dive in. "Is it about, uh, Kyle?"

Her head snaps up and her nose wrinkles. "No. I mean, he's my boss and it got out of hand, but no. Except do you think Grandmissus would leave me alone about it? Ever let it drop?"

"Oh…I think she might never want to think or talk of it again," I say with a chuckle.

Anna smiles. "Maybe, but she would never be able to resist talking about how bad I am at life. Life in general. Look at how she is with Peter, and he grew up being under her thumb. I didn't. I grew up pretty much on my own. I tried, I really tried, but I just can't do it."

There's another gap while I decide how much more I can ask. "So, you and, you know, Kyle?"

She chews, staring down at the table, then shrugs.

"Honey, you think I can't understand, but I do more than most. I fell hard for one of my professors in college. Thought it was real, but all that was real was that he knew how to make an awkward girl feel special. Grown up." I sense her shutting down, so I add real quick. "Not saying anything like that about you. Just talking about myself."

Anna nods. Then putting her elbows on the table, she leans her head on one hand, letting her hair fall down like side curtains. Between the curtains she continues eating her fries. After a bit she flashes her eyes up at me, and it feels like permission to talk.

"For my teacher it was a fling. Just a bit of fun for a couple of weeks. Found out it's not that uncommon." As I'm saying the words I'm realizing just how much this is like my situation. How did I not see it before? An older guy who knows how to talk to young girls and make them feel on top of the world. Thinking and staring out the window, I miss for a moment Anna trying to get my attention.

"Carolina, your phone is buzzing."

"Oh, thanks. Had the ringer turned off." I look at it. "It's your grandmother, I believe that can wait." I drop my phone into my purse. "Want a refill on your Coke? Anything else to eat?"

She leans back and rubs her growing tummy. "No, I've got to start eating better. You heard the doctor. So, on the ultrasound, could you tell what the baby's sex is?"

"No, honestly, I never could tell much from those things. When the technician is pointing I can see real clear, but on my own, not a chance. But you said you don't want to know the sex."

Anna meets my eyes and holds steady. "Just doesn't feel right to know something like that without Will knowing, too."

This is the first time his name has come up. We don't break our eye contact, then she asks, "Is Rose living with Will at your house?"

And my eyes drop.

"Anna, not that… I mean, no."

But she's no longer looking at me and is scooting out of the booth. "Thanks again for lunch, Carolina. I've got to get to work." She doesn't stop until we are near the front of the restaurant and then she turns toward the restroom and runs into me. I'd been following a tad close.

"Oh, sorry," she says. "It's none of my business about him and Rose. She seems real nice. They match good."

"But she's not having his baby" blurts out of my mouth.

Anna jumps like I slapped her and then darts around me. I follow her into the restroom, but it's full of people coming and going. She weaves through the other women and into a stall. Waiting, I lean against the wall beside the hand dryer. When she comes out of her stall she looks at me and smiles. She washes her hands, then steps to where I am to dry them.

My saying I'm sorry gets lost in the roar from the dryer, so I follow her out of the bathroom, down the hallway, and out the side door into the midday heat. She has to stop to let cars go past, and I reach out and take her arm. "Please, Anna, I'm sorry. Thank you for asking me to go with you today. I'm always here for you. Whatever you need."

She looks at the cars passing and asks, "You didn't tell Will?"

"No, I did not. I promise."

"Okay," she says as she takes advantage of a break in the traffic to head to her car. She looks back at me and waves. Then I see it.

She *wanted* me to tell Will.

I sit stunned in the parking lot as the air-conditioning works to cool my car down. She wanted me to tell Will about the sonogram. Of course she did. Nobody wants to go through this alone. I should've told him right in front of Rose. Should've told him about how he'll be doing the laundry in front of her, too. They have it too easy. Way too easy.

Checking my phone, there's a list of unopened emails from just this morning. Every other one appears to be from Missus. Ignoring them is a no-brainer, except as I look, I see that the other emails include one from Betty with an attachment I'm assuming is my invite to her lingerie party. There's one, no, two from Di Rivers. Both with attachments that are full of cruise information, I'm sure. Ruby has sent one out – with an ALL CAPS subject line – saying that she's starting a crime watch committee. (You know that just tickles the police right down to the tips of their toes.) The most recent email is from the high school. The subject line asks me to welcome Coach Colt Jessup. So I guess we have a new freshman football coach, and I have more family to deal with.

My finger hovers over the list. I don't want to open any of them.

With a little buzz, a new email lands in my box, forwarded from Anna. It causes a smile and gives my finger a place to land. Baby Jessup. Sonogram pictures have gotten better. There's a nose and arms, legs. It's a baby. Our baby. Just like that, I love it. In the doctor's office I was so focused on Anna and wishing Will was there, I didn't really appreciate what this means. This baby.

Jackson and I are grandparents. We're going to have a baby. No, not *a* baby.

This baby.

CHAPTER 14

"So let's see it!" Susan says as she comes swinging into Blooming Books late Tuesday afternoon.

"Shh," I whisper with a nod toward Shannon in the back of her shop.

"See what?" Shannon asks as I realize my shushing probably caused more curiosity than Susan's question.

"Oh, just a book I've been looking for. An out-of-print series I've collected since I was little," Susan says as she walks over to me and the back bookshelves. She adds in a completely innocent way, "How are you, Shannon?"

First there's a long, drawn-out sigh. "Okay, I guess," she finally drawls.

Susan whispers to me, "She's getting even more gloomy. Guess the romance with Peter isn't working out?"

"Guess not," I whisper back, then add louder. "Here it is. Mint condition. Knew you'd want to see it as soon as possible." I hand her my phone with the sonogram picture on it.

After a quiet little squeal, she whispers, "Is it a boy or a girl? Can't believe Anna asked you to go." Then louder, "Perfect! So glad you called me."

Shannon steps toward the bookshelves from her worktable,

toward the aisle we're in. "I'm going to make this delivery then go home. You okay to close up?"

Susan grabs a book off the shelf and holds it close so the title doesn't show. Good thinking—her out-of-print series happens to be one of the hottest political thrillers on the *New York Times* list right now. I lower my phone as I say, "Sure. Have a good night."

The young woman sighs again and lowers her shoulders. "Yeah, maybe." As she turns away from us, Susan and I meet eyes and grimace a bit. Susan suddenly turns and walks away from the bookshelves and me. "Shannon, can I ask you a question?"

"I guess. What?" She pulls her keys from her purse, then puts the bag over her shoulder. Her other hand rests on an arrangement of sunflowers in a deep-blue glass vase.

"What's wrong? Why are you so gloomy? Forgive me, but I've got to ask, is it Peter?"

Shannon tucks a twist of dark hair behind her ear and leans on one hip. "Some, okay more than some, but my folks are getting unreasonable. Carolina knows, they act like they don't want me there anymore."

Susan laughs a bit, but shakes her head. "They probably just want you to have your own life. You know they love you, they want the best for you and probably don't think living with them is what's best."

Shannon's eyebrows flatten and her voice raises. "I can't afford to move out. And, well, I don't know how people do all that. It just sounds, well, sounds…"

I pipe up. "Sounds really hard. And you're right. Especially if you're alone. Gotta admit, I hadn't thought of how hard that would be, you know, moving out alone, since I had Jackson."

She lifts the vase of flowers and starts toward the front door. "See? It's hopeless."

Susan strides to the door and opens it for the sad young

woman. "It's not hopeless. Look at this place, you own and run your own business. And another thing, if you really want Peter Bedwell, then you have to decide you want him and go for it. He's so used to having someone, his mother, tell him what to do that he's not real good at thinking on his feet." Then Susan gets a fierce look on her face and bends toward the shorter woman. "He'd be lucky to get you!"

Shannon looks as surprised as I know I do.

Susan pushes her out the door as she pats her back. Nodding at the young woman and giving her a thumbs-up, Susan closes the door, turns around, and leans against it.

I'm halfway across the store, standing next to the chairs near the front window. "Who are you? First you lied so easily about being here for a book and now you're coaching Shannon on getting Peter Bedwell? Has Laney been giving you lessons?"

"Laney doesn't have to give lessons, just being around her every day of my life I guess it's seeped into my brain." Susan rests her head against the door. "Honestly, I'm sick and tired of dealing with a mopey Shannon every time I come in here to see you. And her mother is one of my mother's best friends, and her marriage is suffering because she and Shannon's dad are constantly fighting over her."

"Really? I know Shannon was so ticked when they wouldn't take her on their vacation this summer. For the first time she mentioned he's her stepfather, but everyone says he's always been good to her."

"Good as gold, but he's had enough. So, I figured a little shove from me couldn't hurt." She pushes away from the door. "Okay, now let me see that baby again. I can't believe Anna invited you! But no Will, right?"

"Right, but now I think she did want me to tell him." I hand her my phone and sit in the closest chair. "So I told you about him making his apartment in the basement?"

"Yeah, taking over your laundry space and all that." She sits down also. "Sonograms these days are so clear."

"I know, you see the nose? Oh, and we didn't find out the sex. Anyway, last night I think he had Rose stay over."

Susan jerks her head up. "In your house?"

"Yes. I told him, and her, it couldn't happen again. But, Susan, they acted like *I* was the bad guy." We sit looking at each other and then she shakes her head.

"Sorry, but no. You've got to jerk a knot in his tail."

"I know. I know." I stand up and walk to the door, saying, "Shannon here and Will at home." As I flip the open sign to close, I can't help but sigh. "Didn't you think it would get easier when they were adults?"

"Makes potty training look like a cakewalk," she says.

"And even when they're teenagers, they are still under your control." I turn off the lights beside the front door and walk towards her. With a chuckle, I add, "Why *do* people keep having kids?"

She holds my phone out towards me with the sonogram of my grandchild facing me.

Reaching for it, I smile. "Oh, that's right." I slide back down into the chair I was in before. "Speaking of kids, how is it having them all three in different schools? Leslie still loving college life?"

"Yes, she's loving sorority life, even as a pledge. She never seemed the sorority type to me, but she wanted to do rush so I thought no harm. Then she fell in love with the girls in that sorority, she says. And her daddy apparently has no problem with the bills. I'll tell you, it's awfully expensive. Susie Mae will get her driver's license next month, so that means she can drive herself down the mountain to Chancey High and that will be a huge help."

"No chance Grant will be coming back to Chancey High?"

I ask. "Bryan sure misses him. I sure miss him. Not too fond of Bryan's new friends."

"Darian Academy was made for Grant. He's loving it. Sorry." She lifts her legs to hang over the side arm of the chair, then leans her head back. "It's so quiet here. My little office at the park is so loud. There's practically no insulation, and with all that concrete and open space the sound carries. There's the toddler swim classes and then the senior citizen swim groups, plus the craft and game playing groups I started."

"You never do things halfway, and now you're paying for it. How are things with the opening of Nine Mile?" I lift my phone back up. "Wait, I never did open all the emails from Missus. We had a meeting about the festival this morning, which I left to go with Anna."

Susan waits with her eyes closed as I open the dozen or so emails from Missus. More added since lunchtime.

"Okay, the gist is they decided to go with my idea. Southern Desserts Festival." I look up and nudge Susan with my foot. "Hey, wake up. This concerns Nine Mile. Missus has you down for the world's largest banana pudding out there on the site. Wait, says here she talked to you."

Susan pulls her legs off the chair arm and twists to face forward. "Yes, she did. A conference call with my boss and me and Missus. Where she proceeded to lay out all my failures at the Lake Park. And how my failure to get Nine Mile opened on time is hurting the entire community, both Chancey and Laurel Cove. She had my boss begging to be allowed to sponsor one of the events, so of course she gave us the most expensive one and the hardest one to pull off in such a short amount of time."

"Oh" is all I can think to say.

Susan puts her elbows on her knees and sets her face in her open palms. She lifts up enough to look at me and grimace. Her grimace shifts as a tear rolls out of one eye and down her cheek. "I wanted this job so badly, but I'm tired all the time.

I honestly think I was busier when I worked with the youth at church and did all the gardening at our old house, but I didn't feel like *this*."

"Aw, you've had some big changes this past year." I scooch to the edge of my chair so I'm closer to her. "And Leslie just went off to school, that's hard to deal with. The new house, both you and Griffin with new jobs, and even pulling Grant out of your alma mater and getting used to a new school. All of that is a lot to deal with."

She swipes at her nose with the heel of her hand and sniffles. "Yeah, but all those things are good things. I should be appreciative of it all instead of being a big whiner." She bounces up from her seat and inhales as she tightly crosses her arms. "Like this. Sitting here complaining when I should be making this World's Largest Banana Pudding happen!" Her laugh is forced, and a bit unsettling. "If I'm behind it's all my own fault."

"Susan, that's crazy! You're the only one expecting all this from you," I say. I also stand and reach out to touch her arm.

She pulls away from me and keeps laughing on her way towards the front door. "Ohhh, no. You didn't hear Missus on the phone with my boss. She's been taking very detailed notes on all my failures. And she's not making them up. She's right!"

"That's Missus," I protest. "You cannot be taking her seriously. God doesn't even please her."

At the front door she stops and turns to me. "God doesn't have my boss." She looks up at the clock on the wall beside her. "Great. And now I've missed another appointment with *the best house cleaner in Laurel Cove*. Griffin actually pulled strings for me to get on her schedule, but I can't seem to make the interview. You'd think my filthy house would be enough to remind me." She yanks on the door handle, then looks back at me and shrugs as she steps away.

"Susan, wait…"

But she's already striding down the sidewalk. As I close and lock the front door, I watch until she crosses the street and ducks into her SUV. Her new SUV. She backs out, and I can see in her window that she's already on the phone.

Her straight hair hangs down in a blunt cut above her shoulder.

I miss her ponytail.

The crisp navy and burgundy madras dress she's wearing is perfect for a warm September afternoon. Very classy.

I miss her jeans and muddy shorts.

Then with a pang I remember something that struck me the first time I met her. The tan lines from her gardening gloves. Gone now, of course.

I miss her gardening glove tan.

I'm glad we moved here in time for me to get to know the old Susan. That way I know what things to miss.

CHAPTER 15

There's the smallest bit of red and orange tipping some of the leaves on the hill leading up to our house. Here and there a bush has a whole side turned to a soft rose or peach, but nothing is committed to autumn. Yet.

Shouldn't be long.

A small gathering beside the road causes me to slow down. I see the Kendricks' kids have set up a lemonade stand. I pull my car into their driveway, park, and get out.

"Hey Carolina," a woman about my age says as she leaves the table, her cup in hand. Her car is in the other direction, but she walks towards me.

"Oh, hey, Mrs. Trapp. How's the lemonade?" She's a teacher at the high school, and I worked with her on the last play.

"It's delicious. Well worth the quarter. Met your brother-in-law today."

"Oh, yeah, Colt. He's here for a bit." I turn to the kids. "Hi, K.J. and Katherine. How's business?"

K.J. straightens up the stacks of small cups as he nods and says, "Things are going good, Miss Carolina. You want some? Twenty-five cents."

He pushes Katherine out of the way, and she sits down in her little chair behind the table. She doesn't say anything, but she's licking the palm and fingers of her hand. Then she lays her hand in a puddle on the table, lifts it, and continues her own style of taste-testing.

I focus on the kids, hoping Mrs. Trapp witllgo on to her car, but no such luck.

"So, your brother-in-law, he's not married, right?"

"Right."

"He sure has some of the younger teachers, even at the middle school, all atwitter. If you know what I mean!" She darts her head to the side and winks at me with a chuckle.

My chuckle is short and hopefully doesn't convey whether I know what she means or not.

"So, is he living with you and Jackson? I mean, we know you have plenty of space, but is he looking to buy a house? You know my husband dabbles in some real estate."

"Thank you, K.J.," I say. "Here's a quarter for both of you." The quarter barely has time to get stuck to Katherine's palm before her brother grabs it.

"She can't have the money. She'll eat it," he says, but the words are not out of his mouth before she starts squalling. She's tiny, but she goes from a whimper to a full-alarm siren in the blink of an eye.

"K.J.! What'd you do to your sister?" Kimmy yells as she cracks open the glass front door.

At her mother's voice, Katherine jumps up and goes running to her.

K.J. ignores that his helper has left and asks me and Mrs. Trapp if we'd like a refill for only a dime. "But ya hafta keep your same cup."

We both take a splash, and as the boy is pouring I look up to see Katherine being set down on the front porch by her mother. I wave to Kimmy, but she ignores me and closes the glass door.

Mrs. Trapp leans closer to me and whispers. "Well, looks

like she's found someone to take the place of our Mr. Dollar Store. You see that?"

I nod, because I do see it, but then sipping my lemonade I head for my van. Partly to get away from more talk about Colt and real estate, but partly to see if I can see more from that vantage point. When I turn to look, there's no one in the door or the front window. Katherine is sitting on the front stoop trying to put her flip-flops back on, but her mother isn't visible.

So the two arms that were wrapped around her waist are no longer visible either. The man standing behind Kimmy was in the shadows of the house. I dawdle with my phone, keeping my head tucked so the nosy teacher will leave. If she'd leave I could ask K.J. about the man in the house. But then another car pulls up and a couple teenagers get out to aid in K.J.'s quarter fund.

And no, it's not being nosy if you… well, if you…

Okay, so, I'm nosy.

Even before I get to our driveway, I can see movement through the thickness of the trees as a train blows by. Turning toward the house into the tunnel of weeds and bushes, I ease to a stop at the crossing arm and flashing lights, and put the car in park to wait it out.

It's the perfect time to look at my texts. I'm committed to checking them when that little number on the app says there are ten waiting. I know, my kids have explained how that defeats the whole purpose, and I act all apologetic and untechy. But between you and me, I just really don't care enough to check every time that little bell rings.

I have a couple texts from the school about upcoming events, one from Jackson about his dad's progress in rehab, one from my dad about their next camping trip to the Upper Peninsula of Michigan. See, all that didn't need my immediate attention, right? Every single one of those could've been sent in an email. Texting is way overrated.

But oh, as that little bell rings and a new one pops up, I'm so glad I didn't wait to read it.

From Colt: "I'm bringing home supper tonight. Celebrate my new job!"

I love texting.

With no supper to fix, I'm winnowing down my to-do list for this evening so as to make some time to read. Kids won't be home for a bit with cheerleading and football practice tonight. Same with Colt. Still have Wednesday and Thursday to get ready for guests in the B&B. There's laundry, but Will's in charge of that. Well, as soon as I tell him he's in charge of it. Okay, the rest of the afternoon is free. With the end of the train approaching, I put the car in drive, and then as the arms lift, slowly move over the bumpy crossing.

Shoot! Is that Laney's car in the driveway? What does she want now?

Coming up the front porch steps I can hear the television. However, upon opening the door I see there is no one watching it. "Hello? Laney?" I press mute on the remote control lying on the end table and try again. "Hello? Anyone here?" The response is the same. Silence.

No one is in the kitchen or dining room, but I find Laney and Cayden when I step onto the back deck. "Hi there. What's up?"

She waves at me across the table. "Have a seat. It's so pretty I decided to work out here. Waited 'cause I have some things to ask you."

I scoot a chair around to face the yard instead of the table as I ask, "Why was the TV on?"

"Zoe's watching it since Cayden is asleep. Isn't she in there?"

"No, maybe she's in the bathroom. I'm going to get some water."

"Great, get me some, too," she says as she bends her head back over her papers and notebooks.

As I open the door, Zoe comes through the door to the basement. "Oh! Carolina, you scared me."

"What are you doing in the basement?"

"Nothing. Just, uh, thought I heard something. But it's all good. How was work today? Here let me get that. You've had a long day, I'm sure. Cayden still asleep?" She takes the glasses out of my hands and begins filling them with ice.

"Yes, he's on the deck. Whatcha watching on the TV?"

"You want lemon in your water? I know Miss Laney has her own personal war on lemon in drinks, so she sure doesn't."

"I'll get a piece of lemon," I say as I open the refrigerator, but before I get it opened she's already heading to the deck with our drinks. With my piece of lemon in hand, I duck my head into the living room to look at the muted TV. It's the news, and since it's twenty after the hour, it's not like it just came on.

Back on the deck, I put the lemon in my glass, then sit down. "Where's Zoe?"

"She's walking on home from here. Says she loves to walk along the river, then up the side of the hill to her house. All those years Susan and Griffin lived in that house I don't think I really thought about it going all the way down to the river."

"I don't think that property does. I think she walks under the bridges along the water then comes up at the curve at the top of the hill. How's she liking being in school? Does she miss the homeschooling?"

Laney holds her cold glass to the back of her neck. "It's kind of warm out here. You know, I think she likes school better than she wants anyone to know. Seems she's made some friends. She can't babysit Friday night for the ballgame. Looks like Mr. Cayden here will be making his Chancey High Football debut."

"So what did you need to ask me about?" I put my feet up on the end chair and lay my head back.

"I hear Colt's staying a while. We need his B&B room as of Thursday night, you know?"

"Yes. I know." So much for relaxing. I drop my feet, sit up straight, and turn my chair to face her. "He's moving out of it before then."

"Where to?"

"Will's old room? I'm not sure."

She nods and doodles on the paper in front of her. "Because... Will is in the basement, right? Will and...?"

"Rose is not living here!" I say through gritted teeth. "She's not."

"Hey, okay, okay. That's just what people are saying."

"What people? It was one night."

There's that danged arched eyebrow. "Oh, so she *was* here."

Okay, I'm beginning to get a little mad. "Is this really what you wanted to ask me about? I have things to do!" I stand up and push my leg at the chair in some semblance of a kick.

"Whoa, honey! Don't get your panties all in a wad. Friends let friends know what folks are saying. If you've let Rose move in here, then I'll defend you to the moon and back, but if she's not, then I want to be able to set the record straight. You know I don't give a hoot-'n'-holler about what folks think, but I like to be working with facts when it comes to my people."

Her bright eyes flaring at me remind me who I'm talking to. I sit back down. "I do like being 'your people,' and yes, she did spend last night here." Then I let out a groan. "And for all I know she was here Monday night, too. But I made sure they both knew this morning that that is over."

She rolls her eyes and sits back in her chair. "Lord knows, I could've never in a million years moved back home after living in a dorm for four years."

"I know. What am I going to do with him? They've got the basement done up so nice, but it's almost too much freedom."

"At least you're getting your laundry done. I bet he has Rose doing the laundry, don't you?" Her laugh is cut short when I don't join her. I turn my face to look down the hill.

"Oh, should've known," Laney says. "Well, never mind. As long as we have the Chessie Room open by Thursday night, I'm good. Now, what I really want to talk to you about it what we are going to do in our booth for the Southern Dessert Festival. We've got to claim a dessert. Missus sent out a list to all the businesses and clubs, and they are going fast."

"Guess that was in one of the million emails and attachments she's sent out today. For crying out loud, we only decided on the theme this morning. I don't really care. What do you think?"

She sips her water as she waits on her laptop to respond. "Here's the updated list. I got strawberry shortcake first thing for Shaw and the dealership. His parents do the breakfast for their church every week and make dozens of biscuits, so they'll start making those and freezing 'em. Angie and Alex are doing pecan pie, although let's not tell Missus he's doing something called 'Deconstructed Pecan Pie.'" She looks up at me. "I have no idea what that is."

She shifts the screen toward me. "Here, look. See how many are taken? I think people are so afraid to get left with something bad they jumped in before they even knew if they wanted to participate. Ya gotta admit, Missus sure knows how to turn up the heat."

"See there?" She points to the screen. "Nine Mile is in charge of the World's Largest Banana Pudding. Susan's pretty mad at the way Missus manhandled them."

Laney smiles and scrolls to the top of the page. "Yet, look here. Missus has that 'due to the Grand Opening of the Nine Mile interactive community, they've asked to do the Banana

Pudding' and she feels, quote, 'it would be gracious to grant them their desire.'" She scrolls back down the list. "But Susan'll get over it. She knows how Missus is, and besides, my sister loves to be in the middle of stuff like this. So, what do you think we should do?"

"You know I don't cook. Which of these is the easiest? Of the ones left, chocolate pie is my favorite and my grandma's was the best. Do you like chocolate pie?" We meet eyes and both nod.

"Of course I do." She pulls the laptop toward her and starts typing. "There! I've replied to all that Crossings B&B is doing chocolate pie."

Chewing my lip, I say, "What if we don't get it? I don't really like buttermilk pie, and who wants to cut up all those apples for apple crisp?" I sigh and lean back. "Hope we get it."

"We got it! Missus just emailed me back." She sighs. "Wow, that's a relief!"

We high-five each other over the table and are all smiles. For a bit. Realization soon hits. "Laney? We didn't even really have to do this. We could've said, thanks, but no thanks, couldn't we?"

Laney just blinks at me. "Hmm. But guess we want to be a part of it, right? Right?"

With a ding her email reloads and she grimaces at me. "Too late now. We're on the official list."

We stare at each other with one question on our minds. But we don't ask each other, because we already know the answer.

No, neither one of us has ever made a chocolate pie.

CHAPTER 16

"I wouldn't let you go," Colt says right before he bites into another chicken leg.

Savannah's mouth drops open. "What?"

Now *this* I want to hear. "Really? Why?"

He shrugs and chews for a minute. "I don't trust teenagers when I can see them. Sure don't trust 'em on a boat out in the middle of the ocean. Guess I've worked with them too many years."

"Mom. Don't listen to him. Mr. and Mrs. Rivers will be there. I've never been on a cruise. Please." Savannah has turned her body to block out her uncle, where he's seated straight across from me. Her head is twisted so she can make eyes that communicate just how out of touch her uncle is.

Bryan laughs. "You are so weird. You belong on that boat. They're all as weird as you are at that church."

Now my head twists to the side where my son sits beside me. "Bryan! Don't say things like that!" Then I pause and lower my voice. "So, why would you say a thing like that? Weird how?"

"Mom, they aren't weird. Bryan is just acting like a freshman brat. Don't listen to him." She turns, face and body, towards her uncle. "Congratulations on your new job. Do you like Chancey High?"

Colt grins and lays down his stripped chicken leg bone next to the others on his plate. "Thank you, Savannah. I do like it here. Lived my whole life in Painter, Kentucky, except for finishing up away at college for a couple years. It's time I try somewhere else."

Savannah's dropping the cruise as a subject of conversation is evident, but I don't care. I'll talk to Jackson about it later. Right now the fried chicken is hot. Colt brought two buckets, one of all legs and the other all breasts. He's practically eaten the whole bucket of legs by himself.

"So, do a lot of painters live in Painter? That's really a weird name." Bryan asks. Weird is apparently his favorite adjective this week.

"Not that kind of painter. It's wild cats, cougars, I guess. Back in old times, maybe because they were also called panthers, they were called painters in the mountains. Probably someone saw one around the area and called the area Painter. Name stuck."

"Cool," Bryan says. "Cooler than being named for guys painting houses. Is there more chicken in that bucket?"

I tip over the bucket in front of me for him to reach in and take out another piece. The front door opens and closes, and Will hollers, "Hey, I'm home."

"Just in time for dinner, but you better hurry before Bryan eats all the chicken," I say. "We've got you a plate, just get something to drink."

While he's in the kitchen, we push all the sides toward his end of the table. He swings into the dining room and sits down at the end between Colt and me. "Smells good."

"Your Uncle Colt provided dinner tonight. Wasn't that nice? He's also staying on as the freshman football coach for a while."

"Yeah, I heard that at work today." He's emptying the containers of macaroni and cheese and mashed potatoes. There's quite a bit of gravy left, but he pours it all on his pile of potatoes. I place a nice chicken breast on his plate.

Colt pushes his empty plate away and folds his arms on the table. "Yeah, word flies in a small town. How was work? Sell any cars?"

Will frowns and looks at his plate, then takes a large bite of macaroni and cheese as he shakes his head.

Bryan speaks up. "Where's Rose?"

This causes even a deeper frown and another big spoonful, this time mashed potatoes and gravy.

We're all staring at Will now. Then Savannah snorts, tosses her head, and stands. "I don't want Rose living here. Of course no one cares what I want." She collects Colt's plate, as well as mine and hers, and carries them into the kitchen.

Bryan chokes down his mouthful of food to say, "Wait. Rose is living here? Where?"

Will's face gets closer and closer to his plate.

"Rose is not living here. Right, Will?" I ask, tipping my head in his direction to get a peek at his face.

He rolls his eyes up at me and shrugs.

"No, I'm not really asking. I'm telling you. Rose does not live here."

Colt has folded his arms across his chest and leaned back in his chair. Just watching the show like people who don't have kids do.

Will sits up straight and looks at me. "I'm not a little kid, or a teenager. I'm a man. You understand that, right?"

Colt draws in a chest full of air and then blows it out with a half laugh. "Living in your parents' basement? No, no." He then pushes his chair back and stands. "And a man is grateful when someone else buys his food. Didn't hear you say thank you yet to me or your mother."

Will's jaw tightens, but he doesn't turn toward Colt. Through tightened lips, he says, "Thank you, Uncle Colt, for this delicious fast-food dinner."

Colt lifts his hands out to the side and laughs while shaking his head.

My teeth are clinched as I say, "Will, you are being disrespectful to your uncle."

"He's being disrespectful to me!"

My eyes and mouth snap open. Savannah gasps, and Bryan laughs. Will has always been the obedient, do-everything-right older brother. He rarely got yelled at or punished as a kid because he didn't do anything to be yelled at or punished for. "Will, you apologize right now!"

He bends back over his plate and shovels another forkful of food in his mouth, as he mumbles, "Sure. Okay. I'm so very sorry," never lifting his head or eyes.

I direct my gaze, and clipped words, to my husband's younger brother. "Colt, since we do need your room in the B&B Thursday, you can move into the basement. Will has it fixed up right nice. Will is moving back to his old bedroom on the second floor."

Okay, now my son has lifted both his head and his eyes and is staring at me. "Mom! You can't do that! Rose and I fixed that all up. It's ours, not his."

I stand and pick up both buckets of chicken. "You're right, son. It's not his. It's mine. Mine and your daddy's. Rose wants her things back, fine. And if you want any more chicken you ask your uncle if you can have it. Oh, and I'd suggest asking nice."

Marching into the kitchen, there is only silence behind me.

And the smell of gunpowder hanging in the room.

All right, maybe I've read one too many westerns lately.

"So what's Will doing now?" Jackson asks through the phone. I'm sitting in the dark on the back deck having a cup of decaf coffee.

"Think he left. Probably gone to tell Rose how mean his mommy was to him. He was just so rude. Far as I know he never apologized to Colt."

"Or you. Sounds like you were right about it all. I thought it showed initiative when he fixed up the basement. Sounds like it was more Rose than him, though." There's a pause before he adds, "But he is under a lot of pressure, and we don't want to add to it, you know."

Taking a sip of coffee, I don't answer him that I'm not in the least bit concerned at this point about adding pressure to Will's life. Fry that fish later. After all, there are always other fish to fry. "So what do you think about the cruise? Colt flat out said he wouldn't let her go."

"Speaking of that, Isaac's dad called today. We had a really nice talk. They used to live not far from where we lived in Marietta. Both of them were born and bred in Atlanta. Not many natives of Atlanta around anymore," he says with a laugh.

I'm not laughing.

"Paul is into model trains, can you believe that? Has a layout at their house he's putting up, and he invited us over to check it out sometime. He was quite jealous that I work with trains, the big trains, every day. Seems like a really nice guy. Really nice family." His words trail off and I wait. And wait.

"You there?" he asks.

"Yes, so tell me. Did you and Paul talk about the cruise?"

"Well, of course. I mean, that's why he called, right? It

sounds like a really great opportunity, and honestly, is there really any trouble they can get into out on a boat that they can't get into right here at home? Besides, when will Savannah get another chance to go on a free cruise?"

I sigh because I have to admit he's right. "So you feel okay about it? Think it's a good idea? Maybe it's just hard for me to think of her being so far away from us. Maybe it's me."

Now he's silent. Guess he does think it's me.

"Okay, if you think it's all right," I say. "She'll be thrilled."

He chuckles. "Yeah, I'll miss the dozen or so texts I got today telling me what a good and reasonable daddy I am. Listen, I'll be home tomorrow night. Forgot about my dental appointment on Thursday. I'll just work from there on Friday."

"I don't know where here. This house seemed so big when we moved in. Guess I'll have to clean out that corner of our bedroom again, and you can work there. At least you'll be here tomorrow night when Colt moves into the basement. Will is not going to be happy."

"I heard you sigh. Wish you hadn't laid down the law?"

"Kinda. But no. We've got to get a handle on him, and Rose being here for breakfast is not a good thing. Who knows? Maybe Colt will find another place to live and Will can have the basement back once he starts behaving."

We end our call, and I lay my phone down for just a moment before I pick it back up and type in a search on Google: chocolate pie recipes.

Scrolling and reading while I finish my coffee, the only thing I really discover is that I'm now hungry for chocolate pie. Or chocolate cake. Or chocolate candy. Shoot, chocolate in any form.

I'd texted my parents earlier for my grandmother's chocolate pie recipe, but they don't have it in the motorhome. Mom said it was a pretty standard old-fashioned recipe, so I've found one of those. Looks easy and I actually have everything except a pie crust. I could just make the filling and see how it tastes, right?

Okay, doesn't hurt to try. I can always just throw it away.

Throwing away chocolate—now that makes me laugh out loud.

Chapter 17

"What is this black stuff?" Savannah greets me with instead of 'good morning' as I enter the kitchen. She's pointing to a bowl on the kitchen counter.

"Taste it. Did it get hard?" I move past her to the bowl and stick my finger in it. "Oh, it did get hard. I touch it again. "Maybe too hard. Feels like rubber. Did you taste it?"

She wrinkles her nose. "No. It looks like tar. I took it out of the fridge to get the orange juice. You made it?"

"Yes, it's to make chocolate pie. Oh, yeah, taste it." I dig into the bowl again and hold out my finger with a blob of thick chocolate on it.

She lifts the blob between her finger and her thumb, keeps the wrinkles on her face in place, then smells it. Finally she licks it, then takes a nibble. "Mm," she says as she pops the whole bit in her mouth. "That does taste good, like pudding, but better. It's kind of thick, isn't it? Kind of chewy."

Still chewing my bite, I agree. "Yeah, don't think it's supposed to be chewy. But it's better than the first batch, which was super runny. It's here in a bowl in the bottom drawer of the fridge." I pull it out and stick a spoon in. The spoon doesn't meet any resistance as it falls. "Couldn't slice that," I say as I put it back in the drawer and close the refrigerator. "Oh, some good news for you. Your daddy and I have decided you can go on the cruise."

"Really?! Yes!" She grins from ear to ear and reaches for her phone. (For a moment I thought she was reaching to give me a hug. Must be all the chocolate in my system making me delusional.) "Wait'll everyone finds out."

"Everyone who?" I ask, but she's focused on her phone and already walking out of the kitchen. Bryan rode to school early with Colt for the new before-school weight training session, and we have no one in the B&B. Will didn't venture upstairs before he left this morning and the way he raced out of the driveway looked like he's still angry. So once Savannah leaves I'll have the house to myself and I have nowhere I need to go.

Stepping onto the deck, I take a deep breath, searching for even just a trace of fall. A trail of wood smoke, a hint of decaying leaves, a certain spiciness in the air that comes with an edge of chill. Naw, but almost. The clean of summer air, with its heat and high clouds, is fading, and I'm ready for fall. Maybe I'll get out my fall decorations today. Candles and the autumn leaf door wreath. The table runner quilt that I bought last year for Thanksgiving. I take another deep draw before I go back inside. Almost fall air. Almost.

Savannah is eating a bowl of cereal when I step through the door. With her bowl in hand, she leans against the counter beside the sink. "Just found out I'm on the homecoming court."

"Really? That's wonderful. Congratulations. When is homecoming?"

"October sometime. I'll need a dress."

"Of course. Who else is on the court?"

"Just people." She fishes in her bowl for a final bite of cereal, then puts the bowl, complete with milk and floating pieces of milk-logged cereal in the sink. "Gotta go."

"Have a good day," I say as she grabs her purse and leaves

out the front door. Nothing like an empty-house silence, so I sink onto the couch to enjoy it.

Okay. That's long enough.

Sitting up on the edge of the couch I look around the living room. It needs dusting before I would want to put out any fall decorations. Can't dust and not vacuum. Never did tell Will he was to do the laundry, so there's a pile of that waiting downstairs. Going to need to make dinner tonight since Jackson's coming home. Since Laney had Cayden she's done a great job taking care of the books, but not so much in helping with the cleaning. Wasn't Savannah going to clean the rooms for some extra money? Problem with kids getting real jobs is that they no longer want to work for the pitiful amount I offer.

Pushing myself up off the couch I notice the time. Seven forty-five. Okay. I'll clean really hard for one hour and then take a fun break. Learned this little technique years ago, and it came in handy when the kids were little. Forgot about it, but Bonnie does it at the store. Really seems to help me get things done. So, one hour, then I'll do something fun just for me.

Okay – so it's been two hours. It would be past time for my fun break, except I've gotten nothing done. When I went down to put in the first load of laundry, I started looking around the basement, and it really is a cozy space. Will and Rose did work hard on it. On the coffee table there were some *Southern Living* magazines. They were even splayed out like on a table in a doctor's office. Very neat and inviting, and one had an article about soups. Easy soups, it said, and I did have dinner to think about. So, I managed to get those magazines looked at, and I forgot I don't really like making soups. Too much preparing of stuff.

Then I called Laney and Susan to see what they were doing, but neither one answered. Finally I came up out of the basement to find no one else had done the dusting in my absence. Going to try it again. One hour of work, then I'll have lunch. Yes, it'll only be eleven, but don't you get hungrier at home than at work?

Halfway to the closet where the vacuum is, my phone rings. "Hey Laney. What are you up to?"

"Lunch with Susan up at the club in Laurel Cove. She said to invite you, too. You've been before, right?"

"Yeah. I did go with her. It was nice, but I really need to get some work done here since I don't have to go into the bookstore."

"I have a sitter and we have an invite to lunch," she insists. "Get dressed and I'll pick you up at eleven-fifteen. Tomorrow I'll come help clean, okay?"

I'm off the hook. "That works. Thanks, I'll see you in a bit."

Bonnie's cleaning system works, but mine does, too. Stall until you have no choice, then wait for someone to help you.

Of course, mine's a little less of a sure thing.

CHAPTER 18

"Don't sit at that table," Susan whispers in my ear. She bumps me away from the chair my hand is lying on.

"Why? I mean, I don't care, but what's wrong with that table?"

"Darien snobs," she whispers. She grabs my upper arm and steers me to a table with three ladies on the other side. "Hello ladies, are these seats taken? We need three."

"Not taken at all, honey. We'd love to sit with some young people."

Susan drops her hand away and leaves, saying, "I'll be right back." Laney is over at the drinks table getting us some iced tea, and Susan rushes over to her sister.

"Hello," I say in her absence. "I'm Carolina Jessup. Guest of Susan Lyles. I don't live up here."

"I'm Jean, this is Sara, and that's Margaret Ann. Nice to meet you, Carolina. Where do you live?"

Getting settled, I answer that question and then the string of questions following. All while watching Susan and Laney wander around the room whispering to each other. Finally I stand up and say, "Think I'll walk around a bit before we get started…" But as I begin maneuvering away, Aggie Pearson, the leader of this group, claps her hands and asks everyone to find their seats. "Oh, well," I say with a grin as I sit back down.

"Welcome, everyone," Aggie continues. "Susan, would you introduce your guests? Most know Miss Carolina, proprietor of Crossings B&B in Chancey. If you've not yet attended one of their delightful wine and cheese afternoons, you simply must next time we are invited. What do you think, Carolina? Are we invited for *this* Friday? Weather is supposed to be spectacular."

Laney is still standing, and she waves her arm. "I'm Laney Conner, and speaking on behalf of my partner, Carolina, and my sister, Susan, we'd love to have you ladies on Friday. Let's say four o'clock? Don't want to miss the football game later!"

Aggie nods at Laney and thanks her. Her thank-you seems dismissive, and she actually moves to where she can see me better. "Is that all right with you, Carolina? It is your home."

Laney ignores the slight and rather noisily takes her seat to introduce herself to the ladies already seated.

I speak up rather loudly, "Of course it's all right. Look forward to seeing all of you there."

I turn, and as I do, I punch Laney in the arm. "Way to go, glory hog. She asked *me*." Susan catches my eye and shakes her head. As she takes her seat between us, she says next to my ear. "Don't mess with her. Be nice!"

"She's a bear. She was so snappy on the car ride up here. I get being sleep-deprived having a baby, but don't take it out on me. That's what husbands are for!"

Susan leans back to look at me, then closes her eyes. "Oh, you don't know." Then as Aggie asks us to bow our heads for a prayer, Susan shushes herself and we listen to the prayer. After the communal "amen," I look to Susan, but one of the ladies across the table steals her attention.

"I think we should go around the table and introduce ourselves. Tell us how you came to be in Laurel Cove today!"

Laney charms the rest of the table with her introduction, but she doesn't include me in her glances, smiles, and winks. My introduction is short and sweet since Aggie already put me on the spot. Plus, I'm trying to keep my annoyance with Laney under wraps.

Susan is the final one to share at our table, and she tells of Griffin's new job with Mountain Power, one of the developers of Laurel Cove and a huge contributor to the club, golf course, and parks. And how with the new job they decided a move up the mountain from Chancey would be appropriate. "Also, our son, Grant, is a freshman at Darien Academy. Our daughter Susie Mae is a junior at Chancey High, while our other daughter Leslie is at UGA."

Jean clasps her hands. "So delightful to have ladies here with children still at home. Seems most of the ladies at our lunches are more our ages, with grandchildren the ages of your children. Just delightful."

Instead of talk breaking off into smaller groups, Jean keeps the entire table involved in every discussion, so I can't ask Susan why Laney is being such a snot.

After an hour of such small talk, I couldn't get out of there fast enough. The little slights from Laney during the conversation might have been my imagination, or maybe they weren't. She's very, very good at that Southern girl talk. You know, the kind where you feel like you've been insulted. Where you're pretty sure you've been insulted. Where there is no doubt you've been insulted, but everyone else is saying things like, "Y'all are so lucky to have each other for friends" and "Carolina, you must be so thrilled to have good friends willing to partner in your business" and "Y'all are just as cute as bugs in a rug!"

Yeah, I'm spittin' mad by the time we eat our slices of caramel cake, but I have to keep smiling and saying, "Thank you" and "Yes, I sure am blessed" and "Why, aren't you sweet to say that!"

Get me out of here.

I pick up my pocket book while I say goodbye to the rest of our table. "I just want to speak to Aggie for a quick minute," I explain with another wave.

"Aggie," I say as I walk up to her, "it's so good to see you again."

"You too, Carolina. I've been in your bookstore a couple times, and I'm so happy that Bonnie is enjoying working there. We do miss her at our lunches, though."

"Well, I'll have to arrange it so that she doesn't work every Wednesday, so she can come to lunch. I look forward to seeing you Friday at the house."

"Oh, perfect." She peers over my shoulder. "Well, it looks like Susan and her sister are ready to go, and I need to check on the raffle ticket sale. Lovely to see you again."

Susan is pointing out the door at Laney striding toward the car as I hurry over to her.

"What? She's going to leave me? Tell me what's going on."

Susan pauses with her hand on the door. "Don't want to spoil it, in case you don't know, but did Savannah tell you about homecoming court?"

"Yes, she's on it and needs a new dress. Is Laney mad because Savannah's on the court? It's high school, she just has to get over herself."

Susan rolls her eyes. "It's not really about Savannah, but Jenna, for the first time, is *not* on the court. Savannah got the one spot for a senior cheerleader. They break all the voting down in some crazy way so that it's not just the cheerleaders or just the football players on the court. Each group gets to have one representative. Jenna has always been the cheerleader representative, freshman, sophomore, and junior year. Leslie was on it every year as a member of student government. Susie

Mae is on it this year as junior cheerleader, but last year she covered her bases and ran as a member of a sports group. She played softball just to make sure."

I look out to the parking lot where Laney is sitting in her car with the air on. I can see it moving her hair. Her big hair. Her beauty pageant hair. Then I turn to Susan. "You know these things don't mean that much to me, but what can I do about it? Savannah isn't going to step down, we all know that."

Susan jumps in. "No, of course she shouldn't. And Jenna should have hedged her bets and joined some other group, but..."

"But she thought she didn't need to."

Susan pushes open the door, and we walk toward Laney's car. "So now you know why she's grouchy."

"Okay, thanks. What are you doing this afternoon?"

"Finally meeting with the housekeeper to the stars. Well, at least the stars of Laurel Cove. Then I have a meeting with Grant's teachers at Darien."

"Is everything okay with Grant?"

"Yes," she says, "they do an interview with each student and their parents each year. To make sure things are on track."

"Sounds like a good idea."

"It is, but I don't think I have the stamina to keep up with these Darien parents. The expectations for the kids is intimidating. Griffin is all over it." She sighs and shakes her head.

"What?" I ask as I open the car door to join Laney. "What's wrong? You said Grant loves it."

"He does, but... Griffin wants to force Susie Mae to go to Darien, too. Wants to pull her out of Chancey High, and she's having none of it. When Griffin and she are home at the same time, it's a constant battle."

Laney shifts the big SUV out of park while Susan is still holding on to my open door. Then she says, almost yells, to her sister, "Good riddance to Chancey High, I say. Tell Griffin I'm on his side. Thanks for lunch, Susan, we've got to go."

Susan slams my door as Laney begins backing up.

"You don't mean that about Chancey High," I say.

"No, of course I don't." She pulls out of the parking lot and takes a deep breath before saying, "Jenna didn't make homecoming court."

"Susan told me. I didn't know. I'm sorry."

"It's stupid the way they do it."

"Is she very upset?"

Laney just nods.

We drive in the quiet for a good while, then she laughs a bit. "Sorry I took it out on you at lunch. I just found out as we got here. Kids weren't supposed to know until lunch today, but of course the list got out this morning."

"But you sounded fine when you called me about lunch."

"And this is the worst part, which I didn't even tell Susan and why I'm madder at myself than anybody else. *Angie* Conner was on the list and we thought it was just a mistake because of course, it couldn't be *Angie*." She laughs cynically. "Angie has never been on homecoming court, so of course it meant Jenna. Never gave it a second thought."

"Oh, no. It was really Angie?"

"Yep. Angie never joined a club at school until she and Alex got this food truck business going. She's part of some business and community club and they nominated her."

"Oh, Laney. What a mess."

"Yep. Angie got her sister's place on homecoming court, and Savannah got her boyfriend."

I sit up straight. "Wait. What?"

"Isaac. He dumped Jenna when we wouldn't let her go on that cruise with him. So don't get too attached to him. He won't be around long when you tell Savannah she can't go on the cruise."

Oh.

CHAPTER 19

"I invited the ladies from Laurel Cove to wine and cheese on Friday," I say to Jackson as he stands looking in the refrigerator, "so I'll be going shopping if there's anything in particular you're looking for." He got home a couple hours after I did, so we've been catching up on each other's day for a bit.

"Not really. Just nice to have a full refrigerator to eat out of. Between Shelby and Dad's empty fridge and living in a hotel, I'm appreciating the comforts of home." He pulls out a slice of cheese and eats it as he closes the door. "Whatever it is you have in the Crockpot is making me hungry. What is it?"

"Chicken and dumplings. Got the recipe on the internet. Uses canned biscuits and chicken breasts with some canned soup." I open the Crockpot and we both get a big whiff. "I think it's going to be good. We'll eat around six-thirty. Gives Colt and Bryan enough time to shower."

"Ready to go check the basement? See what needs to be done before Colt can move in?" Jackson asks.

"Are you sure it's the right thing to do?" I start to waffle. "Maybe I shouldn't have…"

"Stop. It'll only be for a couple weeks. I've been talking to Colt and he's already checking out some apartments. He has no huge desire to live with his big brother, believe me. You're right, Will needs to be a bit more grateful, and he definitely needs to slow down this thing with Rose. His room upstairs should help on both those fronts."

At the basement door, I turn and hug him. "Things are so much easier when you're here."

He sighs. "Everything here seems so simple when I'm away. I'm going to try and do better. Be more on top of things." He opens the door, and we head down the steps.

It's messier than it was on Sunday when we first saw it, but it's just dirty clothes, an unmade bed, and some dirty dishes left around.

Looks pretty much like the rest of the house.

I strip the bed and make my way back around to the laundry area. "Not bad. Just wash these sheets and Colt can move in."

"Maybe Rose hasn't had time to pick up her stuff, or maybe she doesn't want it," Jackson says.

"Maybe. I think Will's calmed down, too. He texted me earlier that the basement was ready, so…" I shrug and begin filling the washer. "Either way he'll be home for dinner since its Wednesday and the car lot closes early."

Jackson collects the dirty dishes and brings them to the sink area. "So how did Anna seem Tuesday? Can't believe the sonogram you sent." We lean against the washer and dryer as it finishes filling with water and makes the transition to washing the full load. He speaks up over the noise, "Glad you got to go to the doctor with her. First picture of our grandchild!"

From around the stairwell where the outside door is, Will steps in front of us. A mix of anger and questioning on his face. "What picture? You went to the doctor with Anna?"

We both straighten up from our leaning position. Jackson says, "Will. Didn't hear you come in."

Will tilts his head towards me. "You went to the doctor with Anna?"

"Well, yeah, she, uh…" While I stammer, Jackson pulls out his phone, finds what he's looking for, and hands it to our son.

"This is it? This is the, uh, baby?" Will's face relaxes, and then he blinks his eyes several times. He holds it up to us. "Is that an arm? It's bent like an arm."

My breath catches, and all I can do is nod.

Jackson moves beside his son. "Yes, and see that bump? That's his nose. I spent a lot of time staring at it last night trying to figure it out," he says with a laugh.

Will looks up at his dad. "You said 'his nose.' Is it, is it a boy?"

"Oh, I don't know," Jackson says. Then he looks at me. "Did they tell you yesterday?"

"No. No, Anna said she didn't want to know something like that about the baby unless you knew it, too. I think she wished you were there."

Will cradles his father's phone in both hands and goes to sit down on the couch. He sits without taking his eyes off the phone.

Jackson and I wait to get a feel for what we should do. Slowly we make our way to stand behind the couch, then I go to sit down beside our son. I softly explain, "Anna asked me to go with her and made me promise not to tell you or Missus. But later I realized I'm pretty sure she wanted me to tell you."

He looks at me, then takes his hand off the phone to put it around me in a one-armed hug. "Okay. Thanks for being there for her, Mom. I think she and I need to talk." He stands up and hands the phone to his dad. "Can you send me that picture?"

"Sure, son."

I stand up and give him a hug. Jackson moves around to give him a hug, too, and I turn to start up the stairs.

"Mom?"

"Yes?" I say as I turn to look down.

"That's what you wanted to talk to me about Monday, isn't it? When Rose was here?"

I take a deep breath and then say, "Yes, it was."

Will just shakes his head, then turns to look around him. "Okay. I'll be up for dinner. Six-thirty, right?"

"Right."

"Savannah? Can you come out here?" I catch a glimpse of my daughter in the low light of the kitchen and call her out to the porch where I'm sweeping.

Dinner was delicious, and crockpot chicken and dumplings have gone straight to the top of my menu rotation. Everyone was in a good mood, and you could tell Will was working extra hard to get back in his uncle's good graces.

Savannah sticks her head out the door, clearly not intending to actually come all the way out.

"I want to ask you something. Come on out and close the door." Moving behind the table, I dig out dead leaves and other detritus that have collected in the weeks since I last swept out here. "So, what's this I hear about Jenna and Isaac?"

She moves a chair away from the table and out of my way, then sits in it. "What about them?"

"Were they dating?"

She shrugs. "Not really. You know how Jenna is, she thinks any new boy in Chancey is her property first." She stands up. "I have homework. When can we go dress shopping for homecoming?"

She starts toward the door. I keep sweeping but say, "Isaac asked Jenna to go on the cruise."

That stops her.

"Not really."

Okay, that stops me. "What do you mean, 'not really'?"

She throws her hands up. "Why do you care? Isaac and I aren't actually *dating*. People don't do that anymore. Not like y'all used to." She turns to the door. "I have homework."

"I'm rethinking the cruise," I say, "so you might want to spare a moment of your precious homework time to talk to me."

"Fine!" She flounces back across the deck and throws herself back into the chair she just left. "What do you want to know?"

"If you and Isaac aren't dating, why do you want to go on this cruise with him?"

She doesn't even rolls her eyes at me, just sighs. "Mom. It's. A. Cruise."

Yeah. That's the way to get me to listen. "Cut out talking like I'm stupid. Jenna's parents wouldn't let her go. Why should we let you?"

"Wait. Her parents?" Savannah leans forward. "She said she didn't want to go. Said she didn't even ask her parents." She flops back in the chair, staring out at the dark backyard.

As if they were waiting for a pause in our conversation, the frogs start croaking. It sounds like summer, but a breeze blows across us with just a touch of a chill. Not much. Not enough to send us inside, or even make us wish for long sleeves, but there's a promise. Savannah lifts her face and closes her eyes like she feels it, too. I will not embarrass her by asking if she feels it, so I close my eyes and tilt my head back also.

Then she asks, "You went to the doctor with Anna?"

Back to sweeping. "Yes, I did. How'd you hear?" I push the old leaves, dirt, and sticks I've swept together off the side of the porch.

She shrugs as she sits forward, leaning her elbows on her knees. "So, can I go on the cruise?"

"Who told you I went with Anna?"

"You can't say anything, but I have a friend who saw you there."

"At the doctor's? The OB/GYN doctor's?" Now I sit down to look at her. "Who?"

She just shakes her head. "Don't ask 'cause I can't tell you. I don't think you even know her."

"Then how did she know me?"

"Mom." She looks up at me. "Is Anna okay? Is, uh, the baby okay?"

I nod at her. She says, "Good," and stands up. "I really do have homework."

This time I let her go back inside.

I can't even remember what it was I called her out here to discuss.

Okay, so I do remember, I just don't know what to think, or do, about it.

Chapter 20

"So what time does the freshman game start tonight? And why is it on Thursday?" I ask Colt as I slide in across the breakfast table from him. "Why is this the first freshman game when the Friday night games have been going on a couple weeks?"

He's hunched over his cereal bowl, and he dribbles milk out the corner of his mouth as he talks. "Not all schools have enough kids for a whole freshman team. Those places, the freshmen are just on the JV squad and play before varsity on Friday nights. Although we don't have as many games, it's important to have a freshman team in my opinion. You comin'?"

"I'll be there," Jackson shouts from the stairs. Then, striding into the kitchen, he sets his tennis shoes on an empty chair. "This dentist appointment worked out great."

"Extra bowls and spoons are on the table," I say as he turns around looking for food.

"Dad, if you can't make it, that's okay," Bryan says. "Not like I'll probably play."

Colt laughs. "This ain't the JV team, son. We barely have enough to fill all the positions. You'll most definitely be playing. Not sure what position yet, but you'll be on the field."

Jackson picks up his shoes, drops them on the floor, then takes their place in the chair beside me, across from Bryan and Colt. "See, wouldn't miss it for the world! Right, Carolina?"

"We have guests coming, depends on when they get here. I'm working at the store this morning until noon. When is the game?"

"Five-thirty," Colt answers. "Will, you going to be there? I could use some help on the sidelines."

All of us shift to look at Will who's just come into the kitchen after his first night back on the second floor, in his room next to ours. He stops in the doorway. "Me? I never did sports much. Especially not football." He continues on and sits at the end of the table, pulling a bowl and spoon towards him.

"I'm talking stats, notes, helping me get the kids' names down and their abilities. Don't have to know a lot of football for that."

"Yeah. C'mon, Will. It'd be fun," Bryan chimes in as he stands up and pulls his backpack off the floor.

"Maybe. I'll see how things go today." He fills his bowl with an assortment of cereal and adds milk over it all.

Savannah yells from the living room. "Bryan! I'm leaving."

I yell back, "You don't want any breakfast?"

Bryan answers for her as I hand him his cereal bowl to put in the sink. "FFA is selling chicken biscuits at school this morning."

Colt stands up. "Yep, we don't want to miss that."

"But you just had cereal," I say.

Colt and Bryan have the same confused expression as they look at me.

Jackson laughs. "They're apparently growing boys and need two breakfasts."

Bryan doesn't think about it too long as he knows his sister will leave him. Especially now that he could get a ride with his uncle. But we've been informed by both of our high schoolers that it's not cool to be related to the coach, much less get a ride to school with him. As the front door slams, they are already fussing.

Colt steps to the basement door. "I'm leaving from down here. Thanks, Will, for giving the basement up. Shouldn't be for long. Got some places to check out this weekend. See y'all later at the game."

Left with only the crunching of cereal, the house feels like it took a deep breath, then let it out.

"So you've only got class today, right?" I ask Will.

"Yup." He has his head down so that his spoon only has to travel a few inches to meet his mouth. His hair has gotten longer, and it hangs down, hiding his face. Suddenly he sits up, pulls in a breath, and as he holds it in, he nods his head. Releasing the air, he says, "Meeting Anna for lunch. We're going to talk."

Jackson's eyes meet mine, then we look at our son. Jackson clears his throat. "I think that's a good idea."

I start to agree, but Jackson holds up his hand. "And I don't think you need everybody else's opinion about things right now. Not that your mother is just *everybody else*, but the less you talk to other people about all this right now, the better. Just you and Anna. You never got that time where the two of you figure things out. You were at school, she was here. Then when you were both here, you had, well, you had everybody else."

Will slides his eyes to me. He knows I have questions. Lots of questions. Good questions, but… I swallow and nod. "Dad's right."

Will sits back in his chair, and I can see the questions crossing his face. He needs our help, maybe Jackson is wrong. Maybe we should—

"Good thinking, Dad." He stands up and, without me saying anything, picks up his bowl and spoon and puts them the sink. Then he begins picking up and closing the boxes of cereal.

"You go get ready for school. I'll do this," I say.

But the words are barely out of my mouth before Jackson says, "No! You can't complain about him not taking on more responsibility and then not let him."

I pull my hands off the cereal box I was taking out of my son's hands and smile.

Jackson adds, "Just say 'thank you.'"

Will grins at me as I fold my hands in my lap. "Thank you, Will."

He grins even larger as he responds, "You're welcome, Mother."

He cleans the table, including Jackson's and my bowls. "May I refresh your coffee?"

"Sure," Jackson tells him.

It takes me biting my lip to keep me from telling him I'll get my own. My skin actually feels itchy, him waiting on me like this. Jackson is keeping me in my seat with his stare, so I graciously accept. "Thank you. That would be nice."

He goes upstairs, leaving us with our hot coffee and a clean table. He even wiped down the counters and put all the dishes in the dishwasher. As he climbs the stairs, taking them two at a time, he actually seems to be humming.

"So, it's just us," Jackson says. "When are you leaving for the store?"

"When I finish this *refreshed* coffee. Just stopping in the store for a bit this morning to help Bonnie out—Shannon takes a business class at the college Thursday mornings. We're holding a festival meeting at ten in the store."

"My dentist appointment is at nine, then I'm coming back here to work. Thanks for clearing off the desk in the bedroom. You did good with Will just now."

"I can't believe how hard it was to let him wait on me." I stand up and slide my chair under the table as Jackson does the same.

We meet at the end of the table for a kiss and a hug. Then, looking up at him, I say, "Made me think of something Bonnie said the other day. She said parents think they are raising kids, when they are really raising adults. Or at least should be."

Jackson pulls me to him again and laughs. "That's good. Raising adults. Guess then letting Savannah go on the cruise is a good idea. Show we trust her, right?"

Luckily he doesn't wait for an answer.

CHAPTER 21

"I believe we should carefully consider all vendor requests, if we even get any at this late date, not just grant them willy-nilly. We do not want a junkyard on our square!" Missus' voice echoes around the high ceiling of Blooming Books.

Cathy Stone giggles and then dissolves into belly laughs as she gasps, "Did you say 'willy-nilly'?"

Peter looks across the table at me and the mayor and wiggles his eyebrows, which turns our grins into laughter. Retta and Ida Faye don't find the humor, but they've not thought anything was funny since *Laugh-In* was on TV and Johnny Carson was the king of late night.

Cathy is tipsy or high—or maybe it's just lack of sleep. But she's giggled through the entire meeting. Missus keeps talking over her, since her attempts at public shaming haven't worked. Shannon is back from her morning class and is stalking behind Peter's back, sure that Cathy is trying to attract Peter with her light-hearted attitude. (Believe me, there is *nothing* attractive about it, besides the fact that it's making the meeting more tolerable.)

Missus straightens her back and glares at Cathy. "I did not say 'willy-nilly.' You are absurd. What, Jed? You do *not* need to raise your hand!"

"You did. You did say 'willy-nilly.'"

I look down at my lap. Retta and Ida Faye study the table, and Peter gives his mother a sideways glance and a little nod. This does not aid Cathy in her attempt to settle down.

Missus sighs. "So be it. Retta, looks like you've done a commendable job getting the businesses on board with the dessert booths. The Chamber of Commerce is in capable hands. Peter, the bistro is set up for sandwiches and additional tables on the sidewalk, correct?"

"Yes, all taken care of."

"Ida Faye, you are in charge of the children's area. Are you prepared to give us a full report on that?" Missus asks.

Ida Faye hands each of us a sheet of blue paper. "You'll see here the setup for the children's tables on the sidewalk outside the library. I've enlisted the student government of the high school to provide students to man the table. Counts for their citizenship points."

"Good thinking, Ida Faye." Missus checks her notebook. "Carolina? Do you have anything to report?"

Um... honestly I've been keeping my head low. Shouldn't coming up with the theme be enough? "About our booth? Blooming Books is doing chocolate pie."

Missus just keeps looking at me. Finally she says, "And...?"

Peter speaks up. "Susan and Nine Mile?"

You know, I do think I saw something on one of the thousand emails about me being the liaison for the whole Nine Mile opening thing. "Oh, yes. Well, they're working on it." Not sure what Cathy finds funny now, but she's giggling again, then she sing-songs, "Carolina's in t-r-o-u-b-l-e!"

I flip towards her and snap, "Are you drunk? Quit laughing at everything!"

Missus holds her hands up. "No squabbling. Carolina, you forgetting to take care of your assignment is no reason to act like a child."

"Guess someone forgot to tell me there's a festival meeting," a voice comes booming over the bookcases to the back, where we are seated around a long folding table.

Missus slowly closes her eyes, shakes her head, and mutters, "Gertie Samson."

Gertie picks up a padded chair from the sitting area out front and carries it with one large hand back to our group. "Can't sit on one of the hard metal chairs. Scoot over, Peter. You, too, Ida Faye." She shoves her chair into the newly made spot and sits down. "There now. Who's running this shindig?" She looks around the table with a look of confusion, then chuckles. "I'm joking. We all know who's in charge. Good morning, Shermania. I'd appreciate you not making me have to work so hard to find out about these here festival meetings in the future. After all, I am letting y'all use my idea for this whole rigmarole."

"Your idea? Please don't try and take credit for Carolina's idea. She isn't one for much creative thought, so we should celebrate when it happens."

Of course now Cathy isn't giggling and is ready to talk. "But Missus, surely you know about Gertie's moonshine? The cave? Her flavors?"

Missus waves a gloved hand at us all. "Please. No." She lifts her nose at Gertie. "You are not on this committee. Please leave."

Peter lays a hand on his mother's arm. "You might want to, uh, Gertie has a point."

I speak up. "Hey, it's a good idea. Everyone's excited. Doesn't matter where the idea came from, right?" Looking around I encourage nods from those at the table. I see they all aren't surprised at where I got the idea, and honestly, I kind of thought Missus knew, too.

Apparently I thought wrong. Her eyes get big, and she takes in a big breath. "Are you saying…?"

Gertie jumps in, "That my moonshine is called 'Southern Sweets' and are all about desserts? Yes, ma'am, she sure is!" She digs in the pocket of the long jean dress she's wearing. "Here it is." Unfolding the paper, she lays it on the table, and we all lean towards it. "I'll be doing tastings out on the front sidewalk. Got a big, specially made banner and canopy thing that they'll come set up on Thursday night in the street out front of Andy's Place. Y'all remember my friend Bill? He's got his whole bluegrass band coming down to play all weekend. They can be real hard to book, but I got 'em." She elbows Peter and grins. "Course, don't hurt none that Bill ain't had any of my good lovin' since the spring."

Gertie winks at us all, and Cathy sits up straighter all of a sudden. "Oh, Gertie, wait. Here's my card. Our lingerie comes in all sizes. Big sizes, too. You'll like it."

"Never thought about none of this fancy stuff," Gertie says as she examines the card. Then she slides it into her pocket. "I'll be calling you, girl. So, now, any questions?"

Jed pats the table as he clucks his tongue. "Gotta say, we sure didn't think of having music. Good catch. Really will set a festive mood."

Retta voices agreement and adds, "My businesses were asking if we were going to serve alcohol. Folks do spend more when they imbibe, you know."

"And closing the street, wonderful idea. Less concerns about the children's activities being near the street." Ida Faye smiles as she exclaims, "Oh, mercy! We can even move the children's tables into the street. That makes things so much better. Wait'll I tell the high schoolers, they had too many ideas for our little area."

For the first time in the meeting, ideas are flying, and we are all talking over each other. But you gotta know, Missus doesn't go for all that sharing and excitement.

"Excuse me! Excuse me!" As immediate silence doesn't

fall, she stands up and says it again, louder, "Excuse me!" She waits until we are all looking at her and until all our mouths are shut. "Our permit does not allow for alcohol and—"

"Sure it does," Gertie counters as she digs again into the vast pockets of her dress. "Here's a copy."

Missus sinks back into her chair as she reads the paper. "I did not approve this. This is not the permit I applied for."

Gertie shrugs. "I submitted a new permit."

Missus drops the paper like it's covered in snot. "That is not allowed."

"Sure it is." Gertie grins at us all and winks again. "If you know the right folks in Atlanta." She lumbers out of her chair and stands. "And let there not be any doubt that Gertie Samson knows all the right folks in Atlanta. They love me there." She steps away from the table. "Good to see you folks. Peter, put my chair back for me, okay?"

She takes her time walking to the front, stopping to chat with Shannon and Bonnie on her way. None of us say anything until Jed clears his throat and says almost to himself, "I'm the mayor, and I can't hardly get the streets closed. Takes an act of God."

Missus' head snaps up, and she glares at us all. "Don't let me hear even one of you say *that* woman is God. This meeting is over."

We all stand up quickly. I attempt to disappear behind the bookcases farthest from the door, hoping for 'out of sight, out of mind.'

But she finds me. "Is it true about her liquor? Southern Sweets?"

"Yes."

Missus thinks for a moment, then shrugs. "It's still a good idea."

I only nod in response.

She tugs on her bright white gloves to make sure they are

in place and turns away from me, then she turns back. "You are responsible. If the moonshine samples gets out of hand, if there are any problems at all, it rests with you, Carolina Jessup. After all, how could giving away moonshine lead to any issues?" She raises an eyebrow at me, turns, and walks away.

Hmm. But seriously, when has giving away free booze ever led to problems?

Don't think I need, or even want, to Google that.

Chapter 22

When I think the coast is clear and everyone has left the store, I step out into the open seating area by the front windows. And there sits Retta Bainbridge in all her autumn glory. Her mustard blouse has a scattering of leaf pins in orange and brown across her ample bosom, and her wool skirt is a heavy tweed. She even has on boots.

"Oh, Retta. Thought you'd left."

"Obviously. However, being in real estate, I know how to wait folks out. You can't imagine how hard it is for some people to say no. Especially if you just sit and wait quietly. Do you have a minute?"

I rest on the arm of the chair across from her. "Just a minute. What can I help you with?"

"First I'm wondering if your space is available for my book club meetings? We meet the third Tuesday night of each month at seven p.m. There are only nine of us, so there's plenty of space here. Plus, we would try and buy our books from you. I can give you a list of our upcoming books, we plan a year in advance, and you could try and gather them. We only do books that are available in paperback. Too expensive to be buying hardback books, you know." She smiles at me, closes her mouth, and waits.

Now she just told me how hard it is for people to say no when you just wait, like she is doing now.

"Sure." Okay, so she's right. But also, I think I'd like to be in a book club. I've never been in one, and this would be a good, and profitable, way to try it. "Can I join your book club?"

"Oh, Carolina, you're a librarian, and I'm sure you wouldn't be interested in the silly books we read. You probably read those hard books, or the classics."

I slide down into the chair and smile. "No. Well, sometimes, but mostly I read cozy mysteries and fun books. And, believe it or not, I've never been in a book club."

Retta nods. "Okay. Deal. I'll email you the book list. I hope you like it. Can we hold our October meeting here?"

"Sure, and thanks for letting me join. I'm really looking forward to getting the book list."

She leans forward. "And I've not even told you the exciting news!" She cranes her neck around toward the floral area. "Shannon? Can you come here? Bonnie, come on over, too."

Both women come forward, Bonnie standing to the side of my chair and Shannon scooting over to sit on the chair across from us.

Retta leans over to pull a file folder out of her big leather satchel. "Here we go. First, your Chamber of Commerce member sticker for your front window." She hands it to Shannon, then picks up another sheet and reads aloud from it. "I hereby proclaim Blooming Books the Business of the Month for the Chamber of Commerce of Chancey, Georgia." She pulls out a frame from her bag and hands it to me.

In the frame is a certificate of our being named Business of the Month for November. I hold it up to show Bonnie and then turn it to show Shannon. We make all the appropriate acknowledgments of the honor, and then Retta holds up her hands.

"That's not all! We'll be holding our November Chamber Meeting right here so everyone can celebrate with you! We'll bring a cake and perhaps Peter will provide coffee, or look into one of those large coffee pots."

Shannon frowns. "But where will everyone sit for the meeting?"

"Oh, you'll just need to get some chairs from the church or the funeral home. Maybe some tables, too. We meet on the first Monday of each month, so the first Monday in November at six-thirty p.m. Congratulations!" She stands up and lifts her heavy satchel. "I must be going now. Real estate never rests!" At the door, she says loudly, "Lovely meeting, Carolina. Just lovely." Then she's gone.

We watch as she walks past the front windows. Shannon shakes her head. "It's every bit of seventy-five degrees out there, and the humidity is thick. Them boots have to be swimming in sweat."

Bonnie chimes in. "And that wool! Made me itchy just seeing it in this heat. Can you imagine wearing it?"

I look at the framed certificate in my hands. "Does this seem like a setup to y'all? You're business of the month! Yeah! Throw your own party and invite us!"

Bonnie reaches out to take it from me. "I have noticed Ruby has a couple dozen of these on her walls. Guess it's the thing to do. Besides, we are doing better than I think most folks assumed."

Leaning back in my chair, I laugh. "Better than *I* assumed. I thought it would just be fun, never really thought about us doing so much business."

Shannon stands up. "Law knows you've saved me. Plus, I now sell the little arrangements and bouquets folks pick up when they stop in to look at the books." We all three take a bit to look around and be proud of our creation.

"And I never thought I'd say this," Shannon continues, "but

God bless our landlord, too. Gertie is pretty much amazing."
She walks to the counter, grinning. "She's not only good at
business, but nobody gets Missus' goat like her." She mimics,
"Anyone know who's in charge of this shindig?" We all laugh.

Then Bonnie says, "And what was up with Cathy Stone?
I've never seen her like that. Do you think she was…"

"High?" Shannon asks. "Yes, I do."

"But it's so early. Not even lunchtime."

Shannon pulls her purse out onto the counter and takes her
hairbrush out of it. As she runs it through her hair she tells us.
"You didn't go to high school with Cathy. She was always
wild. I've heard these lingerie parties of hers are a blast. Y'all
going to Betty's?"

Bonnie scoffs. "Absolutely not."

I shrug, "I'm thinking about it. But, you're not saying
there's drugs at these parties? Betty and Jed would never…"

Shannon stuffs her hairbrush back in her pocketbook and
then shoves it back under the counter. "No, not at that one,
definitely not. But apparently there's this pink punch that Cathy
makes called Pink Panty Pulldown. Well, it *is* a lingerie party,
so guess the name's appropriate, but it is delicious I hear, and
very strong. I'm going to go next door and talk to Peter about
this chamber thing. See what he knows. I'll take my lunchtime
now, too. Y'all okay here?"

"Yes," I say. "I need to leave at noon, but it's all good.
Right, Bonnie?"

Bonnie nods and Shannon leaves. I stand and laughingly
repeat the name of the drink Cathy features at her parties.
"Sounds like something from college. Oh, did you hear Retta
talking about holding her book club meetings here?"

"I did, but since you're joining the club you won't need me
to be here, correct?"

"No, unless you want to join us. Wonder who else is in the
club? I've never heard anyone mention it. Did you bring your

lunch today, or do you want to get something from next door before I leave?"

"I brought mine, but I'll eat later. You go ahead and leave whenever you need to. Shannon will be a while, I'm sure." She lets the last word trail off. I know she does it to get my attention, so I walk to where she's straightening books.

"What? Why do you think she'll be a while?"

Bonnie just smiles and tips her head toward the front window. I follow her eyes and watch as Peter and Shannon walk past, hand in hand. "What? Where are they going? Ruby's?"

Bonnie stares at me, then asks with a definite leading lilt, "Or?"

"Or? Oh, Peter's house?"

"Yes, ma'am. Started earlier this week. They aren't hiding a thing."

"But Missus hasn't made a scene or said a word. Surely she has to know, right?"

Bonnie shrugs. "She didn't know about the flavors of Gertie's moonshine. Either her pipeline of information has dried up or she's awfully preoccupied with something."

I step over to the front door and push it open a bit. Bonnie's right, they don't even pretend to be going into Ruby's. At the end of the street they cross at an angle to lead them right to Peter's steps. When I let the door fall shut, I turn to my coworker.

"Got to say I'm surprised, but I don't know exactly why."

Bonnie tsks and shakes her head. "Chamber of Commerce awards, Pink Panty Pulldown punch, and daytime loving. Chancey is just a country song waiting to happen."

149

CHAPTER 23

"Is FM okay?" Jackson asks as I sit beside him on the old wooden bleachers at the freshman football game.

"I guess, why? Where is he?" I hand him the container out of my purse. "Brought you a sandwich. Not near as good as the concession-stand hamburger I was planning on, but better than nothing."

"Thanks, yeah, thought I better call you when I got here and found out they don't do the concession stand for the freshman games." He lifts the lid off the container. "But FM, he was standing over there by the fence, you know where he always stands for the regular games." Jackson points with his head to the section between the ticket booth and the first bleachers, where FM and his buddies hold court on Friday nights. Everyone has to pass by them, and stop and chat, before getting to their seats.

"He's not there now."

"No, he said he needed to go home. Seemed right shaky to me, and I wasn't sure he should drive. So I walked with him to his car, but after sitting there for a bit with him he seemed okay and said he was going to go on home."

"Maybe we should call to check on him."

"He said not to do that. He said no need to worry Missus. Made me promise to not call."

I pull out my phone. "Well, I didn't promise."

Jackson takes another bite and grins. "Good girl. Good sandwich."

"Hey—oh, hey Missus." I pull my phone away from my ear to make sure I called FM's phone. "How, um, where's FM?"

"Right here," she says. "He's tired. I told him to not cut up that fallen tree in our backyard today, but does he listen to me? No. I've taken away his phone and he's going to bed. Please don't keep bothering him. I have to go now."

She actually hangs up on me.

"That woman! How does he live with her?"

I look over to find my husband laughing, trying to keep from losing the food out of his mouth.

"Did you hear that? She's impossible. Quit laughing! It's not funny," I say while trying to stop from laughing myself.

When he can take a sip of water and swallow, Jackson finally speaks. "He didn't mention cutting up that tree. I do feel bad, though. It's the trunk of the huge tree that fell at the end of summer in that storm. Told him I'd help with it."

"Has Bryan played?" I ask. "I see him there on the bench."

"Yeah, but didn't look like he knew what to do. Some of the kids are pretty good. But there's a number like Bryan that are kind of clueless. Did you see Will?"

I look down the row to see Will standing with some of the older students. "Where? Oh, there he is. So he came. Did you talk to him? Did he say anything about his lunch with Anna?" Now I've completely lost interest in the game and am focused on my husband.

He shakes his head as he watches the field and eats potato chips. "There goes Bryan. Colt had to look around for him. Why in the world is he sitting back on the bench? He needs to be more interested in the game. Stand up by the coach."

"Jackson?" I prod.

"Nope. We are not talking about Will and Anna. I'm sick to death talking about them. They are adults. They will figure things out or they won't."

I steal a potato chip to ease my disgust with my husband's new philosophy and look at the field. Bryan lopes around like he's not sure what to do. Finally we watch him get into position and ready for the play. He runs the direction everyone else is running, then he stops and watches when the ball goes the other direction. Suddenly, as he looks toward the sideline where Colt is yelling, he spurts off in that direction. Then he's right in the path of the guy with the football. The big guy with the football. The *huge* guy with the football. The enormous guy who is going to run over my child!

Then Bryan tackles the guy with the football. Like, really tackles him. All by himself.

Bryan jumps up and is met by his teammates. Everyone is patting his helmet, his shoulder, his behind. Colt is clapping with his hand and a clipboard. Jackson and I are both standing up, yelling and clapping. Bryan waves at us then rushes back to the line of play. This time he looks ready, like he knows what he's doing. And you may say I surely can't tell this with all the pads and the helmet and from so far away, but I'm his mother and I can tell.

He looks happy. He really looks happy.

The buzzer announces halftime, and the players run off the field. Bryan is at the head of the pack, running and bumping shoulders with his teammates. Jackson and I remain standing to stretch a bit.

"Did the guests get there? How are they?" Jackson asks.

"Yep. Two couples together and then a man by himself," I say. "He's from Augusta, I believe. The couples are from Chattanooga. The women said they are going to visit and relax while the guys chase trains. They're all a bit older than us."

Jackson finishes his chips, and that reminds me. "Oh, I brought you some Oreos."

"Did you bring enough for me to share?" he asks as he sits down and picks up the plastic grocery bag I delivered his supper in.

"Why, yes, I did. And," I reach into another plastic grocery bag, "a thermos of coffee."

"It's a bit warm for coffee in my opinion, but gotta dunk Oreos in something."

"Never too warm for coffee," I say. I look around and notice for the first time that I don't know many of the faces on the Chancey bleachers. "Kinda weird being here without folks we know."

"Yeah, if Grant was still here, he'd be on the team and then Susan and Griffin would be here." Jackson unscrews the thermos. As he pours coffee into the cups I'm holding, he says, "You know, I haven't talked to Griffin in a while. Not since back in the summer. Guess his new job keeps him busy."

"Apparently. Susan says it's been a real change in their life. She was hiring a housekeeper earlier this week."

Jackson savors a sip from his cup. "You're right, the coffee's good. Why don't you see if they want to come do the wine and cheese thing tomorrow afternoon? Think they'll still go to the Chancey High game? Does Darien Academy even have a football team?"

I shrug as I dunk and eat another cookie. "Okay, that's all for me. Rest are for you. I'll call Susan and see. We can eat dinner at the game, I gotta get my concession-stand hamburger fix."

As the teams come back on the field from their shortened halftime, Jackson stands up. "I'm going to go down to the fence for a bit. See some of the guys from church who have kids on the team. You okay up here alone for a bit?"

"Sure. I'm going to call Susan, and you know me, I have a book if I get bored."

"Of course you do. I'll be right back." I watch as he confidently steps down the bleachers. Must be nice to have long legs—and no fear of tumbling down onto the field in a humiliating heap. I'll be using the stairs.

My call goes directly to Susan's voicemail. "Oh, hey there, it's me, Carolina. Call me. Jackson and I want to get together with you and Griffin tomorrow afternoon." I don't usually leave messages since nobody actually listens to them anymore, but I was watching Jackson and didn't realize her voicemail picked up. After texting her to call me, I lay my phone on the bleacher beside me.

Will is with his uncle on the sidelines. I wonder how his lunch with Anna went. At times I forget there's a baby coming in just a few months. Other times it's like the baby is already here I think about it so much. Where will it live? How will Anna and Will divide their time with it? What will its life be like with its parents not together from the very beginning? What will it be like to have a grandchild? But wait, Jackson is right. I need to back off.

I take a deep breath and watch the players move back onto the field. Yes, Jackson is right. Anna and Will do need to work things out between them. They are adults, and this is their baby, their family. Slowly, I let my breath out.

But they're stupid, and I'm afraid they're going to mess it all up.

Chapter 24

At first our wine and cheese gatherings at Crossings were every Friday for our guests, and on occasional Fridays we'd invite others to join us. However, those occasional people soon began to drop in on the Fridays we thought it would only be our guests. They'd find scant offerings in the munchies and drinks department. This has fallen on my lonely shoulders, since Laney had Cayden to mess with this summer, Susan and Jackson have *real* jobs, and Missus doesn't take with "lollygagging about purely because it's Friday, like the end of the workweek is something people should celebrate." Can you tell I've heard that more than a few times?

Anyway, we decided to not have the wine and cheese gatherings on a regular basis. Sure it took a couple Fridays finding no one home for some people to get the message, but soon they began waiting to be invited. Or calling ahead. Isn't caller ID wonderful?

About once a month now, when we have several guests, we have our little gathering, and on those days we usually invite a few extra folks. It's turned into a wonderful way to get to know people and to make our guests feel at home in Chancey. It's really strengthened our ties to those living up in the gated, la-di-da community of Laurel Cove, which, when you're running a couple of businesses, isn't a bad thing.

"I'm going to put Cayden down in the office," Laney whisper-shouts as she peels off from the front door and heads toward the B&B wing. "He fell asleep on the trip over here. Didn't know you invited the Rivers? Do they drink?"

"The Rivers?" I turn to ask Laney about the Rivers when they come through the front door. "Oh, hello!" I say, and their names slip right out of my mind. "Come in, right through here."

"Thank you for the invitation, Carolina," Isaac's mother says as she steps toward me, arms opened to hug me. Isaac's dad— Mark? John?—leans forward for a two-handed handshake. Still nothing on their names. Laney arrives from down the hall and puts on her beauty queen smile for me, but I give her a side shrug, stick my head in the refrigerator, and decide they can all introduce themselves.

Laney lost her caftans with her baby fat. She's not back in her tight clothes, but has taken to wearing clingy but flowing dresses and wedges. She says her heels will have to wait until she's not carrying a baby around. The dresses accent her curves well, and Laney's never met a plunging neckline she didn't want to get to know better. She meets Mr. Rivers with both her hands outstretched to match him in the two-handed shake game. "Hello, I'm Carolina's partner, Laney Conner, and you're Isaac's parents! Jenna is my daughter."

Still with all four hands connected, Mr. Rivers says, "Wonderful to meet you. I'm Paul and this is my wife Di." (Di. How did I forget that?) Laney drops Paul's hands and reaches for his wife's. "Oh, what a lovely name. And I see where your son gets his height and wonderful manners."

Paul reaches his hand out to lay it on his wife's back. "He couldn't help but get our height, but so glad to hear his manners are holding forth."

"Oh, yes, he's a friend of my daughter *Jenna*." And here I was thinking it was a safe time to leave the refrigerator. "Jenna Conner," Laney says again. I don't have to see her to know her big eyes are wide open and looking for some recognition. She thinks their son was dating her daughter. She thinks she and Shaw turned down their invitation for the cruise. I also don't have to see the Rivers to know they look confused.

Time to leave the refrigerator. "Laney, can you take this platter outside? Di and Paul, make yourselves at home. Everything is outside, so let's move out there and I can introduce you around."

Paul opens the door for Laney. She takes one more look at him and his wife before swishing through the door. Shoulders back, chest and nose high. Poor Paul and Di, they have sinned and fallen short of the glory of, well, Laney. God's okay with it, I'm pretty sure.

It's a perfect afternoon, with the back deck and most of the yard already in the shade. Our B&B guests are talking with FM and some of the ladies from Laurel Cove. Other little groups stand around with plastic wine glasses and little plates of cheese and crackers. Can't help but smile at how hosting something like this would've completely freaked me out this time last year.

This little town practically, no, forget practically, this little town *forced* me out of my comfort zone, and now I don't understand what I was so afraid of. A few platters of cheese, some wine, beautiful weather, it's really easy, actually. And maybe even a little fun.

"This is really nice, Mrs. Jessup," our unaccompanied guest from Augusta, Joel, says as he walks up to me. "Don't guess you have any beer, do you? I'm not much into wine."

"Oh, I think I do. Let me get you one," I say as I dart back into the house.

He waits at the door as I get a beer out of the refrigerator and hand it to him. Then he asks, "And a glass? Plastic ones aren't hardly big enough."

"Sure," I say as I get a glass out of the cabinet. He takes it, says thanks, and wanders back outside. As I step out on the deck, I see the cracker basket is empty, so I go in for the backup box, which I find is not a backup box, but a nearly empty one. Of course my kids feel like having two opened boxes of crackers is better than eating one before opening the next. Saltines are all I have left, so I dump a couple sleeves of them into the basket and take it back out.

A laugh from Laney out on the lawn gets my attention. Glad she's enjoying herself, but maybe I should check on Cayden. As I turn, Aggie, the leader of the Laurel Cove women's group, grabs my arm.

"Carolina, do you have some napkins? There was a little mishap with a glass of wine, and we used all the ones out here to clean it up."

She stands staring at me with her startling blue eyes and all I can say is, "All of them?" She smiles and shrugs before walking back to her circle of ladies.

First Saltines, and now I have to sit a roll of paper towels on the table. I guess I could tear a stack of them off and fold them, but, yeah, no. Of course the table needs replenishing now, and as I carry some more grapes out, I hear Cayden crying. Laney catches my eye as I step onto the deck.

"Carolina, can you check on Cayden? I think I hear him." She turns back to entertaining the group she's gathered around her, and they turn back to being completely absorbed in her story. Didn't miss that the group is mostly men, including my husband and brother-in-law.

The ladies who are staying with us leave their husbands to Laney's storytelling and dash up the steps. "Oh, a baby! Can we come?"

Cayden is all smiles as soon as he sees us, and when the

ladies want to change him and feed him, I let them. They both explain that they have been waiting and waiting for grandchildren, but their kids won't cooperate. I don't tell them I'd really love for my son to have been less cooperative, but I don't have time. The phone is ringing.

"Crossings B&B. Can I help you?"

"Is Griffin there?" a familiar voice asks.

"Susan? Yeah, I did see him earlier. Where are you?"

"At the park. Waiting on my husband. I'll be right there." She hangs up, and I grimace at the phone. She sounded really upset. Looking at the clock I see it's about time to wrap things up. Although it sounds like things are not exactly winding down on their own.

Back outside, I check the food and drink table, which appears to be holding its own. The ice in the wine bin is half-melted, and I throw away a couple empty bottles of red wine. Another laugh catches my attention this time. Gertie's here? Gertie and…

Jackson comes bounding up the steps of the deck, wide grin on his face. "Gertie brought some of her moonshine. We have any more plastic cups?"

"More?" I look around at the table and realize there are no cups there or beside the jugs of ice tea. "Where did all the cups go? I bought a stack of fifty."

Jackson looks around. "Well there's at least that many folks here, don't you think? I'll just get some glasses from the cabinet," he decides as he darts inside.

I walk down onto the grass and to the little card table where Gertie has spread her wares.

"Hey, Carolina. Did you get some cups? Never imagined you wouldn't have cups at a wine and cheese party. Came to tell all 'em how delicious my 'shine is. Figured since this is a private party I'd contribute a bit of fun."

"Yeah, Gertie, I see that," I say. "But you know most of us

are headed to the football game or out to dinner, so we don't want to sample too much, right?"

"Here we go!" Jackson says as he pushes past me. "Coffee cups will work perfect. Everybody grab one."

I step out of the crowd and into Laney. "I really don't like those people," she says as I turn around and see her scowling at the people around Gertie, then I realize she's being very specific about whom she doesn't like. "Think they're so perfect. So tall and thin. So blonde. Went to Georgia Tech, too, did ya know that?"

"Yes, I knew. They seem perfectly nice to me."

Then she bumps my shoulder, causing wine to slosh out of her plastic cup. "Oh yeah, they told me. You're letting Savannah go on this cruise with them? What are you thinking?" Then she looks down at me. "Where's Cayden? You said you were going to check on him."

"I did, and our guests wanted to take care of him. If you haven't noticed I'm the only one working at this little party. You go check on your baby."

She starts toward the house, with a detour to the bin of white wine and ice. She tops off her wine, adjusts the neck of her dress and then sashays inside. When I turn I hear Gertie announce the next flavor is banana pudding. She's holding a tasting right here in our backyard. Colt raises his coffee mug to me in a toast and then puts his arm around Griffin's shoulder. Jackson is right there beside them, and they just look so happy. Relaxing my shoulders, I decide to enjoy myself. Not quite as much as they are enjoying themselves, but it is a beautiful afternoon. I find a chair and sit down, but just as I do someone runs down the deck stairs and past me. I see that it's Susan so I stand back up. She races around the group and then smacks Griffin's back.

"I've been waiting for you for over an hour! Are you

blocking my phone calls? Because Lord knows you don't answer them anymore!"

Griffin turns toward her, but instead of reaching out to comfort her he shrugs. "You knew where I was. I don't see a problem." Then he turns back toward the table. "What's the next flavor, Gertie?"

A gasp from behind me tells me Susan's sister heard that. I turn and step to her. "Laney. Let them handle it." She gives me an eyeful of scorn and flits by me. However, when Susan meets her they both turn back toward the house.

Jackson meets my eyes, then mouths, "What's going on?"

My turn to shrug. Then I follow my friends inside.

Tell me again—what's *not* to like about hosting parties?

CHAPTER 25

"Well, that was a disaster," I say as I flop down on our couch after the ballgame. Ruby's was open after the game, but I didn't want to go. Jackson and Colt rode home with me and didn't go either.

Of course, I didn't give them a choice.

Jackson slogs in from the kitchen and hands me a bottle of water from the fridge. "What were we thinking? That moonshine is dangerous. Just tastes so good."

Our heads turn when the front door opens and Colt pushes through it. He'd stayed out on the front porch to make a quick call, and now he collapses in the closest chair. "I shouldn't sit down here. I should go straight downstairs to bed. Was that the worst ballgame ever? What did we end up losing by? Thirty-something? Thank God I wasn't slated to help coach tonight. It was all I could do to sit in the stands."

"Get used to it. We're not a football powerhouse like Painter. You saw the crowd wasn't taking it bad," Jackson says as he sits on the other end of the couch and turns on the TV. "But it was harder to deal with coming off all that moonshine. Seemed like the game would never end."

"As I said, the whole evening was a disaster. Starting with you two encouraging Gertie with her moonshine samples—

what in the… no. I'm going to bed." I stand and walk to the stairs, then turn to address them both. "You'll be happy to know I cleaned up the backyard when y'all ran off in a hot hurry to go to the game. You'll also be glad to know the dishwasher has run, so we'll actually have clean cups for coffee in the morning."

Colt apologizes. "Sorry, Carolina, but when Will showed up and offered to drive Jackson, Griffin, and me, we couldn't pass up the offer. I really didn't want to miss the beginning." He shakes his head. "Had no idea there was no reason to get there early at all. This team is a disgrace. But, hey," he says as looks over at Jackson, "I did like that Griffin. Seems like a good guy."

With a sigh, I begin climbing the stairs. "Too bad you're not married to him. His wife isn't his biggest fan right now."

Jackson turns on the couch, craning his neck around to look at me. "Yeah, what was up with Susan acting like that? She's usually so calm and together."

"Not now," I spit. "Bryan's curfew is eleven-thirty so make sure he's in before you go to bed."

Now it's Jackson's turn to spit. "What? You want me to stay up? I'm exhausted. He'll be fine. He has his house key, right?"

At the top of the stairs, I stop, place both hands on the railing, and look down. "Do whatever you think is best. He's with those kids I don't like, but you said I'm overreacting. Savannah went to Ruby's with the Rivers, and she just texted me she's on her way home. Will, now that he's free of his designated driving stint with his father and uncle, said he'll be home later and assured me he has his key. So there, I've taken care of two of our three children, cleaned up your mess from your backyard tasting, and I'm going to bed. Bryan is *your* problem." With a regal turn I head to our bedroom. That felt good. Speaking from behind the railing was empowering. Good to know.

Apparently, all I've ever needed was a balcony.

"You said for me to do whatever I think best," Jackson explains as he gets out of bed a few hours later. "So I left the door unlocked and went to bed."

I'm struggling to get my robe on and struggling to not yell. We were just woken with a phone call from Bryan saying he was locked out on the front porch, and we needed to come talk to the officer that brought him home. *Officer!?*

I sling open the bedroom door, and as I rush down the stairs, Jackson is right behind me. I unlock the door, and there is our youngest son and a police officer.

"Hi Officer Pierson. Bryan. Come in," I say as I pull the door wide.

Bryan steps inside then around me. "Going to get some water."

Jackson shakes the officer's hand. "Hi, I'm Jackson Jessup."

"Yeah, I know. Hi, Carolina."

"I know Officer Pierson from the store," I explain. "Denny checks in with all the stores when he's on duty downtown."

Bryan comes back with a bottle of water for himself and one for the officer.

"Thanks, Bryan," Denny says with a nod at our son and a smile. "Sorry to have to wake y'all up like this, but I wanted to let you know Bryan got left out by the ball fields without a ride home. I told him I'd give him a ride, but I was going to have to let his folks know."

My face has to be about a hundred shades of red. Our son is out wandering the country with so-called friends who would abandon him. His parents are asleep when the police bring him home. I'm furious at Bryan, but maybe even more furious at his dad. All I can do is nod.

Denny pushes open the screen door. "Thanks for the water. See y'all around. Better get back to work."

When the front door closes, Jackson and I both turn to our son. "Why were you alone at the ball fields?" I ask.

He shrugs. "Guess everyone left and I didn't realize it. Can I go to bed now? It's no big deal. Won't happen again."

"You better believe it won't happen again! You're never going out with those kids again. I told you I didn't like them!" I spin toward Jackson and repeat, "I told you I didn't like them!"

I whirl back around. "Why were you even at the ball fields in the middle of the night?"

He leans against the back of the couch. "One of the guys knows how to turn on the field lights so we can play Frisbee."

Jackson speaks up. "You were just playing Frisbee?"

"Yeah. What did you think we'd be doing at the ball fields?"

"Guess that sounds right, don't you think?" Jackson asks me. "I mean if they were doing something wrong, would they turn on those big lights?"

"Really? Just playing Frisbee?" I ask my son. I'd already moved over to lean against the couch beside him and smell him. I only smell sweat. No alcohol or smoke. "But you missed curfew. You know the rule. No going out the rest of this weekend or next."

"Mom! I only missed it because I missed my ride. Seriously, I can't be blamed for that!"

I push away from the couch and walk to the stairs. "You can't? Well then, who should we blame? Officer Pierson for not driving fast enough? You messed up. You let your ride go without you. You are being punished."

Jackson opens his mouth, but I close it for him with a look.

"Fine!" Bryan says as he moves around me to march

upstairs. "It's a stupid curfew anyway. Everyone else's is midnight. *If* they even have one at all!"

Jackson says, "We'll talk about all this tomorrow. Also, I want to know why you don't have your house key with you? You're supposed to have your house key with you. I texted you to ask if you had your key and you didn't answer me."

Bryan doesn't answer him now either, just keeps going up the stairs.

Jackson looks at me and shrugs. "Maybe one of the guests locked the door? I know I left it unlocked. At least I think I did."

Working up the energy to take the first step up the stairs, I say to my husband, "I don't know, but I'm going back to bed. I heard Savannah come in earlier. How about Will?"

Jackson shrugs at me. "He is an adult, you know."

As I give him another look, I step to the window and look outside. "His car is here. Now, I'm going back to bed."

He turns out the lamp he's apparently left for our son to find his way home by earlier. In the dark I hear him mumble, "Being home sure is exhausting."

I mumble back, "You have no idea."

CHAPTER 26

"Morning, Ruby. Hey, Libby," I say loud enough to hear over the jangling bell hanging above the door.

"Hey, Carolina," Libby says as she stops to pour coffee at a table along the wall. "Ruby told me you'd be in early this morning for your muffins. Got some early risers up there this weekend?"

"Yes, plus I wanted to sit and have a cup of coffee in peace. I'm not working at the store today, so this will be the only quiet time I get all day up at the house." I sit on one of the stools at the back just as Ruby places a cup and saucer down for me.

"There ya go. Where were you and your crew last night after the game? Savannah was here. Brought those new people. The preacher people out at the big church on the blacktop. They's almost a perfect cross between Laurel Cove people and Chancey folk, don't you think? Seem right normal, but a little high-falutin'." She leans one hip against the counter, then crosses her skinny arms as she talks.

"That is a good way to describe them. Di and Paul Rivers. Son is Isaac." I take a sip of coffee. "Mm, that's good. Any wayward muffins need sampling? Broken ones you've got to throw away?"

She leans over and reaches to the side counter that runs

back to her kitchen area. "As a matter of fact, I did want to try this one out on someone first. Here ya go. Pecan pie muffin. So... last night?"

"We were tired. Wine and cheese thing in the afternoon got out of hand." Taking a bite. I try to figure out what I'm eating. "This is good, but what's in it? Nuts and some other stuff. C'mon, Ruby, you know I'm no good at this food stuff. Pecan pie muffin, you said?"

"I heard Gertie was up there. That one never lets grass grow under her feet, did ya notice? And she don't take no for an answer." Ruby sniffs as she leans back on the counter. "She's right growing on me."

I pull apart the rest of my muffin. "What are these chunks?"

"Pecan pie."

"I know that's the flavor and I taste it, but there's more than nuts and, like, this?" I hold up a piece of light brown something.

She shrugs, reaches out and takes the chunk from my hand, and pops it in her mouth, then talks as she chews. "Pie crust. Had a half a pecan pie left last night so I just chunked it up and put it in a batch of muffins this morning. Real handy knowing freeloaders like you'll show up and I can get free taste-testing."

I push my plate away. "I'da preferred if you'd just kept the pie and served me a piece of it. Although the muffins wouldn't be too bad now, knowing what the chunks are."

She tops off my coffee. "Beggars can't be choosy, Carolina. So what's the story on that brother-in-law of yours? Kinda opened last night to get a look at him."

"Colt? You opened to look at Colt?" Ruby opens after the high school sporting events if she feels like it. She serves whatever kinds of pie she feels like making and stays open just as long as she feels. This being open when you feel like it is another of those charming small-town quirks that get annoying once you live in that small town.

"Colt. That name alone needs a good looksee. And I hear he's going to be the new head coach before long."

"He is head coach of the freshman team," I say as I pick at the muffin I'd pushed away. When Ruby doesn't say anything, I raise my eyes to look at her.

She's got her eyebrows floating high, up near the front line of her hairnet. She shrugs and leans closer to me. "Hear tell the varsity coach ain't long for his job. Not often a championship coach is laid in your lap. Figure that's why you didn't come last night. Let folks talk, let tempers flare, get ready for change, right?"

"What? No, not at all. Ruby, don't start that kind of rumor. Colt's just here for a bit."

Her eyebrows go floating again. "Really? Well, you know Griffin Lyles is still on the school board until they hold the special election in November to replace him. I hear Griffin and Mr. Colt were buddy-buddy last night. First at your place, then all during the game. Griffin took him around introducing him to all the people that are people. If you know what I mean." She pats the counter with both her hands, straightens up, then shrugs. "Just sayin'."

I hiss, "Well, quit sayin' anything!" I take another drink of my coffee as she walks back to the kitchen where a buzzer is going off. Colt, Griffin, and Jackson *were* pretty tight last night. And I don't just mean the kind of tight that comes from drinking moonshine. What if Colt *does* want to stay here? Why wouldn't Jackson have mentioned it? Or maybe Jackson doesn't know?

"My muffins ready?" I ask Ruby, just as she turns around with a wrapped basket in her arms. When we opened Crossings, we arranged to have fresh muffins for our guests to fulfill the second B in our name, Breakfast. One of us runs down and gets a fresh batch every weekend, and Ruby runs a bill for us, which we pay once a month. Well, Laney pays, since she does the books.

"Thanks, Ruby," I say as I turn around, but that doesn't stop her from yelling at my back.

"You bring that Colt boy by here one day, you hear?"

"Sure thing. Bye, Libby."

"Bye, Carolina. See you tonight!"

That stops me. "Tonight? What's tonight?"

Libby sidles up to me with her head tilted down, and her eyes tilted up. "You know. The party? Cathy's party? At Betty's. You know."

"Oh, the lingerie party? That's tonight? That's right, it's tonight."

"Cathy says Saturday night's the best night for women spending money. Don't know why. Of course I'm not going to buy anything, but want to support my daughter. Saturday sure is good for me because I don't have to get up so early for work. You're coming, right?"

"I guess so. I mean, I said I would, but…"

Libby reaches out with her free hand, the one not holding the coffee pot her customers are waiting on. "It sure would mean a lot to Cathy. She looks up to you. A businesswoman, mother, and wife. You are a role model to her, and I sure do appreciate the support you give her. Not everyone's been so kind." She pats my arm, but before I can say anything I notice the tears in her eyes.

"Okay, of course I'll be there. I'll let you go now."

She turns toward the tables, wiping her eyes. With a huge sigh, I push out the door.

Don't you just hate when people think you're kind and supportive, only because you said all the nasty things in your head instead of out loud?

Chapter 27

The air is close and makes my clothes stick to me as I walk across the street to the van. Feels like rain, and we could use it. As much as I like summer, it's time for it to go on its way. We haven't had a single night we could leave the windows open instead of having the air on. A good storm might push some of the humidity and heat away. Even though there are pumpkins sitting on the steps of the gazebo and on Missus's front porch, the decorations don't make it feel like fall. I have a hard time putting up our fall wreath until the weather changes just a little bit.

I make sure the basket of muffins in the passenger seat behind me won't fall over, and then I get in the driver's seat. It's too early for anything else downtown to be open, even Peter's doesn't open until eight. He can't compete with Ruby's early folks, so he concentrates more on the lunch customers. Although there aren't that many of them through the week. Not sure how he's making it, or how long he'll be able to stay open. Sure would hate to see him leave town again. Lord, if I think Shannon is hard to work with now…

Past the railroad tracks and up the hill, I zone out thinking about Peter and Shannon. Wonder what Missus thinks about them? I haven't really talked much to Missus or FM lately.

Maybe we should try to get together with them. Although, getting together with Susan and Griffin didn't work out that well last night. Susan was mad. Real mad. Which means she didn't say a whole lot after their scene in our backyard. Inside the house with me and Laney she just sat and stewed, then left. She was at the ballgame, but working the concession stand for the first half and then sitting with her mama the second half.

Whoa! I slam on the brakes when a car backs out of a driveway to my left and into my path. I miss him by only inches and only because I veered halfway into the ditch on my right. When I look for an apologetic wave, there's only a sneer. A sneer from Kyle Kendrick, who puts his car in gear and tears down the hill. He was at his house. Well, his old house. Kimmy's house.

The front door is closed, there's no sign of lights on or curtains open. Pulling back onto the road, I take one more look in my rearview mirror, but he's long gone. I cross over the railroad tracks in front of our house wondering if Kimmy and Kyle are getting back together. Wondering if Anna and he broke up. Wondering if Anna and Will worked anything out. Just plain ol' wondering.

The wind is picking up and carrying occasional drops of rain with it by the time I get inside. The house is still quiet, so I set the basket of muffins on the dining room table. The table is already laid out with small plates, napkins, juice glasses, butter, jam, knives, and spoons. I set out orange and apple juice beside the glasses and pour the pot of coffee I started brewing before I left into a carafe. The carafe is added to coffee cups, creamer, and sugar, all on a tray on the kitchen table, and I start another pot of coffee. Still there are no sounds from any of the rooms, so I pour myself a cup of coffee and go out to the front porch to watch the storm come in.

The tops of the trees across the tracks are swaying and moaning as the wind announces its growing strength. Every so often the wind carries a cooler breeze, but so far we really don't have any rain. Rocking, I think back to this time last year. Everything was so unsettled. Really threw me for a loop moving to Chancey, not to mention opening a B&B. Now, it feels pretty right. Except I went to bed mad at Jackson last night, *both* times I went to bed last night. After last winter, I said I wouldn't do that again. That I wouldn't hold on to things, but talk about what was bothering me. This time, though, I'm not sure what's bothering me.

Suddenly the rain drowns out the sound of the wind. It comes down in sheets, so much so that I can't even see the railroad tracks or out to the bridge. Not a good day for railfans to watch the area railroad lines, or for playing football games.

"Hey." Will sticks his head out the front door. "Can I join you out here, or you want to be alone?"

"I'd love to have some company," I say. "There's coffee in the carafe and I got extra muffins, so you're welcome to one."

He comes back in a couple minutes and sits in the rocker beside me. His coffee and muffin he sets on the little table between us. "Not a good day to sell cars," he laments.

"Nope, sure isn't." Luckily I'm in the rocking rhythm, and it helps keep my mouth closed.

He's over halfway done with his muffin when he says, "So I had lunch with Anna."

I nod. I rock.

"She looks good. She said to thank you for going with her to see the ultrasound."

I nod. I rock.

"Really loves her job. Guess she's good at it. They're sending her to some training for three weeks later in the fall. Did she tell you about it?"

"No, she didn't."

"It's the beginning of their manager training. She does that, then comes home and does online courses and some other things she'd go to. Apparently the Dollar Store is real good with families, especially single moms. Guess they got some big award last year for how they work with single parents."

He eats some more and sips on his coffee. He clears his throat, then continues. "Mom, now don't go thinking things, but I liked her. Remembered why we liked each other last spring. She's different from a lot of the girls I know. More guarded, more suspicious. Why would I like that, though?"

I rock and then finally admit, "I don't know."

He sighs. "Yeah, me either." Then he stands up, and I want to grab his hand and pull him back down into the chair. I want us to figure this out right this minute. Don't want him going off when he obviously doesn't know what he's doing.

But I don't.

I rock. I nod.

"Thanks, Mom," he says as he begins to open the door. Then he lets it close, and I open my mouth, where my opinions rest, looking for an opening. Since he's coming back, maybe I should say something...

"Forgot to pick up my plate and cup. I'm trying to do better. Thanks for listening, Mom. Needed to talk a bit." This time he makes it all the way inside.

I close my mouth, swallow those opinions...

And rock.

"Jackson and Colt nursed hangovers all day laying on the couch watching football. Bryan barely left his bedroom and Savannah went shopping." I pick from the assortment of veggies and fruit to fill my plate as Susan and I chat. "With the rain all day, it's been like the morgue at our house. As much as

I dreaded this lingerie party, I actually couldn't wait to get out of that house."

Susan moves to a couple chairs in the corner of Betty and Jed's big sunroom. "I know the feeling," is all she says as we sit down.

"How's Griffin doing today? Moonshine catch up with him, too?"

She shrugs. "He was at work all day, so guess he wasn't feeling too awful bad." She pops a cherry tomato in her mouth and looks around the room. It's a really large room of windows, a tile floor, and comfortable furniture. Although the rain stopped earlier, the clouds are low, and so it's darker than it should be at seven p.m. Betty and Jed's ranch house is in one of Chancey's older subdivisions, with nice-sized lots and mature trees.

Betty walks by nervously, even wringing her hands, so I call out to her. "Betty! Thanks for inviting us. Your house is so nice, I especially like this sunroom."

Her smile is almost more of a frown. "Do you? It's awfully big. I've never really known how to decorate out here, and I'm not much of a plant person. Dorothy always had such beautiful plants and flowers out here."

"Oh, Dorothy, Jed's mother?"

"Yes, they own the house. Bought it when they moved here. You do know Jed's daddy was the principal at Chancey High?"

"Yes, Lou and Dorothy stayed at the B&B when we first opened," I say. "Lou's even brought his railfan buddies back for weekends."

Betty laughs and steps closer to me. "Oh, that's right. Silly me." Betty is chunky, doesn't wear makeup, and never seems comfortable. Even now, in her own home, she's worrying her hands and chewing her lips.

I reach up and lay a hand on her arm. "It's lovely. I'm sure

Lou and Dorothy were so pleased to pass along their home to you and Jed."

She shakes her head. "Oh, no. They still own it. We rent from them. I better go see how the tables look. Be sure and eat. And drink." She leans toward me and giggles. "I'm a little afraid to try that pink punch. I hear it's strong." She tiptoes around the edges of the room, and I'm more curious than ever to hear how in the world Cathy Stone talked Betty into hosting this party.

"So did you know Jed's parents still own this house?" I whisper to Susan, but when I look at her I see she's staring straight ahead, not at anyone or anything, just blank. "Hey, are you okay?"

"Me? Oh, yeah, I'm fine." She uncrosses her legs, then crosses them back the other way. She's wearing a sleeveless dress in an orange and yellow flowered print. It looks very sixties, and with her straight hair held back with a yellow headband, she looks really young. Aside from her face, which is pinched.

"You're not fine. What's going on?"

She jumps up, then looks down at me with a smirk. "Let's get some of that pink punch and I'll tell you everything!"

"Okay," I say as I stand up. I'm wearing khaki capris and a black T-shirt. I call it my Sears uniform because one time I wore it to Sears and all their people were wearing the same thing. Khaki bottoms and black T-shirts. Only time I ever came close to wearing a uniform, and I kind of liked it. Felt like I belonged.

"Hide me, Carolina," Cathy says as I reach for a punch cup. She sidles up close to me, then pulls out a bottle between us, tips it up, and it glugs into the bowl.

"Watermelon vodka. It's delish. Betty barely put a taste into it."

"Is it entirely ethical to get ladies drunk to buy your stuff?"

176

She winks at me. "Don't see you turning away?" she says with laugh. "Besides, no one is getting drunk. Just helps loosen things up. Get yours, we're about to get started." I fill the cup in my hand and turn to hand it to Susan, but she's no longer in the vicinity. She's standing beside the window holding her empty cup.

"Hey, you forgot to fill that."

She looks down and shrugs. "Guess I did. This is a nice neighborhood. Did you see the house across the street is for sale?"

"No, I didn't. So, what's up?"

"Just kid stuff. Leslie wanted to come home this weekend. She's not as happy as she's been letting on. Here she was the smartest, and now at UGA, everyone is the smartest. Classes are really hard, and she's second-guessing sorority life now."

"So is she at home? I'll cover for you if you want to leave and be with her."

"No, we told her she couldn't come home. She doesn't have a car there, and we wouldn't go get her. I know she needs to stay there to get used to it, but it's still hard." She looks back out the window. "Wonder what they want for that house?"

"Why? Who's moving? You?" I ask with a laugh.

She turns away from the window and also laughs. "Me? Of course not. I just moved. I'm going to get some punch. Looks like Cathy is starting."

As Cathy holds up the catalog and begins her spiel, I watch Susan. I don't know what's going on, but Leslie being lonely at school isn't it. Last time she was upset like this was when everyone was worried about Susie Mae being pregnant. Then it all came out. How Susan was keeping everything about Susie Mae a secret from everyone, including Griffin. She did say it was 'kid stuff.' Maybe it's Susie Mae again. Or maybe Grant isn't doing well at Darien Academy. I'm sure she's worried some about Leslie, but not this much. Leslie is a land-on-her-feet kind of kid. Scratch kid, *young adult*.

"What?" I ask because Cathy is staring at me like she wants an answer, and the room is quiet.

She says, "I need you to be in charge of one of the small groups. Just say, 'Okay.'"

"Okay." I'd like to blame that easy cave on the punch, but I haven't taken a sip.

Cathy reads off several names and tells them they are all in my small group and for them to go stand beside me. In a few minutes, the room is sectioned off into groups. Before I really see what's going on, she gives us names for our groups. The names are cute, and we're all laughing as she hands out the fancy written signs. Then we see. The groups aren't random and the names aren't just cute. The butter-yellow sign designates the "Willow" group, which Susan is leading. A bright purple sign has "Tinkerbell" written in white glitter, and they are all petite. "Silver Belles" is the name written in glitter on a silver sign, and the sign matches most of the hair in that bunch. My sign is written in cursive with lots of curves and says, "Blossomed."

Now Laney would've taken this sign and stapled it to her forehead, but she's not here. Me and my little group—wait, did I say "little"?—are mortified. Cathy, however, bustles us all around and into different rooms in the house saying, "It's more fun to shop with others who have our same body types, don't you think? I'm going to start helping the Silver Belles, first."

Just as the door to our room, a den and office area, is being closed by Cathy, Betty pushes in. "This is where I'm supposed to be. To help y'all." She sits on the nearest chair and encourages us all to sit, too.

Then she clasps her hands in front of her and asks, "Now, who wants to be our first model?"

Chapter 28

"Church seemed empty today," Laney says as we sit on her porch eating homemade pimento cheese sandwiches.

"It did. Even with the youth all there for the Six Flags trip." Laney's twins and both Bryan and Savannah are at the amusement park, along with Jackson who went as a chaperone. They left right after the service. Laney suggested we bring Cayden home for his nap and enjoy the bowl of pimento cheese her mother was bringing to her. All I had to contribute was a loaf of fresh white bread, which I just happened to have at home.

Gladys Troutman, Laney and Susan's mother, walks onto the porch out the kitchen door. "I can't get enough of that baby. Once Scott and Abby Sue had Ronnie, the grandbabies came fast and furious. After Ronnie, the next year Susan had Leslie and Abby Sue had Ricky. Next came the twins, barely a year before Susie Mae came along. When Susan had Grant we thought that was it. Have to wait for great-grands, but nope! We all got a big ol' Cayden surprise." She settles into the swing with her plate in one hand and her glass of iced tea in the other. She sets her glass on the windowsill to her left. "Can't eat good pimento cheese without light bread. Appreciate you picking up a loaf."

"Did you say 'light' bread?" I ask. "My mom calls store-bought white bread light bread. I thought it was just something she did."

Gladys chuckles. "That's just what we always called it. My momma made her own bread and of course it was delicious, but we kids just loved it when we'd get to have a loaf of Sunbeam sliced bread. Some things just aren't as good on homemade bread."

Laney leans back and stretches. "I was just saying to Carolina that the church seemed empty today. What do you think?"

"I think folks are going over to that church with the new pastor. Reverend Rivers I believe is his name. They are having weekly Bible studies for every group and every topic under the sun. There's one for retirees that's combined with an exercise class, which I must admit I've been tempted to check out. Marjorie Beck goes. So do Mary White and her sister from Canton. She comes all the way up here every week just for it."

"What are the Sunday services like?" I ask, but both Laney and her mother shrug.

Laney grins and rubs her hands together. "Enough about church, though, tell us about this lingerie party last night. Can't believe Shaw and I had to go to that business dinner, but he *was* being honored. Sooo, did you buy anything?"

"I can't believe you weren't there either!" I said. "It was crazy. And Betty sure came out of her shell. You know, I wouldn't be surprised if she wanted to start selling it, too. There were a good number of people there. Susan was there. She had on the cutest dress."

Mrs. Troutman harrumphs as she gives a push to the swing with both feet. "I sure hope Susan bought herself something sexy at that party. Look at that beautiful home Griffin has bought her, and she acts like living up in Laurel Cove is some big inconvenience. Why in the world my three children think this town is the be-all, end-all is beyond me!"

Laney puts a hand out towards her mother. "Please, don't start on that again. Shouldn't you just be happy that we all wanted to be here where you are?"

"No. I understand you staying here since Shaw is from here, and he got this beautiful house practically handed to him. Plus, he has a good business in the area. But Abby Sue and Scott might actually still be together if he'd move down to Atlanta where she works."

The obviously often-run discussion stops as if this is its normal resting place, and as I don't have a dog in this race, I wait.

"Griffin moved here all those years ago just to make your sister happy." Mrs. Troutman barely pauses as she crosses her arms. "He has bent over backwards since the day they married to make her happy." She looks at me. "Susan might seem right easy to get along with, and she is, if she gets her way."

"Mother. Leave Carolina out of this. You can have another go-round about this with Susan later."

"I'm not talking about it with her anymore." She looks at me again. "Carolina, you know how this town can be." She picks up her plate, steadies herself by holding the chain for the swing, then stands up. "It's time for me to go home."

"Me, too," I say. "It was so nice to get to have lunch with you, Mrs. Troutman. Your pimento cheese is wonderful. Maybe I can get your recipe?"

"Of course, dear. Oh, can you hand me my tea glass?"

I lean over and reach for it, then hand it to her as she asks her daughter, "What are you doing this afternoon?"

Laney stands up and stretches. "Taking a nap. I'm glad Zoe got to go to Six Flags with the youth group, but it means I'm on my own with the boy."

I hold the door open for us. "How is Zoe doing in school?"

181

Laney shrugs. "Okay, I guess. She says Kimmy is doing fine without her home."

I exclaim, "Oh, yeah! Speaking of Kimmy, guess who was tearing out of her driveway early yesterday morning?"

"Her husband," Gladys says with authority.

Her solid answer gets my attention. "Yes, but wait, how did you know?"

"Well, it's his home. His wife. His children. Does he seem like the kind of man to let someone else move in on him and what's his? No. A big ol' rooster may take a look over the fence now and then, but don't you be forgetting the coop is his." She hands her daughter her plate, drinks the last sip of her tea before placing the glass in her daughter's hand, then pulls her car keys from the pocket of her skirt. "Nice to see you again, Carolina. Laney, you be pretty now, hear?" She says the last with a look from over her glasses and under raised eyebrows.

Laney rolls her eyes and then holds the door for us both to leave. As I pass her she says out the side of her mouth, "Don't think I didn't notice you not answering about what you bought at the lingerie sale last night."

With a grin, I shrug at her and walk out on the porch. "Bye, Laney. Thanks for lunch."

"You're welcome. And you don't need to tell me anything about the party. I'll just check out Cathy's Facebook page. She usually post pictures there."

The screen door shuts as my mouth opens.

"Ohhh, no." What *is* my Facebook password?

Jackson and the kids won't be home until after dark, and I checked our guests all out between church and lunch at Laney's. Everyone said they had a great time and promised to visit again. As I head up the hill toward home, I reason that leaves only the possibility of Colt and Will at home. Pulling into our driveway, that assumption is borne out. Only their cars are parked near the house.

"Hey, I'm home," I say to Colt, who is sitting on the couch watching a football game. That is as expected, but he's also surrounded by stacks of laundry and clothes baskets.

"Hey. Hope it's okay I'm doing this up here. Bigger TV."

"Are you kidding? You did the laundry? You could be upstairs in my own bed and I wouldn't say a word. Colt, this is so nice!"

"Least I could do." He half-stands in order to pull the laundry basket off the chair beside the window. "There. Now you have a place to sit down."

"You even did the sheets from the B&B rooms." Sitting, I sigh. "Colt, thank you."

"You're welcome, but really I like having something to do when I'm watching sports. And I've been a bachelor for a while, so I'm used to doing laundry. Sorry I didn't make it to church this morning. Didn't set my alarm and overslept."

"Don't apologize to me. Took me forever to get in the habit once we moved here. But now I like it. The preacher is pretty good, and our friends are there." The TV catches our attention as there's a big play, and we watch the game for the couple plays it takes for a touchdown to be scored. Looking around, I see he's got one basket full of laundry for upstairs. "Think I'll take that basket upstairs and get changed. You had lunch, right?"

"Yep, but I think I'm going to take a run down to the mall and do some shopping and eat dinner down there. New job really made me look at my clothes. Think I need to spruce things up some."

There's a somber note in his voice that makes me turn

towards him. "You okay? Guess I haven't really thought that you must be missing home."

He takes a deep breath and sits back. He rubs his empty hands down his athletic shorts and then takes hold of the hems at the knees and tugs on them. He takes another deep breath, which releases in a ragged way. "Sorry, but yeah. Thought it'd not get to me, but…"

I lean forward in my chair. "No one knows more than me how hard it is to do something new. Plus everything happening with your dad. I'm sure if you wanted to go back to your job at Painter High, they'd welcome you with open arms."

That causes him to laugh and shake his head. "Oh, no. I burnt all my bridges there. Burnt 'em to a crisp. I know I told you about the school board member that didn't get along with Dad?" He looks up at me with red, shiny eyes.

"Yeah, you did. But that's just one guy."

"One really important guy, and I was cocky and then there was this girl, this woman. Anyway, it got ugly, and you know how little towns can be. Mom tried to warn me. Told me I was playing with fire, but you know how it is when you think you're smarter than anyone else around. Besides, what could some old man do to me? I was winning football championships!" He goes back to tugging on the hems of his shorts and watching his hands.

"So, did you or do you still have feelings for this woman?"

He twists his head up to look at me. "I wasn't sure, but I think I do. Or is it that I'm just lonely? She didn't speak up for me at all. She was in a rough spot, I understand, but still—to just sit back and act like nothing mattered. That's about the time Dad fell and everything turned upside down. I told everyone I didn't care about my job, and thinking Dad was dying, I didn't. Looking back some folks tried to help, but I blew them off, too. Then when Jackson and Emerson came home, and my brothers both looked so successful and happy, I decided I needed to get out of town, too."

He laughs, closes his eyes, and leans back. "Lucky you. Me not having a plan in mind and you with this big house means you inherited the wayward baby brother." His eyes pop open, and he lifts his head. "Did I tell you I think I have a place to rent? It's a house over behind the library in that little neighborhood."

"No, that's great."

"It's not much, but I don't need much. Will can have his basement back if it all works out. The rental house is empty, so shouldn't take too long."

I stand up, shake my head, and give him a look. "Not sure how I feel about Will and the basement anyway. Plus, he never did laundry. Where is he? Saw his car outside."

Colt starts folding his pile of socks beside him on the couch. "He's downstairs."

"What's he doing down there? Playing videogames?" I walk toward the kitchen, never thinking about going downstairs, until...

"Oh, Carolina. Um, I wouldn't go down there. He's, um... got company."

Turning to look at my brother-in-law, my eyes automatically scan the driveway for a car I might've missed. "Who?"

Colt shrugs. "Honestly, I don't know. He called a bit ago and asked if he could, uh, use the basement this afternoon. Since I was done with the washing and drying, I told him yes."

"So when he came through here..."

"He didn't. Used the outside door downstairs." Now Colt is refolding the socks beside him.

"This is like talking to a teenager, Colt. Seriously, why do you think he's down there with someone else?"

"I heard them talking. And laughing."

"So... it's a girl?"

He shrugs. Eyes glued to the TV.

"Well, O font of knowledge, if you get any more details I hope you'll let me know." I pick up the basket of clothes and lug it around the back of the couch and up the stairs. Colt responds by turning the television volume back up.

Will and Anna? Will and Rose? Will and somebody else? Now that would be even worse.

In my room, I heave the full basket onto the bed, then start undressing. I can't wait to get changed and back into the book I'm reading. This, all of this with Will, is why I read. The people in my book world can act as crazy as they want and it doesn't affect me one bit.

Plus, I like knowing what's going on, and that's just not how real life works.

CHAPTER 29

"Because if it was Anna, I didn't want to interrupt," I explain to Bonnie Monday morning as I sort books and she dusts. Shannon still isn't in so we have the place to ourselves, except for Andy and Patty, whom we can hear moving around upstairs in their apartment.

Bonnie huffs, and it's not because of the dust. "I still think you should've gone down there. See, this is why my kids never moved back home." She looks around the corner at me. "I wasn't nearly as nice as you are!"

We continue in quiet a while. Then with the banging of the door upstairs and stomping on the steps, we both look up to greet Andy and Patty.

"Good morning, headed off to Andy's Place?" I ask.

"First breakfast," Patty says. "We're meeting Andy's parents out at the Cracker Barrel."

"How are your folks, Andy? Haven't seen them really since the wedding."

Andy shoves his hands in his pockets. "Not too good. Church is really dwindling, and of course Dad takes it to heart, seein' as how he started it and all."

Patty puts her hand through his arm and hugs up to him. Still amazes me how these two found each other right here in this store. Seems like they've always been together. Some couples just feel like that, don't they?

I commiserate. "Attendance is down at our church, too."

Andy scowls. "It's that dad-blasted church out at the highway. They've actually just added another service for Saturday night! Folks comin' and goin' there all days of the week."

Patty pats his arm. "Now, honey, we should be happy that so many are getting what they need there, right? Like your dad said, things come and go. Just have to be patient and have faith."

He smiles down at her and sighs. "I reckon. We better go. See you later, Miss Carolina, Miss Bonnie."

"See you later," I say as I stand then follow them to the front. Bonnie joins me as we watch them walk down the sidewalk, still wrapped up together. "They just make you smile, don't they?"

"Yes, they do. They should be a real odd couple, yet they are the very essence of calm and steadiness."

I look at her. "They seem pretty well-matched to me. Odd couple?"

"Yes, her mother is supplying half of north Georgia with moonshine and his father's church picketed next door for it merely being open on Sundays."

"Hmm, I guess I hadn't thought about it. Strange when families get together, isn't it? Well, I'm going to Ruby's, but I'll be right back. Then we're holding the festival meeting here at noon. Missus is bringing sandwiches. Last time we each brought our own lunch and she said the smell of Jed's soup made her nauseous." I laugh. "She asked him if it had squirrel in it."

Bonnie laughs. "If you put half the things that woman says into a movie, people would accuse you of making it up!"

"You are so right," I agree before pulling open the door and leaving. The rain over the weekend left us with a few more fallen leaves and a definite dash of color beginning on the trees and bushes. I put on a light sweater with my jean skirt this morning, but I can already feel that it was a mistake.

Walking into Ruby's I nod and speak to a few people, but Ruby is waving for me to come to the back. When I stop for a minute to say hello to Faun and Flora, two elderly sisters, Ruby shouts, "Carolina! Do I have to come out there and drag you back here?"

The sisters only smile and roll their eyes. Faun says, "Go see what squirrel's got up her tree now. We don't doubt her ability to drag you back there one little bit!"

At the counter, Ruby stops me from sitting on one of the stools and directs me around the counter. Wait, isn't there some law about me not being back here without a hairnet?

"What is it, Ruby? Are you okay?" I follow her right outside her back door and into the bright sunshine. She shakes her head at me and holds a finger to her lips as she firmly shuts the big door behind me.

"Look at this. Every Tom, Dick, and Harry don't need to know," she finally says and she turns to point at the back of her building. Graffiti covers the wall. Although it doesn't look like the graffiti you see in the city, or in the movies. It's more like just circles and lines of green spray paint. Like someone doodling.

"Oh my word, Ruby! When did this happen?"

"Sometime after Saturday night. Nobody much comes back here, not like at your place where you got folks living upstairs and coming and going out the back. I didn't even see it until I brought some trash out here about half an hour ago. It was dark when I parked this morning."

Looking around, I see that, unlike the wide open area behind our building, there's an old shed and a weedy lot here, with just a little path from the parking area out back. There's only room for two cars, so only Ruby and Libby ever park there. On the other side of the little road, which is barely even a real road, is an empty lot, so there's no one to have seen the painting being done.

"Did you call the police?"

"Durn tootin', I did. You won't believe what they said." Ruby is clearly beside herself, she doesn't know what to do with her long, scrawny arms. She crosses them, waves them, plunks her fists on her hips, then runs both hands through her short gray hair, all in a matter of seconds. "What have we come to? Just what?"

"The police, what did they say?"

"That they'll be here when they can get here. They had another act of vandalism to deal with first. Another one!"

We both turn when we hear a car pull up and park on the road behind Ruby's car. It's a police car, and we watch as Officer Pierson and another officer I don't know come to meet us.

"Hello Ruby, Mrs. Jessup. This is Officer Tatum. He's new, borrowed him from Jasper." Officer Pierson lifts his hand at the graffiti. "Yep, looks familiar. We were just dealing with this same paint at another location."

Ruby's arms get back into action. "What in the world? What in the world is even going on here? I don't even recognize my own hometown. I hope these criminals get the book throwed at them! What other landmark have they desecrated now?"

Officer Tatum winces a bit, and his lips turn up. Guess he doesn't see Ruby's back wall as a landmark. I smile at him, and he tries to hide his grin.

Still smiling, I ask, "Yeah, where else was this done?"

Officer Pierson takes a deep breath and looks straight at me. "The ball fields."

"Oh."

I'm not smiling now.

Chapter 30

"Bryan is lucky fall break doesn't start until next week or I'd be all over him. But wait till he gets home! Susan, why did you move Grant away?"

"Believe me, I wish I hadn't," she says. "What did Denny Pierson say? You know he's related to Shaw, don't you? Denny's mom is Shaw's cousin who married into the Pierson family. Does he think Bryan did it?"

I sigh into my phone as I lean against the back of our building. As soon as I came from Ruby's I went to look at our building's alley. No paint there. "He said he doesn't know when the painting was done at the ball field. He just doesn't remember looking in that area when he was rousting the kids Saturday. Plus, it was night. Then with the rain yesterday, no one was out there to see it. Maintenance people saw it this morning. Guess there's some tournament there next week during fall break."

"So maybe it wasn't Bryan. You'll just have to talk to him after school. Now, about the festival. I got your email, *all* your emails, and I can only say we'll do our best."

I wait. But that's it. "What? Susan, what does that even mean? Missus will eat me alive if I try and tell her that. She wants details about the World's Largest Banana Pudding, as in who's donating vanilla wafers and how many spoons you've purchased."

"Well, yeah, I know. But listen, that was her idea. Not mine. I'm not sure we'll be doing it at all, but if I were you I wouldn't tell her that. Just let her find out that day. What's she going to do? Kill me? I've got to go. Just stall Missus. I'm headed out to Nine Mile in a bit and I'll figure something out. Bye."

"The festival is in less—" The dial tone interrupts my sentence, so as I click off my phone I finish it to myself. "... less than three weeks." This move out to Laurel Cove has not been good for Susan. She has completely forgotten how unreasonable Missus can be. Stall Missus. Right. I'll just go do that! While I'm at it, I'll decree biscuits and gravy a health food!

"I don't have all day, Carolina," Jed says with a shake of his head and twist of his wrist to show me his watch. "This is supposed to be a lunch meeting." As if to emphasize his words, his stomach growls loudly.

"What do you want me to do? Missus isn't answering her phone. I'm sure she'll come marching in here any minute telling us we showed up too early."

Cathy comes in the front door of the bookstore. "Got some chips from next door. Missus here yet?"

Retta shakes her head and looks at Peter. "You're sure your mother didn't tell you where she was going this morning?"

"Nope. Maybe we should just cancel the meeting. Try again tomorrow," he says.

Ida Faye speaks up. "Absolutely not! We should at least go through our committee reports. Missus can catch up on it all with my notes."

"I'm in agreement," Gertie says as she opens a bag of Cheetos. "Law, I haven't had these in about a billion years. Thanks, Peter, and thanks, Cathy, for going and getting them. So who has something to update?" She licks the orange dust off her fingers, then picks another Cheeto from the bag.

"Children's area at the library is all set," Ida Faye says. "Weren't there any Funyuns? I won't eat them in my house or at work because of the smell, but I do love them."

"Nope, no Funyuns. Not a real big selection," Cathy says with a shrug at Peter. "Here's some baked potato chips I opened by mistake if anyone wants them. They taste all right, I guess, but the texture is like a damp paper towel." She sets the open bag in the middle of the table, then looks through the selections she brought over. "Oh, and nothing more for me to report."

Ida Faye looks down her nose at the younger woman. "What exactly would you be reporting on? I have yet to understand what you are contributing to this festival."

Cathy doesn't appear high or drunk for this meeting, but her perpetual cheerleading persona gets on folks' nerves anyway. She seems to always be talking and never saying anything.

With a big grin she looks around the table. "I'm here to provide a youthful perspective, I guess. Plus, I have a booth for my business just like the rest of you."

"Girl, that youthful jab was uncalled for," Gertie says from her end of the table. "True, but uncalled for. And I don't recall your business being on the list. Just what dessert are you serving?"

Cathy looks around the table, grins, then puts a chip in her mouth. Grinning at us as she chews with her mouth tightly closed.

Suddenly it hits me how absurd this whole thing is. When Missus is here railroading everything along, it actually appears to make sense. "I'll report," I practically shout. "Susan says there might not be a World's Largest Banana Pudding up at Nine Mile. I can't make a chocolate pie to save my life, and yet I'm supposed to be selling them to the public in just a few weeks. If the debacle at the B&B Wine and Cheese Friday is any example, the Air National Guard won't be able to keep the peace once the moonshine starts flowing. We have less than three weeks to put this together, and Missus can't be bothered to show up. But don't worry, she'll find plenty to yell at us about when she does!"

Everyone stares at me with blinking eyes and open mouths. I drop my head, then look up shaking my head in apology. "I'm sorry. I'm just so... so..." Around me the mouths close into grimaces and the eyes just look tired.

Peter's phone rings, and he picks it up off the table. "There she is. It's Mother. Hello, where are you?" We can hear Missus start talking, then he stands up. "I'll be right there." He's already moving away from the table as he shoves the phone in his pocket. "Dad's had a heart attack. They're already at the doctor's office, but they're taking him to the hospital. I've got to go."

Shannon, standing near the front counter, grabs his arm as he goes by. "I'll drive you. Carolina, I'm leaving," she shouts as she grabs her purse from underneath the counter.

They are both gone before those of us at the table have caught our breath. FM had a heart attack? It can't be a bad one, right? Our mouths droop open as our brains catch up with our imagination, and fear. Imagining what Missus and FM are going through. What our town is going through. What FM means to each of us. Then we look around at each other, and tears spring to Retta's eyes. "Poor FM. So they were at the doctor's office. Did anyone know they were going to the doctor this morning? Was he feeling bad?"

"They were both in church yesterday," Jed says. Then he stands up. "I need to go make sure the pastor knows."

"Good idea," I say. "Peter didn't say what hospital, did he?" Everyone shakes their heads. "I'll text Shannon in a bit and then I'll let you know." I stand up also, and we all begin collecting our notebooks and pens and other things we'd brought.

"Wait a minute. You, too, Jed," Gertie calls to the mayor who's already near the front door. "Come back here."

Jed turns, but he raises his voice, something I don't think I've ever heard him do. "Gertie! There are more important things to do right now than worry about some festival you most likely cooked up just to help you sell more of your blasted moonshine!"

Gertie tips her head at him and smiles. "I agree. Just going to suggest we say a prayer." She holds out her hands, one in the direction of Jed, the other toward me. Chastened, Jed walks back, and we all join hands.

Gertie's voice is strong. "Lord, we're just asking you take care of our friend FM. Take care of his wife and his son, too. Let them all feel your presence in a mighty way. Amen."

Snuffling and swallowing, we all head toward the front of the store. One by one they leave, each calling folks that need to know what's happened. Bonnie went home at lunchtime and I told her to not worry about coming back, so I'm alone. Sinking into one of the chairs in the reading area, I pull out my phone and text Jackson, "Call me."

My phone ringing surprises me. Didn't expect Jackson to be able to call me so soon. Plus, I needed a minute to just breathe. "Hey."

"Hey, you called? I just finished lunch and was headed back out to the site. What's up?"

"Um, FM's had a heart attack. That's really all we know."

"Oh, no," Jackson says. "Where is he?"

"They were apparently at the doctor's office, but now they're taking him to the hospital."

"So, he's already getting care. That's good. Where are you?"

"At the store. Shannon took Peter and Bonnie's off."

"Think I should come home?"

Words don't come, but I shake my head. Then I say, "I guess not. Hopefully it's nothing really bad, and uh, no. No, wait until I find out more. I'm going to text Shannon to call me when they get to the hospital. I'll let you know then, just wanted to call you."

"Of course. Listen, you let me know as soon as you hear anything, okay?"

"Yes," I say with another sniffle. "I need to let Laney and Susan know, so I'll let you go. Love you."

"Love you. Call when you hear."

We hang up and I lay my head back in the chair. FM is going to be okay. I know it.

Chancey just wouldn't be Chancey without him.

"We picked up Anna at the Dollar Store on our way to the hospital," Shannon says when she calls. "The two of them are back there in ICU with Missus, but I haven't heard anything else." She whispers, "But folks here look pretty grave, Carolina. I mean, I know it's a hospital and all, but they looked at us, well, you don't think he could be, you know? Do you?"

My heart squeezes, and I squeak out, "No. He's at the hospital. He'll be fine. Do you…"

"Oh, here's the preacher, and my mom just pulled up. I'll talk to you later."

"Let me know!" I shout as I hear her pulling her phone away from her ear. My teeth grind as I picture them all at the hospital, but mostly I keep going through that moment. How my frustration with Missus was ready to boil over. I'd had enough of her! And then with just one phone call, a couple sentences, what? Half a minute? It was all gone. Like a bubble that pops and no longer exists. How does that happen?

I look around the shop and wonder what to do now. Should I go to the hospital? No, the kids will be home before long, and I need to let them know. Unless they've already heard. No, they would've texted me. I'm still in the chair I first sat down in when everyone left. I called Susan and Laney. Gertie called to say that she'd stopped into Ruby's on her way home and so Ruby and Libby knew. When I talked to Bonnie she said to just close the shop. She offered to come in to work, but she was in the yard gardening and I knew by time she got cleaned up and all the way here, it wouldn't be worth it.

I lay my phone on the table in front of me, then close my eyes. It's better to just stay here until school's out. I don't want to go home to an empty house. I'll go in a bit. Oh, I think as my eyes open. Bryan has football practice and Savannah has cheerleading practice. There's really so little to tell them anyway. Standing up, I lift my phone, make sure the ringer is on high, and put it in the pocket of my skirt.

Grabbing my purse out from under the counter, I shove it under my arm, then reach for the open sign on the door. Flipping it to closed, I walk onto the sidewalk and then lock the door behind me.

What's the use of putting up with all the trouble that comes with living in a small town if you don't take advantage of the thing they do best?

When my hand grasps the worn door handle of Ruby's, my bottom lip begins to quiver. Through the glass, I see other worried eyes, and they meet mine with bits of smiles, little waves. Already Libby is headed toward the door, her arms opening. Shared fear fills the air as much as the scent of strong coffee, and I breathe both in deep.

What do small towns do best?

This. This is what they do best.

Chapter 31

"Surgery went well, but it's going to be a long night," I tell Jackson from my phone in the hospital parking lot. "I brought some brownies and coffee for everyone. Ruby organized some folks to bring them over dinner earlier."

"How are the kids?"

"They're good. Will is actually still here at the hospital with Anna. But before you feel good about that, Rose was here earlier, too. At least that's what Laney told me. She stopped in for everyone to cuddle on Cayden for a bit. Said when her father passed away Grant was a baby, and it helped everyone to have a baby around."

"Still feel like I should come home," he says.

"Apparently they'll know a lot more in the morning. Getting through the night and all, you know. Still, no one but family is allowed back to see him. Colt took Bryan and Savannah out for dinner, so it's good for them to get to spend time with him. Did he tell you he found a house to rent?"

"No, so when's he thinking of moving?"

"Not sure it's a done deal yet, but I'll let you know." I start the car and turn the heater on. "It's actually a little chilly here tonight. Or I'm just chilled from sitting in the hospital, maybe."

I laugh when I look at the outside temperature reading on the van. "Says it's sixty-four degrees, so not really cold, I guess."

"I'll let you go. Call if you hear anything at all, okay? Have a good night and drive safe. Love you."

"Love you, too. Sleep tight and don't worry, I'll let you know what's going on. Night."

As heat fills the car, I relax into it. Jackson has traveled so much in his career that we often spend nights apart. But I know my folks have never been apart. And Missus refused to leave the hospital, even when Peter promised he'd stay.

As I pull out of the parking lot, my phone rings.

"Hey, Laney. I'm just leaving the hospital. No change."

"I guess that's good. Was Susan there?"

"No. Why?"

"She's not returning my phone calls or texts. Well, she's answering my texts but with one-word answers or emojis."

"Where is she? At home?"

"No, that's what got me looking. Susie Mae called me wanting a ride to the hospital to see Missus. Said her mom wasn't around, but she wouldn't say where her mom was. Like she knew, but wasn't saying. It was weird."

"Wait, Savannah's car just passed me pulling into the hospital. Looks like she has a car full." I pull a U-turn. "I'll go check out who's with her and call you back."

By the time I get to the parking lot, Savannah, Susie Mae, and two other friends are climbing out of her little car. I just pull up behind them and roll my window down. "Girls, visiting hours are over."

Savannah rolls her eyes at Susie Mae. "That's because we had to go all the way out to Laurel Cove to get Susie Mae. Told you it would make us late."

Susie Mae rolls her eyes right back. "We're not going in to see Mr. FM. He's in ICU. We're just going to the visiting area to see Missus. She'll want to see us."

The two other girls don't look so sure, and the tall blond, Robyn, pulls at her shorts. "Maybe we should wait. I thought we were just going to go buy a card for her."

Another girl, Candice, echoes her. "Yeah, I don't really like going into hospitals."

Susie Mae smirks at them both and starts walking toward the hospital entrance. Savannah throws her arms up and looks at me. She turns to talk to the other two girls, and I ease the car up to ride alongside Susie Mae.

"Susie Mae, honey, what's going on?" She keeps walking, but I can see now that she's crying. She's small and fine-boned. With her short hair cut in a pixie-style, she looks younger than fifteen. Especially when she's crying. "Come sit in the car and get yourself together."

She only shakes her head and keeps walking. Savannah hollers to her. "Susie Mae, come back! My mom's right, it's too late to go inside."

I pull into one of the unloading spots next to the entrance, leave my flashers on, and get out. A security guard at the front doors opens it to tell us he's locking that entrance since it's nine o'clock. "You can come in right now, but you'll have to leave through the emergency room entrance doors." He holds the door open, but Susie Mae shakes her head and stops.

"No. That's okay."

He smiles at her, nods at me, then closes and locks the door. Susie Mae turns and walks back toward Savannah's car, then she stops. "Miss Carolina, FM's going to be okay, right?"

I put my arm around her tiny shoulders. "I think so. His surgery went good. What's wrong, honey?"

She wipes her eyes and shakes her head. "Nothing. Everything. Why did we have to move up there? We don't belong up there in Laurel Cove." She looks at me, and the wetness of her big, blue eyes make them shine. "We move and

FM almost dies. Things will keep changing and then we won't even belong here anymore. We won't belong anywhere!"

"Let me give you a ride home. Savannah can take the other girls home." I guide her along back the way she came, but then an SUV pulls up behind us. It's stopped, and the driver's door is opening by the time we turn to look at it. Susan jumps out.

"Susie Mae! I told you to stay at home. That I would bring you to the hospital tomorrow. Get in the car." Susan gathers herself, pastes on a smile, and turns to me. "Hey, Carolina. How's FM?"

"Same, I guess." Susie Mae is getting in her mother's car without a word. I whisper to Susan, "What's going on? She seems upset and more than just about FM."

"Who knows? She's a teenage girl. Thanks, but I've got to go." She turns and grabs onto the driver's door to climb in.

I follow her as my car is in that direction. I hold open her door so she can't close it and step into the opening. "Laney's looking for you."

Susan doesn't let go of the door handle and actually tugs on it a bit as if to close it. "I know. I'll call her. I need to get my daughter home and my son in bed, and I still have a long drive to get there. So…"

I step back and let her slam the door. She pulls out. Only the quiet parking lot aisle is between me and Savannah and her friends. "Take them home, and I'll see you at the house," I say, then turn around to walk to my car.

Only nine o'clock, but it feels like it's been a long night already.

Chapter 32

Knocking at my bedroom door wakes me, then the shaft of light from it creaking open wakes me even more.

"Mom?"

I lean up on my elbow and blink. "Will?"

He takes a step forward. "Mom, FM didn't make it through the night."

My heart stops and my throat shuts, so I can only croak out, "What?" I pull myself around to sit, and Will slumps beside me on the bed. We hug and then the door pushes open further.

Savannah steps into the room. "What happened?" she asks, in her little girl voice. "Is it FM?"

Will nods, and she begins crying. She slides onto the bed on my other side. We hug and cry for several minutes, then we begin to pull apart. Will gets up and goes into the bathroom, he runs water in the glass there and brings it out. Savannah takes it first, then I take a drink. He stands in front of us and finishes the glass before he tells us

"Missus told us around midnight that she didn't think he'd make it. She told the doctor she wasn't leaving the room and that Peter and Anna could decide for themselves if they wanted to go back out to the waiting room. Of course, the nurses weren't happy at first, then I think they saw she was right. Or they just got tired of fighting with her."

Savannah sighs and crawls behind me to get under the covers. "We all know how that goes, fighting with Missus."

Will nods. "Anna sat in the chair, with Missus and Peter both on the bed. One on each side of him. I went in and out getting drinks for them and such. Shannon and the minister and some others were out in the waiting room, but Missus said they had to stay there." He leans back against the wall. "You know, I don't think anyone but Peter believed her that he wasn't going to make it. I'm not sure Anna believes it still, but he believed her almost from the first time she said it. I think the three of them had a nice goodbye. Does that sound weird?"

"No. It sounds peaceful. Just like FM would want. I can't believe he's gone." I stand up to hug Will. "I'm proud of you, son."

We hug for a few moments and then he steps back. "I called Dad on my way home. He was going to get up and leave. He said he'd call you once he was on the road home."

"Am I going to school today?" Savannah asks from underneath the comforter.

"Do you want to?" I ask as I open the bedroom door. "Looks like Bryan is still asleep. His alarm will be going off soon. We'll tell him then."

Savannah sits up. "I kinda do want to go to school. I mean, what would I do if I didn't?"

"Then get up and let me get dressed." I turn to Will. "How was Missus when you left?"

He shrugs. "She seemed okay. Peter said they had everything all planned out. She'd texted the funeral home director in the wee hours of the morning." He grimaces. "She texted him before FM even died. Kind of freaked Anna out, but you know Missus."

I nod as I help Savannah get out of the covers. "Probably

made her feel better to think she had everything under control. How was Peter handling it all?"

Will grimaces again. "Not as good. Dazed, but he'll be okay. Shannon actually drove Missus, Peter, and Anna all home in Missus' big caddy. I'm going to get changed. I told them I'd meet them at the funeral home at eight."

We hug again, and Savannah scurries out of the bed to join in the hug. We break apart when we hear Bryan's alarm going off.

Savannah walks down the hall to the stairs to her bedroom, and Will takes a deep breath. "Want me to tell him?"

"Not unless you want to."

Tears spring to his eyes, and his lips press together and down. "No." He leaves my room and walks to his bedroom door. "Mom?"

I step out into the hallway. "Yes?"

He leans his head against the doorjamb, and his voice is husky. "You know FM lived here his whole life."

"Yes, he did."

"Well, driving home last night, I mean this morning... whatever, it was still dark. I took time to go downtown and park for a minute. It was like something was missing." He pauses, and I see his Adam's apple bobbing. "You think a town can miss somebody?"

My mind roams to Ruby's where FM laughed, ate muffins, and drank coffee. Where I first met him ranting about his grandfather's sword. Then to his front sidewalk lined with flowers, where he would garden and watch over the square. I can hear him telling stories from the gazebo steps, or the football field fence, or right here in this house.

I swallow, but my voice still catches. "Son, Chancey now has a hole it never will fill."

Chapter 33

"Carolina, pull that door shut," Missus says from inside her bedroom. "Come over here." She's standing beside the front window looking down onto the town.

"Anna told me you wanted to see me?" I say in a soft voice. "How are you doing?"

"Look down there."

She's pointing outside, so as I get next to her, I look out to where she's pointing. "See? There where Jackson is, beside those tables?" she says.

It's hard to see through the trees as they are still full of leaves, but there are spots where I can see the square and the dozens of tables that are set up there. FM apparently had always said he wanted an old-fashioned dinner-on-the-ground gathering after his funeral, so that's what he's getting. "Yes, I see him."

"Call him. You did bring your phone like Anna told you, right?" Missus has on her suit from the funeral. Her hands are stark white, as her black gloves are lying on the bed. Beside them is the hat she wore to the church. It even has the little black netting, which hung halfway down her face during the ceremony. She puts her hands on her hips and looks back out the window as I dial.

"Hi, um…" As soon as he answers, Missus holds out her hand for the phone. "Here's Missus. She wants to talk to you."

"Those tables are all wrong. I should've seen it this morning, but I had other things on my mind. There should be one long serving table in the middle. The eating tables are to be arranged on each side, slanting away from the serving table." She pauses and stretches to look. "Yes, like that. Once you get the serving table set correctly, I will let Gladys know they can begin bringing out the food." She hits the red button and hands me the phone back. She remains at the window watching and I'm sure Jackson is informing them they have an audience.

"Missus, why don't you sit down?" I try. "Or even lay down and rest a bit."

"Maybe, but not right now. This all has to be perfect." Her head and shoulders move as she studies the dinner grounds through the trees. "What did you think of the service?"

"It was very moving. Beautiful."

"Not as formal as I would've liked, or as my own funeral will be, but it was all to a letter what FM wanted." She still stares out the window, and as the silence grows, I step toward the door.

"Is there anything else I can help you with? Are you okay?"

"Of course, I'm okay. I've been preparing myself for this for years." She sighs and turns to look at the pictures displayed on the old-fashioned dresser. "No one knows, but he'd had other heart attacks. We knew we were on borrowed time. He had always been very matter-of-fact about being so much older than me."

"Other heart attacks? I had no idea."

"No one did. Peter wasn't living here at the time, and other than our son, whom would we have told?" She shifts then to look at me. "You know how hard it is to live in a small town, where if you don't make friends the first time around, you don't get a second chance. FM was my friend. He had many other friends, as you can see from the attendance at the church and all the hullabaloo for this dinner. I do not. I didn't want to share the news of his heart issues with just everybody." She moves back closer to the window.

"I do know how hard it can be in a small town, but Missus, I think of us as friends." As I'm saying the words, I realize they're true.

"That is very nice of you, Carolina. I suppose if I did have friends, you might be one. More likely, we are people sharing the same plot of land for a few years. That's all." She turns and steps to the bed. "Tell Gladys to begin taking the food out." She pulls one glove on, and as she lifts the other to put it on, she looks up at me and scowls. "What are you waiting on? I'll not have you delaying FM's final request because of your dillydallying." She wills me to open the door with her eyes, and I hear a sigh of exasperation as I close it behind me.

"She can't have friends because friends won't let them boss you around," I mutter as I march down the stairs to relay her command.

"Oh my, this is just as it used to be," Flora says to me as I pat her thin shoulder on my way to the food table. Her black dress looks like a stage prop. It's old and elegant, something from another era. The whiff of mothballs? Definitely from a more recent era.

Her sister Fauna agrees. "What a grand idea FM had. God gave us a beautiful day for it, too!"

The sky is September blue, the color of sapphire, the September birthstone. The temperatures are not too warm, which is fortunate as we are all wearing our church clothes. Bryan pointed that out to me earlier that it's not like the other events here in the park where we are wearing casual clothes. The men are in dress shirts, most with ties, some still wearing their suit coats. Of course, for the ladies, there's a preponderance of black or dark outfits. If a visitor were to drive through Chancey this Thursday morning, they would think we were shooting a movie. I can't help but smile—FM would've loved this.

"Haven't you eaten yet?" Peter asks me as I lift a plate at the end of the serving table. "I'm back for seconds. Didn't think I was hungry, but..." He shrugs. "Thanks for helping with all this. Dad would—" He chokes up, then clears his throat. "Dad would've loved this."

"I was just thinking the same thing," I say. "But I've not done much. The ladies of the church have this all down to a science. I just tried to not get in the way and follow directions. How are you doing?" As I start down one side of the long table filling my plate, he goes down the other, taking little bits of food here and there.

"I'm doing okay. He was pretty amazing in the hospital. Mother said we were not going to play those games other people play about him not dying. That we weren't going to waste his last hours playing make-believe."

"Wow. I don't know if I could do that."

"I balked for about one minute, said something about when we got him home, and that was the only time I saw him uncomfortable." Holding a deviled egg above his plate, Peter half-smiles. "He said, 'Son, you know I never could hold with a liar.'" He takes a bite out of the egg, puts the rest on his plate, and shrugs.

"Sounds like he and your mother could write a book on dying."

"Dad also said he hadn't put in all those Sundays sitting in church to lose his faith in heaven when he finally was going to put it to some good use."

"Now there's some sound theology," the minister says as he comes up to Peter's elbow. "Hi, Carolina. You ladies, as always, did a wonderful job with the meal. I'm going to steal Peter away for a few minutes, if that's okay."

"Sure. I'm going to eat." Jackson had waited for me until he saw I was going to be a while. There was so much food we couldn't fit it all on the table, so I had been taking off empty dishes and filling those spots with full ones. I'd suggested just not worrying about getting all the dishes on the table, leaving some for later. However, I was told in no uncertain terms that every dish brought for the dinner would be used *for the dinner*. Apparently there have been hard feelings in the past when a dish didn't get served. Like I said, I'm just following orders.

Will waves me over to where he's sitting. I start that way when I see he's sitting with Rose's grandmother, LaVada. Rose lives with her grandmother on the road to Laurel Cove. I first met LaVada when I stopped to admire her prolific rose bush. I don't like to think about it, but I'm the reason Will and Rose even know each other. Rose did not make an appearance today, and I didn't ask why.

"Hello, LaVada, I haven't seen you in a long time."

"Since my rosebush stopped blooming, if I remember correctly."

"Yes, maybe that was it." I sit in the chair Will has pulled out for me. "Thank you."

"Or maybe it wasn't my rosebush's fault at all. Maybe it was when your son started seeing my granddaughter?" LaVada's lips are pressed disapprovingly at me.

I look at my plate. "Food looks good. I'm starving."

Will had started to sit back down, but with LaVada's last comment, he changed his mind. "Think I'll go see what, um, yeah, think I'll go over here." He wanders off, well, if you can wander in a hurry.

"Carolina, I do not approve of you allowing my granddaughter to shack up at your house."

I choke down a bit of broccoli casserole as I hurry to talk. "Me either. I've stopped it. Moved Will out of the basement and back into a room upstairs. A room next to mine and Jackson's."

"Good. It has nothing to do with my feelings for Will. He seems to be a rather nice young man. However, Rose does have her mother's genes. You've probably heard about the Webster women?"

Squinting at her, I say, "Maybe some, but I don't listen to everything I hear." I laugh and pick up a roll. A homemade roll, I should say. "You know how small towns are with gossip."

"Usually fairly accurate has been my experience," she says as she takes a sip of iced tea.

Now I'm trying to remember exactly what I did hear about Webster women. Susan, no Laney, or was it…

"Would you mind getting me a piece of that pecan pie before it's gone? A cup of coffee also, please. I find myself feeling awfully tired, and without Rose here, maybe I've done too much for myself. This is all so unsettling. Francis gone." She blinks at the tears hanging on her lashes. "It's hard to believe."

I put my unsampled roll back on my plate, then lean towards her to pat her hand. "It's no problem at all. I'll be right back." On the way to the dessert table, I swing by Susan's table and lean down into her ear. "Come with me. I have to ask you something."

Susan stands up and walks close to me. "Thank you! Griffin's mother is driving me crazy. Did I tell you she wants to move in with us?"

"No, but listen. Was it you that told me something about the Webster women? Miss LaVada has cornered me about Will and Rose. Then she practically admitted the gossip about her daughter was true, but I can't remember what that was all about."

"Oh, Lisa, who's Rose's mom, and her sister Janet. They were ahead of me and Laney in school by a good five years. They're close in age and they competed in everything, but mostly boys. Even after they got married, if you get my drift. Might as well get some dessert while I'm here."

I hand her a small plate. "But they don't live here now, right?"

"No, they both moved away over the years. That's all you're getting?"

"It's for Miss LaVada. I haven't even eaten real food yet. So that's it? They were flirts, and maybe a bit more?"

"Yeah, except there was something with Miss LaVada and her sister. I'll ask Momma. Think it was kind of the same thing, just a generation earlier." When we reach her table, she stops. "Go eat. I'll let you know."

Susan moves off speaking to people as she passes different tables. I stand still and the moment stands still with me. Everything in the park seems to be slowing down. Kids that were here have been taken back to school. The food table has more empty dishes than full. Talk is low, and the sun through the trees is no longer overhead. Shafts of golden light wash the scene in sepia tones like an old photograph.

Missus' words earlier in her bedroom come to mind. This dinner, this scene, is FM's final request.

It was a good one.

Chapter 34

Still in my black dress, I'm sitting on our back deck with a glass of wine. Jackson had some work phone calls to make when we got home. Savannah is off with her friends. Grant came home with us from downtown and he and Bryan are in the basement playing video games.

At first I liked the idea of a fast funeral. No long days waiting. However, now I'm not sure it's such a good idea. Missus had everything in motion, as Will said, before FM even died early Tuesday morning. Now here it is, Thursday, sun barely beginning to set, and it's all over.

Tuesday morning was full of the shock and overwhelming sadness. Folks finding out and then calling others. By noon, if not before, the ladies of the church were in full gear. By the time I got to Missus and FM's with two gallon jugs of sweet tea from the store, the kitchen was full of banana breads and egg casseroles. Matter of fact they were clearing those away and putting out bowls of pimento cheese, egg salad, and chicken salad – all homemade, of course. Baskets of rolls and buns and a loaf of Sunbeam filled another spot, while the dining room table held a wide assortment of desserts.

Like waves at the ocean, the house ebbed and flowed all day, and the next. Every door opened and shut letting people and food, in and out. Murmurs would raise to a normal level, then someone would remember and shush them. Again like the waves—soft, loud, constant.

And flowers. I found Gladys Troutman with her face buried in an arrangement of carnations. I tried to turn away and not intrude, but she pulled back and, face shiny with tears, reached out and grabbed my arm. "No, Carolina, don't leave. Carnations are happy flowers, they remind me of Mother's Day or prom corsages. Even new babies. Those, however…" She points across the room at a beautiful lily. "Those I hate. They smell like a funeral." She shuddered. "I can barely stand going to church on Easter because of the lilies. Too many sad memories."

She hugged me and we watched the crowd, ebbing and flowing from living room, to dining room, to front porch. The kitchen door swung open quietly, and another lady in another apron carried another tray of brownies towards us. We made room on the table, then we all took a moment.

The woman whispered, "Missus is handling everything beautifully."

Gladys agreed. "I wasn't sure she'd let us take over, but she knows how these things are done. She isn't to worry one bit with anything. When my Harold died, I didn't understand. I tried to organize things. Worried about the grandkids, chairs, everything, then Maple Hughes pulled me to the side and explained that she was in charge. I was to just take care of Harold, she would take care of everything else."

The aproned lady gave a wise nod. "Missus knows. She and Peter should be back from the church in a bit." She looked at me. "How is Anna?"

"She's okay," I said. "Kind of in shock still. She was going upstairs to lie down, think I'll go find her." Making my way through the people in the main hall, I crept up the stairs and found Anna sound asleep in her and Will's old room.

Anna's the reason I'm sitting here now thinking the quick funeral might not have been such a good idea. She has been in a daze, going through the motions, but not really here for the past two days. I don't think I've heard her say a dozen words, and Will says she won't talk to him. I'm worried about when it hits her. FM worshiped the ground she walked on. She, like most young people, thought he'd always be around.

When you're young, you don't realize how few and far between people are who think you can do no wrong.

It's getting darker, but I only notice when a light in the kitchen is turned on. I hear Will, and I think Anna. As I get up to go inside, the door opens.

"Hi, Mom. Thought you might be out here," Will says as he pushes the door open, then Anna scrunches down to walk underneath his outstretched arm. "Can Anna join you? I could only get my test moved to tomorrow, so I really need to do some studying."

"Of course." I give her a hug and look closely at her. "Is out here all right? We can go inside."

"No," she says, "Will's making me some hot chocolate. I can't seem to get warm, but I have Will's sweater and the afghan off the couch. I want to be outside."

Her face is red and splotchy and clean of all make up. Her hair is flat, but her smile as I hug her again reminds me of someone. "Here, sit in my chair. It's already warm. You get settled, and I'm going to go see if I can get a cup of hot chocolate, too."

Quietly I slide in the door. "I hear you're making hot chocolate. Can I get in on it?"

"Sure, Mom. So how are you? As tired as I am?" Will has dark circles under his eyes and his shoulders droop. "Don't know how I'll stay awake to study."

"Take a shower, get woke up," I say. "I was proud of you

today. You really were a big help to everyone, especially Missus and Peter."

"It's kind of weird being part of the family, but not really being part of the family, you know. I tried to help Anna, but she's not needed anything. Not sure it's hit her yet." The dinging of the microwave causes him to turn around. As he takes one cup out and puts another cup of water in, he asks, "Did you see Kyle Kendrick there at the funeral dinner with Kimmy and their kids?"

"I did. Don't know why I would've expected any shame from him, but…" I shrug. "Kimmy called and asked if she and the kids could come. I suggested just going to the visitation, but she said that 'didn't feel right,' and that she'd already bought some potato salad from the deli to bring." I hold up a hand, palm face out. "Don't get me started on what the ladies in the kitchen had to say about that. Kindest thing was, 'Bless her heart, didn't she even know to at least put it in her own piece of Tupperware?'"

He chuckles as he drops marshmallows into the steaming chocolate. "There you go. Two hot chocolates, marshmallows on top." I pick them up, and he opens the back door. After pushing it open all the way, he grabs his bottle of water and heads toward the living room.

"Will?" He turns at the door out of the kitchen and looks at me. I step back inside the kitchen. "Don't you want to come say bye to Anna?"

He gives me a quizzical look. "Why? Where's she going?" Then he goes on, grabbing hold of the bannister to propel him up the stairs.

Another waste of eye-rolling.

"Here we are. Hot chocolate." Setting the cups on the table, I lean back inside to close the door, then fix the cushion in the chair on the other side of the table before sitting down.

216

I give it until we've each had a sip, then I ask, "How are you doing?"

She wiggles around a bit, getting her hands under the afghan, then poking her fingers out just enough to hold her cup. I've seen Savannah do the same thing, and it makes me smile.

Anna takes a deep breath and says, "Can I ask you something? About FM? Why did he like me so much?"

I'm thrown by her question. "Oh, well, he, well... he once said he saw a lot of Missus in you. And he sure liked her a lot. You're strong-willed like her, then in other ways you're not like her." I find myself backtracking and explaining 'cause it gets tricky comparing someone to Missus. But then things start coming together in my head. "You know, Missus didn't have a good childhood. Her father was abusive and FM pretty much saved her from him. It's a long story, I'll tell you sometime. Maybe he could tell you'd had a rough time with your mom and all."

"I wasn't even related to him," Anna says. "Granmissus had my mom and gave her away to hide it from FM. He shouldn't've liked me at all."

"Maybe, but that's just not how FM is, or was. He forgave easily. Besides, he knew it wasn't your fault. Some people will punish a child for their parent's, or grandparent's in this case, problems, but well, just saying that sounds silly, doesn't it?"

She nods, but is silent as she sips her cocoa. Then she sits up straighter, sitting her cup on the table. "Did you see all those people today? And last night at the visitation thing? There was a line the whole time."

"FM lived here his whole life. Everybody knew him and, even more, everybody loved him."

She turns to face me, half her face lit from the kitchen windows. "My other grandparents had lived in their town all their lives, and no one much bothered about their funerals.

Only folks at my mom's funeral were the people from the church we'd been going to. No one from her past. I know she was a drug addict, but not when she was a kid. Where were her friends from school?"

I open my mouth, but close it with a shake of my head. "I don't know. Not everyone is like FM."

I don't say it, but she goes there as she adds quietly, "Think there'll be that many when Granmissus dies?" She pushes the afghan off her chest. "No, she's not near as old as FM. She won't die for a long, long time." She stands up. "Can you give me a ride home? Well, to Granmissus' house? Think I'll stay there tonight."

With her cup in one hand and the afghan piled on her other arm, she hurries into the house. Guess we're through talking. I take a long drink, get up, and follow her. At the front door, I slide my feet into a pair of loafers sitting by the door, much more comfortable than the dress shoes I've had on all day. "Think they go with my dress?" I ask her.

She smiles, but at the same time leans against the back of the couch, laying both hands on her stomach. "I forget how tired I get, or that I can't move as fast as I used to." A wave of sadness washes over her face, and tears run down her cheeks suddenly. "FM would've really loved this baby, wouldn't he?"

"Oh, yes. Yes, sweetie, he was already crazy about it." Reaching over to her, I wipe her cheeks with my thumbs and look down at her stomach between us. Right then she jumps and her eyes pop open wide. "The baby just kicked big time!" We both laugh a bit as I pull her close and we get mixed up in sad and happy, tears and laughter.

With another big kick, we move apart, and this time when I look closely at her face, I know who she reminds me of...

The old Anna.

Chapter 35

"I'm hoping we'll cancel it. Only thing that makes sense." I lick the peanut butter off my thumb, then I put the empty piece of bread on top of the grape jelly and cut it in half. Realizing Jackson hasn't said anything, I look over my shoulder at the table where he sits eating toast and drinking coffee.

He's staring at me over his cup. "I would like to think you're joking, but I know you're not. The festival is not going to be cancelled. You do remember Gertie Samson, right?"

Shoving the sandwich halves into a little plastic baggie, I sigh. "I know, but you didn't see what the last meeting was like without Missus there. We all know our little parts, but she's such a control freak that we don't know all the important things."

"Who's a control freak?" Savannah asks as she darts into the kitchen. "Can we go shopping for the cruise tomorrow?" She's bent down collecting food in her purse from the snack cabinet.

"You want me to make you a sandwich? I've got plenty of time this morning."

She makes a face, raises her eyebrows, and shakes her head. "No, I'm good. So shopping?"

I tap my finger against my lip in mock thought. "Thought

you said I wouldn't need to buy you anything if we just let you go. Yes, I very much remember you saying that."

She grabs a bottle of water from the fridge and shrugs. "Oh, okay. Just thought it might be nice to go to the mall together." She then takes a plastic throwaway bag from the grocery store, filling it from my cabinets.

"Another food drive? I've got to start buying stuff just for you to donate at school. What's this one get you?"

"Class with the most donations gets to pick the themes for homecoming week. You know, what everyone wears each day."

Jackson laughs. "I can appreciate the school wanting to raise the kids' awareness of people in need, but doesn't all this rewarding of good behavior take it out of the realm of having a good heart and make it just plain ol' 'I'll give as long as it gets me what I want'?"

"Dad, you don't understand," she says as she sits across from him and takes a piece of cinnamon toast from his plate.

"Oh," he answers, "I think I do."

"Whatever," she says as she turns her focus on me.

"Okay," I say. "Maybe TJ Maxx and Target, not the mall."

Savannah grins, and Jackson groans. I ignore them both. Yes, I know Savannah is playing me, but... well, there is no but. I'm going shopping tomorrow with my daughter, so I win. There.

She takes a sip from her daddy's coffee cup before he pulls it away with a scowl, then she asks, "So, anyway, who's the control freak?"

Jackson looks confused. "What?"

I answer, "Missus. I'm hoping the festival will be cancelled."

"It is kind of stupid that it's on homecoming weekend."

"I agree, and that does bolster my point. However, we had the weekend picked before the school changed its calendar."

"Not our fault we got cancelled on." A tornado had

flattened a school southwest of Chancey right before school started. Luckily no one was hurt, but the students had to be dispersed to other schools in the area and their football schedule was cancelled. They just happened to be Chancey High's homecoming opponent. Somehow it missed everyone's notice at first. So now, homecoming week is the week after fall break, and the same weekend as the soon-to-be-cancelled Southern Desserts Festival.

Bryan yells from the living room. "Are we leaving any time soon?"

Savannah takes a deep breath to yell back, but her daddy clears his throat and shakes his head. She sighs, and answers in a voice guaranteed to charm tiny bluebirds into doing your laundry. "Yes, dear brother." She stands, then kisses her father's head as she passes by. "I like having you here in the morning. Bye."

Don't know what happened in the living room, but all we hear is a loud "ow!" from Bryan. Which we ignore as we meet eyes and grimace. Bryan's been a bear since yesterday afternoon with Grant. We took Grant home late last night, and the entire ride home Bryan complained about Chancey High and how he had no friends and why couldn't we send him to Darien Academy? Did Grant's folks really have that much more money than us? Didn't we want him to be happy?

Freshman boy has to be one of the more unusual stages of life. They are the very definition of gawky. Their feet are huge. They slump because they can't come to terms with being tall all of a sudden. Their hair grows like kudzu, and looks kind of like it, too. They mumble, they stomp (when they aren't shuffling), they smell bad, then they overcorrect and smell like a whorehouse on Sunday. Yeah, I don't know how that smells exactly, but it's an old expression for *some* reason. Anyway, they aren't pleasant beings to start with, then add a dose of out-and-out envy, spiked with some self-pity, and you have me actually thinking life with a teenage girl is a good thing.

And we all know that's crazy.

"Wait! He didn't take his lunch!" I grab up the bag I'd set so carefully on the edge of the table and run for the front door. I'm careful on the front porch, as I wave the bag in the air and shout at Savannah's car, which has just started backing out. She stops, and I can see her rolling her eyes from here.

She rolls down her window, and I push the bag in. "Bryan forgot his lunch."

She takes it, and almost takes my arm with her as she hits the gas and continues backing out. I stand in the driveway, robe on, feet bare, and wave, then blow kisses at them. Thank God for school. My kids would have to be still unable to read in the third grade for me to even contemplate homeschooling. Okay, fourth grade.

Jackson meets me on the porch. "And people ask me why I travel so much." He opens the screen door for me. "I'm going to get some work done upstairs. Guests come late afternoon, right?"

"Yep. Laney's going to be here, though. It's some car dealership people she and Shaw know." He starts up the stairs, and I follow him.

He turns around as he climbs. "You're going into town, right? Nail down things on the festival?"

"Yep, and check in on Missus, Peter, and Anna. Last few days have been so crazy. I wonder how they're dealing with it all being over."

He sits down at the desk in the corner, and I open the closet. As he makes a phone call, I get dressed in a pair of navy capris and a navy shirt. After three straight days of black, I want a little color, so I add a bright scarf someone gave me for Christmas. It doesn't look very fall-like, with its pinks and bright greens, but there are little touches of navy, so it works.

Jackson moves on to another phone call while I finish my makeup in the bathroom.

He's just finishing that call as I flip off the bathroom light. "Okay, I'm going to go. Give me a kiss," I say as I step to his desk and lean down. I'm proud to say that after laughing for so many years at my mom and dad making sure to get a kiss every time they parted, we're believers. Since our rough patch last winter, it doesn't seem sappy at all. Just as I straighten up, his phone dings. He picks it up, just as mine also makes the sound for a text message. I walk to the nightstand where it lays.

Jackson says, "Oh, no. It's from Savannah. Someone took the trash bags out of the dumpsters at the Dollar Store, and it's all over the parking lot. Sent a picture of the cops collecting trash blowing all over the road. Guess school traffic is backed way up."

She'd sent the message to both of us, so I look at the same things. Then look up at him.

"Oh, the graffiti. I forgot to tell you. Someone spray-painted the back of Ruby's." I sigh and cock an eyebrow at him. "And the ball field. Last weekend."

Just as he opens his mouth, his phone rings, and he looks at it. "I've got to take this."

"And I've got to go, too." As he presses accept on his phone, we shrug at each other.

Sometimes you feel so much like you're living in a sitcom, you start looking for cameras.

CHAPTER 36

"I'll sue for breach of contract," Gertie says to me and Jed. We're sitting at the table in front of Peter's Bistro. Retta begged off because she said, after losing three days work due to the funeral, she didn't have time to come to a meeting. Ida Faye just said she couldn't come. Cathy didn't answer either the email or my text. And we didn't bother Peter and Missus. We are on the sidewalk because I forgot about Bonnie's Friday morning story time in the shop.

"Don't doubt me. I will sue," Gertie repeats.

"Gertie, be serious. Like there were ever contracts for this thing," I reason, with just a bit of condescension and a mild eye roll.

Then she pulls out a contract.

Jed leans forward and studies the paper. "Yep. That's a contract."

Gertie folds the paper up and shoves it back in the pocket she pulled it from. "Besides, we owe it to Missus. We owe it to Chancey. It'll get the epidemic of vandalism off the front page. Don't you agree, mayor?"

He sniffs, pauses, then like a perpetual-motion toy you get going with just a little touch, his big head nods a little, a little more, then is a full-out nodding party. Then he pushes himself out of the little bistro chair. "Speaking of which, I can't stay. Just wanted to nail down the festival decision, now I've got to get over to the police station. Such a disgrace!"

Gertie and I sigh in agreement. He gives us a little wave with his index finger, then moves across the street to his car.

"Carolina, you didn't seriously think we were going to cancel the festival, did you?"

"No," I say, "but we can't ask Missus to do everything like she was before. She's grieving. The town is grieving. It just seems... I don't know."

Gertie leans her folded arms on the metal table, and it tips toward her. I grab my cup of coffee to keep it from falling. "Child, tell me something. What do you think Missus is going to do today?"

"I don't know. Rest? Answer cards. Make phone calls."

Gertie bends her head forward, then looks up at me. "You know better than that." Then she leans back and lifts her arms off the table. "Oh, wait. You don't know better. You've got your parents, and even still got Jackson's parents. Honey, Missus isn't going to want to sit still no longer than a squirrel does. She *needs* this festival." Gertie stands up and looks across the street at the gazebo and park. Then she smiles.

I smile, too, as I look over my shoulder toward the park where we all gathered yesterday in memory of a great man. "It was a wonderful tribute to FM, wasn't it?"

Her smile widens as she looks away from the park and down the sidewalk behind me. "Not smiling at that. Look." She points behind me, so I turn in my seat and look.

Missus. She's stomping down the sidewalk, well as much as you can stomp in low-heeled pumps. Red, low-heeled pumps. She's still wearing black. Black skirt, black blouse, black gloves. But her shoes are red.

Gertie takes a step away from the table, toward Peter's

Bistro and out of Missus' path. "Morning, Missus," she says as she takes another step away.

"Carolina Jessup! Am I hearing correctly that you are trying to cancel my festival? Do you have so little respect for my dear husband that you would use the occasion of his death to excuse pure laziness on your part? Get up."

"Missus, no, I just thought—"

"Did you hear me? Get up."

I get up. With a glance I see Gertie grinning like a polecat. She's moved all the way to the front window of the bistro.

Missus snaps, "Quit looking at her. Look at me. Now, come with me."

I swear I feel like I'm being called to the principal's office. My stomach is on the sidewalk, and there's a clutch of pure, cold fear where it should be. However, I do follow. When we pass Blooming Books, I look in to see Bonnie give me a look of curiosity over the children's heads. "Are we going to Ruby's?" I ask. But then we pass Ruby's. At the end of the sidewalk, she stops before crossing the street.

She turns to me, and I smile at her. In kindness, I promise.

"What are you smiling at? This is not funny."

I stop smiling, and sadness pulls at my face and heart. "Missus, I know—"

"For goodness' sake, stop that. Everyone is so sad. Yes, it is very sad. It…" She chokes a bit. "It's very sad. But it's over now. However, I do understand why you wanted to cancel the festival."

"For you. It's too much." I reach out to put my hand on her arm and offer some comfort, but her laugh stops me.

"For me?" She laughs again and shakes her head. "Hardly. You can say that. You can even think it, but…" She pauses as she looks both ways then crosses the street. On the other side she doesn't hesitate, but marches straight to her sidewalk. She steps up the two steps, then turns around, and looks down at me—even more than usual. "Of course I don't want, or need, the festival cancelled. You're the only one who needs that."

"Me?" Okay, grieving or not, this is going too far. "Why would I need it canceled?"

She dismisses my look of frustration with a short closing of her eyes, a deep breath, and a tiny shake of her head. She opens her eyes and looks straight into my eyes. "Tell me, Carolina. Have you figured out how to make a chocolate pie?"

Oh. "Well, I've been busy."

"See?" She lifts and drops her stiff shoulders, then turns to walk up her sidewalk, saying loudly over her shoulder, "Follow me. If we're going to be friends, like you seem to want, then I suppose I have to teach you to make a chocolate pie."

This is *not* how I saw my day going.

"So there we were, surrounded by food from the funeral and the food people brought after the funeral. Cakes, rolls, muffins, even pies, and we were making *more* food. We made six chocolate pies." I hold the cardboard box out to Laney as we stand on her front porch. "These are for you."

"Oh, you did meringue, too! Did you tell her we're not doing meringue?"

"Of course I told her. Do you think it made a difference?"

Laney pulls open her screen door. "No."

I carry the box in and put it on her kitchen counter. "And you've heard of conniption fits? Well, I saw one when I told her we were using premade crusts."

As Laney eases the door shut, she whispers, "Keep it down. Cayden is asleep." She is barefoot and wearing one of her pregnancy kimonos. "Let's have a piece. With Zoe in school I have to keep up my energy to take care of everything. Did I tell you I tried a nanny out? She's ten years older than Zoe, but not nearly as mature. Didn't do a lick of work other than looking after the baby. Zoe has me spoilt."

I get two plates out of the cabinet. "Think by the very definition a nanny's job is to look after the baby. Not do your laundry and vacuum. Give me just a small piece, I've already probably eaten enough while we were making them."

"Look how it holds its shape!" she exclaims. "No running over the plate or falling apart."

"And unlike the fillings I made that did hold their shape, it's not like Jell-O Jigglers, where you could pick it up and use it to play catch."

We sit on the stools at her kitchen counter and eat in silence, well, except for the occasional moan of pleasure.

Laney holds her full fork at eye level. "There really is nothing like a homemade crust." Then she looks at me. "Did you help make the crusts, too?"

"Yes. We made it all. Problem is, with Missus it all seemed so easy. She just did it by instinct, hardly measured anything. I didn't even know she could cook. Did you?"

"Well, used to be there wasn't the option of eating out. I think pretty much everyone cooked."

"Probably. Guess it wasn't really something you did because you enjoyed it, you did it to feed your family. Especially out where there weren't a lot of restaurants. I mean, I cook a lot more here than I did in Marietta. It was just so easy to run through a drive-through or get already-made things at the grocery store deli. I probably miss having rotisserie chickens always available as much as anything."

Finished with her pie, Laney is running her finger through any leavings on her plate, and collects a finger-full. "So, how is Missus? Was Anna there?" she asks then puts her chocolate-and-crumb-laden finger in her mouth.

"Missus is just Missus from what I could see." I leave out

the whole idea that she and I are now 'friends,' which she brought up several times in our morning of pie-making. "Anna did spend the night there, but she left shortly after I arrived. Said she needed to get to work since she'd been off since Tuesday night. She seemed pretty subdued. Speaking of work, I need to get going. You're going to the game tonight, right?"

"Yep. Over in Collinswood. You going?"

"Think so." Again I leave out that Missus has asked for a ride to the game. I believe she said something like, "Isn't that something friends do?"

As I walk down the steps, I look back at the porch. "Can't believe next week is fall break. Your girls have any plans?"

"Jenna and I are doing a couple college visits. West Georgia, Georgia State, and somewhere else. I've got Zoe locked in for all week. Think I'll see if I can get her to spend the nights here, too."

"Laney! It's her fall break, too."

"Exactly. Where would you rather be, here with just Cayden, or there with all those other kids?"

"You mean her siblings? Her family?" I resume walking to my car. "Whatever. Just remember that she is younger than your nephew Grant."

"Hogwash. She's way more mature than Grant, or Bryan, or my girls were at that age. She's an old soul." She pauses and cocks a mother's ear towards her house. "Shoot, I hear Cayden." She waves as she goes back inside.

Muttering, I start the van and back out. "Old soul, my foot. I think she just had to grow up fast, and she did it."

CHAPTER 37

***

"She's still living with Kyle Kendrick. Why would I ask Anna to the football game?" Will is standing at our kitchen table, hands on his hips, scowling at me.

"I thought he was back home with Kimmy."

"Yeah?" He drops his hands to the back of the chair in front of him and drops his eyes to the table. "Yeah, well, me too," he mumbles.

"You're sure he and Anna are still together?"

"Let's just leave it at yes, I am sure they are still together." He sighs and adds, "I stopped by the apartment today when I finished my test. Figured he'd be at the store but..." He shrugs, then walks to look out the back doors. "But he was there. She was there." After a bit he mumbles, "It was all rather cozy."

He throws his hands up in the air. "Rose's grandmother read me the riot act yesterday at the funeral. She says as long as I'm a married man, I'm not welcome in her home."

"She's right, you know."

He sighs and looks at me. "I know. I know. Feels like I'm just stuck in everything. My whole life is so messed up."

I give him a sympathetic wince and ask, "Want to come to the game with us? I really do have to leave now to pick up Missus."

"Naw, I'm not sure I want to go at all. I have work all day tomorrow. Don't think I did well on my test today. Rose is off-limits, and Anna might as well be, too. Don't feel much like a football game." He shoves his hands in his pockets. "Maybe I'll see if the guys are around down in Marietta. Although I guess none of them even live there anymore. I'm going to go for a walk."

He opens the doors and heads outside. I watch him walk past the garden and down the hill. At the river, the branches of the weeping willow sway in the little bit of breeze there. They are turning to a watery gold, but they still form a solid curtain.

When we moved here last year, I spent so much time behind that curtain. Crying, talking to a ghost, or I guess it was mostly praying, but whatever it was, it helped. Hope it can help Will now. He has a lot on his plate, and unlike thirteen-year-old Zoe, he's not handling growing up so well.

I turn and see the time. Great, I'm going to be late picking up Missus.

Maybe she'll decide I'm not worthy friend material.

I do need to touch up my fingernail polish… but as I pick up the bottle of polish, I grimace. Nope, can't do it. Can't be late on purpose. I grab my purse and fly out the door.

Missus needs a friend right now, and apparently I'm the chosen one.

Whether I like it or not.

%%%

Home football games are getting tolerable, but I still don't like away games. Learning a new parking scheme, strangers taking tickets, they don't make hamburgers like our concession stand does, everything is different. It's pretty much a nightmare.

That may be an overreaction, but it doesn't feel like it right now. Missus has, of course, been to Collinswood Field over a million times and knows everything there is to know about it. Hard to believe, but everything there is to know about Collinswood's field, traffic, parking, and an assortment of pertinent information can all be laid out in twenty minutes.

I was timing her.

Then the most important points can be reiterated as they are needed due to my not listening the first time.

"The flashing light is where you want to turn. Remember? The one I told you was beside the Baptist church. This is the Methodist church, and that is not a flashing light."

"Not this entrance. The next entrance is where there are boards laid over the muddy parts. Weren't you listening, Carolina?"

"It's much faster to enter at the other end. This is the end close to the concession stand. We don't want to get in that mix, correct?"

"You like the hamburgers at our field, but they do pulled pork sandwiches here, which I believe you'll like even better. But you'll probably not even try one, since I'm suggesting it. That's just how you are."

I'd tuned her out so long ago, that when I finally realize she's asked me a question, a good question, I almost missed it. "Yes, oh yes, you should definitely not climb all the way up there. Sit here with Gladys and the ladies like you usually do."

I think we've established I'm not the most athletic of people, but I scaled those bleachers like a mountain goat being chased by a bear.

"Whew! Made it," I say to Jackson with a big smile. "And by the way, we're leaving Missus here after the game."

Jackson gives me a kiss, then pulls back to look at me. "What?"

"It's either her or me. Or, I know, I'll drive your car home, you take the van and Missus."

He had a work project to drive over and look at that had him driving right back through Collinswood, so he decided to meet us here at the game. He shrugs and says, "Okay."

Taking in then letting out a deep breath, I try to shake the tightness out of my shoulders. I close my eyes as I pull in another deep breath. This has been an awful day. Missing FM has hit in waves, but then each wave would be flattened with another demand, command, or reprimand from Missus. With my eyes still closed, I listen to the bands warm up, the whistles and shouts of the coaches on the field, the chatter around us.

Then Jackson taps my knee. "Hon?"

I look at him and he points down the bleachers. "Don't look now, but here comes your friend."

My head swivels around, he can't mean…

"Scoot over, Carolina," Missus says as the ripple down our row begins under her direction. "Dawned on me those women have had decades to be my friends. It's too late for them now. Besides, I think it best we concentrate on this relationship, don't you?" She settles her hands in her lap, then leaning her head towards me she says, "See, their band leader? He's not very good. Watch, you'll see what I mean. Jackson, when will you be getting our sandwiches? Did Carolina tell you we're having their pulled pork sandwiches?"

"No, she didn't."

Missus purses her lips and looks straight ahead. It's obvious she's trying to restrain from admonishing me for not passing along that necessary information. Then she speaks up, "Jackson? I'll take mine now, thank you."

He stands and looks down at me. "You want one now, too? Game hasn't even started."

Missus lays her gloved hand on my thigh and looks up at my husband. "Oh, I believe she does. Leaving right after halftime means we need to eat early. Plus, she'll just have you making another trip as soon as she smells mine. We'll take chips and water, not soda." She palms a twenty-dollar bill to Jackson. "That's for both of ours."

I make eye contact with him as he stands and waits in front of me. I can feel him encouraging me to speak up. I clear my throat and start, "Missus, I…"

She lifts her hand from my thigh and holds it to my face. "I insist on paying. You drove after all. Jackson, we can't see the field with you standing there. Hurry along."

Jackson moves out of the way as he shrugs, then he lopes down the steps.

Missus lowers her hand. "Now, what were you saying, Carolina? Get it all out now, you don't want to disrupt the game with chitchat."

Again I open my mouth to say—yeah, I don't know what I was going to say either, so I close it and look at the field.

However, Missus leans closer to me and speaks in a low, secretive tone. "While Jackson is gone I wanted to ask about something I heard down with the other ladies. Carolina, look at me. Is it true his brother lost his job up in Kentucky because he was fooling around with one of his students?"

CHAPTER 38

Before I could even process what Missus had asked me, she looked at me more closely and, with her eyes, directed me to look at the people coming in to sit in the row in front of us. She cupped her hand in front of her face, bent her head, and mouthed, "School board." Then she made a motion of locking her lips.

And here I sit. Waiting on a pulled pork sandwich and going over every tiny thing Colt has said to me about why he left Painter. I should've been more suspicious. A grown man doesn't just up and leave his hometown and his job. A school board doesn't fire their championship coach because of some personal squabble. He did say something about a woman. Not a girl, a woman. Didn't he?

Surely, though, our school board has checked everything out. Then some of the past articles in the *Chancey Vedette* come back to me, well, the headlines. I don't actually read the *whole* story. Don't think the school board is actually known for being thorough, if the headlines can be believed. Now that I think about it, they did hire him pretty fast. Oh my word, what if it's true? What if he's a predator? What if that's why he works in high schools?

Jackson will be so upset. What if Jackson knows? No, no way Jackson knows anything.

Is there?

"Here you go. Sandwiches, chips, and bottles of water," Jackson says from the aisle as he hands out our food.

Missus sighs. "Oh, Jackson, bottles? Well, as long as you brought straws."

The look on his face says he didn't bring straws. Just then the whistle to begin the game blows. I stand up.

"I'll get a straw. You watch the game." Again, I'm as limber as a monkey getting out of my seat, around Missus, around Jackson, and heading down the steps. I couldn't eat a bite anyway. More likely than not I would throw up on the school board member who just happens to be seated in front of me.

On my way around the field toward the concession stand, I find a concrete block wall to lean against. This all cannot be true, but then again, look at Colt's father. Having an affair right out in the open. Oh no—and with a much younger woman. Is this why Jackson didn't tell me Colt was coming to stay? No, that can't be true. No way.

Some deep breathing and I'm feeling better. From here I can see down our sideline. I look for Colt. He's right beside the head coach. Colt looks more like he's the head coach. He's so confident and good-looking. How in the world am I going to find out what's going on? Of course I'll ask Jackson, but I wonder how he'll find out. And if it's not true, won't even asking those kind of questions ruin Colt's career?

A laugh bubbles up as I realize I don't have any details. I just took one sentence from Missus and ran with it. Literally. Ran down the bleachers, and now here I stand, practically paralyzed. I push away from the wall, and as I turn to go back the way I came I remember a straw. I turn around and walk to the concession stand, get Missus a straw, and calmly walk back to the guest bleachers. Of course it's all some huge misunderstanding. No need to panic.

"Carolina, this is Richard and Julie Smith. Rich is on the school board," Jackson says as I reach our row. "I was just telling them Colt's my brother."

"Nice to meet you," I say as I shake their hands.

Rich sits back down, but as he does says, "We sure are thrilled to have a coach of his caliber in our district." My back is to him as I ease past Missus. "The kids sure do love him."

With me blocking her, Missus looks up at me and says out the side of her mouth, "Especially the girls."

I need to sit down. I need to sit down right now.

Collinswood 24, Chancey 27.

And just like that, Colt Jessup is a hero. Even Missus thinks now that she must've heard things wrong.

As we wait in a line of cars to leave the grassy parking, Missus is more concerned about making sure we're in the fastest line than she is about recounting what she had heard before she joined Jackson and me in the stands.

"Carolina, you cannot imagine what an extraordinary thing this win over Collinswood is. They went to state last year. We haven't been to state since FM was on the team. If only he'd gotten to see this." She tears up again.

We were already winning at halftime, and she didn't want to leave. Said FM would never forgive her if we won and she wasn't there to see it. That was the first time she teared up, then all while we were tied near the end of the game, she talked to FM like he was sitting in my seat. It was a little disturbing. She would grab my arm, and then look down at her hands, like my arm didn't feel right. Once she even looked up at me and was startled. When we got to the car and I tried to get more details about Colt, she brushed it aside.

"Maybe I heard wrong. Or people in Kentucky are spreading gossip because they are jealous since he's now our football coach." She jabs her gloved finger at a break in traffic. "There, jump in there, those cars will let you in."

Following her directions, I merge into the line near the road, while I agree with her. "Football *is* pretty cutthroat up there. Maybe someone is just telling lies. But tell me exactly what you heard. Were all the ladies talking about it? Does everyone know?"

"I do not believe so. Gladys hadn't heard anything, and if it was going around much, she would know. I'm not saying she's a gossip, but..." Missus shrugs. "Alice told only me and Gladys. She wanted to know if we'd heard anything."

"How did Alice hear?"

Missus thinks as we finally pull onto the highway. "I'm not sure she said. Oh, wait, she said she heard it from her daughter who works at the high school, in the office. Now, turn here to miss the traffic leaving the bigger parking lot. Are you going to Ruby's? FM would always attend Ruby's special evenings, but I did not. However, this might be too big to miss. Yes, it..."

She drones on, and I block her out. Ruby's. Hmmm, that might be a good chance to watch Colt and see how he behaves. Not that I could tell anything, but I hate to accuse him of something so awful without more to go on. It all lost some validity when Missus mentioned Alice Humphries' daughter, Barbara. Barbara Humphries is a little off. She's part-time in the office and thinks she's the kids' best friend. She's not married and thinks all the male teachers are in love with her. Maybe Colt hurt her feelings. Her making up a story about him would not be out of the realm of possibility.

"Yes, I'm going to Ruby's," I say.

Missus clicks her tongue against her teeth. "Well, so glad

you made that earthshaking decision. However, we were no longer even talking about that."

I look over at her. "We weren't? Okay, I must've lost track. What were we talking about?"

"How high the legs of the majorette uniforms are cut. It was like watching them march around in a thong, or some Las Vegas showgirl costume. I will be writing a letter to the editor first thing in the morning."

I roll my eyes and prepare to ignore her again.

"You agreed to have your name affixed to the letter also."

"Wait, I did what?"

But she's moved on. "Park there in front of Peter's Bistro in the handicapped spot. There won't be any handicapped people there tonight. I always park there."

As I ignore her and pull into a spot across the street from her preferred spot, she shrugs and unbuckles her seatbelt. "As your friend, I keep trying to help you, but you refuse to accept it. You won't find many other friends who constantly consider your benefit before their own, but whatever you want."

She pulls down the visor mirror and reapplies her lipstick. Pressing her lips together, she smooths it out, then flips up the visor. "You know me, Carolina, I never want to interfere."

CHAPTER 39

When I see Laney's name come up on my phone screen the next morning, I immediately stand up from my chair on the deck. "I'll start breakfast," I tell Jackson and Colt. "Y'all finish your coffee."

"Hey, good morning," I answer as I walk in the kitchen and pull the door closed behind me.

"Good morning, what ya doing?" she asks.

"Just having coffee. What about you?"

"Same. Sooo, did you go to Ruby's after the game?"

"Yep. Saw Jenna and that new boy she's dating."

"Were they behaving?"

"Seemed to be."

And the conversation dies. I want to ask her if her mother told her what Alice Humphries told her and Missus. Bet she wants to ask me, too, but neither of us want to be the one to start it.

If people had any idea how hard it can truly be sometimes to gossip, they wouldn't be so worried about it.

"Saw you sitting with Missus at the game."

"Yes, did you sit with your mom?"

"Yeah, it's just so much easier with Cayden to sit with her. Cayden's why we didn't come to Ruby's last night."

"That's what I figured."

"Um, was Colt there?" she asks.

"Yep." I close my mouth and make it tight. I cannot give this any validity until I know more, but it is Laney and, well, I would like to know what Gladys thought. If she believes what Alice told her mom. I take a breath and say, "Listen..."

Laney says, "Listen..." at the same time. Then we both laugh.

"So, does you mom believe it?"

"No," she says. "Well, not really. She did at first and then..."

"And then we won the game and the team practically carried the supposed evildoer off the field on their shoulders," I supply.

"Exactly."

"He acted perfectly normal at Ruby's. Humble. Even Coach Daniels was praising him and saying he won the game. The kids adore him." I hold up a finger as though she can see it. "And don't say it! I'm going to talk to Jackson today. Couldn't last night. When we got home that South Carolina game was still on and we all watched it. Then it went into overtime. Then this morning Colt made coffee and was sitting on the deck when we came down."

"Well, I sure don't want to give this any life if it's just another one of Alice Humphries' fantasies, but thought I'd talk real vaguely to a couple of the ladies that work at the high school. See if they have anything to say about anything. Can't talk to Alice, she'll turn it into a big thing if she gets any idea people are actually talking about her. She craves attention." Laney talks to the baby for a minute, then drops her phone. "Sorry, trying to feed Cayden. So what about the girls? Think we should see if they've heard anything?"

I cringe at the thought of confronting Savannah. There was some nasty business with her drama teacher a year ago that I still have nightmares about. "I don't know. Maybe all this is for nothing, and once I talk to Jackson we can forget it."

"That's what I hope. Listen, I need to go feed him. He's wanting my attention and I can't hold this phone between my ear and shoulder. We also need to get this pie thing figured out. I've ordered the little pie crusts, and I'm going down to Costco to get some big tubs of Cool Whip this week. I'm using Shaw's wholesaler number, and I was thinking they do sell awfully big cans of chocolate pudding…"

"Let's think about it, but I've got to go, too. Forgot I was supposed to be starting breakfast."

We hang up, and I rip open a package of small link sausages, then dump them into a warming frying pan. We're having French toast and sausages, then Savannah and I are going shopping. But first, I turn the pan down to low, cover it with a lid, and step to the door onto the deck and open it. "Jackson, can you come in for a minute?"

He stands up, picks up his empty coffee cup, and asks Colt, "Can I get you a refill?"

Colt says, "Sure," and hands him his cup, then adds, "Think I'll go see if there's anything to get out of the garden. I do like a fresh tomato with breakfast." He stands and strolls down the steps.

I close the door behind Jackson. He's not even to the coffee pot when I say, "You need to tell me what led to Colt being fired from Painter High School."

"Oh." He puts the cups on the counter and turns around. "Well, there was some kind of scandal. Folks were pretty ticked because the school board wouldn't come out and say exactly why they'd fired him. Guess they don't have to do that, unless the law was broken. It's considered a personnel matter. Someone even paid for a billboard in support of Colt, didn't I send you a picture of it? I meant to. People were steamed. Some of the letters to the editor were blistering. None against

Colt, but against the school board, especially the president of it. He and Dad go way back as enemies, never did like each other."

"But what did Colt say about it?"

Jackson frowns and thinks. "Not much really. It was pretty muddled up with Dad being hurt and all. Think he might've let them have it when the school board interviewed him. Yeah, I think that was the straw that broke the camel's back. He got angry with them and said stuff he shouldn't."

"And they fired a championship coach for that? There wasn't something about a woman? A girl?"

His frown deepens and he shakes his head. "A woman? No, don't think so."

I'd been leaning against one of the kitchen chairs, keeping a watch on Colt in the garden to make sure he wasn't coming in. I straighten up and walk to the fridge, my back to Jackson. "Never heard anything about, a... a girl?"

I don't see it, but I can hear in his voice he's no longer slouched against the counter. "A girl? Like a young girl?"

I shrug and take out the milk and a container of eggs.

"Carolina, what are you asking me?"

When I turn to look at him, I see he's stepped to the deck door and is looking into the backyard. Quietly I ask, "Could he have been involved with one of his students?"

"No!" Jackson says. "Why would you say that? Is it really that huge of a burden to have my brother staying here? He thinks you and he are getting along really well. He was just telling me how lucky I am to have you and the kids. He said he's really thankful for this time here, as it's given him a chance to get to know you."

"Calm down. It's just a rumor I heard last night, and I wanted to check with you."

Jackson's face has darkened. "You know rumors like this can destroy a person's reputation, not to mention his career."

"Okay, I just wanted to check it out with you. Just needed to make sure."

With his hand on the doorknob, he leans toward me. "Okay, I get that. But, no. Nothing like that was ever even suggested. The whole time I was up there, no one said anything like that to me. Nothing, okay?"

I nod and say, "Okay."

He gives me a quick kiss, then goes outside. I shut the door and watch him walk down to the garden as he talks to his brother. With my forehead pressed against the glass, I mumble, "But would anyone say anything to you? You *are* his brother."

Chapter 40

"It's kind of weird," Savannah says as she leans on the circular sales rack. "I get all excited about the cruise, then I think of FM and feel sad. And guilty, too, I reckon."

I smooth my hand down her hair. "I know. Like at Ruby's after the game, but it was neat Head Coach Daniels doing that toast to him. Even if it was with coffee cups and water glasses."

She stands back and resumes looking at the hanging clearance items. All around us, racks are full of fall and winter merchandise. Sweaters, wool skirts, gloves and scarves displays, despite the warm temperatures outside. The only things suitable for a cruise are on the clearance racks—and that's okay by me. As she pulls out a bathing suit top, she asks, "Do you think Missus is okay? She was kind of, well, rambling last night. Didn't you think so?"

"She was definitely rambling. I think she's trying to do too much, wants life to go on just as it did before. Sometimes you have to just let life stop. Take some time and some deep breaths." I move to the next rack and, turned a bit away from her, I ask, "How do you think your uncle is doing at school?"

"Fine, I guess. Is he moving into that house?"

"Hmmm, you know, I don't know. He was talking about it at breakfast, wasn't he?"

She looks at me and shrugs, then goes on with her shopping. Guess neither one of us were paying attention. I try again. "Do the kids at school like him?"

She nods. "I think so. He's real laidback. Easy to talk to."

"Who talks to him?"

That gets a longer look. "Why? What's going on?"

"Nothing. You want to try those things on?"

She studies me another minute before turning towards the dressing rooms.

I should've known better than to try to get information out of my daughter without her knowing it.

She was born better at this game than I'll ever be.

I'll get Laney to talk to her later.

Once I quit trying to get Savannah to talk about what I wanted her to talk about, we had fun. Shopped and had lunch before heading back home. I waited until it was almost over and we were driving into Chancey before I asked about the cruise. She'd talked about the different excursions and ports of call, but she hadn't mentioned Isaac.

"So, where do things stand with Isaac and you?"

She sniffs and stretches out her legs. She has on shorts and gold sandals. New sandals we found for the cruise that she convinced the cashier to clip the tags off of. "He's okay. Not sure I want him to be my senior-year boyfriend, though."

"I'm still not sure about this whole cruise idea," I confess.

"Mom. It's nothing. I just really want to go on a cruise and he's fun to be with. We're seniors, so neither of us are looking to fall in love or anything."

"But doesn't it strike you as strange that he doesn't want to take a guy friend along? That his parents, as strict as they are, are okay with him taking a girl along?"

"They're not that strict."

"They chaperoned your dates."

"Yeah, but that's just some church thing they do. They really treat Isaac more like a friend than a child. He's really mature, you know. Promise, it'll be fine."

She leans forward to turn up the radio. They are leaving later tonight to drive halfway to Tampa where the cruise leaves Sunday evening at sunset. It's only a four-day cruise, so they'll get back into port Thursday, then home by Friday.

The same Friday the Southern Desserts Festival begins. I have a lot of work to do.

Those cans of chocolate pudding sound better and better...

"I said we should just get two of those big buggies. You're the one who insisted on this thing!" I kick out at the big metal contraption I'm trying to drive around the warehouse store. I make sure to not actually kick it, as it is a big metal contraption.

Laney stands with her hands on her hips. "Well, we're buying a lot. Maybe it's easier to push. Try that."

"I have! I've pushed and pulled and begged." We are both in our dresses from church. After Sunday school, when Shaw and Jackson said they'd take the kids to lunch after church and we could go ahead to Costco, they didn't have to say it twice. We even skipped the service so we could get down here early. We have this big, flat thing loaded with cans of pudding, Cool Whip, plates, napkins, and spoons. It's also loaded down with all the other stuff we each are getting for ourselves. We've been here a while, but now we can't get to the counter to pay for all our stuff.

Laney pushes by me. "Here, let me try." I move out of her way as my phone rings.

"That's probably Jackson asking if we've run off a cliff or something. Oh, it's Savannah. Hi, honey," I say into the phone. "You getting ready to get on the ship?"

The first sound I hear turns my knees to water. She's crying. My tough-as-nails daughter is crying—no, sobbing. I step backwards and sink onto a box of canned goods.

"Come get me," she says between sobs. Then she takes a long breath and is able to talk more clearly. "Come get me. I'm not going on that cruise."

"Honey, what's wrong? Are you okay? Where are the Rivers?"

"I'm still in Georgia, not all the way in Tampa. Just come get me. The Rivers are gone."

My heart leaps out of my chest. "Gone!? What do you mean gone?"

"They had to leave to make the cruise. I'm still at the hotel where we stayed last night. Near Valdosta." She takes a ragged breath. "Can you come get me?"

That gets me on my feet. "Of course." I say to Laney, "Call Jackson. Tell him to come get me here—we're going to Valdosta." She nods, then I go back to talking to Savannah.

"Now tell me what happened. You are okay, right?"

"I'm okay, just they weren't, they—his sister who I was supposed to be rooming with ended up not coming and so they cancelled Isaac's room. We were going to be in the same room. And when I told them I didn't think that was a good idea, they were so mean. That I wasn't paying, so I didn't have the right to tell them what to do. They kept saying they trusted me and Isaac. That we had earned their trust and respect. It was creepy, Mom!"

"So they just left you there? Why didn't they call me? Let me know?"

"Well, they got kind of mad at me, and then I went and sat in the lobby. I knew they wouldn't do anything in front of other people. They hate causing a scene."

"Is that what you did that they got mad about?"

"Some, they didn't like that, but it was when they all three came down with the bags, even mine, and saying that we had to leave. Again they started with the whole thing about trusting Isaac to be a gentleman. Well," I hear her laugh a bit. Shaky, but still she was laughing. "Well, then I shouted at them, right there in the lobby, 'Trust him all you want, I don't trust him as far as I can throw him. Did he tell you I sprayed him with hairspray last night to keep him off me?'"

"Honey, what in the world!"

"Mom, he thought I was going to sleep with him. His mom was supposed to be sleeping in my room here, and him and his dad sharing a room, like they told you. But he came into the room and acted like I was crazy for believing that, that *of course* we were a couple for the trip. He just assumed we were going to be together. And honestly, I think his parents assumed it, too. What is wrong with them?"

My mouth won't work. I'm completely flabbergasted.

"But Mom, don't worry. I've got my bags, and the hotel is nice. The manager is a mom, too, and she's been so sweet. There's a McDonald's next door, so I'm going to go get something to eat. I'll be fine until you get here. Sorry I was so upset earlier. I feel better now."

"Of course you were upset!" I say. "I'm beside myself. What were they thinking? And just leaving you there, it's beyond anything I've ever heard."

"One thing his mom kept saying was, 'Why do you care? No one will know anything.' His dad said basically the same thing, and he's a preacher!"

"Well, honey, I don't know what they were thinking, but they are wrong and you are right. You did the right thing."

She sighs. "Good. Thanks, Mom. And you were right, too, but it's all okay now. I just want to come home."

I burst out laughing. After a pause, she says, "Mom?"

"Sorry, honey. But you should see Laney corralling this big metal cart in Costco in her high heels and Sunday dress."

I can hear a hesitant grin breaking on her face. "Then take a picture. Miss Laney always likes being on Facebook."

Then we both laugh—and it feels so good.

CHAPTER 41

"I've been thinking," Savannah says as she hold the end of the blue-and-white gingham fabric we're going to decorate our festival stall with next weekend. "You know the Rivers will be home tomorrow from the cruise."

We're out on the sidewalk in front of the store where there's plenty of room, since I needed to man the store this Thursday afternoon. Plus it's too nice out to be inside. They're mowing the square, so while it smells good, it is a little noisy out here. Savannah and I are standing close to each other so we can talk without others hearing.

However, I step a little closer to her at her statement. She's not talked a lot about what happened since we got home. While she talked non-stop *during* the trip home, it was like she got it all out then didn't want to think about it anymore.

"Yeah, I know," I say. "Days have gone fast. Are you worried about seeing them?"

She holds the fabric up for me to cut. "I was, but that's what I was thinking. Why should I be worried? They're the ones who are putting on an act. Isaac and I didn't even act like boyfriend and girlfriend here. I was actually kind of mad at him for not wanting to be closer at school. I really think he didn't want to be tied down to me in Chancey. But on the cruise we'd be a couple. Do people really think they can have two separate lives?"

I hand her the end of a new piece of fabric, and she steps away from me to stretch it out so I can measure it. "I think people do. When I was growing up one of my friends wasn't allowed to wear a two-piece swimming suit at home because her folks felt it was indecent, but when they went on vacation she could. That never made sense to me. Or people that cheat on their spouses, that's like having two lives, I guess. Seems to me that trying to live two lives is a good way to make sure neither life is very happy."

"Looking great, Carolina!" Laney shouts as she strides up the sidewalk towards us. "Hey, Savannah. Thanks for your help." She gives Savannah a side-arm hug.

Savannah has been a huge help this week. Like with the blue-and-white gingham. That was her idea. I was fine with just the white tables, but once I saw some of the other dessert booths plans, I was extra glad for her help.

And thankful for Colt's help, too. Neither Laney nor I have heard even one more peep about Colt and Kentucky. That may be because school is out and Alice Humphries went on a trip to the mountains. Colt actually drew up a plan for our booth to make it more than just some bare, long tables borrowed from the church arranged in a square. (Which was *my* plan.) He made us a façade piece that he painted white and blue. He's also helped keep tabs on Bryan this week. They've worked in the garden and been working out down at the school gym. The rental house is almost ready, he's been told, and Colt plans to move out next week. I honestly will miss him.

Savannah pulls her phone out of her back pocket and checks the time. "Oh, I better go. The Williamsons are supposed to check in around four." She looks at me with eyebrows raised. "You good?"

"Yes. We're good. Thanks for taking care of the B&B while I'm here."

She waves as she heads toward the street, studying her phone.

Laney and I watch her walk off, then Laney says, "So she seems okay."

"Yeah she does, and thanks for not saying 'I told you so' about the cruise."

She winks and bumps me with her shoulder. "Well, I was thinking it."

I roll my eyes at her and grin, then turn to look up the sidewalk. "Oh, no. Here she comes."

Laney shifts her focus, too. Then grins. "Your best friend! You and Missus exchanged friendship bracelets yet?"

"She's driving me crazy. I'm trying to have patience with her, but…"

"Carolina," Missus butts in. "I'm hosting a dinner party for the committee Saturday evening. It's all quite short notice, but I'm sure you'll be there, correct?"

"Well, I don't know—"

"Then tomorrow night? Or is Sunday better?" She's standing in front of me with her new iPhone resting in one hand, and her index finger on the other hand poised over it. "Whichever evening you decide will work."

Laney laughs, picks up the stack of cut fabric, and walks to the door of the store. "I'll see you inside."

I sigh. "Saturday works."

Missus' index finger gets busy, and she precedes me in moving toward the store's front door. Funny, she looks like she's mimicking how Savannah just left. Head turned down, both hands busy. I step around to open the door for her, and she doesn't even look up as she walks inside.

With everything going on, the biggest event in Chancey this week may be that Missus got an iPhone. She now rules her kingdom through texts and apps. Her weather app is now all of the committee members' weather app, as she sends festival weather updates hourly. Not only are our calendars synced, but she's synced to everyone's on any committee she's on. I'm up to date on all the decisions surrounding her upcoming fiftieth class reunion, the yard sale her women's group at church is holding, and her dentist appointment next Wednesday at ten-thirty. I have to assume half the county, likewise, knows everything our festival committee discusses.

Retta blocked her, saying it was interfering with her real estate work. Let's just say the scene at Ruby's *that* resulted in has served to warn the rest of us it's not a good idea. Kind of like how Caribbean islands used to hang pirates in their harbors to warn other pirates of the consequences for pirating there.

We have all been warned. Give Missus access to all your information, calendars, and whatever else she wants. Who do we have to thank for all this?

My daughter-in-law, Missus' iPhone pusher. Yeah, that means I can't even complain about it out loud.

Anna and Will went to the doctor this past week and found out the sex of the baby, but they aren't letting the rest of us know yet. Peter and Shannon are throwing them a gender reveal party next week. No, Anna and Will are still not together. Yes, Peter and Shannon are.

Shannon's moved into his house, in fact. People want so badly to talk about this development, but there are those hanging pirates to think about. Missus hasn't mentioned it, even to me—her best friend. Does she not know? Does she not care? Doesn't there have to be a reaction of some kind? I'm not asking, of course.

Laney wants to run a lottery on when Missus will figure it out and her head explode, but after Laney's last stint of gambling got her dismissed as city treasurer, she's restraining herself.

"I put the fabric on your book table in the back. Where's Shannon?" Laney comes through the shelves as she asks about Shannon. She's talking to me, but looking at Missus to see if Shannon's name elicits a response. Missus doesn't even look up from her phone.

"She's taking some time off this week. Next week with homecoming flowers I guess is crazy for her." I push it a bit. "She's getting settled in her new place." We both watch Missus. When she drops her phone a bit, we both draw in quick breaths.

"About that," Missus says and our eyes widen. "Laney, how is Jenna feeling being left off the homecoming queen ballot? I feel for her and would like to buy her a corsage, unless that would just rub salt in the wound."

"Oh," Laney says after a pause while her brain redirects. "She's okay, now. College visits this week helped, I think. That's super nice of you, though. Maybe not a corsage like the other girls, maybe some roses for her to carry? Looks a little less planned."

Missus's iPhone leaps back into action as she punches in whatever she's punching in about ordering Jenna flowers. Laney and I just smile at each other.

I ask, "Which college did she like best?"

"She was really impressed with Georgia College, over on the other side of the state. It's a public school, but they're keeping it small. Want it to feel like a private school."

"Maybe I can get Savannah interested in it. She has no interest in next year. Says she wants to go away to school, but doesn't want to think about it right now. After that episode with Isaac, I think she's even more reticent about making any decision."

That gets Missus' attention. "When those people get back

255

I'm letting them know that is not how our young women are to be treated! How dare they leave her alone in a hotel! Makes my blood boil. They are just fortunate FM isn't here. He'd run them out of town with a bucket of pitch and a bag of chicken feathers!"

Laney and I stare at her. Who is this FM she's talking about? This past week he's taken on traits he never possessed while living. FM would no more run someone out of town with tar and feathers than I would. He was a gentle soul, but apparently not in Missus' memory. I've heard of departed loved ones being thought of as more kindly, or with a more loving and generous spirit. She's turned our sweet FM into John Wayne on steroids.

However, we ignore her. We all ignore everything. We let her grant superhuman testosterone to FM, text us at all hours of the night, and cause traffic jams because she won't look up from her phone. All because we understand she's in mourning and needs our patience.

Plus, there are those hanging pirates to think about.

Chapter 42

"Wonder if she'll serve food left from the funeral?" Jackson asks as he pulls his head out of his closet. "Are you sure she said men had to wear ties?"

"Yes. Serving funeral food would make sense, I guess. Freezer was full of it, unless she's found an app that cooks dinner on that blasted phone of hers." I kick off my just-put-on shoes. "I don't care if she said she wanted women wearing heels and dresses. I'm wearing flats."

"That mean I can forget the tie?"

I shrug. "Heels she said were optional, ties were not. I *am* wearing a dress."

Turned away from the mirror and his fingers busy tying his tie, he asks, "You think Shannon will be there with Peter?"

"Oh, most definitely. It was all Shannon talked about yesterday at work. I'm anxious to see them as a couple. Still can't actually picture it. I rarely actually see them together, except when they pass by the front window downtown."

Jackson grabs me from behind and hugs me close. "All I know is I'm glad he's over his little infatuation with you. Hard to believe this time last year he was playing ghost on our hillside."

"It has been an interesting year." I slump back against him. "Do we have to go tonight?"

He squeezes me. "Yes. Because if we don't your *bestie* will come find us and drag us there anyway." He rests his chin on my shoulder. "Actually, maybe I don't have to go. She probably wouldn't come hunt me down." Turning me around in his arms, he kisses me and pulls me tight again. "However, I want to be with you just as much as Missus does."

We kiss again, and he whispers in my ear, "Plus I want to see Shannon and Peter in front of his mother."

We laugh, and I push him away. "Fine, let's go."

I call out Savannah's name in the hallway to see if she's upstairs or downstairs.

"I'm down here," she yells from the kitchen. By the time we get down the stairs she's sitting on the couch.

I tell her she looks nice as I walk behind the couch into the kitchen. Jackson goes to sit in the chair by the window and says, "So you and the girls are going to a movie?"

"Yep, Jenna and Angie are picking me up in twenty minutes. Aren't y'all going to a dinner party? Why is it so early?"

Jackson raises an eyebrow and answers, "Missus."

"Oh. Yeah, that explains it," she says as I come back into the living room. Then she presses a button on the remote muting the show she had on. At Jackson's chair, I stop and wait as Savannah has turned toward her daddy. "Dad, I just want to say thanks for talking to Mr. Rivers."

Jackson came home yesterday afternoon saying he'd already made an appointment to meet Paul Rivers at Ruby Tuesday's at the interstate that evening. Later he reported there was very little said by Isaac's father. An off-the-cuff apology for leaving Savannah, but then he added it was something they felt they had no control over. He admitted they should've called us, but didn't want to embarrass Savannah in case she didn't tell us what had happened. *Like she had a choice after they left her on the Florida-Georgia line!*

Anyway, as Jackson predicted, the family denied and lied and mostly acted like Savannah was an irrational teenager. He told them that we and our friends all knew the true story, that Isaac was no longer allowed near our house, and that he thought they'd find he wouldn't be welcomed in several other homes. Paul responded that they had found Chancey High wasn't up to the educational standards they required for Isaac, and he would be attending a private boarding school in South Carolina immediately.

Jackson leans forward, his elbows on his knees. "I realized they were the type of people who would protect their son, the victim in their eyes, and make everyone else out to be evil. I had no intention of letting them anywhere near you with that garbage." He lifts up a hand and grabs hold of one of mine. "Didn't want them to get a shot at your mom either, because she knew better. I'm the one that thought it was fine. I was wrong. Way wrong."

Savannah grimaces. "Yeah. Guess now we have to listen to Mom, like, all the time." She grins as she looks up at me.

"Yes! All. The. Time." I take a step and give her a hug over the back of the couch. "Have fun tonight. You handled yourself well in this whole thing. You and your hair spray."

She laughs. "The hair spray was more because I was mad about missing the cruise. He was honestly surprised that I wanted him to leave, but he was leaving. The hair spray just made him move faster."

Jackson stands and then hugs her, too. "Well, it's all over. Maybe he'll be more cautious next time."

Savannah sighs. "I hope so. I know I'll pay more attention." She holds onto her daddy's hand and smiles up at him. "Gotta remember all guys aren't like you."

He winks. "That is absolutely right. So no dating until you find my clone!"

I push him toward the door. "C'mon, Mr. Perfect. Missus is waiting."

As we pull the door shut, Savannah has already unmuted the television and is back into her show.

"She seems okay?" Jackson asks.

"I think so," I say as we walk to the car. "It's been wonderful she had the week off. And even better that she doesn't have to see him again. Like our daughter, I want to say thank you to you. For talking to Paul Rivers, but also for coming to this dinner with me instead of going fishing with Colt and the boys."

"You know fishing isn't something I enjoy." He opens my door as he adds, "Unless it's beside a railroad bridge. Plus, it's been awhile since we've gone out, so while I would've enjoyed their company, I'm glad to be with you." He closes my door as I get settled in the van, then walks around to his own. As he starts the engine and turns around to head across the track he says, "And another thing..."

Together we say, "You want to see Shannon and Peter."

Stephen and Cathy Cross arrive at Missus' sidewalk at the same time we do. Cathy has on a blue dress with heels, and Stephen not only is wearing a tie, but also a jacket. He grumbles as he shakes Jackson's hand. "Can't believe she planned this for tonight. Georgia game is at seven."

"So we'll all be home in plenty of time for most of the game," I say. "Maybe that's why she scheduled dinner so early."

Cathy loops her arm in Stephen's and pulls him up the sidewalk ahead of us. "I'm just glad to be out of the house."

Again Stephen grumbles, "You're out of the house most every night. Forrest sleeps more nights at your parents than at our house."

"You could go get him instead of hanging out with your old friends at that bar," she responds.

Jackson and I raise eyebrows at each other as we follow the bickering couple up onto the porch. However, at the door, Cathy is all sweetness and light, and Stephen employs his good looks and smooth talk on Missus. The look on Missus' face is like she forgot she'd invited them.

I hang back to let the younger couple get past Missus before we reach her. "Hello, thanks for having us. Are you okay?" I ask.

She frowns and shakes her head a bit. "I was sure Cathy had a lingerie party over in Dalton this evening. It was on her calendar and one reason I selected this date. Just my luck her on-again, off-again marriage happens to be on again tonight. Come in." She shakes Jackson's hand, then leans in to kiss my cheek. As she pulls back, she sighs. "At least as uncouth as Mr. and Mrs. Cross are, she followed the dress code. Hope your feet are comfortable, Carolina."

She turns away, and Jackson is grinning so big I bet his lips hurt. I jab him hard with my elbow to make sure at least something hurts. "Shut up."

A beautiful buffet is laid out, and I quickly realize she's had the dinner catered. The large dining table is already set, but I see Missus is instructing changes to it. I guess she really didn't think Cathy was coming. I follow Jackson to the living room and echo him, telling a young lady in all black that I'd like a glass of white wine. Peter is standing at the end of the room beside the front windows. Ida Faye and Retta are holding down a love seat near him. Shannon is in a chair on his other side. I nod at the older ladies, but head to the other side of Shannon.

"Hi there. You look lovely, Shannon. That's a really good color on you."

She smiles and looks up under her lashes at Peter. "Thank you. Peter helped me pick it out."

Usually she wears younger-looking clothes. Colors and prints and odd silhouettes. Lower cut or tight to show off her large chest, in lots of shades of purple. She really likes purple. The dress she's wearing tonight, though, is burnt-orange linen. She has on a large gold necklace and earrings. With her short haircut, I've always thought she looked like a fairy. But it's styled different now, and it's not so unnaturally black. She's wearing dark brown pumps—heels, of course.

Peter shifts his wine glass to his other hand, then reaches his now-empty hand out to lay it on Shannon's shoulder. He winks at her, then looks up at me. "Hello. Good to see you tonight." He leans forward a bit. Up close he still looks drained, as he has since he left our meeting to go to the hospital only a bit over a week ago. "Can you believe Mother doing this now? I tried talking her out of it, but she wouldn't hear of it. Glad you and Jackson could come."

One of the staff clears her throat to get our attention, then says to us, "Mrs. Bedwell asks everyone to make their way to the table."

I step over to say hello to Retta and Ida Faye as I take Jackson's arm. When I turn toward the door, I watch Peter bending over Shannon, her arm tucked next to him. He's whispering as they walk, and she's smiling. She looks like a different person almost. Taller. Older. Better.

Jackson is looking at her also, and again, we meet eyes and smile.

Jed and Betty are the last to arrive, so we didn't have the

chance to chat with them. Soon we are all seated, and Missus calls us to attention.

"This dinner is to thank all of you for your aid in this inaugural Southern Desserts Festival. It's been a trying time for a variety of reasons, but I have no doubt it will be a resounding success next weekend. I also appreciate you being here tonight. Some might say, including my son, that it's too soon after recent events, but I say different. I prefer to be busy and surrounded by friends." She abruptly sits down with tightly pressed lips and bright eyes.

Peter looks into his lap, as do Ida Fay and Retta. Jed pushes to his feet. "I'll say grace."

His prayer is sweet and just long enough for everyone to catch their breath and wipe their eyes. We eat and talk and laugh. It was all in all a much better evening than I could've imagined. Eventually I forget to even watch Peter and Shannon. Missus treats her like she always has—she ignores her. She, as usual, fawns over Peter, whom she had seated at the other end of the table. Cathy and Betty keep up a steady conversation about the lingerie business, so that's boring. Stephen has his phone in his lap—checking on football scores, I assume.

Dinner went fast, dessert was served immediately, and before it was even dark, we were heading out the front door. Stephen was walking down the sidewalk a good two yards in front of Cathy. He'd already expressed his desire to not miss kickoff. Betty and Jed were right behind them. Retta and Ida Faye had been the first to leave. They didn't want to get caught out after dark, they said. Although both live within five minutes of Missus' home, no one begged them to hang around.

Missus had just closed the front door, leaving Jackson, Peter, Shannon, and me on the front porch.

Peter whispers, "Want to go check out Gertie's cave?"

Jackson answers quickly. "Yes! Good thinking." We four scurry off the porch, down the sidewalk, and then up Gertie's sidewalk. We can hear voices as we let ourselves in the front door and make our way down the hallway, then the stairs.

A small crowd is enjoying the games, most gathered around the biggest screen where the Georgia-Vanderbilt game is getting ready to start. We talk to some of the others there and find seats. Jackson is in awe as he's never been down here before.

Just as we sit down, the door at the bottom of the stairs opens, and we hear a familiar voice.

"Did I get here in time?" Our heads all swing to see Missus standing at the open door. She exclaims, "Thought I'd never get rid of them all."

Chapter 43

"She just left?" Bonnie asks from the other side of my Monday morning book sorting table. When she came in, I told her to forget dusting or shelving books for a bit and to pull up a chair.

"Yes. You've heard the phrase 'turned on their heel'? Well, that's exactly what she did when Gertie moved aside for her to see our table. Missus drew in a sharp breath and turned right back up the stairs. Peter chased after her, but she ignored him."

"Have you talked to her since?" Bonnie asks this in a whisper. The bell over the front door rings, and she takes to her feet.

"Yes, well tried to," I respond quickly, "but it was like it never happened. Gertie won't talk either."

Bonnie holds a finger up at me as she turns to the front. "Welcome to Blooming Books. Can I help you?"

I listen just long enough to hear that I'm not needed or being asked for, then let their talking fade into the background. At church yesterday, Missus acted as always. Maybe even stiffer than usual. I tried to sit with her since I assumed it would be hard to not have FM beside her. You'd've thought I was dressed in full clown garb the way she looked at me. After her up-and-down examination, she said, "Yes, Carolina? Can

I help you?" Organ music started, and she turned to face the front. She even pulled her purse over closer to her like I was going to steal it. So I went back to sit with Jackson.

When I hear the front door bell again, followed by my name, I look up. Peter is striding through the shelves toward me. I motion him to the chair Bonnie left. "Morning. What's up?"

He scratches his head with both hands in frustration and then tucks them under his arms. He ignores the proffered chair. "Mother. She's grieving, I know. But what was she doing in Gertie's basement Saturday? She won't say. Won't say anything. It's driving me crazy. Is she having a mental breakdown? I mean, honestly, that's the only explanation I can come up with. Plus—well…"

"Well what?" I ask when nothing else is forthcoming. "What else?"

"She hasn't said anything about, you know, about Shannon…" He lets his words dwindle, and then he leans on the table looking down at it.

Well, there's one big question-about-town answered.

"Nothing?"

"No, nothing." He looks up sideways at me. "You think she knows?"

I shrug. "Who knows? Anyway, Shannon looked really nice Saturday night. And it was fun to hang out with you and her. Well, once we got over the shock of your mother showing up."

"Yeah. Shannon did look nice. Never thought I'd enjoy her company as much as I do, but I keep waiting for my mother to jump in. But why? It's my house. I'm a grown man. If I enjoy being with Shannon, who is she to say anything?" He straightens up. "Right?"

"Right," I say as I stand up. "So, what's the problem?"

He shrugs. "I don't know." He looks around the back area, then folds his arms tight again as he turns to look out the front window. "I miss my dad." Then he turns quickly back to me. "Do you think he liked Shannon?"

"FM? I guess."

He chews on the inside of his mouth, then starts nodding slowly. As his nodding speed increases, he takes a deep breath and unfolds his arms, like a bird opening huge wings. "Okay. Okay." Then he strides to the front door and leaves.

I've always heard you should not make decisions in the aftermath of a death. Now, with Missus and Peter, I've seen why.

"What's that smell?" Savannah asks with her nose wrinkled up. She leads three other girls into the shop after school, and they all flop down in the sitting area close to the front window.

One of the girls sniffs and responds, "Smells kind of like dirt, but better."

"I like it. Mums right?" one of the others says. She takes a long slurp of her coffee drink from next door.

Shannon is busy working and doesn't answer them, so I do. "Yes. Chrysanthemums. Flowers for homecoming. How was Pajama Day?"

The girls, all wearing pajama pants and cute T-shirts, grin, roll their eyes, and start with the OMGs. Soon they are all laughing and talking. "We told the junior cheerleaders they could wear more revealing stuff since it was pajama day. Like, really wear what they sleep in! Of course, they believed us!"

"Mom, didn't Miss Susan call you?" Savannah jumps up to come to the shelf I'm working on. "Susie Mae got sent home. She had on this tiny, sexy outfit." She arches one eyebrow. "Granted, she doesn't have a lot to show, but what she had was right out there to see!"

Shannon walks up to the group. "Wait, Susie Mae wore something like that to school? How could she not know better? How could her mother not know better?"

One of the girls says, "Oh, she knew better. She just wanted the attention." The girl drops her voice like no one else would hear her. "Besides, who hasn't seen what Susie Mae has?"

Savannah's eyes widen. "Char!"

The girl looks at me, then Shannon, then shrugs. "Sorry."

I pull out my phone to see if I missed any calls or texts from Susan or Laney, but I didn't. "I bet Susan was hot by the time she got to school to pick her up."

Savannah turns her back on her friends and says low to me. "It was her dad."

"Griffin? Wonder where Susan was?"

One of the girls says loudly, "I heard her dad was really mad."

"I bet," I say, "her pulling a stunt like that."

But then the girl continues. "She had regular pajamas like we're wearing over her sexy ones. She took them off between second and third period, paraded down the crowded hall, then right into class wearing next to nothing. Her dad wanted to know why she couldn't just put the regular pajamas on and stay at school. My mom was working in the office, and they could hear him yelling at the principal over the phone!"

I step forward. "Wait. Griffin was mad at the principal? Not Susie Mae?"

The girl nods her head, then takes a long sip of coffee.

Savannah shakes her head as she sits back down. "Apparently all the junior cheerleaders had sexy pajamas under their other ones. They were showing them to each other in the bathroom, and teasing the guys in class with peeks. Susie Mae was the only one to go all out, though. Only one to take off the outer PJs."

Just then, the front door opens and Zoe is standing there

in jeans and a T-shirt. Her smile dies the minute she sees the senior girls sitting in the store. She actually starts to back out, then I call her name. I try to make eye contact with Savannah to also welcome the freshman, but she's buried in her phone and talking to her friends.

"Hey Zoe, what you up to?" I ask as I near her.

"Nothing." She hurries past me to the bookshelves and I follow her.

"How was school today?"

"Okay." Then she looks down at herself. "Except it was this stupid homecoming week dress-up thing, and I didn't know it was something people actually did."

"I'm sure everyone didn't."

"Everyone that matters did. Like them." Her eyes cut to the front of the store. "I'm so stupid at school."

"Honey, you are hardly stupid," I say. "You actually skipped a grade. Just ignore the other kids."

Even as those words come out of my mouth, I hear the lameness. Zoe doesn't even roll her eyes at me. Just dismisses me with a turn back to the shelf.

"So, what's the theme for tomorrow?"

Zoe shrugs.

"It's Tacky Tuesday, right?"

She shrugs again.

I straighten books on the shelf in front of me as she pulls a book off another one. When the girls burst out in laughter at whatever they're talking about, she pushes the book back onto the shelf and brushes past me. She's out the door before I catch her, and I just let her go.

I wouldn't go back to being a teenager for all the peaches in Georgia.

Or mums in this shop.

It does smell weird in here.

Chapter 44

"This is just too much. What in the world have the police even been doing?" Ruby erupts, and by the murmurs and head-nodding in the crowd, she's not alone in her disgust. The windows in the abandoned storefront next to Ruby's were shattered sometime last night.

Dawn has barely broken, but Ruby has gathered a crowd. She called the other shop owners when she found the glass all over the sidewalk as she opened at six a.m. We look like our own version of Pajama Day. Peter, Shannon, and I are joined by Gertie, Patty, Andy, and the others she rousted from bed. Then there are the fully dressed customers who showed up for coffee and a muffin, but got more excitement than planned.

Charlie Spoon is taking pictures for the *Chancey Vedette*, although it's still practically dark, asking questions, and writing as fast as he can in his notebook. He sputters as he writes, "This here is vandalism, you know. Other stuff has been more like pranks, but this here is serious."

"Pranks!" Ruby yells. "Taking my plants, defacing my building? What about the Lake Park? Breaking into the concession stand. *Possibly* this lazy attitude by our so-called *press* is why the authorities have been so lax! Pranks, my foot!"

"Ruby, now, you know what I mean, you know," Charles

explains. "Your plants, for cryin' out loud, were Dollar Store plastic jobs that were faded and needed throwing away. The spray paint turned out to be chalk paint that washed right off with a water hose. The trash from the dumpster could've been considered a driving hazard, I suppose, but it didn't really hurt anything. And you know nothing but a couple candy bars were taken from the Lake Park, plus Susan don't rightly even know if it was locked. But this? This here is real damage. Real damage, you know."

I pull my jacket tighter, it's gotten cold out. "What did the police say? You called them, didn't you?"

She waves her hand in the air. "Yes, that Pierson boy got here, but then there was a wreck out at the blacktop he had to go attend to. He said since it's an empty building there's nothing to secure. I'm telling you, we are on our own!"

Peter wraps his arm around Shannon and starts walking away, but Ruby catches him. "Peter Bedwell, where do you think you're going? This requires action. Don't you be slinking off to that love nest with that, that floozy!"

Shannon whirls around. "Why, you old bird! You don't call me names!"

Peter steps in front of Shannon and states, "Ruby, I'm going to get dressed and come back here with a shovel, a broom, and a trashcan to clean this up. Is that okay with you?"

She sniffs and flings her arms out. "'Bout time someone does something productive. I've got muffins to make." Turning back to her store, she hurries away. I think she's afraid Shannon's coming after her.

Shannon, however, has already turned back down the sidewalk. Peter looks after her, then turns back to look at me and shrugs before jogging after her.

Gertie has been quiet, but after a big sigh, she says, "Patty, you and Andy go on up to the house and start some breakfast. I'll be there in a minute. Carolina, need to have a word."

"But Ma, can't we just go back to bed at our place?" Patty whines. Andy stops, as he'd already started down the sidewalk toward his store and his mother-in-law's house.

Gertie's face scrunches up at the pushback. Patty is usually more than compliant with her mother. Heck, with everyone. Even more surprising, Gertie gives. "I guess. Go on." The young couple hurry past us to their apartment above Blooming Books.

"Hmm," Gertie says looking after them. "Think her being pregnant would make her develop a backbone?"

"Patty's pregnant?" I ask.

"Not that I know of. But I keep looking for signs, don't you know. I mean, if they're trying, what's taking so long?"

Oh, its definitely too early for this conversation. "Uh, um. What do you want to talk to me about?"

"Your boy," Gertie says. "Not fond of those friends of his."

"Will or Bryan?"

"That Bryan. Not fond of Will's girlfriend, but that's just 'cause he's already married, and messin' with Webster women never turns out good for a married man. But no, Bryan's been seen where he shouldn't be seen."

"Where? When?"

"Just around. I don't trust that group, and with all this vandalism, well, just think you and Jackson need to step up. Take care of it."

"Gertie, I need some more details. Like where was he seen? Doing what?" The door to Ruby's opens, and the smell of coffee almost makes me feel faint.

"Told you, just around. Aw, there's the cops now. I'll go get Ruby. She won't want to miss this." Gertie lumbers off, and I realize she's in the old bathrobe I got so used to when she lived at the B&B all those months.

I wish I could just dismiss her advice on Bryan, but she's

smart and she notices things. "Good morning," I say to Officer Pierson. "Guess it's happened again. Got any leads?"

"Morning," he says then he steps across the broken glass and looks into the empty building. He spends a minute there, then comes back toward me just as Ruby's door flies open, releasing more coffee smell and her voice.

The officer lowers his voice and leans toward me, "Mrs. Jessup, let's talk later. Okay?"

Nodding okay, I back away and let Ruby and Gertie have center stage. I'm going home.

There's a boy I need to yank out of bed.

"Where the devil is he?"

Leaving Bryan's empty bedroom, I dash down the hall to Savannah's door, but it standing open usually means she's not in her room.

"Savannah!" I shout, but I only wait a minute before stomping to the stairs and then down them.

"Mom?" I hear as I get to the bottom. Turning around I see a half-asleep Will standing at the railing. I'd forgotten him. Guess I did get at least one of my kids out of bed. He asks, "What's going on? Are you okay?"

"Where's your brother?"

He shrugs. "I don't know. Why?"

I roll my eyes and plant my fists on my hips. "It's not even seven o'clock and he's out of bed and gone?" Then I remember. "Oh, yeah. Weight practice. Colt was taking him." I turn around for the kitchen and say, "Go back to bed. Sorry. And cheerleaders are selling chicken biscuits this morning, so that's where Savannah is," I continue as I fall into a kitchen chair.

I stare at the coffee pot, willing it to fill magically. I can't work up the strength to stand, much less deal with coffee grounds. Laying my head on my crossed arms on the table, my chin quivers, my chest tightens, then the burning behind my eyes becomes more than I can stand. In one sob, everything releases—my chest, my eyes, my jaw. Things have happened too fast. FM, Savannah being left at a hotel hours away, Bryan brought home by the police, the ultrasound of my grandbaby, Will and Rose, Colt, and even Missus being crazy.

As it all pours out, with a healthy dose of self-pity and loneliness, I blame Laney for being so busy with Cayden. I blame Jackson for being gone so much and bringing his brother here, which takes time away from us. I blame Susan for moving up the mountain when she said it wouldn't make any difference. I blame them all in another round, but by then I'm running out of steam. There's nothing left to cry out, and my yawns start taking over sobs. With my head still on my arms, I give in and fall asleep.

For about five minutes.

Someone's at the front door.

Chapter 45

"Kimmy? What did she want?" Laney asks as she adjusts Cayden in her arms. We're sitting on my back deck Tuesday afternoon after cleaning the B&B rooms. We'd cleaned in silence for the most part. Laney worrying about Jenna and how upset she is about the homecoming court now that it's so close, and me worrying about, well, you've already heard that list.

"Crack of dawn and she wanted to talk about Paul and Di Rivers," I say. "Kimmy's been going to a Bible study at their church, and when Zoe told her what happened, which, how did Zoe find out about them leaving Savannah, Laney? Do you know?"

Laney smiles at me. "Well, you know Zoe's like part of the family. I'm not good at editing myself when I'm emotional, and I was very emotional about how that family treated Savannah." She shrugs. "Sorry, but not really."

"Whatever. Anyway, she said she needed to know if it was true. I told her it was. She said she'd gotten a lot of good from the class there, but she'd have to rethink everything."

"Kimmy say anything about that husband of hers?"

"Not really. I just asked how things were going and she shrugged saying she was waiting to see how things played out. Whatever that means."

275

Laney picks up her phone and looks at the time. "Why hasn't Susan called me back? I still have to go home, fix something for supper, and get dressed for this reveal party at Peter's."

"…and Shannon's," I add.

"And Shannon's. Just shoot me. Peter Bedwell winding up with someone like her."

"Oh, I didn't tell you. Peter asked me yesterday morning if I thought FM liked Shannon."

We make sad faces at each other, and Laney sighs. "Can't believe he's gone."

"I can't believe how Missus has gone off her rocker," I say. "I understand grief, but does she have to kill the rest of us? She's called me half a dozen times today about things for the festival. New things. Things we can't do. Aren't doing! An hour ago she wanted to open the festival Friday night. I reminded her it was Homecoming, and she said, 'Okay, after the game.' I keep trying to remind her this is a trial run for this festival. Just one day to see how it goes."

"She still hasn't mentioned Gertie's?" Laney asks. "I mean, we all know she's a huge Georgia football fan. Is it truly that strange for her to watch the game there?"

There's a pause, before we both admit it would be very, very strange.

Laney holds her sleeping boy out to me. "Hold him so I can get out of this chair. I can't wait any longer on that sister of mine. I am holding her feet to the fire next time I see her. She has to make more time for us. She just has to."

Laney stretches and turns to the kitchen as I struggle to stand up with her heavy son in my arms. "I've got to admit, I'm glad to find out you feel that way, too. I was feeling way too needy this morning."

Laney laughs. "Oh, never you fear. If I'm around, you will never appear *that* needy!" She hauls the diaper bag over one shoulder. "Can you carry him out?"

"Sure."

She follows me out of the house, and as we get to her big SUV, a police car pulls into our driveway, parks, and Officer Pierson steps out.

Laney stashes her things inside the vehicle, then takes the baby. "You go on. I've got this." She winks at me, and I move over to the sidewalk where the officer waits.

"Good to see you, Mrs. Conner," he says, then waves at her as I walk up the sidewalk ahead of him.

As I start up the steps, he says, "We're good out here. I just want to speak to you for a minute. Mr. Jessup wouldn't happen to be here, would he?"

"No, he's at work. South of Atlanta actually, but he's coming home tonight because we're having a reveal party for our grandchild." I physically have to stop my mouth from talking as I turn to him. My heart is beating so hard. I take my foot off the step, but tighten my hold on the end post of the railing. Maybe if I have a heart attack I'll slide down more gradually if I'm holding onto something. No need to crack my head on the sidewalk, too.

"No problem," he says as he takes that stance you see military people and police officers take. Feet spread, loose knees, thumbs tucked into his belt. "Mrs. Jessup, I'm not sure we have a problem with Bryan, but I want to make sure you and his dad have talked to him about being out late."

"Oh, most definitely." However, as my head nods yes, my brain is saying, 'Did we? There was FM dying, and Savannah, and well... did we?'

"Okay, good. Talk to him again. Make sure he's not getting out after, after he's supposed to be inside. Not sure when the windows were broken, but can't imagine it was before midnight." Pierson looks off to the side and takes a deep breath. "You saw down there this morning, tempers are high. Folks don't like things like this in Chancey."

"Absolutely. But it was an abandoned store."

His eyes swing to me and harden. "Whoever is doing these things needs to realize it's a crime. A crime we're taking seriously, even if others aren't."

"Oh, of course. I was just saying it was, um, I was, it's serious. Yes, most definitely. Do you…" My question fades on my tongue. Don't think I want to know if he has any suspects.

He tips his head at me and takes a step back. "Appreciate your time. Be sure and have a talk with Bryan." He walks back to his car and then turns over his shoulder. "A serious talk."

"Yes, sir. Absolutely."

A train whistle alerts us that it's headed our way from across the river. Pierson's squad car is across the tracks before the arms come down, and I stand to watch the huge engines, four of them, pull the dozens of cars south, down the tracks. It's mostly empty automobile carriers headed back to Florida for another load of brand-new vehicles unloaded at the ports. There are some assorted boxcars and tank cars, too.

As the last one crosses, I wait because, underneath the train, I'd seen a car on the other side of the tracks, also waiting. Savannah is talking on her phone, but she does check for another train as she pulls across the crossing. All thoughts about fussing at her for being on her phone while driving dissipate when I see her brother in the front seat with her.

"Don't you have practice?" I greet him as he opens his side of the car.

Savannah gets out of her car carrying nothing but her purse. She's explained to me that seniors don't actually have to take books home. I do a double-take on her outfit: an old pair of khaki pants that are baggy on her and one of my shirts, which also hangs on her.

"Why are you wearing my shirt?" I ask.

"Tacky Tuesday, remember? You weren't here this morning for me to ask. Where were you?"

"Ugh, was that just this morning? Seems a million years ago." I look at her brother who does have to bring books home and is struggling to get his half-opened backpack out of the back floorboard of his sister's car. He's wearing a Hawaiian shirt I bought Jackson for a Jimmy Buffett concert we went to years ago. "Did they cancel football practice?"

He grunts, and when he faces me I see why he was struggling with his backpack so much. His left hand is wrapped in a bandage.

"What happened?" I step closer to him to take his backpack.

With another grunt, he lets me take it. Then he says, "I cut my hand. Couldn't practice." He begins walking up the sidewalk behind his sister.

"Wait, what? You cut your hand? How? Is it bad?"

He shrugs and keeps walking. "Nurse says it doesn't need stitches, just to take care of it."

I'm right behind him and can see that the bandage is mostly around his palm. His fingers or thumb aren't wrapped up. "So, you cut it at school?" I have to say, hearing it happened today and not last night is a relief.

Savannah holds the door for him to enter the living room and explains. "No, he did it this morning cutting his bagel. How stupid."

"So, you saw him? What happened?"

Savannah shrugs at me. "I don't know. He had it wrapped up by the time I came down. Took forever to dress tacky. It's a lot harder than a normal day. Hard to believe, but it was. What time is this party at Peter's tonight? You said we have to be there?"

"Yes, it's for your new niece or nephew." Bryan is headed up the stairs, and I'm still standing on the porch with Savannah in my way. "Bryan, wait," I say. "We need to talk."

Savannah looks from me to her brother and raises her eyebrows. "Okay. Well, I've got to put in some time on the homecoming decorations, but I'll meet y'all at Peter's. What time?"

"Seven. He said they're having munchies, so I'm not fixing dinner. Besides with Atlanta traffic no telling what time your dad will get here. Bryan, I said, wait!"

"Mom. Come on! I want to go upstairs and you're going to talk to Savannah all day." He stops on the stairs and looks down at us.

Savannah moves inside, then runs up the stairs past him, saying, "Nope, brother dear, sounds like she's going to talk to *you* all day. Have fun!"

As I move to sit on the couch, Bryan slogs down the stairs and over to the chair near the dining room door.

"So the nurse bandaged your hand at school? Why?"

He holds it out and looks at it. "It was bleeding through the Band-Aids I put on it. It's not that bad. She said I could practice tomorrow, but to keep it wrapped up today and tonight. She gave me a new big Band-Aid to put on it tomorrow morning."

"So how did you cut it?"

"Savannah told you. Cutting my bagel." He stares at his hand.

"You didn't cut it last night?"

He finally looks at me. "Why would I be eating a bagel last night?"

"Last night downtown. Where some windows were broken. Were you there?"

He looks back down, but only shakes his head.

"Bryan? Were you there?"

"No."

"What do you know about it?"

"Nothing. 'Cept everyone talking about it at school today." He sits back in his chair and looks at me, then out the window. And for the thousandth time I lament that I can't tell when this kid is lying. And I'm better at sniffing out a lie than his dad.

"What about the other things? Ruby's flowers and the spray painting at the ballpark and downtown? The Lake Park concession stand being broken in?"

"What about all that?"

I stand up, this makes me too antsy. I'm acting guiltier than he is. "Do you know anything about any of that?"

"Not really. Just what people say."

I walk to the window and wipe dust off the table with my hand. "So what do people say?" Looking back at him, I force myself to stand still, so I cross my arms and widen my feet, like Officer Pierson earlier.

"That it's a shame, but it didn't hurt nothing."

"Last night was different is what Officer Pierson says. He was up here this afternoon. Wanted me and your daddy to talk to you. To make sure you are taking this all seriously. Are you?"

He looks at me. Looks me straight in the eye and says, "Mom. I didn't break those windows. I didn't."

Dang, wish I could believe him.

CHAPTER 46

"I don't make cupcakes for just anyone!" Ruby announces to us as we all lift our cupcakes up and prepare to take the revealing bite, which will tell us if the baby is a girl or a boy. "But these were kind of fun. I had Libby do the icing because she's more particular than I am with things like that."

The cupcakes have a thick coating of white icing on them, swirled on top with blue and pink pearl candy sprinkles. It's not a big gathering, but in Peter's house, it feels like a lot of people, especially when we're all gathered around Will and Anna.

While Peter's house is as old as the other houses on this side of the square, including his mother's house where he was raised, it's a smaller version of the huge antebellum houses. I haven't seen it in several months, but his remodeling has paid off. It was practically falling down when he bought it. He obviously used his remodeling skills on his girlfriend as well, as she's wearing another dress that makes her look taller, older, altogether—*better*. And now she has highlights in her hair that I know weren't there yesterday. They light up her face and make her hair look grownup, intentional. She's also playing hostess, which Laney, Susan, and I are watching, sure that any minute Missus will realize what's going on right under her nose. Missus is staying close to Anna and ignoring the rest of us. Even me.

I'm not complaining.

"Everyone ready?" Ruby shouts. Jackson and I meet eyes and get ready for our bites. Savannah and Bryan are standing to the side of Will, and I love that I can see all three of them at once. I've decided to ignore my annoyance with my youngest for tonight. Plenty of time for that tomorrow. Will grins at me, and then Ruby yells, "Now!"

There's a brief moment where we all are taking sweet bites. Then "It's a girl!" swirls around the room as we all see the center of pink in the middle of each cupcake.

"A girl," I say and reach out to kiss my husband. We mingle our pink-cupcake-crumbed lips. Anna and Will knew, so they are laughing, and then Will steps back to take off his collared, long-sleeved sport shirt. As he pulls it over his head, we see he has on a pink T-shirt that says, "That's my girl" on it. He looks happy. Anna looks happy. Missus looks happy, but as she takes a deep breath, she looks at Peter and they share a sad smile. FM would've loved this.

Anna stands up and takes off the blue scarf, which matched the pink one she was also wearing. So now she and Will are both wearing pink. The rest of us are wearing an assortment of blue and pinks. I have to admit I'm wearing blue. It didn't matter to me, but I had to pick a side. Jackson is very proud that he's wearing a pink golf shirt, although I believe it's the first time he's taken it out of his closet. He's not a pink shirt kind of guy.

Will holds up his hands. "Thank you everyone for coming tonight. Thanks to Peter and Shannon and Ruby for making it so fun to share with you all. Anna has something to say."

Anna steps back and reaches to her Uncle Peter. He takes her hand, and she pulls him forward. Then she reaches down to hold Missus' hand, where she is still seated on Anna's right.

"It's hard not having my grandfather here tonight, but babies come whether the time is right or not." At that she looks up at Will and sighs with a small smile. "Anyway, Will and I found out we were expecting a little girl last week and we've come up with her name." She looks down at Missus as she says, "Her name is Frances Marion Jessup. Not sure we'll call her FM, but she will make sure we never forget him."

Peter is beyond words as he wraps her in a hug. Then Anna sits down to hug her grandmother. Will reaches over the table to shake his daddy's hand and to hold my hand for a moment. It's so real now. She has a name!

Missus clears her throat and holds up a hand. "I'm very touched, but I'm also hoping you are using the feminine form of Frances. I do not altogether approve of names being used for either gender. The male for Francis has an *i*, not an *e*. No reason to start my great-granddaughter off wrong."

Will laughs out loud. "Anna called it! She said she didn't care, but Missus would!" We all laugh with him, but I see a tear or two being wiped away.

"Frances Marion," I whisper. "My granddaughter."

As people move around the room chatting, I find myself next to Missus in the kitchen. We're fixing cups of decaf coffee, and as we start drinking them, we stand next to the back door and look outside. Patty and Andy are sitting outside with Savannah and Bryan on the deck that Peter added at some point.

"He's really done a great job with this house. I didn't even realize he was putting on this deck," I say. Then the joy of the evening bubbles up in me (or maybe it was the glass of champagne), and I do it. I ask what everyone's been wondering. "So, Missus, what do you think of Shannon moving in here?"

"What do you mean?" she asks as she turns to face me.

Of course the champagne was only good for one question. Now it's all me. "Well, obviously you see that they're a couple, right? I mean, they threw this party for Anna and Will together."

"Obviously," she says, her gaze never wavering.

"So, how do you feel about it? What do you think? Are you surprised?"

She takes a sip of her coffee then pauses. She settles the cup in the saucer, then looks back up at me. "Surprised? Me? She's from Chancey and not leaving Chancey. I know her entire family. She's a good businesswoman and, most importantly, she's young enough to have children. I chose her months ago. So, Carolina, on the contrary, I'm the only one *not* surprised."

She turns and sets her cup and saucer on the kitchen counter. She straightens her gray sweater on her shoulders and checks her hair in the glass panes of the cabinet beside me. My mouth is still hanging open when she looks at me and finishes with, "I believe a spring wedding would be nice and *obviously*—I get what I want. Good night, Carolina."

CHAPTER 47

"After looking at it, I believe he could climb out his window onto the porch roof and easily jump down to the ground," Jackson says as he sits down across from me out on the deck Wednesday morning. Savannah, Bryan, and Colt have left for school. "How did we not think of that?"

"Does the screen look like it's been messed with? Those things don't go in and out easily." I push the container of watermelon I'm eating out of over to him, and he picks out a piece.

"It actually does. It's bent, but I'm not sure when that happened. So, you didn't ask him about sneaking out, just about if he was involved, right?"

"Yeah," I say. "Don't know why I didn't think to ask. I guess I just can't fathom our son out running around town while we're lying in bed." Through the glass doors, I see Will in the kitchen. "There's Will. Tell him to come out here."

Jackson leans to the door and pulls it open. "Hey, Will, can you come out here a minute?"

Shortly, he walks out sipping his coffee. He flips one of the cushions, which is wet from the dew, and sits down. "Pass me the watermelon. What's up?"

I blurt it out. "Did you sneak out of the house after we were in bed?"

He stops with a piece of watermelon in midair. "Last night? No. I was exhausted."

"No." Jackson gives me an indulgent glance. "Your mom means when you were a teenager. Like Bryan's age."

"Where would I have gone? We didn't live close enough to anything to walk in Marietta."

"That's true," I say. "Do you think Bryan sneaks out here?"

Will chews, selects another piece of fruit, and thinks. "Maybe. It'd be easy with the porch roof right out his window. We've sat up there on the roof a couple times."

"What?" Jackson exclaims. "Doing what?"

Will grins at his dad. "Watching trains. What else?"

The furrowing of Jackson's forehead tells me he's seeing all new possibilities. He shakes his head at his son. "Why haven't you guys told me before?"

I steer the conversation back on track. "Jackson, no. We're not talking about trains right now. The police came to our house to talk about our son, we have more important things to think about."

"Whoa! The police were here about Bryan? What'd he do?" Will asks.

I shrug. "We don't know that he did anything, but you know, all the vandalism. The broken windows downtown." A honk out front causes me to look that direction and causes Will to stand.

"There's Rose. I've gotta go." At the door, he looks back at us and shakes his head. "Don't worry about Bryan. He's a good liar and all, but I don't see him destroying things. See you later!"

Jackson and I stare at each other. I sigh when he says, "Well, good to know our son the liar probably doesn't destroy things."

"And Will just left with Rose? He and Anna looked so happy last night. I wish he'd straighten all that out."

As he pulls the watermelon bowl to him, Jackson laughs. "Hard to believe, but right now our good child is Savannah."

"What is wrong with her?" I shout as I throw the Wednesday afternoon *Chancey Vedette* onto the Blooming Books counter, which I'm standing behind.

Shannon bends to pick up the pieces of the paper as she says, "Knew you'd want to see it as soon as I read it, so I came straight here when it was delivered at Peter's. I didn't even finish lunch." We both look as the front door flies open.

"Tell me this is not what I think it is," Missus says, holding out her copy of the newspaper. "Tell me you did not give that woman an interview."

I shout back. "Who knew she was working for the newspaper?"

Missus slams the paper down on the counter and takes out her phone. "I've already called Charles twice, but he didn't answer. I still own that newspaper—"

"Peter owns the newspaper," Shannon interjects.

Missus frowns and looks down at the woman she hand-selected for her son. I'd laugh, but I'm really not in the mood right now. Kimmy Kendrick is apparently the *Chancey Vedette*'s newest cub reporter. Her early morning call at my house the other day was not out of neighborly concern, or even old-fashioned gossip. I would so love to think it was just gossip now. No, apparently it was an exposé of the Rivers' church she's been working on. She doesn't mention Savannah by name, but it's not hard to figure out.

Never taking her eyes off her future daughter-in-law—

according to her—Missus draws in a deep breath and says, "Yes. Peter owns it, but it's in my family and I find this completely unacceptable." She turns away from Shannon, taking another deep breath. Then she continues, directing herself to me. "Not the facts about that church. We all know my stance on nondenominational churches, but about Savannah. This makes her sound like she ran off to some down-state motel with that boy. Why on earth would you tell that woman these details about your child?"

"I didn't! I barely told her anything. The one quote she attributes to me, I actually did say, but not for the newspaper." I pick it up and read, from the front page, "'The young woman's mother, a well-respected Chancey businesswoman, said, "She (her daughter) called crying from a hotel near the Florida line. They just abandoned her there and didn't even call us. We thought it was going to be a nice family cruise, but the Rivers apparently had no problem with their son sleeping with our daughter. We are livid."'" I drop the paper again. "That's basically all I said. Who knows where she got the other stuff?"

Just then Missus' phone rings and she says, "It's Charles." She listens for a moment, then hangs up the phone. "Well, that explains it. Savannah is their secret source. She's a minor so he didn't quote her, but she and Kimmy did this together. Kimmy's been working for Charles and this is her first big piece, but they wanted to keep it secret until it came out in the paper. Savannah knew she was asking around, so she told her she had a big scoop about the family. Understandably, she wanted to help ruin the Rivers. Apparently he assumed you knew since Savannah was involved."

We stand there, all looking down at the papers on the counter. Finally Shannon begins collecting them and states, "Well, Missus, you're always going on about women standing up for themselves and having a voice. Looks like Kimmy and Savannah thought you meant it." Then, leaving the papers in a neat stack on the counter, she turns toward the back of the store.

Missus' mouth is actually gaping. I don't think she's breathing as she stares at Shannon walking away.

My first smile since reading the paper crosses my lips. "So. Still excited about that spring wedding?"

"This is the last good meal for the week, people," I say as I sit the platter of beef roast, potatoes, and carrots in the middle of the dining room table Wednesday evening. "After tonight, it's frozen pizzas, chicken nuggets, and hot dogs until Sunday. No, Monday. I'm taking Sunday off from everything."

It's late, but everyone is here. Wednesday practices are early because Wednesday night is traditionally a church night in Chancey. Colt and Bryan had time for a quick shower as they raced in from practice. Will's been upstairs studying, so he just managed to make it down the stairs. Jackson and Savannah set the table and helped finish things up for dinner while we talked about the newspaper. Savannah sees nothing wrong with it, and honestly, why hide it? So I reckon we're okay with it, too.

"I'll help out at the festival," Colt says. "My rental house still isn't a sure thing, can you believe it?"

Will sighs, and Colt hands him the gravy boat. "Sorry, Will. Hoped to have the basement back to you by the weekend."

"What's the holdup?" I ask.

"Not sure," Colt says. "Thought it was for some fixing up the owner was having done, but that's done. I'm afraid the owner is going to back out, and there is just nothing else much out there to rent. Hey, did y'all see the paper? Savannah, is that the article you were talking about working on?"

Jackson and I stare at her, but she spoons peas onto her plate and nods. "Yep."

"You told Colt about it?" Jackson asks.

"Well, he was worried," she says.

"And we weren't? Give me those peas. Don't just sit them down, pass them along," I say holding out my hand. I hate when people stop passing food because they've got theirs.

Savannah hands me the peas. "I meant to tell you, but I just kind of forgot. But isn't it cool that Kimmy is like a real reporter now?"

Bryan has his head down, stuffing his mouth. Football has toned him and made him even hungrier. I'm not sure if his food requires all his focus, or if he's staying out of the line of fire, but it's not going to work. I dive in headfirst. "Bryan, have you been sneaking out your window and going out at night?"

He lifts his head, a carrot half in his mouth. He pops it all the way in with his hand and shrugs. "Just once."

Will points his fork at me and Jackson and nods, adding, "Told ya."

He's so helpful, isn't he?

"Where did you go?" Jackson asks.

"Just out. Guys called and they were hanging out. Didn't want to bother you."

My appetite is waning as my temper builds. Just as I begin to let him have it, Jackson puts his hands up. "Stop. We're eating dinner. Son, we will be addressing this later. Okay, Carolina?" He waits for me to nod, then continues, "Now, nice talk. Fun talk. Nothing about the newspaper or sneaking out. I want to enjoy this fantastic meal your mom made, okay?"

For several minutes we all are quiet. It takes a bit to get our minds in a different gear.

Colt brightens up. "Hey, I talked to Dad today. He's moving out of the rehab center tomorrow. Going home."

"Shelby still doing okay with everything?" I ask.

He grins and looks around the table, stopping at his brother. "She's doing real fine, apparently. They're getting married."

"What?!" is the general consensus.

I add, "I thought maybe they were already married."

Jackson falls back in his chair. "Didn't I just say I wanted to enjoy this meal? Surely they are doing it at the Justice of the Peace and we don't have to participate. Please tell me that." He leans back up and spears a chunk of beef while looking at his brother, waiting for confirmation.

Colt shrugs and dips his head towards his plate as he lifts his fork. "Guess we'll talk about it later. This is delicious, Carolina. So tell me about the dessert festival, how's that going?"

I stare at him, and my shoulders fall. "Really? You think I want to talk about that fiasco? Missus objected to us using premade crusts, but she took us buying cans of chocolate pudding as, let me quote, 'a deeply hurtful personal insult.' She took me under her wing, and I've stabbed her in the back. She's completely out of control! Between the newspaper— thank you, Savannah—our chocolate pudding, and—"

When Will jumps up and runs out of the room, it stops me, but before I can get on him about just leaving the table, I hear what he's doing. There's soft jazz music coming from the television.

He turns it a little louder than we usually have for background noise and comes back into the dining room. "There. Let's just eat and listen to the music. Okay, Mom?" He takes his place back at the table, lifts his glass of iced tea in a toast, and says, "Doesn't appear to be any safe topics at this moment. This is an awesome meal, Mom."

The music-only eating lasts long enough for most of the meal to be eaten. As Colt stands up and begins clearing the table, he says, "I was serious about wanting to help this weekend. With the B&B or dinner or however I can help out."

"I appreciate it," I say. "With homecoming also this weekend, Savannah won't be around for the guests, so that's a great idea. Wait." I turn to my daughter. "Homecoming. Weren't you going with Isaac? I completely forgot about that." Savannah stands up, picks up a couple bowls, and heads to the kitchen. "Yeah. I might not go."

Again, the general consensus is "What?!"

"I mean I have to go the game," she says. "I'm cheering and on the court, but not going to the dance isn't that big of a loss."

Those of us still in the dining room look at each other.

Then Bryan speaks up, "I'm going."

I motion for him to stand up and take the plates in my hands. "I know. You and the guys."

He grins as he slowly stands up. "Not going with the guys anymore."

Colt walks away from the table and I note that he's heading into the kitchen kind of fast, but I look back at my youngest. "Who are you going with?"

His grin only grows as he reaches for the plates. "Brittani. Uncle Colt said he noticed her watching me at practice and told me I should ask her." He easily takes the stack of plates in one hand and lifts the half-full pitcher of tea with his other. "She said she liked the way I was looking like a real football player." Savannah giggles at him. Then Will flat-out laughs.

Colt comes back to the table to get another load and apologizes. "Didn't realize they had a history. I just noticed her watching him."

"Thanks, Colt," I say as I join everyone else in the kitchen, which quickly empties as Will excuses himself to study. Jackson proposes that he and Bryan take a walk out back to talk about whether he'll even be allowed to go to homecoming. I try to convince Colt to go on so I can talk to Savannah alone. She's being a little too quiet. But my brother-in-law won't take the hint, so I actually listen to him.

"So if that's okay?" he's saying. "I really meant to have my own place by now."

"Sorry, what? I wasn't paying attention."

Savannah rolls her eyes at me. "His girlfriend is coming, and he wants her to stay downstairs with him this weekend."

"I didn't know you had a girlfriend," I say. "You mentioned a woman, but it sounded like it was over."

He leans against the counter, drying his hands on a dish towel, and sighs. "Thought it was, but…" He doesn't finish, but as he hangs the towel back on the oven handle, he looks at me and winks. "Guess it's not. No worries, though, we'll stay out of your way. Thanks, Carolina."

He strides to the basement door, through it, then we hear him loping down the stairs. Savannah closes the dishwasher and wipes her hands on the towel her uncle just hung up. "So, think his girlfriend is the one that was in his class?"

Chapter 48

"Did you have any doubt my sister would make it work?" Laney and I pull into the Dollar Store parking lot as she finishes telling me Susan's setup for the World's Largest Banana Pudding up at Nine Mile. We get out of the car and walk across the hot pavement. We're having one of those early fall heat waves. They don't usually last too long, but we are all so over the heat by now.

"That is pretty ingenious, using those long plastic gutters," I say. "I've seen them used for long banana splits, but never banana pudding. Phew! I can't believe it's so hot. All these desserts are going to melt."

We're in shorts, T-shirts, and tennis shoes in October. Today is our errands day. Some are part of my duties resulting from being on the festival committee, some from being the mother of a homecoming candidate, and some from being the mother of a son who, at the last minute, decided to take a date to homecoming.

Laney volunteered to run errands with me since her in-laws are staying at her house. They're fulfilling their obligation to the strawberry shortcakes Laney signed Shaw's dealership up for. They only live half an hour away, but as she volunteered them to make the biscuits for the shortcakes without asking first, they invited themselves to stay while they fulfilled their duties—which include babysitting, Laney decided. There's a whole lot of passive-aggressive stuff going on there, but who am I to judge? I may need lessons from them just to survive my father-in-law's wedding to my husband's ex-wife. Let's just say it sounds like we'll be going to Kentucky next month.

"Of course it won't be anywhere near the world's largest banana pudding, but measured out in length, it'll be pretty big." She pulls open the Dollar Store door and motions for me to walk through. It's cool and quiet, and as I always do when I enter, I say a little prayer that Kyle Kendrick is not on the floor, but either in his office in the back or completely off the premises. He gives me the creeps. Can't see how Kimmy or Anna can stand him.

Speaking of Anna, I see her sitting on a stool down the first aisle working with a pricing machine. "Hey there," I call out.

She leans back, and we can see how her stomach has grown. It's pushing at the buttons on her white shirt, and she pulls the shirt down to help the buttons stay buttoned. With one hand on the shelf in front of her and the other pushing on her knee, she stands up.

"Carolina, Laney. What can I help you with?"

"Law, I can't believe I looked like that just a few months ago!" Laney exclaims, then she stops herself. "Not that you don't look great, honey. Just great. I just can't believe sweet little Cayden ever fit inside me. But never mind that. Susan ordered two cases of vanilla wafers from Kyle, and he called to tell her they're in."

"Oh sure, follow me," Anna says as she heads to the back.

Laney follows her, but I say I'm going to do the shopping up front while they're back there. Missus has given me a list a mile long of things to bring back to Dessert Central—as she's named the back of our shop. Setup in the park begins tomorrow and needs to be done by game time at seven. Then the festival is only from ten a.m. until four p.m. on Saturday. I'm proud of us on the committee for managing to keep Missus from expanding the festival by hours, or even days. It helped our case when we found out Cathy had forgotten to do the PR she was actually on the committee to do, so we're expecting a very small turnout.

Just as I make my way to the counter with my full buggy, I hear Laney coming towards the front of the store. "Carolina? Can you pull your car up front? Mr. Kendrick is going to bring the vanilla wafers out for us."

Anna is following her, and as she gets to the front she weaves around the counter, puts a key into the register, and turns it on. "I'll start checking all this out if you want to go get your car. Nobody else in here right now."

By the time I get the car lined up, with the trunk open to the store's front door, Kyle is out there waiting with two cardboard boxes on a dolly.

We get the boxes in, but as I head back inside to pay for my purchases, he reaches out for my arm. I can't help that it makes me flinch.

"Sorry, didn't mean to startle you," he says. "But I wanted a word with you."

I look through the glass windows where Laney and Anna are in a conversation, both absentmindedly rubbing their stomachs. "Okay. What do you want?"

"I know you don't like me, but I just want to let you know how highly I think of Anna. I'm not just blowing smoke about her taking some managerial classes and being a manager with us, the company. She's a hard worker, and real pleasant."

"I agree. That's good news, if that's what she wants." I fold my arms tightly in front of me, and even though wrapped like that, I might look like I'm cold, I'm actually melting in the morning heat. Kyle looks so calm and cool, like a reptile—no body temperature.

"It is what she wants. Oh, and something else. I'm going to be leaving this store." He cocks an eyebrow at me. "I'm sure you'll be happy to hear that."

He's right, so I don't get all polite and tell him he's wrong. I only nod.

"New store for me to open up near the Tennessee border."

"Congratulations."

"Thanks, but why I'm telling you is, well, I figure you could pass word along to your son that Anna's going with me."

A chill goes through me, and now I clasp my arms closer to me to stop from shaking. Anna is going with him? The baby? "What about Kimmy? Your kids?"

He shrugs. "Kimmy's got a new life. Church and that newspaper job and all her friends here. Besides, she has Zoe. Anna and I can start over fresh."

"With my grandbaby?" I hiss. "Anna truly wants this? I thought you were saying she'd be manager here."

"Didn't say here," he says. "She's doesn't want to be stuck in this hole, and she might not even want to work once the baby comes. And we'll be having our own kids, she'll be busy. Your son won't be too heartbroken, his girlfriend and him are tight. They'll have their own little family to worry about soon enough, I bet."

I whirl around to look at Anna and Laney, but they're laughing. Kyle Kendrick rolls the dolly to the front door, then opens it. He waits for me to walk through, so I do.

Laney keeps looking at me as I pay at the checkout. She knows something is wrong, but I just can't talk about it with Anna yet. So I suffer Laney's looks until we are in the car. I turn the key and flip the air-conditioning up as high as it'll go. Then—I start crying.

As she rubs my back, I confide in Laney. It all spills out, but even as it does I'm telling myself it's not true. Anna wouldn't just up and leave Missus. And Will. And even us. They're naming the baby after FM. She and Will were so much like a couple two nights ago. Savannah and I were planning the nursery at our house just last night. Planning on starting it as soon as Will moves back into the basement and his room is empty. This baby is too real now for it to live somewhere else. No, it can't be true.

Repeating that mantra helps me dry my tears and finally drive back to town.

"You can't tell anyone until I talk to Will and Anna. Don't tell anyone. I'm serious, Laney." The car is stopped in front of Blooming Books, but I'm holding her arm tight.

"Okay. Promise I won't say a word." She raises a weary eyebrow. "Why would I? This is awful, awful news. You really don't think Will knows about it?"

I release her arm and think about last night. "No. He was happy last night. Joking around with Bryan. Oh, Bryan." As I open my door, I roll my eyes. "Did I tell you Bryan is taking Brittani to homecoming? Oh, and Savannah says she's *not* going to homecoming."

That gets Laney sitting back down in her seat. "What? It's her senior year. Of course she's going." Then she inhales, exhaling a long "ohhh." "Isaac was her date. Oh man, that stinks. Want me to call Ricky down at Georgia State? Maybe he doesn't have a game this weekend."

"I wish, but no. She'll be fine. It's one dance, right?"

Laney laughs as she gets out of the van on her side. "I'm still talking my daughter off the ledge from not being on homecoming court. She planned on winning, and now she won't even be out on the field. So don't try to make it sound better to me. I know better."

We load up with the bags from the back of the van and carrying as much as humanly possible across the sidewalk. Out of nowhere, Laney starts laughing, then says, "Oh, how the mighty have fallen! Maybe this is good, for Savannah and Jenna to not be the queen bees for once."

I can't bring myself to laugh just yet. "Maybe. Doubtful. But maybe. Now, Laney, Missus is in here. Not one word about Anna and that creep."

Shannon opens the door for us and steps out onto the sidewalk to let us by. "Thank God you are back, Carolina. That woman is driving me crazy."

I'd told Laney about Missus' plans for Shannon and Peter, so she and I meet eyes. I say, "I don't know, Shannon, seems to me you were giving it back to her pretty good this morning."

My coworker lowers her voice. "Of course. She already hates me. Why try and be nice to her? She's like that queen in *Alice in Wonderland* yelling, 'Off with their heads!' all the time. Not giving anybody a chance."

Wow! Shannon smack-talking Missus!

That stops Laney and me in our tracks. We look at each other again and burst out laughing. Savannah and Jenna apparently aren't the only queen bees in town with their crowns out of whack.

CHAPTER 49

"Really? It's for me?" I bury my nose in the huge, creamy chrysanthemum Jackson hands me Friday morning in our bedroom. I'm finishing my makeup, and he sits on the edge of the bed after his floral delivery.

"Yep. I had no less than a dozen people tell me I had to get you one. Including Shannon, who basically just handed me the bill for it last week and told me to pick it up this morning. Wasn't sure she'd be open this early, but after I got the muffins for the weekend I stopped by and she's up and going strong."

Flipping off the bathroom light, I come to him and lean down for a kiss. He tries to pull me onto the bed, but I resist with a laugh. "Nope. No time this morning. Full day for both of us. So glad you took today off."

He tightens his grip on my hand. "My taking the day off doesn't qualify as deserving of special treatment?"

I stop and step back to him. "Well, now that you mention it… Okay, you can choose a muffin first!" Jerking my hand out of his grasp with another laugh, I move to the door. "Did you see Will downstairs? He say anything?"

Jackson stands up. "Didn't see him. I feel sure he has no clue about what Kendrick said to you. It's good he's roped

Bryan in to working in the dealership booth tomorrow, though. It'll be easy to keep an eye on him."

I pause before I open the door. "Makes me so mad at Bryan that now I completely freeze every time I see Officer Pierson. I'm just sure he's coming to tell me something else about our son. Bryan just acts so blasé about it all. Savannah always seems fearless, but out of confidence. Bryan out of…"

"Stupidity," Jackson finishes my sentence, and I nod at him.

"Exactly." I turn, open the door, and enter the hall.

Jackson follows and sighs as we start down the stairs. "But from what I remember, that's pretty much status quo for teen boys."

When I hear Rose's laughter from the kitchen, I look over my shoulder. "And grown boys, too."

"Good morning. What are y'all up to today?" I say entering the kitchen.

Rose stands up straight from where she'd been leaning on the counter. "Morning." She wraps both hands around her coffee cup and stares down into it.

Will is facing the counter beside her, but looks back to say, "Good morning. Making my lunch for work."

Jackson pulls a notepad and pen out of the junk drawer. "I'm putting a note on the muffins. Everybody only gets one this morning. Got it?" He digs for tape in the drawer. "Anybody know when Colt's friend is getting here?"

That gets Will to turn all the way around. "Yeah, his girlfriend is staying downstairs all weekend?"

My face gets hot, but before I open my mouth, Jackson growls, "Son. Don't push it." he doesn't even look at Will, but our son immediately folds with a quick glance at Rose, who's still staring into her coffee cup.

He goes back to fixing his lunch, and I open the fridge to help my flushed face. Grabbing a bottle of water and an apple, I say, "Rose, I hope your grandmother will be at the festival tomorrow. And Will, thanks for letting Bryan work in the dealership's booth."

Will collects his lunch items in a plastic grocery bag. "Yeah, salespeople want to work on the lot tomorrow selling cars and making money. Laney's working with you and Mr. Conner's parents are kind of old to have to do all that by themselves. Oh, and I talked to Bryan about the whole being out after y'all are in bed. He said he wasn't going to do it anymore." Will stops and looks at me. "Said folks were getting things all mixed up, and he agreed that going out until everything settled down was stupid. Then he got all ramped up talking about it and said going out now was probably a little dangerous."

We all think about that, and I shake my head. "What? Why can't that boy just say, 'Cool. I won't do that anymore.' He is such a drama king!"

That makes Rose laugh out loud. Will grins at her. "That's what Rose said."

Rose follows Will out of the kitchen. With the jangle of car keys and the opening and shutting of the front door, they are gone. Jackson and I shrug at each other.

I really hate how much I like Rose.

"Kimmy, hi!" Seeing her come through Blooming Books' front door gets me up from our couch, where I'm counting out change for our pie booth tomorrow. "Haven't seen you since the paper came out. Congratulations on the new job."

"Thanks, Carolina. Think I'm going to enjoy it. I need the layout for where our booth is going to be. Charles said to come check with y'all." She's wearing a pair of old jeans and a tight T-shirt. Her hair is up in a high ponytail, and she looks younger than usual. Maybe working at the paper is good for her.

"Okay, here's the layout map. But can I talk to you for a minute?" I motion her over to the children's section.

She rolls her eyes but follows. I am still holding the layout map she came for. I step behind the bookshelf and wait for her. She's talking before she even gets behind the shelf.

"Carolina, I could not tell you I was working on an article about that church. You understand I was working undercover. Finally found something all those years living with Kyle Kendrick was good for: detecting bull!"

"But…"

She holds up both hands. "No, you don't understand. Those people had to be taken down. The new folks at that church love the Rivers, but the people that have been there all along knew there was something wrong. They are what ya call sheep in wolves… no, wolves in sheep's clothing. It had to be done, Carolina, I'm telling you, it had—"

"I agree with you!" I finally have to shout. "As long as the article was fine with Savannah, it was fine with me. And if she'd told me she was helping you, I would've told you even more. But Isaac is gone and his parents will be, too. Soon, I hope. Either way, I'm all good with all that. But you, what's going on with you?"

"Me? Well, I'm working for the paper and, uh, why?"

"Are you getting back together with your husband?" I ask.

"Now that's a tad personal like, don't you think?"

"Really? Now you're going to be secretive?"

She steps away from me. "I'm working on things. Things you don't need to know about." She leans toward me and takes hold of the layout map. "Kyle Kendrick is a complicated man, and he's not easy to handle. It takes time." She jerks the map out of my hand and darts around the bookshelf.

With a sigh, I mutter, "Kimmy, Kimmy. You may not have as much time as you think."

"Here, Missus. Take a seat," Gertie says as she pulls a cushioned chair out from the table in the tented area in front of her house/shop/cave. Since Gertie had rented the tent, it went up fast. Everywhere else on the square, folks are struggling with tables, canopies, and homemade displays like ours.

"Why, thank you. I believe I will." Missus eases onto the chair and fans herself with one of the layout maps. We've been walking the square, reviewing everyone's progress, and the afternoon is getting hotter.

Gertie sits in one of the other chairs, and I lean on the table as I say, "Looks like everything is on target. Some of the more bare-bones booths are stepping up their game, since they've seen how the others are going all out."

Missus nods once. "Competition makes people either rise to the occasion or bow out altogether."

"Or cheat," Gertie adds. "Cheating has always appealed more to me than working hard. Besides, what is cheating except working hard in a different direction?" She grins and leans a sweaty forearm on the table. "A direction most normal folks just ain't thought of yet."

Apparently I'm just tired enough and just hot enough to not have good sense. "So, since it's just the three of us here, Missus, I want to know... What was up with you coming into the cave to watch the Georgia game that night after the dinner party?"

Gertie side-eyes Missus. Missus studies the map in her hand.

I raise my own hands in befuddlement. "What's the big deal? Your refusal to talk about it, both of you, makes it more interesting to everyone. What's going on?"

Missus tilts her head up and over towards Gertie. "You didn't tell anyone?"

"No. Weren't no thing to me, but weren't my business to tell."

"Hmm," Missus says. She folds the map in a square and taps the corner of it on her knee. Finally she says, "FM had been making private visits to Gertie's since she moved next door."

"Um, okay. For the moonshine? Right?" I ask hopefully.

Missus frowns at me. "Of course for the moonshine. What *else* would he *possibly* be over there after?"

"Hey!" Gertie says.

Missus rolls her eyes at me but doesn't even turn to Gertie. "Get over yourself, Gertie Samson. It was *only* for the moonshine and, well, football." With a tiny, disgusted shake of her head, she says, "So after his... his... after he was gone, I asked Gertie if I could come watch the game with her. That's all."

"So why didn't you stay and watch the game with all of us? Peter asked you to stay."

Her bottom lip disappears, and her eyes suddenly fill with tears. Gertie leans up to put a big hand on her back, and I lean toward her to rest my hand on hers. "I'm sorry I asked."

"No, no." Her voice is shaky and gets shakier as she explains. "I made the last few weeks a living hell for my husband because he would go next door to enjoy that godforsaken moonshine and football." She looks over her shoulder. "And yes, I can admit it, Gertie, your company also. Gertie knows how to laugh and enjoy a ball game."

She looks up at me, one of the only times I've ever seen her look confused. "Why did I refuse to share that with him? Everyone knows I'm a fan of the Bulldogs, but I don't actually watch the games. I ridiculed him for wasting that time for *years*. I'd bug him with to-do lists and turning the channel to watch a news broadcast. Then he started going to her house and I swore I'd never..."

She breaks down crying. It's the first time I've seen her lose control since FM died. Gertie leans closer to her, her one arm encircling Missus back, and we sit like that for a long time. When her crying begins to slack off, she takes a deep breath and sits straighter. "It was embarrassing that particular evening because Peter knew how badly I'd treated his father through the years about fun things like watching a football game. To see Peter there that night, it taking his father's *death* to get *me* there? Well, I couldn't. Just couldn't." She lays her hands on the table and pushes to stand up. Gertie helps her stand, and then we wait as she regains her strength. "I'm going to go in the house."

"I'll go with you," I say, and just like that, the steeled-eye Missus is back.

"Why?"

"Well, to help you, to..."

"You really want to help me, Carolina? Get this mess out here finished so we can go to the ball game in peace. You are picking me up, right? You will not be late, correct?"

"Correct."

By the time she steps out from the tent's shadow, her back is straight and she's tapping on her phone. Gertie and I look at each other. The big woman twists her mouth, half grin, half grimace. "That woman there and I have fought since we were kids here in this town. Two more different people have never existed in the same square mile. Yet all these years later, here we are living side by side. Neighbors. Anyone think God don't have a mean streak, just show 'em that."

"You don't mean that." I squint my face, then challenge her. "I think you kind of like her."

Gertie's grin fades, and she sinks back into her chair. "No, honey, no." She pauses, then with an upward jut of her chin, she says, "I loved FM. Always did. If he wasn't such a good man and a kind soul, if he hadn't felt he had to rescue that one from her pathetic excuse for a father, he would never have married her."

I shrug. "Maybe, but maybe not. No way to know that now."

She smiles, but this time it's wistful and sad. "Except that I do. You see, only reason I didn't already have FM's ring on my hand the day he gave it to her was I told him to wait when he asked me. He asked me the week before that stupid county fair where all this got set in motion."

I drop to Missus' chair. "What? Why did you tell him to wait?"

"Stupidity. My pa was in jail for moonshining, and I said he had to wait and ask for my pa's permission. He was getting out in another four weeks." She lifts her hands. "What was just another four weeks? FM was feeling pretty low. Me wanting to wait for my good-for-nothing pa, when here was this good, good man wanting to marry me. You've heard the story, I'm sure. He saw Shermania's father being mean to her, took her away from that sorry excuse for a man, and married her that night. He came to love her, sure. But that's just FM. You know, some folks can will themselves to love." She points a finger my direction. "Those are the happy people."

She stands up and I do, too, but I can't think of anything to say.

Gertie looks around her empty booth. "You better get on doing what she told you to do. She may be getting old, but she can still scald a hide with a look. I'm going to go find Patty and Andy and kick them back into gear. I don't even have to see them to know they're not doing what they're supposed to be doing."

She lumbers off, and I look around the square. So much activity. So many busy people. It's hard to remember that everybody has a life full of stories behind them. A history that might shock or distress, or perhaps even relieve us, if only we knew it.

Standing in this spot, the reality of growing up and living in a small town washes over me. It's knowing the histories of everyone around you. It's knowing that everyone around you knows *your* history. It's getting up each morning wearing your story, whether you want to or not.

Small-town living will break your heart. If it doesn't turn it hard as a piece of coal first.

CHAPTER 50

"I see Savannah opted to cheer tonight," Laney says as she sits down beside me in the stands.

"Opted? She didn't mention having an option." But there are fewer cheerleaders, then a look at the student section shows Jenna, Susie Mae, and several other girls in nice dresses. Not formals, but church dresses. "Why isn't Jenna cheering?"

Laney studies me. "Don't you remember anything from last year? I know Savannah wasn't on homecoming court then, but you act like this is all new. Or did you even come to the homecoming game last year?"

"Lord knows, Laney. I was a tad distressed about the whole move to Chancey, the ghost, fighting with you and Susan. That may have been around when I was avoiding everyone."

She nudges me with her shoulder. "And look at you now. Best friends with the town's matriarch. You know Peter's a bit put-out that his mother chose to ride with you instead of him tonight."

"Why didn't he say something? I had no idea. Believe me, I'd gladly forego the honor of listening to her tell me how to drive the mile to the field, how to park, and even how not to dress as the mother of a homecoming candidate." I stretch my hands out at my jeans and jersey top. "I see you got the memo, and look, here comes Susan. She also got the memo."

Susan stops at our row and asks, "What memo?"

Laney shoves me down the bench with her hip to make room for her sister. "We didn't tell Carolina how to dress. I figured since it was her second year she knew, but now that we're thinking about it she probably didn't come to the game last year."

Susan pulls out a padded seat cushion and lays it down. "My behind can't take these hard benches. And don't worry, you look fine."

I ignore the look that passes between the two sisters. They are both wearing church clothes. Susan has on black slacks and a plaid blazer. Laney is wearing a long skirt, short boots, and a cream turtleneck under a paisley shawl. Susan nods at me. "Most important, you have the corsage. That's what really matters, right, Laney?"

"Of course," she nods. "Jackson and Shaw went to get us hot dogs. Where's Griffin?"

Susan adjusts her flower, although it looks fine, and mumbles, "Griffin? He's around here somewhere, I guess."

"Didn't you come together?" Laney asks. I love having Laney around. She asks exactly what I want to know.

"Of course not. I've been at Nine Mile all day. I came straight from there." Susan looks at me and points. "You tell your best friend, Missus, if she ever, *ever* signs me up for something like this World's Largest Banana Pudding again, I'll hang her from one of these goalposts." She grins a bit and lowers her voice to say, "However, it has forced everyone to get on board up there at Nine Mile, and we'll be ready to open. I think it's going to go over well. Can't wait for y'all to see it. Best part is once it's open, I can hand it all over to Carter May."

As she finishes she stands up. "Here come the guys. I think I'm going to go sit with Mom tonight. Y'all enjoy!" she says as she runs down the stairs to the lower section where the older folks sit. Where I'd left Missus to watch the game.

We get settled with our food and drinks just in time for the game to start. Laney and I are sitting together, with Jackson on my other side and Shaw on her other side, on the end of the row.

"You said Peter wanted to bring his mother to the game? So why didn't he?" I ask.

"I shouldn't have made it sound like he's mad at you," Laney says. "He thinks his mother is avoiding him since FM's death."

"Oh. Okay. He may be right, but I think it'll pass. Anyway, keep an eye out. Colt's girlfriend is supposed to be coming straight here when she gets into town."

Laney leans across me. "Jackson, do you know Colt's girlfriend?"

He shakes his head and chews as he watches the play on the field. When the pass is dropped, he looks at her and says, "No. She was in a class or something, but I never met her."

"What!" I exclaim. "She was in a class? So he *is* dating one of his students?"

Jackson grimaces. "Oh, no. No, he wouldn't, um…"

"I asked you that very thing. You actually got mad at me for even asking. Is she eighteen? Oh my gosh, do you know how much trouble he might be in?"

Jackson grumbles, "Then keep your voice down. I wasn't really paying attention when he told me the other day. We were watching practice. You know, Bryan may actually get in the game tonight."

I slap his thigh. "Well, pay attention. If some little girl shows up for your brother tonight, there is no way she is staying in our house. Do you hear me?" I look over at Laney, who's grinning from ear to ear. So I slap her thigh, too.

"Ow! I didn't say anything." Her grin comes back quickly,

though. "I can think of lots and lots of things to say, but I did not say them."

"Shut up and eat."

I find Colt on the sidelines and scan the fence behind him. I'm assuming she'll show up there when she gets here. Just then, someone runs along the fence, bumping into people walking between the fence and the stands. I halfway stand to see who it is. It looks kind of like Kyle Kendrick, and when he stops I can see it is him. Then I see that he has his hand around Anna's upper arm.

"Jackson, look!" I point, and we both stand. Laney and Shaw also stand, and we move past them to the aisle. Kyle is talking with his face down in Anna's face. Then she turns away, just as Kimmy comes walking up. They are clogging up the flow of traffic, and now more people are standing up so it's hard for me to see what's going on.

I hear Kimmy screech, "Like hell!" And then everything seems to explode.

Jackson pushes past me, and I hear him shout, "Will!"

As I step down onto the pavement, I keep my eyes focused on Anna's pink shirt. People are jostling around, and I push back to get through to her. When I get to her, I'm stopped in my tracks. Kimmy clutches Anna's shoulders with one arm, and her other hand slaps her husband. When Anna sees me, she lunges towards me.

"Are you okay?" I ask once I have her safely in my arms.

She's crying and shaking. A man taps me on the shoulder as he stands and says, "Here, sit in our seat." So I pull her down to the metal bench. When I look up, Kimmy is reading Kyle the riot act. Words like *commitment* and *vow* and *kids*. She's letting him have every bit of that tough love Bible study she was in. And wonder of wonders, he's listening. Really? I've heard of slapping some sense into someone, but never seen it.

As the crowd disperses, I spot Will and Jackson near the

fence. Jackson has his arm around our son's shoulders. They look grim as they move toward us.

Will asks, "Anna, what happened?"

"The move. It was all about the move," she says as Will steps closer to her, shaking off his dad's arm.

He looks stunned. "Dad just told me. You're moving? I thought we were going to talk things out before we made big decisions. Raise the baby together. Try to act like adults, and now I find out in the middle of a football game you're moving? No! No way. You're not doing it."

Anna jumps up and shouts back in his face. "Oh, yes, I am! Neither you nor Kyle Kendrick get to tell me what to do. I'm moving in with my grandmother, and I don't care if you're happy about it or not." As the words come out she seems to be thinking and her voice softens. "But wait, you wouldn't be mad about that. That's what you suggested. Why are you mad?"

Will looks at Jackson. Jackson looks at me. I look at Kyle. "He told me you were moving with him away from here."

Anna turns to him. "You what? You told people that? No. No." She turns to Will. "No, that is not happening. Was never happening. I've been staying with Granmissus on and off for weeks, just like I told you. Kyle is just making things up."

Kimmy steps to her husband's side and wraps her arm around his arm. "My husband just needed to be reminded of a few things. I'da preferred do it in a more private place, but when I saw him chasing after you, Anna, I knew it was here and now." Kyle rubs his face where it's still red from her slap. We hear a cheer, and the gentleman whose seats Anna and I are sitting in yells, "Chancey scored!"

"Here, you can have your seats back. Thank you." As I stand and move out of the way, Officer Pierson walks up.

Jackson shakes his hand and says, "Officer Pierson. Things are fine here now. Just a little misunderstanding."

Denny nods and looks around, then he bends his head forward and clears his throat. "Can I have a word with you?"

His policeman voice makes my stomach flip. This doesn't sound like chitchat, or like he's just passing on a little information. This sounds serious. I let go of Anna as I look up at Jackson and nod. "Sure." Jackson echoes me and we step toward the officer.

"No, not you. The Kendricks."

Kimmy's eyes fly open as she objects, "I just slapped him to calm him down. It wasn't hard, I promise."

Kyle immediately covers his reddened cheek with his hand. "She's right, officer. I needed to calm down. It didn't hurt."

Denny says, "It's not about that. It's about your daughter, Zoe. Let's step over here."

They follow him around the corner. Will has his arm around Anna, and he says to her, "Let's go sit with Missus. Do you want anything? A drink? Something to eat?"

She smiles up at him and wraps her arm around his waist. "No. Let's just sit down." They walk past us, and Jackson and I both let out long breaths. Jackson holds out his hand for me to hold as we walk up the steps back to our seats.

Shaw and Laney move to let us in, but as soon as we sit down, Laney says, "Did they get arrested? What happened?"

"No, it wasn't about that. Something about Zoe? Is she here?"

Laney stands up to see the student section better. "I don't know. With Shaw's parents here we didn't need her to watch Cayden tonight." She sits down. "You don't think she's hurt, do you?" She grabs her purse and puts it on her lap. Her hands are shaking as she pulls out her phone.

"Wait," I say as I lay my hand on hers. "Here comes Kimmy."

Kimmy makes a weird face as she climbs the step and nears

315

us. Not upset, more confused. As she reaches our row, Laney asks, "Is Zoe all right?"

Kimmy takes a deep breath. "I guess, but I need a favor. We need to go talk to the officer for a bit. Can y'all keep a lookout for K.J.? I brought him to his first football game, what a disaster. He's playing with the other kids in the end zone down there. Zoe was supposed to be watching the other two kids, but I guess she had bigger ideas."

"Are they okay?" Laney asks, then says, "And of course we'll take care of K.J. He can come home with us if you need him to. That precious Zoe takes care of our family so well, it's the least we can do."

Shaw reaches out and pats Kimmy's shoulders. "Anything you need. Zoe's like family to us."

Kimmy rolls her eyes. "Sure wish she was your family right now. You know all that vandalizing around town? Looks like it was Zoe. All Zoe."

CHAPTER 51

"It needs to rain," Missus declares. I pull open the door to Ruby's, and she marches in. "This very minute. The game is over and festival prep begins early in the morning. If it's going to rain, it better do it fast. Did you see they're calling for a gully washer?"

Charles Spoon steps up to us. "Carolina, I need to make sure you're okay with that article thing, you know. And, ah…" His eyes shift around the café, and he leans closer to me. "What was all that about at the game? You know, with… ah, the Kendricks?"

I widen my eyes in shock. "Why, Charles Spoon, are you asking me to ruin, simply ruin your new ace reporter's own scoop? I never!"

We push past him, and Missus half-turns to look at me. "What was that all about? What happened at the game? I have absolutely no concern with that family, but I do not like being in the dark."

By some miracle, Missus missed the whole thing. Apparently the people standing blocked that area. "Nothing. There's Angie."

Angie Conner, the new homecoming queen of Chancey High. Yep, and while she's toned down her black makeup, she

317

still kind of looks like the vampire wannabe I first met at the Piggly Wiggly. She's matured, owning her own business, and I can't deny that having won, and held onto, the hottest guy in Chancey hasn't hurt her stature in our small town. But to win homecoming queen? No one saw it coming. Well, except for possibly her sister. Savannah told me and Laney after the game that Jenna milked not being on the ballot and garnered support for her twin. Her main concern was her cousin Susie Mae not winning the honor as a junior. No junior has ever won, but wearing skimpy, practically see-through baby-doll pajamas at school appears to be a winning strategy. An *almost* winning strategy. As Laney said, and is still saying rather loudly, "Susie Mae can win next year!"

Laney is sitting beside her daughters and swaying with emotion, joy, and that half-flask of bourbon she drank after getting the news about Zoe. She sent Shaw to the car to get it for her, and he almost missed his daughter being crowned queen. Missus veers off to sit at a table where Charles and some of the other older folks are seated.

I take a seat at an empty table as Jackson is on his way. He went down to the locker room area to see his son, the football star. Bryan did get in the game and made an important tackle. Jackson's also hoping to run into Colt and his girlfriend. We never did see her at the game. Jackson got quiet, and I think he's a little fearful about his brother's new squeeze being underage. Or barely above it.

"No, thanks, Libby. No coffee for me tonight," I say when she tries to turn over the cup sitting in front of me. "No pie either. I need to get a good night's sleep before the festival."

"I hear ya. Ruby wasn't planning on opening, but when she heard they'd made an arrest for all that vandalism and then when little Angie Conner won queen, well, she couldn't resist." She says from the side of her mouth as she moves on, "So the pies are frozen, not fresh. You're not missing anything."

Arrest? I get up and make my way to the back counter. Then I break all protocol and step behind it. "Ruby, hey."

"Hey, you. I hear you were right there for the arrest."

"Not really. What have you heard?" Kimmy had called Laney and told her K.J. was going to spend the night with his friend Cas so everything with him was under control. She hung up before Laney could get any more information.

"Just that Denny caught them in the act tonight, then nailed them at the football game. Folks say you were talking to him. That there was a scuffle. Did they try to escape? Who was it?" Ruby finishes cutting the pies in front of her, tosses the knife in the sink, and turns to me for the full story.

"No, that was about something else. So, he caught them in the act doing what?"

She shrugs. "Didn't hear." She picks up a pie in each hand and places them on the counter. "Shoot. Thought I was going to get the whole story when you got here." She flicks a towel at me. "Get back on the other side of the counter if you ain't got nothing to say. Go!"

Hurrying back to my table, I stop to give Angie a hug, Laney a high-five, and a general shrug to say I don't know any more about Zoe. Then Laney waves at who's coming in the door, and I turn to see a couple of the football players, including Bryan.

Jackson is behind them, then Colt and... and a woman. A woman as old as me and he has his arm around her. That's his girlfriend? I turn to Laney, and her wide eyes match mine. In a bit of a daze, I walk over to give my son a hug, and when I do the same to my husband, he whispers in my ear.

"Yes. That's her. Remember the school board member that's been fighting with Dad? The guy the age of dad? That is, well, *was* his wife!"

I pull back and roll my eyes. "No wonder he got fired. But she's at least my age!"

He shrugs at me, then turns. "Rebecca, this is my wife, Carolina."

I shake her hand and can't help but stare. She's beautiful. She's wearing a wrap dress and high-heeled slides. She looks like a movie star. An aging movie star, but a movie star nonetheless. Her hair is red, her boobs are high, her jewelry looks real, and she's wearing long, glamorous false eyelashes. Colt looks like a puppy in a YouTube video with his favorite toy. But she's staying at my house? Oh, Lord, look at her nails. She might as well have high maintenance stamped on her forehead.

A blur bumps past me. "Hey, don't think we've met. I'm Laney."

People talk about macho men trying to out do each other with their handshake, well, it's nothing to well-endowed beauty queens attempting to out-pose each other. Hand on hip, shake of hair, presenting of boobs, and, being in the South, a thickening of accent.

Well, Queen Angie had center stage for at least a little while.

Peter sidles up behind me. "Who's that?"

"Colt's girlfriend."

"Your Colt? Coach Colt?" His eyes are wide. Matter of fact, looking around—everyone's eyes are wide. "Hmm. Can I talk to you?"

"Sure, let's sit down." I sit, and he takes the chair across from me.

"Is Mother avoiding me?" he asks before his behind hits the seat.

"Probably. I got the lowdown on her leaving the cave that night. She's actually embarrassed about how she treated your dad in front of you."

He falls back against the seat of his chair. "Seriously?"

"What she said. But listen, don't think she's getting soft. She's not. Matter of fact, I think this goodwill tour of hers is already wearing thin on her. So tell me, how are things with Shannon?"

He thinks as his eyes drift over to where Shannon's sitting. "It's like the most normal relationship I've ever had, and that worries me." He leans up, elbows on the table. "Honestly, I keep waiting to get tired of her. One of the reasons I let her move in. Figured that was the quickest way to get over her, to get tired of her, but…"

"But… what?"

He grins. "I think some of it is how unhappy it makes Mother. I left Chancey all those years ago because I didn't know how to be my own man here. Not with her making all my decisions for me. Running my life. Feels good to be bucking her like this." He stands up. "Don't worry, I'm not using Shannon, I honestly like her. But knowing Mother doesn't approve does add to the mix." He walks over and leans down to kiss Shannon, surprising her midsentence. When I see his eyes flash toward the front where Missus is seated, checking to see if she saw, I cringe.

Poor guy, he hasn't got a chance.

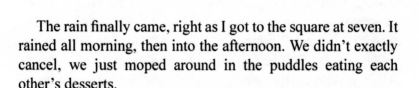

CHAPTER 52

The rain finally came, right as I got to the square at seven. It rained all morning, then into the afternoon. We didn't exactly cancel, we just moped around in the puddles eating each other's desserts.

Missus was right. Our chocolate pies were disappointing next to everyone else's homemade treats. Laney is donating everything we had left to a children's home not far away. Kids will love the little individual pies. She loaded her SUV up, put Cayden in his car seat, and set off for the drive to the children's home during his nap time. Which means our booth closed at noon.

Angie and Alex never even took their deconstructed pecan pie out of their food truck or opened their booth. They just headed down to Canton to sell them near the shopping center.

Bryan had a blast with Shaw's parents and the strawberry shortcakes on biscuits. They only unfroze and heated up a small batch, but they were heavenly. Bryan had a heavy hand with the strawberry goop, as he called it. They also let him spray the Reddi-whip on top of each one, and what kid doesn't like doing that? Watching him was the best thing about the whole day. We didn't tell him it was Zoe, but we did tell him he was in the clear on the vandalism. For some reason I think he knew it had been Zoe all along.

We didn't see hide nor hair of the Kendrick family. And no one mentioned any new vandalism from last night, so I still don't know what she got caught doing.

We also didn't see hide nor hair of Colt and Rebecca until almost one o'clock. Don't even want to think about them sleeping in down in my basement.

"Wish I'd thought of those," I say to Rebecca when she walks into Blooming Books with Colt trailing along. He still looks like a puppy, just a more tired, satisfied puppy. You know I'm rolling my eyes. "Those boots are adorable. My tennis shoes are completely soaked."

Rebecca has on navy leggings, navy boots with little green whales on them, and a long silky shirt. Over that she's wearing a clear plastic raincoat. She looks like she just walked out of a magazine. Same heavy makeup as last night, but her hair is poufed up and back in a high ponytail.

"Carolina! Your shop is adorable," she says. "So sorry about the rain. I was looking forward to all the yummy desserts. Can I just look around? I'm needing some new books."

She walks off, and Colt steps over to the counter and leans against it. "So what d'ya think? Isn't she great?"

I turn to face him. "She's not what I expected."

"I was afraid she'd go back to him. Or move away and forget us all. But she's made her decision." He's beaming, absolutely beaming.

"Is she from Painter?"

Scorn fills his face and his voice. "Carolina. Be serious. No, she's not from Painter. She's originally from Florida, I think, but Old Man Scarborough met her out in Vegas, dumped his wife, and married her. But poor Rebecca didn't really love him. She was just lonely and scared. You know how that goes."

Yeah, I know how that goes. I've read more romance novels

than Vegas has showgirls. Poor, lonely, scared showgirls. But I just nod. Yep, I just nod.

And Colt continues. "When he got her back to Painter it didn't take long for her to see he didn't really love her. He just wanted to show her off. Lord her over his old friends. Makes my blood boil to think about it!"

Are guys really this stupid? Better question—are guys I'm related to really this stupid?

"How long were they together?" I ask.

"Hm, let's see. He's a judge, so divorce went real smooth. They got married in Vegas and so, she's been in Painter for I'd say eight, yeah, eight months."

Am I on some kind of reality show?

"Colt, that's not very long to know that you don't want to be married."

He leans on his elbow and lowers his voice. "But we had such chemistry right from the beginning. We met in an exercise class at the gym and we just knew. You don't understand." He steps past me to look at his girlfriend. "Hey, hon, find some books?" I turn to see them together.

She holds up three books. "I did. If it keeps raining like this we can just snuggle and read, right?" She leans over, and I swear she licks his ear.

Okay, maybe I'm imagining things, but would you be surprised?

"Oh darn," I say. "Looks like the rain is stopping."

I walk behind the counter and bite my tongue while I sell her the books. I didn't even write down what they were for our inventory like I'm supposed to. Only thing I want to know now is: how long is she staying in my house?

As rays of sunshine appear, things get busier outside. Most folks had hunkered down at Ruby's or Gertie's to wait out the rain since the forecast was that it would end midafternoon. I'd retreated to the store since I knew it would be empty. Too much togetherness with the good folk of Chancey is not good for my health. Now everyone is venturing out to clean their booths and pack up.

Colt says to his chemistry partner, "Let's go see if Jackson needs any help. Or you can stay here with Carolina."

She leans over to him—being forewarned now, I don't watch—and purrs, "I'm so anxious to start this book. Is it okay with you if I stay here in Carolina's sweet shop, right there on that couch, and read? I really wouldn't be much help out there."

"Of course! Right, Carolina?"

"Of course. I'll probably need to step out there, but you'll be fine here. I'll put the closed sign up. Don't believe there'll be any customers anyway."

When Colt opens the door, a brisk, cold wind pushes in. We both catch our breaths. "They said the rain was bringing in a cold front. Looks like it's here."

Since none of us showed up dressed for the cold, only wearing rain jackets, we hurry with cleaning up and are making great progress.

"Do you know where Laney is?" her mother asks as she walks up to what's left of our booth. Susan is trailing a bit behind her talking on her phone.

"Yes, although she should be getting back soon. She took our leftover pie stuff to the children's home. Are you okay?" Gladys Troutman is usually calm. An efficient woman, you know, has things under control. But she's pulling at her hands and looks sad.

"Oh, I'm fine. Just need to talk to Laney. Oh, hello," she says when Colt comes back for another load.

"Well, hello, Mrs. Troutman. Good to see you again. You know Carolina, my sister-in-law, right?"

"Of course. She and my daughters are good friends."

"Oh, you did say that," he says as he folds up another table.

I help push the table together for him. "Didn't know you knew Gladys." Susan walks up as she hangs up. "Hey Susan. You know Colt from school and the Lake Park, right?"

Colt says, "Yes, I know Mrs. Lyles. As for Mrs. Troutman – Gladys, I was hoping she'd be my landlady. House I wanted to rent belongs to her. You haven't changed your mind, have you?" He picks up the table. "I'd still be interested."

Gladys shakes her head and presses her lips together. When she speaks, her voice also shakes. "No. I *wish* you could have it." Tears spring to her eyes. I step to hold her elbow as I look to Susan to help her mother, but she looks more mad than concerned.

"Mom, please," Susan snaps.

"Susan? Is everything okay? Your mom seems upset."

Susan sighs and closes her eyes. "Coach, you can't rent my mother's house because," she opens her eyes and says, "because I'm renting it. Griffin and I are getting a divorce."

My shock is mirrored in Laney's face as she walks up behind her sister. She's carrying Cayden, and she looks so stunned I worry she might drop him. Colt sees the same thing, and he sets down the table, then reaches out to shore up Laney's elbow.

Susan turns to see Laney, and she automatically speaks to her nephew. "Hi Cayden. Want to come see your Aunt Susan?"

As she reaches for him, though, Laney pulls back, says "No," then turns and leaves, hurrying back towards the SUV she just got out of.

Susan looks at me, then her mother.

Gladys dips her head, then shrugs. "What did you expect? I tried to tell you, but as always, you're the smartest one in the room." Then she also walks off.

Colt picks up the table he'd folded and, with a quick wave, goes while the going is good.

"Susan, what's happening?" I ask.

"Surely you can see what's going on, right? Griffin and I have nothing in common anymore. I never wanted to live on that awful mountain. That house is an embarrassment. It's all about his ego. There's not even a flat place for me to plant tomatoes. I belong in Chancey. Here where all of you are. My mother. My sister and brother. Laney will come around." Susan is so defiant, so decided, that it takes me aback. "But the kids and you and Griffin. I just can't imagine..."

"Well, start imagining, because I'm done. So done. Kids will be fine. Susie Mae hates it up there, too. She's thrilled to be moving back. Grant will get used to it. He's becoming as big of a snob as his father living up there. It's best for him to move home, too."

Jackson comes strolling up. "Hey, Susan. So how did things go up at Nine Mile? You get as much rain as we did?"

She smiles at him. "Yes, but luckily I cancelled the World's Largest Banana Pudding before we set anything up. Took everything to a homeless shelter in Dalton, they were thrilled. But I've got to go. Moving to do!" She strides off, and Jackson frowns at me.

"What's she moving?"

I shake my head and grab onto him. He automatically hugs me back, although he has no choice since I'm holding onto him like the earth would swallow me up if I let go.

Now that I know, I realize she's right. I should've known all along. I should've been paying better attention. How can you lean on your friends in a bad time if your friends are stupid?

Finally Jackson pushes me away enough to see my face. "Honey, what's wrong?"

Opening my mouth, I search for the words, but they just won't come out.

Maybe if I don't say them, they won't be true. I don't know, but whatever, they won't come out of my mouth, so instead

I say, "I'm freezing. My feet are wet. I've been here since dawn."

He lets me get away with that because he's a good husband. He kisses my forehead. "Let's go home. We'll talk there."

Nodding, I shiver and wipe away a tear that wants to be the first of many.

The first annual Chancey Southern Desserts Festival is over.

CHAPTER 53

A big storm in Florida, a hurricane in some places, sent the rain we'd had all day. As it left the area, cold northern air filled the vacancy. All that resulted in one of the most beautiful sunsets I've ever seen. Jackson and I are wrapped up on the front porch, watching the sky turn to even brighter shades of orange when someone hollers "hey" from the other side of the railroad tracks. It's hard to see who it is in the shadows, but then we realize its Kyle Kendrick.

Jackson nudges me. "Want to meet him and walk out on the bridge? Bet the sunset is even prettier out there."

"Sure. That way I don't have to have that man in my house." We get up and stretch, then walk down the steps to meet him.

"Want to walk out on the bridge with us?" Jackson asks as he shakes the man's hand. I ignore him.

"Sure. Don't want to bother you, but wanted to let y'all know what's going on. Figured a walk couldn't hurt either."

There's more color in the trees on the hills around the river now, although some of it may be the reflection of the deep orange of the sky. The air is still, as it often seems to be right at dusk. Kyle looks around and as we get near the center, he shoves his hands in his jeans pockets and shakes his head.

"I've never been up here. Now that I think about it, Zoe's talked about it a lot."

We stop and all lean on the railing looking toward the west, watching the sky shift and change.

Okay, I've been silent enough. "How is Zoe?"

He seems to chew on his words for a moment, then says, "She'll be okay. Did you hear what she got caught doing last night?"

"No. No one seems to know," I answer.

"She put Katherine and Kevin to bed, then lit out of the house and walked to the Dollar Store. Left them alone. She said she had to get out of the house. Guess looking back we should've thought more about her going to the high school game than us. Kimmy wanted to take K.J., and I, well, I was trying to hold on to Anna. I mean, I guess that's what I was doing. Don't rightly know now."

He's looking down at the river and repeats to himself, "Don't rightly know. Anyway, she was scratching words into the windows of the store with a rock. Our alarm system is pretty good, and she set it off. It's silent, so she didn't know until the officer pulled into the parking lot that she'd been caught. However, he said he thought she was fine with being caught."

"She wanted your attention," I say as I turn to face him, one elbow on the railing.

"Apparently. We sat down and had a session today with the school counselor. It was good. It was hard to see how much we'd put on her, but she never complained. Always seemed to want to do more. You know?"

I chuckle and have to admit, "Yes, I know. I often wished my kids were more like her. I'm glad she's getting some counseling. She'll be okay, I think."

He brightens, "Counselor thinks so, too. And about last night at the game. I'm real sorry about all that. Anna just seemed so easy to, uh, no. No excuses. I did her wrong and did Kimmy wrong. I moved back home today, too. Kimmy's taking me back if I straighten up. School counselor is getting us someone to talk to, and I'm going to go to some of those classes she's taking out at that church."

Jackson asks, "You're not moving?"

"I'll be working at that other store up near the border, but no, we're staying here for now." He steps away from the railing. "Thanks for listening and for how much y'all have helped Kimmy and the kids and Zoe. Sorry again for the pain I caused y'all." He shoves his hands back into his pockets again and turns to walk back down the bridge toward home.

Jackson lays his arm across my shoulders, and we watch the last bit of yellow fade into gray. As he turns with me toward the house, he says, "If anything, the Kendrick family should give us hope for Susan and Griffin. If they can get back together, then…" He lets his words drift off with a shrug.

"That's true. That's very true. Now, what about this Rebecca? Did you talk to your mom?"

"Yep. She can't believe Colt is still head over heels about her. She figured it was just an infatuation. Rebecca is really something. Really set Painter back on its heels when she showed up. Mom wasn't living there then, she'd already moved to the coast, but her friends were beside themselves. Rebecca is a hurricane apparently."

"But what does she see in Colt?"

"Exactly! Mom said she thought Rebecca was just bored when they started seeing each other, but to divorce for him? She's not getting any money divorcing Judge Scarborough. He had a prenup. Mom figures she'll be leaving Colt behind soon. At least she kind of hopes so."

I cringe as I wonder, "Could they actually be in love?"

A car bouncing over the tracks gets our attention. "Well, looks like that's the lovebirds now," Jackson says.

They are out of Rebecca's car and on the porch by the time we get there.

"Did you see that sunset?" Colt asks. "Turned the whole sky orange." He reaches for Rebecca's hand. "We've got good news! We're going to rent Anna's apartment!"

"What? Really?" But wait. I freeze. "Did you say 'we'? You're moving here, too, Rebecca?"

Rebecca smiles and bats her eyes at Colt before turning to give us her full smile and a showgirl pose. "Yes. Isn't it wonderful? We're so happy!"

Colt gazes at her and says, "Tell them what else."

"Yes, what else?" I say as I lean on the porch column. My legs are feeling weak.

She beams at me. "Carolina, you and I will also be business neighbors. The building where that little vandal broke the windows earlier this week? Well, that is no longer unoccupied. It's the new home of the Phoenix Dance Studio. Phoenix was my, uh, dancer name."

"Imagine that," I manage to say without my smile slipping much.

She tosses her ponytail and shimmies her shoulders. "Those big windows right on Main Street will be perfect for people to see what they can do, what they can *look like* if they join."

It's Jackson's turn to say something, so I nudge him. His oh-so creative mind spits out, "Well. Imagine that."

Colt opens the front door and holds it open for Phoenix—I mean, Rebecca. I follow behind her, and Jackson brings up the end. The lovebirds walk into the living room, while Jackson and I move on towards the kitchen.

Colt laughs as he and Rebecca sit down on the couch. He says loud enough for us to hear, "Rebecca was just telling me how one of the more popular classes is the pole dancing class, you know for teaching ladies how to pole dance." He laughs even louder. "Carolina, you might want to look into that!"

Jackson and I just stare at each other. Pole dancing in downtown Chancey, right next door to Ruby's.

Imagine that.

CHARACTER LIST

Jackson and Carolina Jessup – Moved to Chancey one year ago. Operate Crossings, a bed-and-breakfast for railfans in their home. They have three children: Will, 22, a recent college grad; Savannah, 16; Bryan, 13. Jackson works for the railroad and is out of town often. Carolina also runs the bookstore side of Blooming Books.

Jackson's family – Mother Etta lives at the beach in South Carolina. Father Hank is married to Shelby and lives in Kentucky. Two brothers, Emerson and Colt. Emerson is the oldest, ane he and his wife have three daughters and live in Virginia. Colt is the youngest, is single, and lives in their hometown in Kentucky.

Carolina's family – Parents Goldie and Jack live in Tennessee. Carolina is an only child.Missus and FM Bedwell – Lifelong residents of Chancey.

Peter Bedwell, 45, lives two doors down from his parents. Owns Peter's Bistro on the square.

Anna Jessup, 19, Missus' granddaughter. Her mother was **given up** for adoption and died when Anna was 16. Anna found Missus and came to Chancey. Married Will Jessup when she got pregnant. They are currently separated.

Laney and Shaw Conner – Both from Chancey. Shaw owns an automotive dealership. Laney partners with Carolina in the B&B. They have three children: twins Angie and Jenna, 17; Cayden, 4 months.

Susan and Griffin Lyles – Susan is sister to Laney and manages the Lake Park. Griffin recently got a big job with the electric company and moved his family to the well-to-do community on the mountain of Laurel Cove. They have three children: Leslie, 19; Susie Mae, 15; Grant, 13. Laney and Susan's mother is Gladys Troutman.

Gertie Samson – She has one child: Patty, 28, married to Andy Taylor. Gertie was raised in Chancey and returned after her daughter, Patty, settled there. She owns a lot of property in town. She lives in the house she, Patty, and Andy run their businesses out of.

Ruby Harden– Owns and runs Ruby's Café on the town square. Lifelong Chancey resident.

Libby Stone – Works with Ruby at the café and is married to Bill Stone. Daughter

Cathy Stone Cross, Libby and Bill's daughter is married to Stephen Cross, a teacher at the high school. They have a young son, Forrest. Cathy sells lingerie through at-home parties. Her previous role as a high school cheerleader still has a profound impact on her life.

Kendrick family – Moved to town for father Kyle to open new Dollar Store where he hired Anna Jessup as assistant manager and then began an affair with her. Currently he lives with Anna. Wife Kimmy and their four children live in Chancey. Kyle's daughter, Zoe, from a previous marriage lives with Kimmy and cares for the younger three children.

Shannon Chilton – Operates florist part of Blooming Books. Lifelong Chancey resident. She's 30 and in a relationship with Peter Bedwell.

Bonnie Cuneo – Works in Blooming Books. Retired teacher who lives in Laurel Cove.

Don't miss...

Next Stop, Chancey
Book One in the Chancey Series

Looking in your teenage daughter's purse is never a good idea.

After all, it ended up with Carolina opening a B&B for railroad buffs in a tiny Georgia mountain town. Carolina knows all about, and hates, small towns. How did she end up leaving her wonderful Atlanta suburbs behind while making her husband's dreams come true?

Unlike back home in the suburbs with privacy fences and automatic garage doors, everybody in Chancey thinks your business is their business and they all love the newest Chancey business. The B&B hosts a senate candidate, a tea for the County Fair beauty contestants, and railroad nuts who sit out by the tracks and record the sound of a train going by. Yet, nobody believes Carolina prefers the 'burbs.

Oh, yeah, and if you just ignore a ghost, will it go away?

Chancey Family Lies
Book Two in the Chancey Series

Holidays are different in small towns. You're expected to cook.

Carolina is determined her first holiday season as a
stay-at-home mom will be perfect. However...

Twelve kids from college (and one nobody seems to know)
Eleven chili dinners (why do we always have to feed a crowd?)
Ten dozen fake birds (cardinals, no less)
Nine hours without power (but lots of stranded guests)
Eight angry council members (wait, where's the town's money?)
Seven trains a-blowin' (all the time. All. The. Time.)
Six weeks with relatives (six weeks?!?)
Five plotting teens (again, who is that girl?)
Four in-laws staying (and staying, and staying...)
Three dogs a-barking (who brought the dogs?)
Two big ol' secrets (and they ain't wrapped in ribbons
under the tree, either)
And the perfect season gone with the wind.

Derailed in Chancey
Book Three in the Chancey Series

Should she jump?

When the train is headed for disaster, the engineer can jump out, right?

Carolina knew moving teenagers from the Atlanta suburbs to a small Georgia mountain town was a horrible idea. She knew opening a B&B was an even worse plan. She can't see around the next curve, but...

Should she jump?

Oncoming headlights aren't only aimed at her family, the town of Chancey is being set up for a collision that could change everything. And as that unfolds, Carolina's husband Jackson is smack dab in the middle of it all, his hand on the throttle, going full steam ahead.

Should she jump?

Would you?

Chancey Jobs
Book Four in the Chancey Series

Aren't small towns
supposed to be boring?

Overnight, a shiny new business opens on Chancey, Georgia's Main Street, with a manager straight from New York City who doesn't find the South charming, at all. Carolina's bookstore is also opening on Main Street. *If* she can keep Patty's mind on books instead of a new romance.

Then, when a secret wedding catches everyone off guard, a springtime tornado in Chancey just seems like icing on the cake. (Wedding cake, that is.)

Trains still run by Crossings, the B&B for rail road enthusiasts. Ruby still sells coffee and muffins. And kids still get out of school for the summer.

However, even in a small town, change is constant.
New jobs mean a move for long-time Chancey residents. Cancelled plans lead to moves across the state—and broken hearts. Graduations mean new chapters. And babies mean...well...

Babies mean nothing will ever be the same again.

Kids Are Chancey
Book Five in the Chancey Series

"A mother is only as happy
as her unhappiest child," they say.
But is it true?

What if your children are all miserable, Carolina wonders, but your life is finally coming together?

Will's new marriage and new job, are already old. Savannah's reduced to chasing a guy and she's playing the Southern Belle to do it. Bryan is labeled a stalker. Maybe worse, is he a world-class liar?

Carolina's friends are having kid worries, too. Laney's finding the age gap between high school senior and newborn grows with her exhaustion. Susan's kids too quickly get accustomed, and attached, to their new station in life in their ritzy mountain community. Missus schemes to have her great-grandchild living under her roof, but that means living with a pregnant teenager first.

Why *do* people keep having kids?

CPSIA information can be obtained
at www.ICGtesting.com
Printed in the USA
FFOW02n1222080718
47317234-50320FF